PENGUIN BOOKS

WHIP HAND

jockeys. The winner of over 350 races, he was champion jockey in 1953/1954 and rode for HM Queen Elizabeth, the Queen Mother, most famously on Devon Loch in the 1956 Grand National. On his retirement from the saddle, he published his autobiography, *The Sport of Queens*, before going on to write forty-three bestselling novels, a volume of short stories (*Field of 13*), and the biography of Lester Piggott.

During his lifetime Dick Francis received many awards, amongst them the prestigious Crime Writers' Association's Cartier Diamond Dagger for his outstanding contribution to the genre, and three 'best novel' Edgar Allan Poe awards from The Mystery Writers of America. In 1996 he was named by them as Grand Master for a lifetime's achievement. In 1998 he was elected a fellow of the Royal Society of Literature, and was awarded a CBE in the Queen's Birthday Honours List of 2000.

Dick Francis died in February 2010, at the age of eighty-nine, but he remains one of the greatest thriller writers of all time.

Books by Dick Francis

Books by Dick Francis and Felix Francis

Dick Francis Novels by Felix Francis

WHIP HAND

Dick Francis

PENGUIN BOOKS

PENGUIN BOOKS

Published by the Penguin Group
Penguin Books Ltd, 80 Strand, London WC2R 0RL, England
Penguin Group (USA) Inc., 375 Hudson Street, New York, New York 10014, USA
Penguin Group (Canada), 90 Eglinton Avenue East, Suite 700, Toronto, Ontario, Canada M4P 2Y3
(a division of Pearson Penguin Canada Inc.)
Penguin Ireland, 25 St Stephen's Green, Dublin 2, Ireland (a division of Penguin Books Ltd)
Penguin Group (Australia), 707 Collins Street, Melbourne, Victoria 3008, Australia
(a division of Pearson Australia Group Pty Ltd)
Penguin Books India Pvt Ltd, 11 Community Centre, Panchsheel Park, New Delhi – 110 017, India
Penguin Group (NZ), 67 Apollo Drive, Rosedale, Auckland 0632, New Zealand
(a division of Pearson New Zealand Ltd)
Penguin Books (South Africa) (Pty) Ltd, Block D, Rosebank Office Park,
181 Jan Smuts Avenue, Parktown North, Gauteng 2193, South Africa

Penguin Books Ltd, Registered Offices: 80 Strand, London WC2R 0RL, England

www.penguin.com

First published by Michael Joseph Ltd 1979
Reissued in Penguin Books 2014
001

Printed in Great Britain by Clays Ltd, St Ives plc

ISBN: 978-1-405-91677-6

www.greenpenguin.co.uk

This book is for

Mike Gwilym
Actor

and

Jacky Stoller
Producer

with gratitude and affection

Prologue

I dreamed I was riding in a race.

Nothing odd in that. I'd ridden in thousands.

There were fences to jump. There were horses, and jockeys in a rainbow of colours, and miles of green grass. There were massed banks of people, with pink oval faces, indistinguishable pink blobs from where I crouched in the stirrups, galloping past, straining with speed.

Their mouths were open, and although I could hear no sound I knew they were shouting.

Shouting my name, to make me win.

Winning was all. Winning was my function. What I was there for. What I wanted. What I was born for.

In the dream, I won the race. The shouting turned to cheering, and the cheering lifted me up on its wings, like a wave. But the winning was all; not the cheering.

I woke in the dark, as I often did, at four in the morning.

There was silence. No cheering. Just silence.

I could still feel the way I'd moved with the horse, the

1

ripple of muscle through both of the striving bodies, uniting in one. I could still feel the irons round my feet, the calves of my legs gripping, the balance, the nearness to my head of the stretching brown neck, the mane blowing in my mouth, my hands on the reins.

There came, at that point, the second awakening. The real one. The moment in which I first moved, and opened my eyes, and remembered that I wouldn't ride any more races, ever. The wrench of loss came again as a fresh grief. The dream was a dream for whole men.

I dreamed it quite often.

Damned senseless thing to do.

Living, of course, was quite different. One discarded dreams, and got dressed, and made what one could of the day.

CHAPTER ONE

I took the battery out of my arm and fed it into the recharger, and only realized I'd done it when ten seconds later the fingers wouldn't work.

How odd, I thought. Recharging the battery, and the manoeuvre needed to accomplish it, had become such second nature that I had done them instinctively, without conscious decision, like brushing my teeth. And I realized for the first time that I had finally squared my subconscious, at least when I was awake, to the fact that what I now had as a left hand was a matter of metal and plastic, not muscle and bone and blood.

I pulled my tie off and flung it haphazardly on to my jacket, which lay over the leather arm of the sofa: stretched and sighed with the ease of homecoming: listened to the familiar silences of the flat; and as usual felt the welcoming peace unlock the gritty tensions of the outside world.

I suppose that that flat was more of a haven than a home. Comfortable certainly, but not slowly and lovingly put together. Furnished, rather, on one brisk unemotional afternoon in one store: 'I'll have that, that, that and that . . . and send them as soon as possible.' The collection had gelled, more or less, but I now owned nothing whose loss I would ache over; and if that was a defence mechanism, at least I knew it.

Contentedly padding around in shirt sleeves and socks, I switched on the warm pools of tablelights, encouraged the television with a practised slap, poured a soothing Scotch, and decided not to do yesterday's washing up. There was steak in the fridge and money in the bank, and who needed an aim in life anyway?

I tended nowadays to do most things one-handed, because it was quicker. My ingenious false hand, which worked via solenoids from electrical impulses in what was left of my forearm, would open and close in a fairly vice-like grip, but at its own pace. It did *look* like a real hand, though, to the extent that people sometimes didn't notice. There were shapes like fingernails, and ridges for tendons, and blue lines for veins. When I was alone I seemed to use it less and less, but it pleased me better to see it on than off.

I shaped up to that evening as to many another. On the sofa, feet up, knees bent, in contact with a chunky tumbler and happy to live vicariously via the small screen: and I was mildly irritated when halfway through a decent comedy the door bell rang.

With more reluctance than curiosity I stood up, parked the glass, fumbled through my jacket pockets for the spare battery I'd been carrying there, and snapped it

4

into the socket in my arm. Then, buttoning the shirt cuff down over the plastic wrist, I went out into the small hall and took a look through the spyhole in the door.

There was no trouble on the mat, unless trouble had taken the shape of a middle-aged lady in a blue headscarf. I opened the door and said politely, 'Good evening, can I help you?'

'Sid,' she said. 'Can I come in?'

I looked at her, thinking that I didn't know her. But then a good many people whom I didn't know called me Sid, and I'd always taken it as a compliment.

Coarse dark curls showed under the headscarf, a pair of tinted glasses hid her eyes, and heavy crimson lipstick focused attention on her mouth. There was embarrassment in her manner and she seemed to be trembling inside her loose fawn raincoat. She still appeared to expect me to recognize her, but it was not until she looked nervously over her shoulder, and I saw her profile against the light, that I actually did.

Even then I said incredulously, tentatively, 'Rosemary?'

'Look,' she said, brushing past me as I opened the door more widely. 'I simply must talk to you.'

'Well . . . come in.'

While I closed the door behind us she stopped in front of the looking glass in the hall and started to untie the headscarf.

'My God, whatever do I look like?'

I saw that her fingers were shaking too much to undo

5

the knot, and finally with a frustrated little moan she stretched over her head, grasped the points of the scarf, and forcefully pulled the whole thing forward. Off with the scarf came all the black curls, and out shook the more familiar chestnut mane of Rosemary Caspar, who had called me Sid for fifteen years.

'My God,' she said again, putting the tinted glasses away in her handbag and fetching out a tissue to wipe off the worst of the gleaming lipstick. 'I had to come. I had to come.'

I watched the tremors in her hands and listened to the jerkiness in her voice, and reflected that I'd seen a whole procession of people in this state since I'd drifted into the trade of sorting out trouble and disaster.

'Come on in and have a drink,' I said, knowing it was what she both needed and expected, and sighing internally over the ruins of my quiet evening. 'Whisky or gin?'

'Gin . . . tonic . . . anything.'

Still wearing the raincoat she followed me into the sitting room and sat abruptly on the sofa as if her knees had given way beneath her. I looked briefly at the vague eyes, switched off the laughter on the television and poured her a tranquillizing dose of mother's ruin.

'Here,' I said, handing her the tumbler. 'So what's the problem?'

'Problem!' She was transitorily indignant. 'It's more than that.'

6

I was going to have to tread lightly.

"Well, what I didn't tell you was that James lives in London."

"Oh, that's brilliant," she replied as she turned on the dishwasher. Then the penny dropped. "Oh, wait." She faced me, her eyes narrowing. "So, what does that mean for us? You're going to drop me to spend time with James, aren't you?"

I would never have done that. Cat is my best friend in the world, and I only saw her in person every couple of years. Time with her was exceedingly precious to me.

But I did want to see James again before heading home to Australia.

"No, of course not. We can still do all the things you've planned—except I thought that, maybe on Tuesday night, instead of going to the pub quiz with you and your friends, I could see James. You'll hardly even miss me and, besides, I'm not that good at trivia anyway." We both knew that last part was a lie.

She crossed her little arms—she's a very small person—and the scowl intensified.

"Sarah Jane," she started. Uh oh, she was already using my full given name. I held my breath *and* my tongue. "I barely got to see you before you went to Greece and now that you're back, I have the whole week planned out perfectly. You know how much it means to me to have you here, *and* for you to meet Mich and my other friends—"

She was right, but I saw an opening and jumped in. "Well, you're teaching tomorrow, so I can see James then, right?"

7

"What?" My logic seemed to baffle her. I think she'd been ready for more of a fight. "Well, yes, of course. I mean, our plans don't start until Saturday, so ..." She cut herself off with a loud yawn. "Sorry, I've got to go to bed. I have to be up in six hours." She crossed the room and smacked a kiss onto my cheek before disappearing down the hallway to her room.

"Goodnight, Cat," I called after her in a loud whisper. She flapped her hand in response.

I glanced at the pile of bedding next to the couch. Both of Cat's flatmates were in residence that night, and I had been relegated to the pull-out I was sitting on. Normally, that would have been fine, but a lengthy sisterly debrief, the drama surrounding my suitors, and far too much red wine had curdled into a nasty flavour of exhaustion. I didn't think I could muster the energy to make up the pull-out.

With a heavy sigh, I dragged myself off the couch and into the bathroom where I brushed my teeth, splashed some water on my face instead of running through my typical three-step skincare routine, and staggered back to the couch. I plopped a pillow on one end and pulled a doona over me as I stretched out along its length. I promised myself I'd make up a proper bed the next night.

As I drifted off to sleep, I realised with a start that I hadn't responded to the text James had sent earlier, asking when he could see me. In a feat of imperfect timing, it had arrived right after I'd said goodbye to Josh and was in a taxi on the way to the Athens airport, steeping in post-trip blues and already missing the cute American boy.

I flicked my eyes to the clock on the wall. 12:57am. I'd text James in the morning.

*

I woke to the sound of the kettle revving up, the promise of tea the only thing stopping me from smothering myself with a pillow. Whose idea was it to open that second bottle of rioja? Oh, right, it was mine.

"Sez, are you awake?" half-whispered Cat.

I rolled over onto my back and wiped a stream of drool off my cheek. "Yep," I replied, wincing at the sound of my own voice.

"I'm making tea." Ah, the Parsons sisters' motto.

"And here, take these." She held her closed hand above mine and I gratefully accepted two headache tablets. I knew from *vast* experience that along with tea, they were the sure-fire way to kerb a massive wine hangover.

I popped the tablets in my mouth and pulled myself to an upright position. Oh, crap. Water. I needed water. As if by magic, a glass of water appeared in front of me. Have I mentioned how much I love my sister?

I swallowed the tablets with a gulp of water and downed the rest of the glass. "How are *you* feeling, Cat?" She was moving around the kitchen, making up two bowls of cereal with yoghurt while the tea brewed.

"Oh, I'm all right." I eyed her with concern. Cat didn't usually suffer from hangovers like I did, but she certainly wasn't her typical "morning person" self—my doing, I was sure.

9

"Sorry we drank so much last night—and that we stayed up so late." I stood slowly, steadying myself before I began folding the doona.

"Pfft, don't worry about it. I loved hearing about your trip, especially your *suitors*, as Gerry would say." She chuckled to herself, clearly at my expense, but I didn't mind. If she was teasing me, she was probably okay. I put the folded doona onto the pile of untouched linens and added my pillow, then pulled out a stool at the breakfast bar and sat waiting for my tea.

"It was such a wonderful trip, Cat—and not just 'cause of Josh and James." An unbidden smile broke across my face as I mentally transported myself back to the boat, our "floating home" we'd called it.

Cat handed me a mug of tea and I took a sip—strong and milky, just how I liked it. "Seriously, Greece is sublime. I mean, it's *beautiful*. Just being there, seeing those craggy islands with the whitewashed boxy buildings, that pop of Santorini blue, *gorgeous* bursts of bougainvillea everywhere, it made my heart sing." We shared a smile across the kitchen counter and I sipped more tea.

"And time just seemed to go slower there, you know. I really felt like I was squeezing the most out of every day, like each one had a hundred hours in it." I could feel the tea coursing through me, calming me and easing the pounding in my head. Or maybe it was thoughts of Greece working their magic.

"I really needed that trip, Cat, that fresh perspective on everything. I've been so stuck."

"I know, Sez." Her voice was gentle and her eyes so filled with kindness, I was a millimetre from succumbing to a bout of self-pity and regret. How had I let myself get so lost? How had I let so much time pass without *living*?

"I'll have to take you there someday," I added brightly, shaking off the strong pull of wallowing.

"Next time. We need to work out the timing better, though."

"Yeah. Sorry 'bout that." It had been entirely my fault. When I'd booked the trip, I hadn't even considered Cat's teaching commitments. All I'd known in that dark moment as I scoured the internet, credit card in hand, was that I needed something to look forward to, something just for me.

"No, that's not what I meant. I just ... I miss you when you're not here. I wish ..."

She left the thought unfinished, but I knew what she meant. It was a shitty thing living across the world from someone you loved.

"Me too," I replied quietly.

We were back in melancholic territory again and Cat rescued us by changing the subject. "So, what are you and James going to do today?" She pushed a bowl of cereal and a spoon across the counter. There was no one in the world who was a better hangover nurse than my sister.

"I haven't texted him yet, so I'm not even sure he's free. And I have no idea where he lives. He said London, but that could be anywhere inside the M25." I ate a spoonful from my bowl.

"True. But if he's as wealthy as you say, it's probably some-where in the single digits."

"Mmm," I said, chewing and covering my mouth. "Single digits?"

"You *can't* have forgotten," she ribbed. "We're in E14—double digits. He's probably in Kensington or Notting Hill, could be Knightsbridge, *maybe* Hampstead Heath. Or, he could live in Richmond. It's double digits, but it's posh. Oh, I love Richmond," she added wistfully.

Cat's early morning geography lesson was doing my head in and I struggled to keep up. Besides, when we'd lived in London together, our flat was in N8 and that was *not* a posh suburb.

"Crouch End has a single digit postcode," I said, through a mouthful of cereal.

"Right," she acknowledged. "Not exactly posh, but it's brimming with hipsters now. *Anyway*, you know what I mean. He probably lives in a *central* single digit. Or Richmond."

She was right about Richmond, by the way—it *was* beautiful. I loved it too, especially the part along the Thames. I had some lovely memories of long afternoons spent at riverside pubs. It also had great charity shops—people with money donate the most incredible things. I'd once snagged a gorgeous, fits-me-like-a-glove, black leather jacket for fourteen pounds from Oxfam on Richmond High Street.

The whole conversation was moot, however, because I had no idea where James lived. "Yeah, maybe," I replied noncommittally.

Cat seemed to be faring far better than me by the time we finished breakfast. As she tidied up the kitchen, she chatted cheerfully about all the plans she had for us. Meanwhile, I considered it a major accomplishment to keep my breakfast down and my body upright. I tried to concentrate on the multitude of details she was spouting, but my mind kept drifting off.

Finally, and please keep in mind that I adore my sister, she left the kitchen to have a shower and I was plunged into welcomed silence.

Left alone, I turned my attention to the most pressing matter at hand—replying to James. When I retrieved my phone from my (beautiful and much-loved) leather handbag, I realised I had neglected to charge it the night before. Drunk Sarah is useless at remembering such mundane but necessary tasks. Thankfully, though, it still had 15% battery left. I opened James's text.

Hey beautiful. Can't wait to see you. What day should we get together? Jx

I took a deep breath and typed my response. Then deleted it, then typed it again. I followed this pattern twice more before settling on this:

Hi. Are you free today?

Before I could talk myself out of it, I tapped the "send" icon. *Look at me, casually texting a super-handsome man to make plans for a date.*

Who was I kidding? There was nothing casual about a text message that took more minutes to compose than it had words.

I heard Cat leave the bathroom and I grabbed my toiletries bag from my backpack so I could take the next shower. Along with tea and over-the-counter drugs, only a hot shower can complete the hangover cure trifecta.

When I emerged from the shower ten minutes later, feeling somewhat human again, I dried off, then ran some moisturising product through my hair. My plan was to let it dry naturally and I silently begged my curls to behave themselves. Then, wiping steam from the mirror above the sink, I made the joyful discovery that I looked like an extra from *The Walking Dead*. Thank god for makeup. Yes, Rimmel, I'd love the London look, thank you very much—*way* better than "zombie chic". But makeup could wait. I wanted to see if James had replied.

Back in the living room, clad in Cat's borrowed and far-too-short-for-me bathrobe, I picked up my phone, seeing that the battery was down to 8%. *8%?* What the hell had it been doing while I was showering? Computing pi to a thousand decimal places? I needed to plug it in immediately, or it would chuck a huge wobbly, die, then need a two-hour charge before it would turn back on.

I did *not* want to spend the next two hours fretting over a text message.

I dug the charger and an adapter out of my backpack and looked around for an outlet. My phone buzzed at me angrily. 5%. *Argh!* Why was it being so infuriating? *There!* I hurriedly unplugged the kettle, ready to forgo a much-needed second mug of tea, and plugged in the phone.

When I opened my text messages, I saw that James had replied, and my stomach did a little flip.

I was hoping for today, so a yes from me. Where are you and what time can I come and get you?

My heart started racing and it suddenly occurred to me that James was a *real person*.

I know that must sound weird, but James was The Silver Fox—capital letters intended—and our brief time together had been more like an episode of *Sex and the City* than real life. He was my very own Mr Big, and all I had to do was send an address and he'd soon be standing at my door. Well, Cat's door, but you know what I mean.

My little stomach flip evolved into a round-off followed by a handspring. I was beginning to FREAK OUT. Just then, Cat came into the kitchen and caught me looking at my phone as though it was covered in Ebola.

"Uh, Sez?" I blinked at her, feeling the crease between my eyebrows deepening. "What's wrong?"

I pointed at the phone and she came over and read James's message. "The silver fox?" she asked. I nodded and started chewing on my thumbnail, something I'd never done before in my entire life.

"Well, great. You get to see him today." I nodded again. "So, what's going on? Are you all right?" She looked really concerned, which made me even more freaked out. "Sarah, you're going out with him, right? You said you wanted to see him again."

I re-read the message, and it dawned on me why I was so rattled.

"Cat, what if he realises I'm just a silly schoolteacher from Australia, that I'm—" I stopped.

I'm what? Nothing special? No, worse. What if he realises that I'm not the kind of woman who dates the handsome silver fox she met while sailing around the Greek Islands?

Cat was obviously waiting for me to finish my thought. "What if he realises, I'm just *me?*" I steeled myself for the inevitable sisterly dig. Instead, she put her little arms around me and gave me a tight squeeze.

"If he realises that, then he is a very lucky man, because you are wonderful." She let go of me and rooted around in the catch-all on the counter for her keys. "Go on the date. Let him spoil you. Have *fun.*"

"But ..." I trailed off.

"But what?" I saw her glance at the clock. She needed to go.

"Nothing. You're right. I'll text him back." She looked relieved.

"All right, I'm off. Have a fantastic time with your billionaire boyfriend." She kissed my cheek as I started to protest that he was neither a billionaire—just a millionaire—nor my boyfriend, but she ignored me and called out, "Bye-eee," over her shoulder as she walked down the hall and out the door.

I was on my own once more with my wretched, worrisome thoughts. What I was going to say was, "But, what about

Josh?" And what about Josh? Sure, I had plans to see him in December, but I could still meet up with James, right?

Right?

I chewed on my thumbnail again. I was really going to have to stop that. I picked up my phone— now up to a whopping 20% battery—and typed out my response, asking him to pick me up at eleven. That would give me plenty of time to wash my boat-filthy clothes and do something about my zombie face. I added Cat's address and sent the text.

Moments later, he replied.

Perfect. I know a lovely spot for lunch and afterwards I'll take you to one of my favourite places in London. See you soon! Jx

So, it was happening, a date with the silver fox. Then it occurred to me—what do you wear to have lunch with a millionaire?

I did a mental inventory of my backpack, but boating clothes and bikinis would hardly do, and eleven o'clock was only three hours away. What on earth had I been thinking? I wasn't going to have time to wash clothes, fix my face, *and* find something suitable to wear!

I only had one option. I was going to have to raid my sister's wardrobe, which would have been fine if I wasn't five inches taller and several kilos heavier than her.

Crap-a-doodle-do.

Chapter 2

After receiving no less than seven frantic text messages, my sister finally responded to my clothing emergency with excellent news. She'd bought an Alannah Hill dress during her last trip to Sydney and had never got around to altering it. It was in my size!

I found the dress hanging in the back of her wardrobe. It was gorgeous on the hanger, and it looked even better when I put it on. I retrieved my strappy sandals from my backpack—even though I knew the dress would have looked much better with heels, flats would have to do. Before I knew it, it was close to eleven and all I had done for three hours, was get ready and fret.

I wasn't sure whether I was excited about my date with the silver fox, or nervous, but whatever the feeling was—perhaps a little of both—it was doing some spectacular gymnastics in my stomach. And even though I was expecting it, the bleat of the door buzzer made me leap. A grainy black and white image of James appeared on the wall console and I pressed the button so he could hear me.

"Hi James!" I said *way* too enthusiastically. *Cool it, Sarah.*

I deliberately dropped my voice an octave. "I'll be right down."

"Wonderful!" he said, grinning into the camera. I took a step back even though he couldn't see me, such was the impact of that smile.

During the elevator ride to the lobby, I attempted to calm myself by breathing in through my nose and exhaling long slow breaths out of my mouth. It was a shorter ride than I needed, though, because Cat only lived on the fourteenth floor.

Why does he make me feel so squidgy inside? I thought, as the elevator announced its arrival at the lobby. Then the doors opened and there he was, in all his glorious gorgeousness. *Oh yeah, that's why.*

He smiled at me, reaching for my hand as I approached. I gave it willingly, transfixed by that smile, and he gently pulled me towards him, kissing me lightly on the lips. "Hello, beautiful," he said, his voice like honey being poured over gravel.

"Hello, handsome," I replied, as though I was someone way cooler than me. His eyes roved over my face and my shallow breaths reappeared, the traitors.

"We're just out here," he said suddenly, seeming to remember himself. He led me out of the building to his car, which was idling at the kerb. I don't know what kind of car I was expecting him to drive—maybe a Jaguar or Mercedes—but I was pleasantly surprised to see a Peugeot RCZ in metallic marshmallow-white.

I knew what kind of car it was because I like cars—a *lot*—and the RCZ was at the top of my "if I won the lottery, I would buy this car" list. It suited him perfectly, just as elegant and sexy as he was.

James opened the door for me, and I climbed in as gracefully I could, settling into the soft leather seat. As he got in the driver's side, he flicked me a look. His mouth turned up at the corner and he reached across to squeeze my hand. It was almost like he couldn't believe I was there with him.

That made two of us.

As he turned his attention to driving and deftly pulled away from the kerb, I noticed two things. First, James smelled divine. It was the same scent he'd worn in Greece—sunshiny, citrusy and manly. And second, it was a spectacular day in London, which anyone who lives there will tell you, is super rare in early September.

It was sunny, with bright puffs of clouds dotting an azure sky. Glancing at the dashboard, I saw it was 26°C outside—practically a heatwave in London terms, but I was both delighted and relieved. I was wearing a floaty Alannah Hill dress and I didn't want to freeze to death, *or* inadvertently flash my bum because of a chilly gust of wind.

"So, how was the end of your trip?" James asked.

You mean the end of my trip where I slept with Josh and maybe fell for him a little and then made plans to see him in a few months? That?

He obviously didn't know how much of a loaded question he'd asked. He glanced at me, still smiling, and this was when a normal person would reply. I'd have to gather my wits.

"It was lovely. Um, yeah, the last stop, Mykonos, that was, uh, really lovely." Hardly an eloquent response, but my dastardly wits had abandoned me. How could I avoid talking about one would-be suitor to the other without sounding like a twit?

"Was Mykonos your favourite island?"

"No. I mean, I liked it. It's beautiful—all the islands were—but I think I liked Naxos best."

Oops. Naxos was where James and I had officially met, where we'd gone on that sort-of date *and* where he'd kissed me. It was also where he'd asked me what was going on between me and Josh. I had played it down at the time, but things with Josh had progressed since then and I needed to redirect this conversation—pronto.

"Uh, we had an incredible lunch there at this tiny café with no name." Food was a safe topic, right?

"One of Duncan's gems?" Phew. Another safe topic—Duncan.

Relieved that I'd steered the topic away from my romantic entanglements, I leapt back into the conversation with gusto. "Yes, exactly! He seemed to know all these great, out-of-the-way places. And in busy towns, we'd come across a row of restaurants—they'd look *exactly* the same, but he'd know the best one to eat at, *every* time. He never steered us wrong."

"He's great with local knowledge, always has been."

"How did you end up hiring him?" Duncan had once worked for James, skippering James's boat in the Caribbean.

"He answered an advertisement. He was qualified and as soon as I met him, I liked him. It was a good fit."

I felt a surge of fondness for Duncan the Skipper, wondering if I would ever see him again. I also wondered how things were going with him and his girlfriend, Gerry. They were dating long-distance, and I was heavily invested in their "happily ever after" because they were just gorgeous together.

It was also easier than championing my own—*and* far more likely.

I'd met two men who lived across the world from me. That it would work out with one of them would be a minor miracle, one I wasn't sure I wanted. Yes, I needed to shake up my life—like Josh and I had talked about in Greece, I wanted my life to be bigger. But that was about reconnecting with my friends, taking more initiative at work, travelling more. It didn't necessarily mean leaping into a long-distance relationship—with *anyone*. I wasn't sure my heart was ready for that.

What the hell am I doing?

I was having some fun, damn it—well-deserved fun.

After a string of horrid men, not one of whom was able to keep his hands off someone else, I was on a date with a seemingly nice man who thought I was beautiful. Where was the harm in that?

Not to mention, that if I wasn't on a date with James, I would be at Cat's flat, alone, watching bad daytime TV—is that a tautology?—eating too many digestive biscuits, and googling how to get the boat stains out of my clothes.

I turned my attention back to James and watched him navigate the rabbit warren of inner London roads with ease. He was a sexy driver. He probably looked sexy peeling potatoes too, but there is something attractive about a man who looks both confident and comfortable driving. His tanned hands rested lightly on the steering wheel and he frowned ever-so-slightly when he checked his mirrors.

"So, where are we going?" I asked after a few moments of silence.

"Have you been to The Summerhouse?" he asked. No, I had not. I hadn't even heard of The Summerhouse, but if the millionaire was taking me there, it was bound to be good.

"No, not yet, but I've heard it's lovely." There was that word again, "lovely". I felt like asking if we could make a quick stop at Waterstones so I could buy a thesaurus.

"It's fairly close to home for me—not overly fancy, but good food and it's in a nice spot. I think you'll like it."

"So, where is home?" I asked, remembering my conversation with Cat that morning.

"Paddington," he replied. And then he added, "W2," the way people who live in London sometimes do.

Cat had been right. "Single digit," I accidentally said aloud.

"Sorry?" He hadn't quite heard me, thank goodness.

"Paddington's lovely," I replied. *Good grief.*

*

As predicted, I liked The Summerhouse.

It was situated on a canal in an area of West London called Little Venice. I'd been to actual Venice, and the similarities ended with the canal, but it was—dare I say it—a *lovely* part of London.

The restaurant was bright and airy, with furnishings in crisp white and light wood, and on each table was a small bouquet of yellow flowers. There was even a compact hedge of lush green foliage which made a sort-of wall between the restaurant and the canal. The waterway was dotted with canal boats, some moored and some on the move, and with London putting on some brilliant sunshine, the restaurant and its surrounds literally shone.

We were shown to our table—which gave us a front-row view of the canal—by a petite, dark-haired woman with a severe fringe and a perfect red lip. She smiled politely as she handed me my menu. I glanced over it and just seeing the offerings made me hungry. Thank god my hangover was over.

"You cannot go wrong here. Everything's terrific," said James.

"So, you come here a lot, then?" I asked.

He laughed, seemingly at himself. "I do, yes. Probably more than I should, but as I said, it's close to home and I love the food."

"James!" A large man in a white chef's coat called out and made his way across the restaurant, gracefully navigating between the tables.

"Paulie." James looked up at the chef and they shook hands warmly. I wondered if James was one of those people who knew everyone everywhere he went. "This is my friend, Sarah. She's visiting from Sydney."

Paulie turned towards me and took my offered hand between his large ones. "Welcome, Sarah. We'll have to make sure we dazzle you with something tantalising. You have some incredible seafood restaurants in Sydney." That may have been true, but I wasn't the sort of person who frequented the incredible seafood restaurants of Sydney. Still, Paulie didn't know that and I *was* dressed in Alannah Hill, so I decided to play along.

"Oh, we absolutely do, but I'm very much looking forward to this lunch. James has raved about your restaurant." Paulie seemed to like that and when I caught James's eye, he winked at me.

"In that case, may I design a special menu for the two of you?" I looked at James and he shrugged good-naturedly as if to say, "why not?"

I grinned up at Paulie. "I'd love it."

"Terrific. Anything you don't like?" he asked.

"No, not really."

"Excellent." He clapped his hands together in a way that was utterly endearing. "James, the sancerre will be perfect with what I have in mind."

James closed his menu. "Sounds good."

The dark-haired woman suddenly appeared by Paulie's side and he murmured something to her. She smiled her polite smile at us, took our menus, and disappeared.

"Maria will bring the wine. You two, sit tight." With that, Paulie was gone and James and I were left alone. I realised, with some gratitude, that I was no longer nervous. Perhaps our encounter with the larger-than-life Paulie had quelled my nerves. I grabbed the moment to take in more of the view, glad James didn't feel the need to fill the silence.

"It really is beautiful here," I said after a few moments.

"The weather helps," James replied. "Although, it's just as beautiful on a cold, wet day—only a different kind of beauty. They wind down the awnings, so it's quite cosy. And, it's a great place to watch the world go by."

Just then, a canal boat drifted past. I smiled to myself.

"Literally." I turned towards James. "You know, I used to live in London. Did I tell you that?"

"No, I don't think you did. How long ago?"

"Quite a while. I was in my twenties. Actually, my sister and I moved here together. I went back to Australia after a couple of years and she stayed."

"So, London wasn't for you?" Was he just making conversation, or did I detect something more in his tone? "Uh, I don't know if I'd put it that way, exactly. I loved my time here—well, eventually. Cat and I arrived with all these grand ideas of what life would be like, but for the first little while, London nearly chewed us up and spat us out."

"In what way?"

"Well, it's expensive, even compared with Sydney." He nodded, but I wondered if a man who was worth millions could truly understand what I meant. "We *were* lucky—we got work right away. I'd been teaching a couple of years, and Cat was a recent graduate, so we signed up with a teaching agency. But it took a while to get established, you know, to figure out where we wanted to live and to meet people.

"The teaching paid quite well, even though the work was gruelling, so we were able to move out of our bedsit within a month—which was a good thing. I mean, I love my sister, but sharing a bedsit ..." I let the thought hang in the air, smiling to myself at the younger Parsons sisters who'd bickered the whole time. "And then we moved into a flatshare with two other girls and it became more fun, less of a grind. I started touring not long after that."

Maria arrived at our table with two wine glasses and the

bottle of Sancerre, interrupting our conversation. One-handed, she placed a glass in front of each of us, then showed the bottle to James. He gave a slight nod, and she nimbly removed the cork and poured a sip for him to taste.

"I'm sure it's fine, thank you, Maria. Please go ahead." She poured a glass for me, then one for James and, without a word, disappeared with the rest of the bottle.

"So, you said you toured? I'm not sure what that means."

"I worked in travel, leading tours in Europe. I started with Ventureseek a few months after we moved to the flatshare, but I kept my room, so I had a home base."

"So, you've seen quite a lot of Europe, then?"

"Yes," I laughed. "Lots of the *touristy* parts and I always had fifty other people to worry about, so there wasn't a lot of time for *real* travel, to immerse myself. That's why this trip to Greece was so important to me. It was the first time I'd been there by myself and it was kind of perfect, you know, the pace of it. Lots of time for contemplation."

I knew I was treading dangerously close to Josh and all our discussions about that bigger life. My delinquent wits finally showed up, telling me to steer the conversation in another direction, but James did it for me. "Did you enjoy it, the touring?" he asked.

"Yes—mostly. And eventually, I wanted to move back to Australia." I left it at that, and he didn't press, which I appreciated. I could talk ad nauseum about my touring days, the places I'd been to, the people, the *loneliness*. Not exactly great date conversation, that last part.

"So, where was the flatshare?"

"Crouch End," I replied. Then I added, "N8."

"Oh, Crouch End is terrific. Good coffee."

I was amused and a little dubious. "You've spent time in Crouch End?"

"Of course. It has a wonderful arts scene. I have quite a few artists on my books that I found in boutique galleries in and around Crouch End." *Ahhh, of course.*

I took a sip from my neglected wine glass. The Sancerre was delicious.

"To reunions," said James, holding his glass aloft.

"Oh, sorry. Here I am drinking without a toast. To reunions," I said, smiling to cover my embarrassment. We clinked glasses and each took a sip. When James placed his glass back on the table, his mouth bore a hint of a smile and he seemed to drink me in with his eyes. My heart sped up under his gentle scrutiny, and I held his gaze unflinchingly.

He truly was a magnificent-looking man.

The night before, I'd told Cat that James reminded me of a salt-and-peppered Richard Armitage. Sitting opposite him, I was seeing hints of Gerard Butler too. That should give you an indication of the level of gorgeousness I was dealing with.

"I didn't tell you before how beautiful you look today," he said, out of nowhere. Or maybe he had read my mind and wanted to return the compliment.

Regardless, I blushed. And I don't usually blush, but I felt the warmth creep up my chest and fill my cheeks. I hoped I didn't look like I'd just downed a giant bowl of heavy-hitting Tandoori.

"Thank you," I replied, as graciously as I could. Where was the food?

In a moment of truly perfect timing, two plates of crab cakes and grapefruit salad arrived at the table—exactly what I would have ordered for a starter.

"Happy?" asked James. I knew he was talking about the food, but when I considered my reply it encompassed a whole lot more.

"Absolutely." I smiled at him and took a bite of crab cake. It was divine.

*

The rest of lunch was just as delicious. Paulie prepared pan-fried seabass for the main course and sent out a cheese board for dessert. I love sea bass—*and* cheese. Paulie was clearly a genius.

Just as we were finishing the cheese course, I asked James where he grew up. I'd been listening closely to him all through lunch and even though I'm usually good at picking accents, I still hadn't pinned his down. It seemed to be a hodgepodge of several western European accents.

"I was born here in London—Surrey, actually—and we stayed until I was five, and then every year or so we moved to a new European country—Belgium, Germany, France, Spain, the Netherlands. I didn't settle back in the UK until I went to university." So, I *had* picked it. I skipped my usual self-congratulations, however, because James's description of his childhood had left me cold.

I couldn't imagine moving around so much in my formative years. I'd gone to one primary school, which had fed into one high school, and I had friends I'd known since I was five.

"But this is home now, right?" I asked, concerned. Everyone needs a *home*, somewhere to come back to after the whirlwind and excitement of travel.

I took a tiny sip of wine as I waited for his reply. James was sitting on one glass, because he was driving, and I had limited myself to two, because I wanted to maintain the façade that I was a sophisticated woman, which tipsy Sarah is not.

"London is, yes, although I've lived in various places. Paris was a favourite." Paris was a favourite city of mine too, to *visit*. The longest I had stayed there was a week. *Maybe James will take me to Paris*. I put my inner voice back in her box. Wangling an invite to Paris was hardly good manners on a first date.

"And what about you? Have you considered living outside of Australia again?" he asked, his sky-blue eyes staring into mine. Something was making my mind fuzzy. It was either the wine or those eyes, but my fuzzy mind was a millisecond away from saying, "with you?"

I recovered in time to respond like a normal adult person. "To be honest, I haven't really thought about it."

His smile was unreadable. Did it mean, "you're adorable, you unsophisticated Aussie," or, "I've got a villa in France I think you'd like?" Either way, I wanted to change the subject— *again*.

"So, you said something about taking me to one of your favourite places?"

"Yes, but I'm going to keep it as a surprise until we get there." He winked at me again and, believe me, he could pull off a wink without being cheesy. In fact, such was its power, I felt a tingling warmth ignite between my legs. I wondered what the protocol was for inviting a silver fox back to my sister's flatshare for mind-blowing sex. That would be okay, right?

James signalled for the bill. Although I usually went Dutch on a first date—and second and third and fourth dates too—I knew James was not the sort of man who would expect that, or even want it, so I sat quietly while he settled it.

"Thank you for lunch," I said when Maria left the table.

"You're more than welcome."

"Paulie is something of a genius, I think."

"Did I hear my name?" Suddenly the big man was beside us. How was he so stealthy? James and I stood, and I collected my handbag from under my chair. Paulie shook James's hand again while James thanked him for lunch.

"And how did we do, Miss Sarah? Did you enjoy your lunch?"

"Paulie, it was divine. Thank you."

"Excellent! I'm so pleased. We will have to have you and James back again soon." Before I could respond, Paulie leant down and kissed me on both cheeks.

"I'd love that," I said, laughing a little at his infectious ebullience. *I would love to come back here with James sometime.* The thought arrived unbidden, but I was starting to think I'd love to go anywhere with James. *Uh oh.*

Chapter 3

Riding through the streets of inner London in James's car, I looked out of the passenger window as we passed pristine rows of terraced houses, lush gated gardens, and pubs that had been standing for centuries, their window boxes brimming with bright bouquets of flowers.

London was putting on a spectacular show, and if I hadn't known better—that she had dark corners where filth and poverty and loneliness dwelled—it was the sort of day that could make me fall in love with her again.

"I'm taking the long way," said James as he turned onto Bayswater Road. "I just adore Hyde Park."

I did too and on that day, Londoners were out in full force sunning themselves and revealing a vast array of flesh. Mums and dads with small children pushed prams with fat little feet poking out; business people walked barefoot on the grass with their shoes in their hands; young women wearing swimsuits sunned themselves on towels; and older men and women sat on benches, fanning themselves with newspapers and tossing chunks of bread to the swans.

Everyone in Hyde Park seemed to be making the most of the early autumn sun.

"Are you really not telling me where we're going?" I asked.

"Don't you like surprises?" James asked, flicking me an amused look.

"Not really," I replied honestly. I *didn't* like surprises. I liked to know what to expect so I wouldn't be blindsided. Sure, some surprises were good, but in my experience, most of them were awful, like finding out your boyfriend is sleeping with your yoga bestie. That was Neil the cheating bastard, by the way.

Still, I didn't want to appear ungrateful. "Sorry," I said, glancing at James.

He gave me an understanding smile. "Not at all. We're going to the British Museum. I have a friend who works there and she's going to give us a private tour of the Parthenon Sculptures."

Oh, so it was a *good* surprise. "That sounds amazing, James." I meant it, but it sounded feeble to my contrite ears.

"Have you been before, to the museum?"

"Oh, for sure. It's a favourite of mine too." When I'd lived in London, the British Museum was one of the places I'd retreat to when I was having a hard time. I'd wander slowly around the Great Court or visit the Marbles from the Parthenon. Mostly, though, I went to the Reading Room, sometimes to read, sometimes just to sit quietly. It was the closest I came to meditation.

"I thought it was fitting, since we met in Greece. Did you get to the Acropolis?" James asked, pulling me from my thoughts.

"Oh, no, not on this trip, unfortunately. The only time I had in Athens was a rather harrowing taxi ride to the airport. I've been before, though. I'm guessing not much has changed in only a decade. You know, it being an ancient ruin and all."

He smiled. "They have made a *bit* of progress on the restoration, but they also have the most incredible museum now. It's definitely worth going next time you're there." *Or you and I could go together.* See how my mind gets ahead of itself?

"That museum, do they have many original artefacts? Aren't most of them here?" I asked.

"About half and half, so there are a lot of replicas in Athens, I'm afraid, but I know Greece is actively campaigning to take ownership again. Valentina will likely know how they're progressing."

Ah, Greece. Glorious, beautiful, heart-filling Greece.

It was only days before that I'd been eating *horiatiki* and basking under the Greek sun. I was already missing it. And Josh, I realised with a jolt. But I didn't want to think about Josh, especially as James chose that moment to cover my hand with his and give it a gentle squeeze.

Was holding hands cheating? Could you cheat on someone who wasn't really your boyfriend, someone who had called you his "travel buddy"? The whole situation was too confusing for words and I wanted Josh out of my head immediately.

Thankfully, the familiar cupola of the museum appeared ahead of us and thoughts of Josh receded into the background where they belonged. James pulled into a parking space and turned off the engine, then turned towards me.

"Sarah," he said, a glint in his eye. God, he was sexy. I tried not to hyperventilate.

"I thought I could wait until later, but that is not going to happen." He reached over and cupped my chin in his hand and pulled me towards him. His mouth was warm and soft against mine, and he tasted faintly of the wine. I responded to the kiss as though we were somewhere private and not in the middle of London. How far away was Paddington, anyway? Perhaps the Marbles could wait.

We broke the kiss with shy smiles, and he rested his forehead against mine. "Sarah, you take my breath away." *I do?* There I was having to steady my breath every time he merely glanced at me and, apparently, I was having the same effect on him. *Me!*

"And as much as I'd like to skip out on Valentina, she's a good friend and she's promised us something special."

I was siding with skipping out, but then again, I do hate to be rude. "Then we shouldn't keep her waiting," I replied before giving him a quick smack on the lips and climbing out of the car. I didn't know who this super-confident Sarah was, but James seemed to like her. I didn't mind her either.

The private tour of the museum was incredible and so was Valentina. If James hadn't been explicit about fancying me, she was the kind of woman who could induce some heavy-hitting jealousy. She was Italian, tall, slim, and blonde. She was also one of the most beautiful women I'd ever seen in person. She greeted me with two cheek kisses—James's friends were so affectionate—and a warm smile.

"*Buongiorno*, Sarah. A pleasure to meet you."

It was a pleasure to meet her too and I hoped I could get through the tour without drooling on her shoes, especially as they were suede. I was forming a serious girl crush.

And I needn't have worried about James fancying her. Valentina was married to his closest friend from university, Marcus. She also treated James like a brother, teasing him good-naturedly about me.

"James must think very highly of you, Sarah. The last time he introduced me to someone he was dating was two popes ago." She raised her eyebrows at me and James shook his head, smiling.

Valentina was the fourth of James's friends I'd met—if you counted Duncan, which I did—and they all obviously adored him. I took it as a sign that he was one of the good guys. Armando, his friend in Greece, had alluded to him playing the field, but Valentina was saying the opposite. And based on the embarrassed look on his face, she seemed to be right. That was both flattering and terrifying. It certainly didn't play into my "just have some fun" approach to our date. I'd have to unpack it later.

As well as giving us a tour, Valentina snuck us behind the scenes to see a collection of artefacts that had just been uncovered on Crete. She was leading the curation of the collection and it was fascinating to gain some insight into the laborious process of identifying and cataloguing dozens, if not hundreds, of pieces.

She also gave us an update on Greece's claim on the remaining pieces from the Acropolis, which was that there was no update. Greece still wanted them back and the Brits were still holding onto them. Such an odd, and somewhat heart-breaking, situation.

Eventually, we said reluctant goodbyes to Valentina, who was due at a mid-afternoon meeting. James promised to see her and Marcus soon and asked her to send his love to her oafish husband. She laughed at that.

I truly hoped *I* would see her again.

As we made our way back through the Great Court, I walked slowly so I could stare up at the glass ceiling and its mesmerising geometric shapes. James took my hand and leant down. "I love watching you take it all in," he said. And I was enjoying taking it all in. The Great Court is an incredible space. It's the kind of place that makes you feel small and vulnerable, and grand and capable of anything, all at once.

I pointed at the Reading Room. "I used to spend a lot of time in there after I first moved here," I said.

"Oh yes?"

"It was a sanctuary of sorts—a good place to collect my thoughts."

"I can understand that. Would you like to go up?"

I smiled. "I'd love that."

He led me up the left staircase, still holding my hand. We stepped into the large, round room and without saying anything, we both headed off in a different direction, me to the left and James to the right.

We circled the perimeter of the room slowly, connected only by our eyes.

The room smelled of leather and paper, of humanity, history, and contemplation. Snippets of whispers filled the air, but mostly there was the stillness. It felt familiar, like home. As I embarked on the bigger life I'd promised myself, I knew I would need to find somewhere like it in Sydney, somewhere I could just *be*.

I kept my eyes on James as we walked, first away from each other, then ever closer. We met on the opposite side of the room, oblivious to the other people in the space. When we were toe to toe, we shared a smile. "Hello," he whispered.

"Hello," I whispered back, a tingling sensation rushing through me.

He took my hand again and led me from the room. When we stepped outside, he stopped on the top of the staircase and kissed me fervently and quickly. It lasted just long enough to elicit an, "Ahem!" from someone nearby, but I didn't care about propriety.

It had been a magical afternoon. Even going to a place I knew, somewhere I'd been dozens of times before, was a new experience with James. As he drove us through London, heading east towards Cat's flat, I thought about that bigger life I wanted. That afternoon had been a great start.

And maybe I *did* like surprises, especially when they came in the package of a six-foot-something, blue-eyed silver fox. I hadn't wanted to meet anyone in Greece, yet here was a man who was bright and exciting and sexy.

Quite simply, James was a wonderful surprise.

*

"You got a private tour of the British Museum?!" asked Cat, obviously impressed.

I was bustling around her kitchen making a frittata for our dinner. With toast being her biggest contribution to the culinary world, she was sitting at the breakfast bar, keeping out of my way. We were both sipping wine—*not* a stunning bottle from the Loire Valley, but a cheap and cheerful chardonnay she'd picked up at Sainsbury's on the way home.

"Not the whole museum—that could take a week."

"True."

"But she did walk us through the Acropolis exhibit. Cat, she's amazing. She's brilliant for a start. She gave us the most incredible insight into—"

"Enough about the gorgeous Italian woman," Cat waved her hand at me impatiently. "I want to hear more about your date with the silver fox."

"But Valentina is an important part of my date." She rolled her eyes, so I skipped ahead to the Reading Room and the kiss on the stairs. Cat's mouth popped open.

"No way," she said after a moment of incredulity.

"*Way*," I replied mock-seriously.

"You have the most incredible fucking life," she said, a generous measure of jealousy in her tone.

"You say that like this sort of thing happens to me all the time." She made a little noise in the back of her throat. I read it as, "it does—you lucky, lucky cow." "It doesn't! You know that better than anyone. My love life has been a parade of cheating dickheads for years now, and just because I go on one date with James, doesn't mean my whole *life* has changed."

I punctuated my point by expertly cracking an egg onto the edge of the bowl.

"But it's not just the date with James, though, is it? There's the hot American too. Maybe this is a turning point for you, for your love life." I continued cracking eggs while she gave me a dose of her "I know you better than anyone" rhetoric. "And anyway, history with men aside, you *do* have an incredible life. You travel, you have a good job, you live in *Sydney* where there's actual sunshine more than four days a year—"

It was my turn to cut her off. "True, yes, all true. And, I do need to focus more on the positive, but this whole trip— meeting Josh and James—that's all new. That's not me having 'an incredible fucking life' as you put it."

"You're right." Who was this woman and what had she done with my sister? "I'm a little jealous, that's all." I whisked the eggs and eyed her suspiciously. Cat didn't typically tout her shortcomings.

"It's just that *I* wouldn't mind a handsome millionaire schlepping me about London in his fancy car and adoring me."

"Hang on ..." I stopped whisking—seriously, who *was* this woman? "Did I just hear Cat Parsons say she wouldn't mind having a *boyfriend*?"

I could see the gears turning behind her eyes as she realised what she'd said. Because Cat didn't *do* boyfriends. She didn't do dating, casual or otherwise, and she *certainly* didn't do "adoring men".

Cat was anti love. Full stop.

"You know what I mean," she back-pedalled. "I could go for a handsome millionaire *lover*, is all."

"Cat, he's not my lover." *Yet.* I didn't voice that last part. I rarely won arguments with my sister, and I wasn't about to lose on a technicality.

"Well, he's *something*—and there's Josh—*two* hot lovers, Sez. They're gunna make you hand in your sisterhood card." She punctuated *her* point with one of her looks. Crap, she was going to win this one.

"Okay," I conceded, "I get what you're saying. But really, this thing with James, it's just a bit of fun, like a karmic reward for all the crap Neil put me through. And if I spend more than five minutes thinking about it ... well, it's just *bizarre*, like it's not even real," I added before going back to the eggs.

"Well, of course! That stuff in the museum, that's soppy romance-novel stuff. That's a frigging Nicholas Sparks novel. Julia Roberts will probably play you in the film." She got me laughing with that.

"Julia Roberts is a bit too old to play me. Maybe Emilia Clarke."

"Oh, she's *fab*."

"She is. I bet she could do an Aussie accent, too."

"Definitely. So, who'd play the silver fox?"

"James? Well, I told you he reminds me of Richard Armitage."

"Oh, I *love* him. *Ocean's Eight*—I mean, he's so delicious in that, even though he's the baddy."

"I love him from the *Vicar of Dibley*. Remember when he asks Geraldine to marry him—"

"Oh, yes, yes, that's right and she thinks he means to perform the ceremony to *another woman*—and then she realises that he's *proposing*—"

"—and she starts making those burbling noises." Cat and I made the noises, then laughed so hard, I stopped frittata-ing and she stopped drinking. I still can't imagine how Dawn French got through that scene. "God, that was funny," I said when I'd recovered my ability to speak.

Cat sighed one of those loud sighs you do after a good laugh and I got back to the frittata mixture, pouring it into a pan and sliding it into the oven. "Okay, that should take about twenty minutes."

"Top-up?" she asked rhetorically as she leapt off her stool and retrieved the wine from the fridge. I pushed my glass towards her.

"So, when are you seeing him again?" she asked.

I took a sip of wine—Dutch courage. "Well, that's the thing. It turns out that Tuesday *is* good for him. In fact, he wants to take me to a gallery opening in SoHo." I took another sip of wine, knowing this could go either way.

"You should go," she said matter-of-factly.

"Really? But what about the pub quiz? And your friends?"

"We can go out with them on Wednesday, or maybe Thursday. We'll grab drinks after they finish work, or something."

"But the quiz ..." I trailed off. I didn't want to leave her in the lurch.

"Sarah, we win nearly every week—*without* you. I think we'll be fine."

I put my glass down, ran around the other side of the kitchen island, and scooped her up in a huge hug. "Thank you. Thank you. Thank you!"

"You're welcome." I stepped back, a massive grin on my face. "Now," she said, "what are you going to wear?"

Oh, crap. I hadn't thought about that.

Chapter 4

Two wardrobe emergencies in one week! Well, maybe "emergency" was too dramatic. It was only Friday and I had until Tuesday to figure out what to wear to the gallery opening.

"Show me what you've got," said Cat.

"I've got sailing clothes. You know—shorts, bikinis, sarongs."

"And clothes for this week, yes, for booting about London?" She was leaning against the doorframe of her room, watching me rummage around in my backpack.

"Well, yes, but that's just skinny jeans and tops."

"Hmm. Besides the Alannah Hill, I don't have anything that's going to fit you and you can't wear it again. Or, can you?" I threw her a look that said, "no".

Then I remembered the dress—*the* dress. The one Josh bought for me in that boutique on Mykonos, right before the end of the trip.

"Hang on," I said, digging into a pocket of the backpack. I pulled out the dress and held it up.

"That's not skinny jeans," said Cat dryly.

"No, definitely not skinny jeans." I hugged the dress to me, remembering Josh's expression when he saw me in it for the first time. "Josh bought it for me," I added quietly. When I met Cat's eyes, her face was unreadable. "What does that look mean? Don't you like it?"

"Uh, *hello*, it's gorgeous. Put it on." I quickly undressed, stepped into the dress, and pulled the straps up over my shoulders. I turned away from Cat so she could zip it up and when I turned back around, I stood silently chewing on my lip.

"Well, it looks amazing."

"It does?" I looked down at the dress again. It was long and hugged my body, with slits up both sides, and it was all the colours of a sunset, an ombre of yellow, orange, pink, and red.

"Sez, c'mon, you know it does."

"But ..." I hesitated.

"But, what? You have to wear that dress." Didn't she understand that *Josh* bought me the dress, and I couldn't wear it on a date with *James*?

Or *could* I? While I contemplated my mini moral dilemma, a more pressing thought popped into my head. "Crap. I don't have any shoes and I can't wear it to a gallery opening with my sandals—they're flats."

"You're right. We'll go shopping tomorrow."

I stepped in front of Cat's full-length mirror. I really did look good in the dress. "Hair up or down?" I asked, pulling my hair into a loose knot on top of my head.

"Up, definitely." Cat stood behind me and looked at me in

the mirror. "I can help if you like. Oh, and I have an evening bag that will look great with the dress."

"Oh, thank you, Cat." Feeling my excitement mount, I threw my arms around her.

"You know," she said, her voice muffled by my hug, "that evening bag is rather roomy. You can even fit a toothbrush and a clean pair of knickers in it."

My sister is hilarious.

*

Cat and I had a *fantastic* weekend. We mooched about Portobello Market, had a tipsy sing-along to an Ed Sheeran cover artist in the local pub, enjoyed a couple of chatty dinners in cheap and cheerful cafés, and when we weren't out and about, we hung out at Cat's place solving the problems of the world while downing copious amounts of tea and chocolate digestives.

I met Cat's bestie, Mich—such a darling—and her lovely flatmate, Jane, who joined us at the pub on Saturday afternoon. Cat's other flatmate, Alex, had gone to Scotland for a long weekend and I still hadn't met him. In truth, I was beginning to wonder if he actually existed. Still, with him away, I had three nights of sleeping in a real bed and not on the pull-out. *Thank you, Alex, whoever you are!*

Most importantly, though, I got to do one of my favourite things—spend time with my sister.

She is one of the very few people on the planet who I can be myself with—*completely* myself. Sometimes I'm brilliant,

47

funny, and brave, but mostly I'm a bit of a dork who loves photos of cats sleeping in weird places and can tie a cherry stem in a knot with my tongue. That last thing is a party trick I cultivated at uni, and it's never failed to impress my audience, especially if it's an audience of one. I'll just leave it at that.

We went shoe shopping on the Saturday morning, and I found a gorgeous pair for my date with James. They were cherry-red, suede heeled sandals with a fringe across the top of the foot, and I'd hit the jackpot. They were beautiful *and* I could walk in them. They also matched the red hues of my sunset dress. Cat's evening bag was a large fuchsia clutch and she was right, it completed the look perfectly.

She was also right about the toothbrush and knickers part. I had no idea how the night with James was going to end, but why not be prepared, right? I borrowed a small makeup bag from Cat and packed it with a G-string, my toothbrush, some moisturiser, concealer, and lip balm. I tucked it into the corner of the clutch and added the usual going-out paraphernalia—lipstick, tissues, my phone, and a credit card.

Before she left for the pub quiz, Cat came through with a very sexy up-do. Magically, it looked like I'd scooped up my curls and piled them on top of my head, then pinned them with a single hairpin—implying that my up-do could be undone and shaken loose in one fell swoop, just like in old Hollywood films. She's clever like that.

I, however, was not the sort of woman who could pull off a move like that. Also, my hair actually had twenty-five hairpins in it, so even if I tried to shake it free, I'd end up looking like Tippy Hedren in *The Birds*.

James was sending a car for me at 8:00pm, another reminder that he was wealthy and sophisticated, and I was about to step, once again, into an unfamiliar world.

At ten minutes to eight, I locked up Cat's flat and took the elevator to the lobby. The driver was supposed to call when he arrived, but I was so nervous, I'd been pacing a hole in the carpet of Cat's hallway since 7:40. I figured a change of scenery was in order and, if needed, that the lobby was long enough for some advanced pacing.

The nerves were nothing new to me. I was prone to bouts of nervousness, but sometimes the nerves became full-blown anxiety. It was that tipping point I was hoping to avoid by heading to the lobby. Being nervous was one thing, but when you're having an anxiety attack, it doesn't matter that your mind knows there's no real reason for your survival instincts to be activated. You're in it and you have to ride it out.

Of course, being nervous was understandable. Until I met Josh and James, my romantic history was a series of train wrecks. No doubt, some part of my unconscious mind was bleating, "Run away! Run away!" like King Arthur in *Monty Python and the Holy Grail*.

At exactly 8:00pm, a black town car pulled up in front of the building and my phone rang inside my clutch. I didn't bother answering it. Instead, I walked outside and when the driver climbed out of the car, I called out, "Hello, it's me." He looked confused, so I started waving. "Hi, I'm Sarah. You're here for me." *Okay, calm down, Sarah. You're not going to the Oscars.*

He smiled politely and walked around the car to open the

back door for me. I got in by sitting on the seat and swinging my legs around—a trick I'd seen on TV—and settled back against the dark leather seat. The car was immaculate and smelled of new car and fancy air freshener. I hadn't expected anything less.

"Would you care for some bottled water?" asked the driver, as he pulled away from the kerb. If I had been in an Uber on the way to dinner with my girlfriends, I would have said yes. But I was nervous. If I said yes, I would either A) spill the water down the front of me, or B) successfully drink the water without spilling a drop, but have to pee the moment I arrived at the gallery. I wasn't chancing either.

"Uh, no thank you."

"We will arrive at the gallery before 8:40pm, madam."

Madam? Isn't "madam" reserved for older ladies? I'm only thirty-six, for crying out loud.

"Is there a type of music you would prefer to listen to?" he asked. I hadn't realised I would have so many decisions to make during a forty-minute car ride.

"Um, sure. How about Adele?" Now I was asking *him*, as though we had to come to some sort of consensus. I silently thanked him for having the good manners not to make me feel like more of an idiot. Adele started singing at a moderate volume and I took a deep breath.

Geez, Sarah. Anyone would think you've been living under a rock. You've been in a limo before—twice!—and those are way fancier.

It was cute how I was tricking myself into believing that the *car ride* was making me nervous.

A Sunset in Sydney

I looked out the side window, focusing on the beauty of London at night. I know Paris is considered the City of Lights, but London is a close second in my mind. When we drove past the Houses of Parliament, they reflected their twinkling, golden lights onto the Thames.

It was a calm, still night, without a cloud in the sky— another rarity in London—and I hoped to steal some of that calm for myself. I knew I just needed to be myself—but the brilliant, funny, and brave Sarah, rather than the dork who loved cat photos.

I saw the driver discreetly text someone as we pulled up outside the gallery and when he opened my door, James was waiting for me on the footpath, offering me his hand. I took it and as I stepped out of the town car, the slit of my dress revealed my recently tanned thigh.

I saw James's eyes flick down to my thigh, then back to my eyes, the flash of lust obvious. He leant in to kiss my cheek, the most unchaste cheek kiss I'd ever received. Between that and his lusty look, my nethers were on high alert.

"You're breathtaking," he whispered in that honey-gravel voice. I surprised myself by keeping my cool and leaning into the kiss.

"Thank you," I half-whispered back.

Keeping my hand in his, James led us up two steps, through what looked like someone's front door, and into the gallery. The first room was filled with people, many sipping bubbles or drinking a bright red cocktail from martini glasses. There was a general hubbub echoing off the wooden floorboards, but no distinctively loud voices.

Until I heard a loud, throaty laugh coming from the next room.

"That's Valentina," said James. Valentina! My girl crush from the museum! "Come with me," he added as he manoeuvred us through the artsy crowd with ease. He stopped to take a flute of bubbles from a passing waiter, handed it to me, then took one for himself, all while holding my hand. When we stepped through the doorway into the next room, there she was.

As soon as she laid eyes on me and James, she excused herself from the woman she was talking to and made a beeline for us. Or rather, for me. "Sarah!" she called enthusiastically, as she kissed me on both cheeks. "You look divine!"

I smiled back at her brightly, "Thank you, and so do you." She did, trust me.

You know those women who can pull off tight leather pants and a flimsy, almost see-through blouse and look totally incredible and not at all like a tragic fashion victim? That was Valentina. Her hair fell down her back in a slick sheet, like Cher circa 1975, only blonde. I was in *love*.

She turned to James and gave him a quick kiss. "Marcus is in there." She pointed to the next room. "He can't get away from Sir Percy. Can you please rescue him, *bello*?"

James looked at me questioningly. "Go, I'll be fine. Anyway, I want to meet Marcus, so you'd better go get him." He disappeared into the crowd and then it was just me and Valentina, who was staring at my shoes.

"*Mi amore*, where did you get those?" she asked. I pointed a toe and turned my ankle from side to side.

"You like them?" I asked, knowing the answer. If two women both love shoes, it's enough to build a friendship on.

"They are simply gorgeous," she said, still staring.

"Shoe Embassy in Camden."

"Oh, I love that place, but I haven't been in so long. I must get back there."

"They were the last pair. I was super lucky they were in my size."

"*Fantastico.*"

James appeared at my side. He looked down at my shoes, as Valentina was doing, then up at me. "Great shoes." His eyes twinkled with good humour.

"Apparently, they're a hit," I quipped back.

"Sarah Parsons," he said, turning his attention to the man standing beside him. "Marcus Aurelius."

Marcus, Valentina's husband, was another handsome silver fox, but I doubted his name was really Marcus Aurelius. "Nice to meet you," I said, holding out my hand.

He ignored it and kissed me on the cheek—my cheeks were getting quite the attention that night. "Likewise," Marcus said with a crisp London accent that reminded me of Hugh Grant.

Valentina and James both beamed at Marcus, and it was clear there was a lot of love between them. Then, for a moment, no one said anything, so I did what I usually did in those situations—I filled the silence. "So, Aurelius?" All three of them laughed, and I felt a little put out that I didn't get the joke.

"It's a nickname Marcus earned during a mini-break the three of us took to Rome—an aeon ago," said James, filling me in. "It's a juicy story, but perhaps one for another time," he added, almost conspiratorially, and I felt like I was back in the fold.

"So, Sarah. Have you been to this gallery before?" asked Marcus.

"No, I haven't. Actually, I don't even know which gallery we're at."

James raised a hand. "That's my fault, I'm afraid. I don't think I ever told you. Sorry." He leant his head against mine as though we were already a couple who shared in-jokes. "It's called 'Laz Inc.' and it's the brainchild of that man over there, Steve Lazarides." He nodded towards a bald man, with strong features, who looked about forty.

"Is he a friend?" I asked.

"A colleague, of sorts." I searched James's face for more information, but it didn't seem like he was going to reveal anything more. "Did you want to have a look through the exhibit?" he asked, changing the subject.

"Sure," I smiled brightly at him.

"We'll come and find you later," he said to Marcus and Valentina before taking my hand and leading me into the next room.

To be honest, I was less interested in the art than I was in James. He was dressed in a casual grey suit with a pale blue shirt opened to the third button. God, he was gorgeous. He also looked so at ease—in his clothes, in that environment with all those people—that I envied him a little. In contrast, I felt like the great pretender.

We stopped in front of a large square painting, which I

regarded with a tilted head. It was frighteningly ugly and I found myself frowning at it as I took in the rough texture of the paint and the various shades of grey and brown.

"That dress is quite something, Sarah." His voice was low and deep in my ear, and his breath tickled my neck.

The image of a grinning Josh popped into my mind, but I dismissed it as fast as it came. "I got it in Greece," I said, omitting the most important part of that story. When I looked up at James, he nodded approvingly.

Then a tiny furrow appeared between his brows. "Sarah ..." It was a small shock to realise that James seemed nervous. I kept my eyes on his and squeezed his hand in encourage-ment. "I know I invited you to this event, and we haven't even seen the art yet, but ... I just want to take you home and make love to you."

Oh. My. God.

"May I do that?" With his gravelly voice and his eyes intently locked on mine, my nethers went to DEFCON 1. The only reply I could muster was a nod.

Chapter 5

We made a quick getaway, with a brief stop to say goodbye to Marcus and Valentina. I truly hoped I'd see them both again, especially Valentina. I was certain we were destined to become best friends.

As we rode in the back of the town car, James's hand resting on mine, anxious Sarah made a highly unwelcomed appearance. My stomach was doing Olympic-level gymnastics at the thought of going home with the silver fox. I reminded myself I was sexy, smart, well-travelled, and a grown woman. The driver had even called me "madam". I was also incredibly grateful for Cat's insistence that I get a "just in case" bikini wax.

Cat! I should text her to say I'll be late. "Uh, James?" He looked at me, the desire in his eyes nearly setting me on fire.

"Yes?" There was that bemused smile again.

"Do you mind if I send a quick text to my sister? To, uh, let her know I won't be home 'til late?"

He broke into a full smile. "Of course not. But you may want to tell her you won't be back until tomorrow."

My surprise was genuine. "Really?"

He tilted his head to the side, "I'm fairly certain I won't want you to go."

"Oh," I replied, and I couldn't help smiling back. I hadn't wanted to be presumptuous about sleeping over, but there was nothing ambiguous about James's invitation.

I took out my phone and shot off a quick text to Cat.

Left gallery early. Going back to James's place. Be home tomorrow. Eeek!

I put my phone away and reached for James's hand. *Keep calm, Sarah. You're just going home with the silver fox to make love with him. No biggie.*

My phone bleeped, interrupting my internal pep talk and James looked at the pink clutch on my lap.

"That was quick."

"Oh, Cat is never without her phone. I think she'd have it surgically implanted if she could." *Well, that's complete bullshit, Sarah.* Cat was no more a slave to her phone than I was. We both thought of our phones as a convenience, not something we couldn't live without.

"Did you want to check it?"

"Uh, yeah, sure." I took out my phone out and opened the text without checking who it was from.

Josh. It was from Josh. *Oh, crap.*

I read it quickly, trying to keep my expression neutral.

A Sunset in Sydney

Hey Sarah. I hope you're having a great time in London.
I'm almost on Chicago time again and started back at
work yesterday. Brutal. Missing our boat and the gang.
Missing you. Catchya later. Jx

As texts went, it was fairly innocuous, but I was sitting next to James. On my way to his house. Where we were about to have sex.

"Everything all right?" said the handsome man next to me.

"Absolutely," I said, flashing a completely fake million-watt smile. I put my phone on silent and tucked it away at the bottom of the enormous clutch. I knew Cat would be fine with my sleepover plans, and I *certainly* wasn't going to reply to Josh while I was with James.

Having two suitors was hard.

I wished I had Gerry to talk to, or one of my other girl-friends from the boat, Marie or Hannah. They'd all met Josh *and* James, so I knew they'd understand I was torn in two—except that Marie was definitely "Team Josh".

I had no idea what team I was on, or if I was on either team. Was there a "Team Sarah"?

James took my hand again and lifted it to his mouth to kiss it. "Good, because we're here."

I looked out my window to see an immaculate white terraced house with black trim surrounding two bay windows on each floor and steps up to a glossy black door with tall topiary trees standing sentry either side. It was very "London". It was also magnificent.

The driver came around to my side of the car and opened

the door for me while James got out on his side. By the time I had gathered my wits, there were two men standing on the footpath waiting for me to exit the car. James reached past the driver and like he did at the gallery, took my hand.

I nodded my thanks to the driver and James thanked him by his name, Fergus, which explained the slight brogue of his accent.

James escorted me up the steps and took his keys from his pocket, then opened the front door. It led to a warmly lit entryway with wooden floorboards and a hallstand along one wall. On the opposite wall were two sets of stairs, one going up and one going down. I looked upstairs, but it was dark.

"The bedroom," he said as he placed his keys on a hook next to the hallstand.

"Oh, lovely," I replied. *Really, Sarah? Buy that thesaurus already.*

"This way," he said, leading the way into the most beautiful, most grown-up living room I had ever seen. A black Eames chair and ottoman took pride of place against one wall and opposite was a long, white couch with just enough throw cushions in various neutral shades to look comfortable, but not too "showroomy".

"Have a seat. I'll get us something to drink," he said, motioning to the couch. Did I mention it was white? Me on a white couch with a beverage was a recipe for disaster. "What would you like?"

"Um ..." I hoped I didn't look as stricken as I felt. My nervousness about the lovemaking had taken a backseat—I'd probably make a clumsy fool of myself and we wouldn't even get that far. Thankfully, James either didn't sense my panic or was gentlemanly enough to ignore it.

"Well, I whisked you out of there before we finished our champagne, so how about a bottle of that?"

I nodded enthusiastically and said, "That sounds perfect," just like a normal human being would in the same situation.

Bubbles *were* a good way to go. They made me a little tipsy, but never morose and never rolling-around-on-the-floor drunk like I'd been once or twice on other drinks, like red wine and tequila and rum and Cointreau. Okay, that had happened more than once or twice.

Champagne was also a good choice, because if I did spill—and I was going to try *very hard* not to—it wouldn't leave a mark on James's luxurious couch.

While James disappeared downstairs to what I presumed was the kitchen, I examined the rest of the room from my perch on the couch. It was accented with wood—teak?—which appeared in the sideboard, the low asymmetrical coffee table, and the floating shelves that dotted the walls, each with its own subtle lighting and showcasing some kind of knick-knack. *Do rich people even have knick-knacks? Artefacts? Objets d'art?*

I heard the pop of a cork from downstairs. Any moment now, James would be back, and I'd have to find something interesting or intelligent to talk about. I turned around to look at the giant painting above the couch, splashes of vibrant blues and reds on a white canvas. It wasn't really to my taste, but it *was* striking. I wondered how much of a conversation I could elicit about a painting I didn't like.

Glancing around at the rest of the room, my eyes landed on the two bay windows that looked out over the street. And—*Oh, my god!*—beneath each was a window seat! Ever since I'd met James, I'd pictured him in a fancy apartment, sipping his morning coffee and reading the Sunday papers as he casually lounged on his *window seat*. And there were two of them, one for James and one for me.

"Here you are." James was standing right in front of me, holding out a flute. I'd been so lost in my fantasy of whiling away a Sunday morning together on twin window seats, I hadn't even heard him come upstairs. I took the glass and he settled in beside me on the couch.

"A toast," he said, looking intently into my eyes. *I could get used to being looked at like that.* "To you, a woman like a breath of fresh air and warm sunshine." Something like a shiver, but much nicer, shot through my body. I clinked the rim of my glass against his and took a sip. It was definitely a step or two above what we'd had at the gallery. I'm not saying I knew a lot about actual champagne, but the bubbles were fine and silky, and it had that toasted honey flavour I loved.

And I'm not sure if it was the toast or the first sip of bubbles that emboldened me, but I couldn't wait any longer. I needed to kiss James. I placed my glass delicately on the table in front of me, without spilling a drop, and then took his from him and placed it next to mine. I took a steadying breath as subtly as I could, turned back towards James and kissed him, tenderly at first, and then the longing I felt took over.

James lifted a hand to the nape of my neck and pulled me towards him, his mouth on mine, the intensity of our kiss building. He tasted like the champagne and his tongue against mine sent more of those magic shivers through me. He broke the kiss and for just a moment I was disappointed, until his mouth found my throat and sensation took over conscious thought. His lips trailed down my chest as he held me to him with one hand and caressed a nipple through my dress with the other.

I was in heaven.

"Sarah ..." A throaty whisper broke into my reverie. He looked up and met my eyes. "Bedroom." I nodded, understanding completely. We needed each other, completely, unencumbered by the logistics of sex on a couch covered in throw pillows.

He stood quickly, but gracefully, pulling me up with him. He grabbed my hand and, with what seemed like a sense of urgency, led the way upstairs. He dropped my hand only long enough to flick on a lamp next to the bed.

Then he turned me around gently, kissing my neck and trailing kisses down my shoulder. I felt his hand on the zip of my dress and he pulled it down in one swift movement. He pushed the straps over my shoulders and the dress fell to the floor.

I stepped out of it and turned to face him. He looked the length of my body and met my eyes. "My god, you're beautiful." I had never felt more desired and any self-consciousness I'd felt, all the nerves I'd battled during the car ride, vanished. I wanted James in a way I'd never wanted any man before.

I wanted to lay myself bare before him and let him ravish me. Which is exactly what I did.

*

We were lying next to each other, both of us staring content-edly at the ceiling like they do in films—only I didn't have a sheet pulled up to my chest for modesty. James had explored me so thoroughly, and enough times, that I didn't feel the need to cover myself.

When he'd said in the gallery that he wanted to make love to me, he had meant it. I felt utterly worshipped, and I'd shared something with him I had never shared with another man—even Josh. For the first time ever, I didn't think, I didn't worry, I didn't try to please. I just let myself *be*, right in every moment. I had let James make love to me. It was glorious.

I rolled over onto my side and propped my head up on my hand, so I could look at him. "Hi," I said, smiling at him.

He turned his head towards me, "Hi."

"You are very handsome—do you know that?"

He laughed. "Thank you." He looked back at the ceiling, a slightly embarrassed smile on his face. It was nice to see James being self-conscious, even just a little bit. It made him more human, more accessible, more like someone who would want to spend time with me.

"I'm going to ask you something," I said. That got his attention and he looked at me. "Normally, I would ask if I could ask a question, but I've already decided I'm going to ask this, so here it goes."

The smile was back, this one clearly at my expense. Still, I was not going to be deterred.

"Why me?"

Confusion flashed quickly across his face, but in less than a moment, his face settled; he knew what I meant. I could see him considering his response and I resisted the urge to speak, to follow up with more questions and a litany of reasons why I was such an odd choice for him.

"Because of what I said when I toasted you earlier. You're a breath of fresh air. You are honest, you're open, you have no agenda. You, Sarah, are genuinely interested in people and willing to know them without guile. I get the sense you've been hurt in the past, but you're still willing to give of yourself. You haven't become cynical or jaded."

I haven't?

Until that moment—seeing myself through James's eyes—I thought I had. Wasn't that why I got annoyed with Cat for hoping I'd meet someone in Greece? Or why I wanted my ex, the cheating bastard, to fuck off and die? Because I'd been screwed over. Because I was cynical about love?

Lying there with James, however, I realised he was right, that despite everything, I *had* met someone. I'd met *two* some-ones. And in different ways, I had let them both in. Maybe the hopeful romantic in me *hadn't* been obliterated.

Maybe I wasn't broken.

"You're frowning," James said, shaking me from my poorly timed self-exploration.

He reached over, smoothing the frown lines between my brows with his thumb. I let him. Then he cupped my face and pulled me towards him for a soft, sweet kiss.

"And of course, there's that ridiculously sexy body of yours," he said between kisses. I laughed, relieved to be out of my head and back with James, back with a man who made me feel attractive and appreciated, who was far kinder to me than I was to myself.

"Well, there is that, yes," I said, pretending to be serious. "It is rather sexy, if I do say so myself." We shared a smile.

"Hey," I said, suddenly flashing on a memory of the first time we met. "You were smoking a cigar when I first saw you in Santorini—a slim one."

He nodded. "That's right, I was."

"Do you smoke? Cigarettes, I mean?"

"No, not anymore. I did for a long time, but I quit about twenty years ago. Cigars, though, yes, from time to time. My friend in Santorini always gifts me a box whenever I see him."

"I like cigars," I said. "I mean, I love the smell of the smoke."

"Have you ever smoked one?"

"Nope."

"Do you want to?" he asked, raising his eyebrows.

I grinned. "I'd love to." And that's how we ended up sitting side by side on one of the window seats as James taught me the finer points of enjoying a cigar. I didn't know you weren't supposed to inhale them like you did a cigarette, that it was about the taste of the smoke. I quite liked it.

I also liked the view from the window seat. "It's pretty here." As views went, there were probably more spectacular ones in the world, but the houses across the way were as opulent as James's and the lights from the homes gave off a warm glow.

"You asked me earlier why you." I stopped looking out the window and met his eyes. "One of the reasons is that you notice things, you appreciate the little things." I smiled.

"Last year, I briefly dated a woman"—*Whoa! Do I want to hear this?* My smile vanished—"and one night in particular, there was a clear sky and a full moon, and I suggested we go for a late-night walk." I thought about how magical that would have been. "There I was, thinking it was romantic, something enjoyable to do together, and she just looked at me as though I had lost my mind and said, 'Why?'"

"I wouldn't have said that."

He shook his head gently. "No, you would have put your shoes on, and we'd have gone for the walk." I nodded. He leant in and kissed me. "And that's why *you*, Sarah." He kissed me more deeply, and we put out our cigars and went back to bed.

It wasn't much of a *sleepover*, but I did get a few hours of shut eye.

Chapter 6

I woke up in a dreamy state of satiation, with just a hint of self-satisfaction. Yes, I'd just complicated my love life further, but I could take a moment to bask in the afterglow of the night before. James was a *spectacular* lover. *Well done me.*

It wasn't quite daylight outside, but there was a promise of morning in the thin light seeping into the room either side of the curtains. James was still soundly asleep next to me, his back a wall of lithe muscle. I looked around the bedroom, keeping still so I didn't wake him.

It was as tastefully and expensively decorated as his living room. There were hints of him—the man, the person—in the tight cluster of small paintings on the wall opposite the bed, all different styles, but all featuring the same hue of blue— "robin's egg", I think it's called.

On his dresser, minimally designed and in dark wood, was a framed black and white photo of a couple on their wedding day—his parents, I assumed—and another framed photo of two men throwing their heads back, laughing. I couldn't make out their faces well enough to see if one of them was James. I'd sneak a peek later.

I gently propped myself up on my elbows so I could see the clock on James's side of the bed. It was 6:17am. I didn't know if he had to be somewhere that morning, or what time he usually woke up on a weekday, but I wasn't keen to just lie there, waiting. I also desperately needed a shower—all that ravishing, you know.

I pushed back the covers, climbed out of bed naked, and quietly made my way into the bathroom. I'd left Cat's evening bag in there the night before after I'd brushed my teeth and used my moisturiser to take my makeup off. This gal can be innovative when it comes to skincare. I'd also unpinned my hair from its fancy up-do before I went to sleep, and I saw in the mirror that it was taking advantage of its freedom. I looked like Merida from that film *Brave*—only a brunette.

My phone buzzed from inside the evening bag and I dug it out. I hadn't packed a phone charger, so it was telling me it was in the death throes of ebbing battery life at 18%. There were also two new text messages. The first one was from Cat:

Woo hoo! Will leave a key with the concierge if I go out. Text when you're coming home.

The next one was from Josh:

Hey, just home from work. Was hoping we could FaceTime later. Miss ya. Jx

A twist of panic snaked its way through my stomach. *WHAT. AM. I. DOING?*

Less than a week before, I'd woken up next to Josh, miserable about saying goodbye and asking myself if I loved him. And there I was in the silver fox's bathroom after I had made love with him—*made love!*—practically all night long.

I shot off a quick text to Cat:

Just woke up. OMG. So much to tell. Home soon—def before lunch.

Replying to Josh was more difficult. It was late at night in Chicago. What if I replied while he was still awake, and he wanted to FaceTime me right away? I decided to hold off until I was back at Cat's and knew he'd be asleep. I turned off my phone. There was no sense in listening to it die completely. That buzzing could drive a person mad.

James's bathroom was perfection. As well as two sinks, there was a giant soaking tub and a separate shower with a rain-water shower head. I opened a cupboard under the closest sink and, as I hoped, there was a stack of fluffy towels. I pulled one out, hung it on a hook next to the shower, and stepped in.

The water felt great, but when I turned it off, I realised James was knocking on the bathroom door. "Sarah?"

"Yes," I called out. I reached for the towel and clutched it to me in an act of unnecessary modesty.

"Tea or coffee?"

Oh, how lovely! "Uh, tea please. White, no sugar," I replied.

"See you downstairs in a tick."

I dried off quickly. I didn't really have much in the way of toiletries or cosmetics with me, so I brushed my teeth, slathered on some moisturiser, touched up under my eyes with concealer, dotted some lipstick on my cheeks and rubbed it in for that freshly flushed look, and pinned the curls around my face on top of my head, out of the way. Like I said, this gal can innovate with just a handful of products.

But what to wear? I didn't really fancy putting on my dress for a cup of tea. I opened the bathroom door and there on the bed, on the side I had slept on, was a folded-up bathrobe—a *woman's* bathrobe. James was not only thoughtful and generous in bed, it seemed. I put on the robe and descended two levels to the kitchen.

Now, I know I've raved about James's house, but I nearly had another orgasm when I saw his kitchen. It was exactly what I would have designed if I owned my own house and had an unlimited budget. There was a giant island cupboard—bench space for days—a six-burner gas stove, two ovens, and twin sinks with draining boards on each side.

And the fridge! It was massive! And it had some seriously fancy controls. Even from the foot of the stairs, I could tell it made sparkling water. I would have bet a million pounds he also had a great knife set, and that the best cookware you could buy was tucked away somewhere. He'd set two places, cloth napkins and all, at one end of the breakfast bar, which seated six.

I managed to take in all these details in about seven seconds. That's how much I love a good kitchen—even more than a dream bathroom.

"Good morning," James smiled, as he poured hot water into a teapot. It was probably from the Ming dynasty. I noted he was also wearing a robe.

"Good morning," I smiled back. "James, your home is really beautiful—all of it—but this kitchen!"

"You like it?"

"I could happily live in this kitchen for the rest of my life. Really, I would sleep on the floor."

He laughed heartily, throwing his head back. I thought about the two men in the photo in his room and realised I'd forgotten to take a closer look before coming downstairs.

"Well, you're most welcome to cook in here if you like, but as far as sleeping goes, I'd rather have you in my bed."

I blushed at that. I mean, how could I not? It made me think of all the things he'd done to me in that bed.

"I made us some toast. My housekeeper, Janice, gets in the most exquisite bread from a bakery not far from here *and* she makes her own jam." He pointed a knife towards several jars of jam on the countertop, then used it to butter the toast that popped up.

I took a seat opposite him at one of the place settings. "It smells amazing."

"I've brewed us a pot of tea, too. I usually use teabags, but it's nice to have someone to share a pot with. I also have an espresso machine if you'd like a coffee later"—*of* course *he does*—"but I prefer tea first thing."

"Me too. And I may say yes to a coffee later. Are you any good?" He cocked his head to the side, then added a bemused smile.

"I couldn't say. Am I?"

Oh god! "No, I ..." *How embarrassing.* "I meant coffee. Are you any good at making coffee?" I put my face in my hands and shook my head. "You're laughing at me," I said through my hands.

He came around to my side of the counter and gently pulled my hands from my face, taking them into his. I couldn't look at him.

"I am laughing at you, yes. I am an utter bastard. Will you forgive me?" I raised my eyes to his and my breath caught in my throat. "Please?"

I nodded. He leant down and kissed my mouth with a quick smack. "Good. Now I'll finish making breakfast, so we can eat, and then I shall have you at least once more before we start our day properly." He waggled his eyebrows at me a couple of times.

My stomach did a flip-flop and I giggled in response. As hungry as I was—and I was pretty much starving after all the physical activity we'd had the night before—I was very much looking forward to being in James's bed again. He grinned at me from his post across the counter. I was starting to think he really *could* read my mind.

We ate side by side at the breakfast bar, chatting about Paddington and what he liked about living there. He was right about that bread, too. It was grainy and delicious, and he'd toasted it perfectly. I can't abide people who would wave a piece of bread over a candle flame and call it toast.

It was also impossible to choose between Janice's fig, strawberry, and rhubarb jams, so I had some of all three. With several slices of toast and more than my share of a giant pot of tea, I had managed to make quite a pig of myself.

"Yum!" I said, wiping toast crumbs from my mouth with a cloth napkin.

"Happy?" he asked, as he got up and took my plate. He'd asked me that before, the week before at lunch. And like then, I knew he was just asking if everything was okay. I realised, though, that I *was* happy being there with him eating toast and drinking tea.

"Deliriously." All I needed was to move the whole thing upstairs to the window seats and I'd be living out my fantasy. I got up and started helping to clear away the detritus of breakfast.

"Good." He took the mugs from my hands and placed them in the sink. "Let's leave all that for now." Then he kissed me deeply, his hands on the small of my back pulling me towards him.

He broke off the kiss and I bit my lip. "Bedroom?" I asked.

He nodded, his eyes narrowing. "Bedroom. Now."

I have no idea what got into me, but I replied with, "Race you there." Then I turned and ran up two flights of stairs, James fast on my heels. In his bedroom he captured me around the waist, flinging us both onto the bed. I dissolved into giggles, breathless from running up all those stairs. James's face, just inches from mine, broke into a broad smile. I sighed, contentedly.

"Hi," I said.

"Hi," he said. Then he enveloped me in his arms and kissed

me. I wrapped my arms tightly around his neck and happily let him ravish me again—twice.

*

I was lying on my side, my head on James's chest while he stroked my hair. I pushed myself up onto one elbow and our eyes met. "I meant to ask you something earlier, but only just remembered."

"What's that?" His hand continued to play with my hair. I had no idea how bad it looked unfettered and sex-mussed—most of the hairpins had flown out during my run up the stairs.

"The photo over there ..." I looked towards the photo of the two men. "Who is that?" He must have known exactly what I meant, because he didn't even glance towards his dresser. "That's me with my brother, Christian."

"Oh, you have a brother? Are you close?" I thought about Cat, how she was my bestie, and that I always felt sorry for people who didn't have that kind of relationship with their siblings.

"We were, yes, very close. He was my dearest friend." The past tense of his words and the shadow of grief that momentarily crossed his face prefaced an awful "but ...".

"What happened?" I whispered. "Did you have a falling out?"

"No." His eyes glistened, and he sighed out heavily. "He died. Just a few years ago now. Car accident." He pushed a thumb into his eyes, one after the other. "Sorry."

"Oh, no, James. *I'm* sorry. I ..." I felt like crap and wanted to say so, but that was unfair. No matter how badly I felt for putting my foot in it, my feelings paled in comparison with James's grief, which was palpable.

"You did nothing wrong, Sarah."

I stroked the side of his face and pressed my forehead against his cheek. "I am sorry, though. I'm sorry you lost someone so precious to you." There were tears in my eyes. James pulled me tightly to him and I snuggled up against his chest.

"I guess I don't really talk about him very often, and it's been a long time since anyone else was up here."

"You don't have to explain."

"But I want to." He paused and I held my breath waiting for him to speak. "My father died more than ten years ago, so when Christian died, it was just me and my mother to deal with the grief together. But she couldn't be there for me. It was overwhelming for her. She loved my father, and he'd gone. She loved Christian, and ... well, I think I was too much of a reminder of what she'd lost." I hugged him tighter. "I think it hurt her more to see me than not to."

"You both look really happy in that photo," I said, barely more than a whisper.

I could hear the smile in his voice. "We were." Then he laughed, a quiet but warm chuckle, almost to himself. "We were at Valentina and Marcus's place, some party in the summertime, and he'd just told me the most pornographic joke. God, he was a character." I smiled to myself. "I didn't even know there was a photo of that moment until Tina gave it to me, framed, right after Christian's service."

I lifted myself up, so I could meet his eyes. "Really?"

He smiled. "Yes."

"That's the most thoughtful thing ever. You know, I kind of have a crush on Valentina."

"We all do, darling," he said, pulling me close for a kiss.

"James?"

"Yes."

"I really am sorry about Christian."

"I know."

"But I'm also glad you were close, that you had that kind of relationship with him. My sister is ..." How could I even begin to describe what Cat meant to me? Tears prickled my eyes and I swiped them away with the back of my hand, annoyed that I couldn't articulate my thoughts.

"I know, Sarah. I know just what you mean."

And there it was, James making me feel understood without me having to explain.

I snuffled and looked around for a tissue. James reached for the box next to his side of the bed and handed it to me. Then we each took a handful and cleaned ourselves up.

"James."

"Sarah."

"I have one more question."

"Uh oh," he teased.

"Whose bathrobe is that?" I pointed to the item in question, which was lying on the floor where James had flung it earlier.

He laughed—heartily this time.

"Why, darling, that would be yours." I looked at him and my confusion had to be obvious. "Just think of it like the toothbrush you popped into your evening bag." He was teasing me. "There was a brand new one under the sink for you, by the way." Make that, *seriously* teasing me. Not that I minded, not really.

"Right," I said. "Well then, as it's mine, where do I hang it up?"

*

"He actually bought you a bathrobe?" Cat really did home in on the most bizarre details.

James had driven me back to Cat's mid-morning, holding my hand as much as it was possible while navigating the narrow, winding streets of London. When we pulled up, he came around to my side of the car to open the door and to kiss me goodbye properly—that's what he'd said, "properly".

Swoon.

I'll admit, though, even after having the most amazing time with James, I'd been looking forward to talking it through with Cat so I could get her take on things. But after the bathrobe quip, I was beginning to question her ability to debrief properly. I needed my best girlfriend, not an annoying little sister.

"Everything I just told you, and that's what you get hung up on?"

"I'm not hung up. I'm intrigued. It's very *Pretty Woman*."

"Except the part about me not being a prostitute."

"Well, yes, *obvs*. So, are you falling in love with him?" I spat out half a mouthful of tea. So far, this conversation was not going as planned. I was glad it was too early for us to have cracked a bottle of red—much harder to get out of the carpet. Cat jumped up to grab a dishcloth.

"Well, *are* you?" she persisted.

Was I falling in love with James? The truth was, I didn't know. I had certainly fallen in *lust* with him—he was gorgeous by anyone's standards. I'd thoroughly enjoyed all the sex, and we'd had some interesting conversations, but *love*? Surely, it was way too soon to be thinking along those lines, especially as half the time I was with him, I felt like an unrefined pretender.

Cat finished cleaning up the tea I'd spat out, then brought a packet of chocolate digestives from the kitchen. She knew me so well. Without thinking, I took a biscuit out of the packet and ate half of it in one bite, chewing pensively as I considered Cat's question.

And then I remembered what James had told me about Christian—how he'd opened up to me, and that I'd desperately wanted to take away the hurt I saw in his eyes. Was that falling in love, or something close to it?

I swallowed and popped the second half of the biscuit into my mouth. More pensive chewing. But even if I set aside what we'd shared about our siblings, there were all those lovely things James had said about me. Apparently, I was a "breath of fresh air", and if I was completely honest with myself, it felt wonderful to be appreciated like that.

I swallowed again and looked at my sister, who was curled up on an armchair watching me. "Perhaps I am falling for him."

She nodded, seemingly to respect the weight of what I'd just said. "And you also think you might be falling for Josh," she said simply.

I bit my lip. Oh god, she was right. I had serious feelings for two men. I could no longer kid myself that this was all just a bit of fun.

And then I burst into tears.

Chapter 7

Goodbyes are hard. They are the single most excruciating thing about being a traveller. Forget jet lag and lost luggage and having your wallet stolen. Saying goodbye to loved ones is hands-down the worst part. And there's always that tipping point, just over halfway into a trip when the time to say goodbye starts to loom ahead.

My time in London was coming to an end, and the thought of saying goodbye to Cat was eating me up inside. I knew when I was back home in Sydney, the distance between us would start to feel less acute, but there would be weeks, maybe even months before it would hurt less. The hardest part was not knowing when we would be together next.

And even though my sister was my number one person, the person I loved more than anyone, I felt almost as rotten at the thought of saying goodbye to James.

After the sleepover, we made plans to see each other one more time before I flew home. But when the invitation came on Thursday morning, I was torn. Saying "yes" would mean less time with Cat.

Surprisingly, Cat insisted I go. "We have today, tonight and tomorrow, then we'll have the whole of Saturday together—*and* Sunday morning before I take you to the airport." The word "airport" made me nauseous.

"Are you sure? This is my Cat time. Who knows when you'll be in Sydney next, and I'm not sure when I can get back to the UK."

"With how things are going with James, you'll probably be back here before you know it. Ooh, you might even move here!"

As much as I loved Cat's enthusiasm, she'd made a giant leap into the improbable and I'd have to rein her in. "Let's not get ahead of ourselves."

"Oh, bollocks to that. That's something old Sarah would say. You're new Sarah now. And new Sarah is falling in love with a sexy millionaire, and she's gunna move to London and live in that gorgeous house in Paddington and I'll see her all the time." She punctuated her fantasy-fuelled diatribe by doing a little dance.

I rolled my eyes and tutted at her.

"So, you're going to see him, right?" I re-read James's message on my phone, even though I'd already read it enough times to have it memorised.

Hello, beautiful. Please say I can steal you away from your sister tomorrow evening. I promise I'll have you back first thing on Saturday morning. I want to say goodbye properly. Jx

I looked at Cat, who was staring at me expectantly. "Oh, fuck it," I said. I sent this reply:

I'd love that.

Short, simple, and to the point.

Perfect. I'll pick you up at 7. Looking forward to it. I missed you next to me last night. X

I sighed, half in resignation at saying goodbye, and half in anticipation of the "properly" part of his text. James may have used that word a lot, but he never threw it away. He always meant it.

Cat looked smug. "You can stop that right now," I said in my big-sisterly voice.

She replied with a grin and waggled her eyebrows at me.

"Oh, crap." I realised I had no idea where we were going or what to wear. So many wardrobe considerations in one week!

"What?"

"Dress code."

"Ahh, yes, very important."

I shot off another text—so much for short, simple, and to the point.

Hi—me again—just wondering what the plan is for tomorrow night—and the dress code.

The reply zinged back in almost an instant.

The plan is a secret, but dress code is casual.

Casual? Did that mean the same thing to him as it did to me?

Jeans okay?

Perfect. See you then. And bring your toothbrush. X

I laughed out loud. "What? What did he say?" My sister—so nosy!

"Never you mind."

"Hey! No fair."

"He told me to bring my toothbrush."

She nodded in approval. "I like his style."

"Oh, and I get to wear jeans."

"Jeans? Really? How intriguing." I completely agreed.

*

Cat and I spent Thursday and Friday doing touristy London things from Cat's list of "Things I Never Do Unless Sarah is Visiting". She always makes out like I drag her along, but she has as much fun as I do. Besides, Madame Tussaud's really *is* amazing, even the third time, and who would pass up last-minute twenty-pound tickets to see Benedict Cumberbatch *and* David Tennant onstage? Yes, really! Although, it was

Waiting for Godot and I don't really like that play—absurdism was never my favourite—but again, Cumberbatch, Tennant, and twenty-pound tickets.

And even though I was soaking up as many moments with my sister as I could, Friday evening rolled around before I knew it.

I was in Cat's room and she watched while I put the finishing touches on my "natural looking but actually took me twenty-five minutes to apply" makeup. "You look great," she said as I smoothed on some coral-coloured lipstick.

I turned to her and smiled. "Thanks!"

"So, because there's no pretence and you're definitely staying over, you can take an *actual* overnight bag, right?"

"I guess so. I mean, I don't want to look like I've decided to move in or anything, but I think I'll at least pack a nightie and my facial cleanser this time."

"I've got just the thing," she said, standing on her tippy-toes and reaching into her wardrobe.

"Do you want help?" I expected a "no". Cat was quick to remind people that she was "just little" when it suited her, but she hated having to ask for help.

"Yes, please." One for the record books!

"What am I looking for?"

"Leather tote bag. Somewhere up there." She pointed to the top shelf of her wardrobe, which was reasonably well-organised, but tiny. I commiserated with her. My wardrobe in Sydney was four times the size. I thought I could see the handle of the bag she meant. I gave it a good tug and we stood helpless under a cascade of bags.

I looked at her. "Sorry," I said. "Avalanche."

"Bagalanche," she replied, deadpan. We fell about laughing as we gathered no fewer than thirteen bags from her bedroom floor.

"You have a lot of bags."

"Kettle? This is pot. You're black."

"True, but mine don't fall on my head every time I open my wardrobe."

"I need a bigger wardrobe."

"Or fewer bags."

She threw me a look. It meant, "you did not just say that".

"Sorry. Forgot who I was talking to."

"Here." She handed me the tan tote in baby-soft leather, and I lost the ability to speak. It was stunning. I wondered if A) she'd miss it, and B) if it would fit in my luggage.

"You can't have it."

Bugger, she'd read my mind.

"But you can borrow it."

I gave her a quick hug. "Thank you!"

James was due in less than twenty minutes, so I had to get a move on. I unzipped my backpack and pulled out the only other decent (and clean) pair of knickers I had besides the ones I was wearing. Then I found a nightie—the sort-of sexy one with spaghetti straps, not the one with a cat drinking coffee on the front—and a cute top I could wear the next day with the jeans I had on. I had already packed a small toiletries bag with the basics and some makeup. I just needed my phone charger and my wallet, and I was all set.

I was wearing a pair of dark denim, super-comfortable

skinny jeans and a floaty blue and white tie-dyed top which looked like I'd picked it up from a street vendor in Greece, but I'd actually bought from a boutique on Oxford Street in Sydney for a mint. My hair was half-up, half-down and a few loose curls framed my face. On my feet were my strappy flat sandals.

"Do you need a wrap, or a cardigan, or something? What if you're going somewhere outdoors?" I hadn't thought about that.

"Is it going to get cold tonight?"

"Not cold, but definitely cooler, probably below twenty."

"Oh, right. Have you got something I can borrow?" She looked at me like I was a complete idiot. Of course she had something, and of course it was perfect. It was a pashmina, the same blue as the swirls on my top. I folded it up and put it in the tote, then had a final look in the mirror. I fingered a wayward curl, but quickly gave up trying to make it behave. "I think I'm going to wait for James downstairs."

"Nervous?" *She knows me so well.*

"A little."

She reached up and gave me a big hug. "Have the most amazing time."

I hugged her back tightly. "I will."

"And if he proposes, say yes!"

I broke the hug so I could give her a chastising look, which she brushed off by laughing. She clearly thought she was hilarious.

"Go!" She pushed me out of her bedroom into the hallway. "Go pace in the lobby."

"I will then!" I said with faux indignation.

"Love you," she called as I went out the door.

"Love you back!" I replied over my shoulder. I shook my head as I waited for the elevator. *I adore my mad little sister.*

Just then, she popped her head out of her front door.

"And get a photo this time!"

I take that back. My sister is a massive pain in the bum.

*

"Hello, you," said a very handsome silver fox. He took my tote from me with one hand and pulled me in for a kiss with the other. It was a lovely kiss.

"Hello to you," I said, smiling dreamily. He opened the car door for me and while I got settled and seat-belted, put my tote in the boot. When he climbed into the car, I checked him out properly and he looked *good*. It was that Ralph Lauren model look again. Black jeans, slim fit—not skinny—and a light-blue dress shirt, untucked, with the second button undone and the sleeves rolled up to show his tanned forearms. *Wowser.*

When we pulled away from the kerb, I couldn't contain my curiosity any further. "So, where are we headed?"

"Well, I've actually planned an evening in," he said, and then added, "sort of."

"Now I'm really intrigued."

"I'd prefer to keep the details a surprise." He glanced at me and returned his eyes to the road. "Would that be all right—the surprise part?"

"Absolutely." I had already started to reassess my dislike of surprises, mainly because James was so good at them. My excitement built as I watched London pass by my window.

Could I live here again? I wondered. London *was* an incredible city, and Cat was there. And James, of course. A life with James ... It was one thing to fantasise about Sunday mornings and window seats, but what would real life with the silver fox even *be* like? When we were in Greece, James had said he was looking for that, for something real, but that didn't mean he wanted it with me. And even if he did, could I give up my life in Sydney? My *home*?

James reached over and took my hand and I squeezed it in return. Then a niggling thought taunted me from the back of my mind. If I allowed myself to fall for James, if I *did* pursue something more serious and long-term with him, where did that leave me and Josh?

Josh and I had said all those things when we were on Mykonos—almost a pact. Off the boat and away from the others, we'd had a lengthy heart-to-heart, promising each other that our friendship—even if that was all it turned out to be—would stay intact for the rest of our lives. We were important to each other. There was love there, maybe not the kind of love you build a relationship on, but real, tangible love.

But I knew that no matter what Josh and I had told each other, or how much we had meant it at the time, there was no way we could remain friends if James and I were together.

Please don't see that guy, James. That's what Josh had said to me on our last day together in Greece. And yet, there I was, sitting in James's car, holding James's hand, and very much looking forward to the evening ahead.

Did I feel guilty? Yes and no.

No, because—and I realise this is going to sound very Disney princess of me—I needed to be true to myself and what I was feeling. And what I was feeling was that I was falling for an incredible man, a man who hadn't hesitated at all about expressing his feelings for me, a man who made me feel desired and perhaps even *hopeful*.

And, yes. Because I cared about Josh, and I'd put him off that week. I'd had to, mostly for my own sanity, but by the time I'd got back to Cat's the morning after my sleepover with James, Josh had texted a third time.

Hi Sarah, I hope everything's okay. Would love to hear from you and maybe to FaceTime later. I miss you. Josh xxx

He'd gone from a casual, "miss ya" in the first two texts, to "I miss you". He'd even added two extra kisses.

Cat had watched me agonise over my reply for nearly fifteen minutes, as I typed and deleted and typed and deleted a response. When I threw my head back with an exasperated sigh, she offered her help.

"Let me see," she said, signalling for me to hand her the phone. I did and she read his three texts quickly. "He's keen, I'll give him that. Do you want to FaceTime him?"

I chewed on my lip. "I don't know." She threw me a look. "Well, I don't."

"Do you miss him?"

"Honestly, no, but only because you and I've had such a great time together—"

"And you and *James* have had a great time together."

"Right. That too. It's just that there hasn't really been any time to miss Josh. But, when I'm back home, and I don't have you, *or* James, *or* Josh ... well, I'll miss him then."

I couldn't read her face, but I figured she was digesting what I'd just said. I kept chewing on my lip. *You're going to wear it away at this rate, Sarah.*

"Look, I get it," she said, and I sighed, relieved. "Do you want to know what I'd do?"

Uh, yes, duh. I signalled for her to get on with it.

"Text him back to say you're having a great time with me, because you *are*, and that you want to make the most of the time with your sister, but you miss him too, and you can't wait to FaceTime when you get back to Sydney next week." She paused, probably for effect—she was quite dramatic sometimes. "How's that?"

That was genius. And that is exactly what I did.

Except, as I held hands with James and thought about my reply to Josh, my stomach twanged—and not the good kind of twang, but an angsty one full of guilt.

Please don't see that guy, James.

Chapter 8

James parked the car out front of his house, and I looked at him quizzically.

"I'm not saying anything to spoil the surprise," he said, which made me even more intrigued. "I'll get your bag."

I let myself out of the car, climbed the steps, and waited for James at his front door. When he joined me, reaching past me to unlock the door, I got a waft of his cologne—god, he smelled delicious. I hoped his surprise included lots of canoodling. "Go on in, but wait just inside," he said, snapping me from my less-than-pure thoughts. "I'll put your bag upstairs. Oh, is there anything you need?" He held up the leather tote. "We'll be outside."

"Uh, let me just grab one thing," I said, unzipping it and pulling out Cat's pashmina.

"All good?"

I nodded, and James took the stairs two at a time. He was back on the main level of the house before I knew it. "Come with me," he said, taking my hand.

He led me downstairs into the kitchen, out the back door, and into a small courtyard bordered by potted plants.

In the centre, sat a small café table and two chairs. I moved towards one of the chairs, but James tugged gently at my hand.

"Not here. This way." He led me to the corner of the house where a wrought-iron spiral staircase rose to the roof. I smiled. This was becoming quite the adventure.

"After you. Or shall I go first?"

"You go," I said. "I'll follow."

It was too steep and narrow to keep holding hands, but I followed closely behind James with one hand gripping the railing. When I emerged onto the rooftop, he was smiling down at me mischievously.

Then he stepped aside.

I gasped, my fingertips to my mouth, then I took in every heavenly detail of the rooftop terrace.

Strings of fairy lights ran along the high walls, creating a sparkling rectangle of light and at each corner, potted topiary trees stood proud, dense with twinkling lights. Dotted about were dozens of tealight candles forming tiny tableaux of soft light, and in the centre of the terrace was a large blanket covered with plump cushions. On one corner of the blanket sat an enormous picnic basket—an actual wicker basket with two flip-up lids either side of the handle—and next to it was a bottle of champagne in an ice bucket with two flutes at the ready.

"Oh, James." I had no other words—it was a rare moment.

It was so pretty, so thoughtful. And even though we hadn't eaten a thing or tasted the champagne, even before we sat on the blanket, I thought it was the single most romantic moment

of my life. I wished I could have taken a photo to show Cat—
and everyone else I'd ever met—but I knew it would break
the spell.

"Come, sit." I walked over to the blanket and slipped off
my sandals before nestling in, a giant pillow at my back. James
busied himself with the bubbles and poured two glasses,
handing one to me.

"I actually have a stunning bottle of red in the basket, but
I thought we could start with this, and a toast, to celebrate."

Celebrate? Holy crap, is *he proposing? He's not, right? That
would be mad.*

"So, what are we celebrating?" I asked as casually as possible
for a woman who thinks she may be getting proposed to.

He hesitated, just for a moment, but long enough for a
shot of terror to jolt through me.

"We're celebrating ... well, us." *Gulp.* "I know it's only been
a few weeks since I first saw you in Santorini, and even less
time since I've got to know you—*properly*, I mean—but I do
know you're someone special. You've become important to
me, Sarah."

My eyes were locked on his, my heart racing.

"And I don't say this lightly, because I haven't felt this way
for a very long time. I'm falling in love with you."

Oh. My. God.

I was holding my breath, and I realised my mouth was
hanging open. I shut it. Looking like a goldfish when a man
is pouring his heart out to you is less than optimal.

"And I know it's early days for us, and that you go back to
Sydney soon—too soon in my mind—but if you have feelings

for me, then I want to find a way for us to be together, to see what this can become."

So, there it was. Not a proposal, thank goodness. I was surprised at how relieved I felt, but really, it would have been far too soon. And it would have made me question his sanity or his motives—or both.

But James wanted me. He wanted *me*.

As I held his gaze, I wondered if he expected me to say something and I seriously hoped he didn't.

Because I didn't know what to say. I knew I felt *something* for him, but to label that and say it out loud seemed so formal, almost like a commitment, one I wasn't ready to make.

Talk about having a bigger life. It was all incredibly overwhelming.

"Don't feel like you have to say anything—or decide anything—right this minute." Relief flooded through me. *Could this man be any more perfect?*

But I had to give him something of myself. He had laid his heart bare.

So, I did what mine told me to. I leant forward and kissed him, pulling him close with the front of his shirt. I didn't know if a kiss could convey everything I was feeling, everything I wasn't quite able to parse or ready to say, but I hoped so.

When we broke apart, I realised I had a fistful of his shirt and I quickly smoothed out his shirtfront. "Sorry about that," I said.

He touched his forehead to mine. "Sarah, don't ever feel you need to apologise for kissing me like that."

I smiled.

"So," he said, lightening the mood with a single word, "I hope you're hungry. We have a delectable assortment of fine foods for our picnic dinner." He opened the basket and with a flourish worthy of Nigella Lawson, began to decant its contents onto the blanket. I giggled in response and he winked at me.

He took out an array of cured meats, two cheeses—one soft and oozing and a blue—a bowl of plump, glossy olives stuffed with blanched almonds, crispy flatbread, quince paste, pâté, and a mini baguette. Oh, and a bottle of gamay from Beaujolais.

"That's quite the spread," I said, genuinely impressed. "I'm guessing we have a few countries represented here."

"We do." He pointed to the meat, "Tuscany—wild boar and prosciutto," then to the cheeses, "France—Meaux and the Pyrenees," then to the olives, "Spain." I popped an olive in my mouth. *God, I love olives.*

"Good?" I nodded enthusiastically and popped another one in my mouth. James would have to move fast if he was going to get any.

From the basket, James produced two plates, two napkins, and cutlery, including cheese knives and a pâté knife. And there I was, already helping myself to a slice of prosciutto with my fingers. *Oops. You can't take me anywhere.*

James either ignored them or didn't care about my bad manners. "Are you happy with the champagne? We could switch to red."

I held up my flute. "This is perfect for now, but I'm keen on the red for later. I *love* a wine from Beaujolais."

"Oh, you do?" There was obvious interest in his eyes. *You're not the only one who can be surprising*, I thought.

"I've been places and seen things, you know. I'm a proper, experienced world traveller."

He laughed, "I have no doubt. So, tell me, how did you come to *love* a wine from Beaujolais?"

"Well, I told you how I used to run tours in Europe." He nodded. "One of our overnight stays was at a *château* right in the heart of the Beaujolais region. It even had its own vines and there was this ancient vintner who lived in a cottage on the property. For anyone interested, he'd conduct these little tours of the winery. He had very limited English, but he could get his meaning across with a few words and gestures, that sort of thing.

"And, he *especially* loved the ladies. I'm pretty sure it was his intention to keep us tipsy the whole time we were there. He'd greet the coaches with carafes of his latest vintage, straight from the barrel and, before my feet hit the ground, he'd hand me a globe-shaped wine glass filled to the brim."

James grinned at me while he cut off a generous piece of the gooey cheese and slathered it onto a hunk of bread. "And did he?"

"What's that?"

"Keep you tipsy?" He took a bite and groaned a little.

"Is it as amazing as it looks?"

"It is. Here, you try it." He handed me the rest of the bite he'd prepared. "It's one of my favourite things in the world to eat."

I popped the bite into my mouth and savoured the combination of crusty bread and creamy cheese. He was right. It was delicious. If I did end up spending the rest of my life with James, I'd probably gain about fifty kilos.

"Anyway, sorry, I interrupted—the old vintner, keeping you tipsy."

"Oh, right. And, yes, he did. His wine was just so drinkable." I took another sip of my bubbles, also dangerously drinkable.

"We'd arrive at the *château* mid-afternoon from Paris, and by the time I went to bed that night, I'd have drunk seven or eight glasses." His eyes widened. "*And* we didn't leave until after lunch the next day, so I'd have a sneaky glass or two with lunch. I swear I'd be half-cut by the time we left for Antibes. This was just the tour managers, though. The drivers couldn't drink before a travel day, so they never got to have any wine. I'm sure it drove them batty."

"Pun intended," he joked.

"Oh, pun definitely intended." It wasn't.

"So, how many people at the *château*? How many tours at once?"

"Only ever two tours with around fifty people on each." He shook his head as though in disbelief. "It was a big place, but even so, we all shared rooms. It was crowded, but fun—well, *mostly*. I'm guessing you've never really travelled like that."

"Oh, I think you'd be surprised." I grinned. "I've not gone on a bus tour, but I certainly had some escapades backpacking around Europe—in my *youth*, that is." His eyes twinkled with amusement.

Just then, my mind alighted on a memory from Greece,

when James had introduced me to his friend, Armando. "Wait, were you called 'Jimmy' then, in your *youth*?" I asked, loading up the word like he had. His head cocked to the side. "It's just that Armando called you that, and you're old friends, right?" I took a sip of my bubbles.

"Depends what you mean by *old*."

The bubbles went down the wrong way, leaving me spluttering and coughing, and James reached across to pat me on the back. How had I wandered so blindly into "age difference" territory? Yes, James was in his fifties, but I certainly didn't consider him *old*.

"Are you all right?" Concern etched his face.

I cleared my throat, then nodded. "All good, thank you." I took a deep breath and saw his concern ease. "You know, I don't ... it's not ... I don't really care ..." *Good grief, Sarah.* You'd never know I was an English teacher.

"Are you talking about our age difference?" he asked, saving me from another bout of verbal diarrhoea.

"Poorly, but yes. It doesn't matter to me."

"Nor me."

Our eyes were locked onto each other's and I wondered if he was thinking what I was. *It doesn't matter, but just out of curiosity ...*

"I'm thirty-six, nearly thirty-seven," I blurted.

"Fifty-two," he said and I decided, right then, that fifty-two was the sexiest age *ever*. I saw the smile twitching the corner of his mouth and moments later, we were grinning at each other.

"And yes," he said, as he topped up my bubbles.

"Yes?" I'd completely lost track of what question he was answering.

"Jimmy. Armando and I met when I was twentyish."

I searched James's face for a glimpse of twenty-year-old Jimmy, but James was such a *man*, it was futile.

"He's the *only* person who calls me that, however."

"Is that so, Mr Cartwright?" I lifted my chin, challenging him, even though I would *never* call him "Jimmy".

"It is, Ms Parsons." He tipped his head and finished his glass of bubbles. "Now, back to you. Did you enjoy touring? You didn't say when we were at lunch last week. And I'll be honest, it sounds like a difficult job." He made himself another bite of bread and cheese and I took the moment to consider my response.

"It was a difficult job. I know a lot of people think it's very exciting and glamorous to get paid to travel around Europe. And, of course, there were days when I had to pinch myself. We went to some incredible locations, did these amazing things, like paragliding in Greece, and all those tours of ancient sites and historical buildings. I loved that part. I could go to Rome a thousand times and never get sick of it. *And* I met people who've become treasured friends, like I said.

"But there were other facets, the stuff no one talked about, the difficult stuff. Twenty-hour days, hardly any sleep, borders and visas and lost passports and stolen credit cards, clients with hangovers, *me* with hangovers—just lots of hangovers. Anyway, with the long drives, subsisting on fast food, and never exercising, I often felt like rubbish."

"So, not an ordinary job, then."

"No, never ordinary. Probably the best and worst time of my life," I said, then added, "So far, anyway." I loved how attentive he was being, but it also made me a little self-conscious. "Sorry, I'm talking incessantly about myself."

"No, not at all. I like hearing about you, about your life."

"In any case, that was the long way around to answer your question, but I love Beaujolais, probably as much for the memories as for the wine."

"Let's switch, then," he said, sitting upright and feeling around in the picnic basket. After a moment, he pulled out a wine opener and I clapped my hands together softly in anticipation.

I didn't think there could possibly be anything left in the basket, but then he took out two red wine glasses—globe-shaped glasses, like I'd drunk from in France—and I squealed with unconcealed delight. "That picnic basket is like the Tardis. Anything else tucked away in there?"

He squinted into the basket, as if trying to see to its depths. He looked up. "No. This is all." He indicated the impressive spread between us with a nod of his head.

"So," I said as he opened and poured the wine, "You did all this yourself?"

"I had a little help—with the candles—Janice lit them just before we arrived." He handed me my glass and clinked the edge of his against mine. "But, everything else, yes, that was me."

So, the millionaire, who could have paid someone to shop

and to set up our terrace picnic, had gone to a lot of trouble to tell me he thought he was falling in love with me. *Double swoon.*

"Well, it's divine." I took a sip of wine and I could *taste* the sunshine of central France. The wine was both familiar and something entirely new, far more elevated than any wine from Beaujolais I'd had before.

"Do you like it?"

"I'm out of superlatives," I replied.

He laughed lightly. "I find that very difficult to believe." I didn't mind the gentle teasing. It made me feel like he appreciated *me*—all of me, even the things I agonised over, like being too effusive, or worried I was constantly making a fool of myself.

What a wonderful feeling to be appreciated like that, to be loved. *Loved.*

James had said he was falling in love with me. And I'd said nothing. How could I leave him wondering like that? I had to tell him *something.* "James, thank you—for the dinner and this week and for, well ..."

And in the absolute worst timing, a lack of superlatives was the least of my worries. I had lost the ability to say how I felt. I looked at my wine for inspiration, feeling the crease form between my brows. Why couldn't I tell James how I felt? What was wrong with me?

He was watching me intently, letting me have the moment I needed to collect my thoughts, to find my words. And after what felt like aeons, I was finally able to say, "I do have feelings for you." It was just above a whisper, and my voice caught in my throat as the emotion threatened to overwhelm me, but I said it.

He stood, then, and reached out for my hand. "Come here," he said.

I placed my glass on the blanket, then reached for his hand and let him help me stand. I was careful not to tread on our picnic, which would have been the perfect way to obliterate the moment. He didn't say anything more, just wrapped his arms around me and pulled me into a hug. I held onto him tightly as he rested his chin on the top of my head. We stood like that for a long time.

And then very quietly, he said, "Oh, Sarah."

*

I woke on my second-to-last day in London well before the sun came up, lying on my back with my stomach in knots. The goodbyes were coming thick and fast. First it would be James and then it would be Cat. I didn't know which one I was dreading the most.

And that morning, the glow of the night before—the things we'd said, the incredible meal on the rooftop, our lovemaking, the possibility of a future together—receded, and in its place was dread, thick syrupy dread.

"I can practically hear you thinking," said the gravelly voice next to me. He rolled over onto his side to face me. I smiled weakly.

"I hate saying goodbye," I said, forgoing any pretence that our situation was tolerable. He snuggled closer and nuzzled my neck with his mouth, peppering me with tiny kisses. It annoyed me. I was not in the mood for nuzzling.

"Goodbyes *are* awful, but it won't be for good."

I hoped not.

"I hope not."

He lifted his head, suddenly serious. "It will be all right, Sarah. I'll visit, or you'll come here. Actually, we'll do both until we know for sure, and then we'll sort it out. All right? We don't need to decide anything right this minute."

Maybe I was being over-sensitive, but I thought he was being condescending. I didn't mention it, though. "Okay," I said, even though it wasn't.

"Can I make you breakfast before I take you home?"

Take me home.

Only, it wasn't my home. It was Cat's home, and soon I would have to leave there too. And the only thing worse than a goodbye, is a long, drawn-out goodbye.

"Actually, I think I'll just have a shower and then we can head out."

"Oh. It's very early. It's not even seven yet."

"I know." *Tell him. Tell him it's the situation and not him. You're not mad at him.*

But I couldn't. I was behaving like a child, and I knew it. And I was pretty sure he knew I knew it. I just couldn't help it. Maybe I thought it would be easier to part if we were annoyed at each other. Maybe I had lost my damned mind.

"Okay, then. You take a shower, and I'll get dressed. We can leave as soon as you're ready."

I am really screwing this up.

He flung back the doona and reached for the jeans I'd pulled off him the night before, which were on the floor next to his side of the bed. He didn't bother with underwear and with his back to me, he pulled them up. I heard the zip.

Yep, I'm totally and completely screwing this up in the worst way. Fix it, Sarah, for fuck's sake.

"James." He stopped, his shirt on but not yet buttoned. I climbed over to his side of the bed and knelt behind him. I slid the shirt off his shoulders and let it drop to the floor, then wrapped my arms around him and ran them up his torso, resting them on his chest. Pulling him towards me, I leant my forehead against his bare back.

He turned suddenly and grasped my face roughly between his hands, kissing me with an intensity that held everything we were both feeling. I fell backwards onto the bed, pulling the weight of him onto me. We both fumbled at the waistband of his jeans, until his impatience won out and he practically tore them off and pushed them onto the floor. He made short work of the condom he retrieved from his bedside table, then he was inside me.

We clung to each other and moved with a ferocity we'd never had before, until he collapsed, spent and breathing hard, his face in the groove between my neck and my shoulder. I held him close to me and stroked his hair.

Whatever this was, this feeling, I wasn't sure I was ready for it.

*

I was fidgeting. I fidget when I'm anxious, mostly with my hands, and at that moment I was interlocking and unlocking my fingers in quick succession. I glanced across at James, who was driving with the same ease and confidence I'd seen before. In the midst of everything I felt, I lusted after the confident, sexy man who made driving in London traffic—there is *always* traffic in London, even on a Saturday morning—look easy.

My phone bleeped from my lap. Cat. I had just texted her to let her know we were on our way.

I want to meet him.

What? No! No way! James meeting Cat was not part of the plan. I was barely able to admit I had feelings for him. I was *not* ready for him to meet the family.

No.

Her reply was so quick I was surprised she could type that fast.

I know you know your no is bollocks. I'm meeting him.

I'm going to kill my sister.

NO! I'm not ready.

I lifted my thumb to my mouth and nibbled on the nail.

When am I going to meet him then? At the wedding???!!!

Grrr! I was not in the mood for Cat to prolong her proposal joke by playing the "future brother-in-law" card.

No wedding. UR not meeting him. That's final.

I don't usually go for abbreviations in texts, but I had to type fast to get Cat to back down. Not only was I not ready for Jámes to meet Cat, but I wanted to say goodbye in private, not with my little sister ogling us. *Surely*, she could figure that out! My phone bleeped again.

See you out front!

Yep. I was definitely going to kill my little sister. Maybe I could convince James to run her over with his fancy car. "Everything okay?" James asked, glancing over at me. I hid the screen of my phone with my hand, just in case reading tiny type with a mere sideways glance was amongst his hidden talents.

"Uh huh. Just texting Cat about our plans for the day." *That sounded breezy, right?*

"So, what's in store then?" Crap, I hadn't thought that far ahead. Lying was hard.

"Oh, she wants to go shopping, but I'm thinking of the National Gallery. I love that place." Or, maybe lying wasn't that hard.

"You'll get to see sunflowers," he said. I didn't get it.

"Sunflowers?"

"Van Gogh. *Sunflowers* is my favourite painting in the National Gallery," he replied.

I caught up. "Oh, yes, it's mine too!" That part wasn't even a lie. I *love* that painting—or rather, that series of paintings. I'd seen two of them in person—at the Van Gogh Museum in Amsterdam and the one in London.

"In between tours, I'd go to the gallery and sit in front of *Sunflowers*, just taking it in—sometimes for an hour or more," I said. "It was a way of stilling my mind, catching my breath after the intensity of the tour." I smiled to myself. The gallery visit had started as a lie, but I wondered if I could talk Cat into stopping in that afternoon.

"So, kind of like your visits to the British Museum then?" he asked.

"Yes, in a way. Although, they served different purposes. I'd head to the museum if I was feeling homesick or just blue, whereas *Sunflowers* was more of a palate cleanser for my brain—a reset. Does that make sense?"

"I know just what you mean by that." Maybe I had explained myself better than I thought. "And each time I see that painting—although, I haven't been for a while and must go back sometime soon—I see something different in it. It's remarkable."

"Yes!" I exclaimed, "I do too. It's both elegantly simple and compellingly complex." We exchanged a quick smile and I had to bite my tongue, so I didn't invite him to the gallery with us. I didn't even know if we'd end up going, and I really couldn't drag out our goodbye. It was hard enough as it was.

Not long after we discovered our shared love of Van Gogh, we pulled up outside Cat's building. As promised, there she was, grinning like an annoying little sister.

"Uh, James?"

He parallel-parked the car—expertly of course—and looked at me. "Yes, Sarah."

"Heads up. You're about to meet my sister."

"Oh? Really?"

"Yes. And I apologise in advance." He laughed. I didn't.

We both got out of the car and as James got my tote—sorry, *Cat's* tote—out of the boot, I tried to cut Cat off at the pass. All I managed before she pushed past me was a quiet, but pointed, "Behave." It came out like a growl.

"Hi, you must be James," said my ridiculously infuriating but utterly charming sister. She held out her hand and James took it and then kissed her on the cheek.

"And you must be the much-loved sister, Cat."

They stood there beaming at each other. I don't know which one I wanted to slap more.

"Here, I'll take that," said Cat, signalling to the tote. Well, at least she was being helpful. "It is mine, after all." *Argh!* Killing her would have been too kind. Torture came to mind.

James gave her the tote. "Well, thank you for loaning it to Sarah *and* for sparing her as much as you have this past week. I know this was supposed to be your time together."

"It's no problem at all, really. We've still got the rest of today and tomorrow morning." Listening to them talk as though I wasn't there was both fascinating and bloody maddening.

"Oh yes! Sarah said you're thinking of going to the National Gallery." *I what? Oh crap.* Lying was hard again.

To her credit, Cat didn't miss a beat. "Sarah loves her *Sunflowers*," she said, saving me and being a condescending cow in the same breath.

My level of angst increased as the ridiculous conversation went on. James didn't seem to notice—or if he did, he was an excellent actor. "So she said. I'm glad she'll get to see it before she goes home. And, I'll make sure to put it on the itinerary when she's here next."

Well, that shut her up. Cat's mouth formed a perfect O and her eyebrows nearly leapt passed her hairline.

After a moment of rare silence from my little sister, she just smiled and said, "How lovely." Then she seemed to come to her senses. "Well, I'll just take this upstairs and leave you two to ... leave you two alone."

James leant down and kissed her cheek again. "So lovely to have met you, Cat."

I think she blushed. "And you, James. Bye."

"Goodbye." She turned back towards me, her eyes wide with approval and a silly grin on her face, and left James and me to say goodbye.

I walked over to him and reached up for a hug. He wrapped his arms around me. "I think you know how much I hate this part," I said, my voice muffled by his chest.

"Me too, darling." We stood like that for some time.

I pulled away, keeping my arms around his neck. "Kiss me." He did, sweetly. When the kiss ended, I said, "I need to go inside now and not see you drive away. Okay?"

113

He just nodded, the sheen of tears in his eyes. "Goodbye, Sarah." I stood on my toes and pressed my mouth to his. Then before I could drag it out any longer, I turned and walked into the building. I pressed the button for the elevator several times, impatient for it to come and take me away—away from where I knew James was still standing and watching me.

It finally arrived with a "ding" and I chanced a glance outside. He raised a hand and I raised mine. Then I stepped into the elevator and dissolved into tears.

Like I said, goodbyes suck. They're even harder than lying.

Chapter 9

Cat was waiting for me with the front door open and even though she is a tiny woman, she threw her arms around me and enveloped me in a huge hug. I boo-hooed for a good couple of minutes before I let her go.

"Come inside," she said. "We don't want to scare the neighbours." It wasn't even that funny, but it had the desired effect and I smiled a little as I wiped tears and snot from my face.

"You didn't let him see you looking like this, did you?" asked my not-so-subtle sister.

"No," I wailed. "I was very dignified. I waited until I got in the elevator."

I followed Cat into the living room, and I could hear the kettle boiling, so I knew tea was on its way. *I love my little sister.*

"Sit down," she said, handing me a box of tissues. I sat. "Wipe your face." I did. She could have told me to do pretty much anything and I would have followed her instructions to the letter. I was not in a state to make my own decisions.

She brought over a plate of chocolate digestives. The plate was overkill. I could have happily tipped my head back and let them pour into my mouth from the packet. I took one and ate it in two bites. While I chewed and snuffled and got myself together, Cat made us tea. When there was a giant mug in my hand—really, she'd busted out the big ones—she sat opposite me.

"Before you tell me what happened, let me say one thing," she said earnestly. I nodded and swallowed my biscuit. "James is hands-down the hottest frigging man I've ever seen in real life."

That did the trick. She got me laughing.

"Seriously, Sarah. What the actual F? I mean, you're a catch, you know I think that, but ... I'm ... well, I'm in awe. Go, you." She raised her mug in a toast and I clinked mine against hers, grinning through my tears. "Okay, now, what the hell happened? Are you engaged? Are you moving here? What?"

"Enough with the proposal stuff, already," I wailed.

"Fine. But *something* happened. Look at you." She made a face that encompassed the giant mess that was me. It was not flattering.

I sighed. "He says he's falling in love with me."

"Wow."

"Yeah."

"And do you feel the same way?"

"I don't know."

"So, is that a solid maybe?" I chewed on my lip. "Stop chewing your lip. You'll gnaw right through it." I stopped and lifted a nail to my mouth and started nibbling. "And stop that too. It's nasty. Here." She pushed the plate of biscuits towards me.

"Getting fat on biscuits is better?" I took a biscuit.

"What did you say to him? Did you say anything?"

"I said that I have feelings for him."

"Huh, well that's good, right?" It must have been a rhetorical question, because she didn't wait for me to answer. "So, what does all this mean, *logistically*?"

"Logistically?"

She got impatient with me. "Is there any possibility that you might be moving to London?"

"I'm not moving to London, Cat."

"Well, you can't blame me for hoping." She gave me an encouraging smile. "So, how did you leave things?"

"We both think there's something there and that we need to see what it is, and he said we'll work it out." I stared at the surface of my tea, not really seeing it.

"Oh."

"Yeah."

"So, no firm plans?" I shook my head. "Are you all right with that?"

I lifted my eyes. "Yes, I guess so. I mean, I'm sad. It's hard to say goodbye when you don't know when you're going to see someone again." I realised that the same would be true when I said goodbye to Cat, but I pushed the thought aside. One crisis at a time.

"But you think it will be soon?"

"Yes." I was relieved to discover how certain I felt. "James has means, obviously, so he can come to me, or fly me here. There's my job, but the terms are only ten weeks long, and then I can travel again." I was starting to feel better.

"But you didn't talk about any of that?" she asked.

"No. It didn't seem the right time to dwell on all that. But, I know we'll see each other again. Like he said, we'll work it out." Calmness washed over me. Talking it through with Cat had helped immensely, and I really did believe it would be okay. I would miss James, yes, but we'd be together again, and as soon as we made plans, I would have that to look forward to. I leant back against the couch and took a sip of tea.

"So, Sarah?"

"Hmm?"

"What about Josh?" Cat asked, hesitantly. "How does he factor into all this?"

Oh, crap. Josh!

I hadn't given him *one* thought since ... I realised I couldn't remember the last time I'd thought about Josh.

Josh—the guy who made me laugh until I couldn't breathe, whose smile made me feel all squidgy inside, and who shared the longing that now fuelled me, the need for a bigger life. Josh—the guy I was seeing for New Year's in Hawaii.

My sexy American boy.

"Oh, Cat. What am I going to do?" I looked at Cat, stricken, and her face was riddled with concern.

But there was no answer she could give. It was my mess, and she seemed just as flummoxed as I was.

We finished our tea in silence, and I chewed on my thoughts, contemplating how I had let myself fall for two men at the same time.

Then, tea drunk, Cat shooed me off the couch with some

much-needed tough love, telling me to freshen up so we could go out for the day. Apparently, she had plans for us and none of them included me moping around her flat. We rode the train and then the tube into central London, and popped up at one of my favourite places—Leicester Square.

It was awash with tourists, as it usually was, and there was a street performer who was doing things with a giant hoop that would have impressed me on any other day. Cat took one look at my morose face and dragged me towards my favourite bookstore in London, Foyles on Charing Cross Road. It wasn't a long walk, maybe five minutes, and she handled it like she does all crowds—elbows out and barking "excuse me" a hundred times. I followed closely behind, not wanting to get lost in the melee.

"Was this part of the plan?" I asked as we stood roadside opposite Foyles and waited for the little man to go green.

"The plan for today?" I nodded. "Well, no. Not originally. But you didn't seem too keen on mooching about Leicester Square, so ..." She let the thought go unfinished.

"I don't know that I'm in the mood."

The light turned green and I started to cross, but Cat pulled me back onto the footpath. A woman, who bumped into us, apologised passive-aggressively, as only the English can do.

"Really? It's *Foyles*."

"I know. Can we just do something else? Maybe see a movie or something?"

"You want to spend our last day together seeing a movie?" She didn't sound particularly impressed.

"Sorry."

She grabbed my wrist and led me away from the road into the entryway of a tiny shop that sold antique jewellery. "Sarah, I love you—I do—but this is *my* day with you and I really don't want to spend it moping about London or hiding in the dark at the cinema."

She was right. "Sorry."

"Stop saying 'sorry'. It's really frigging annoying." She was probably right about that too. "Look at me." Great, she was resorting to old-school parenting techniques. I must have been more of a mess than I thought. I looked at her. "Do you want to go home? To my place, I mean."

I didn't, not really. I'd just sit there and stew in the mess of my own making and—*worse!*—waste time I could be having fun with Cat.

"No," I said, sounding reasonably sure. Fake it 'til you make it, right?

"Okay, so what do you want to do?"

"What did you have planned originally, before, well … everything?"

"Benefit brow bar, mooch about Oxford Street for a bit of window shopping, then oysters and champers at Bentley's Oyster Bar, then cocktails at Bar Termini. Not sure after that."

"That's a lot of bars."

She laughed, "I suppose it is. We can even throw in a quick trip to the National Gallery if you like, for some *Sunflowers* time. I mean, everything's right here." By that, she meant in central London and within walking distance.

"I would like that. *Sunflowers*, I mean, even just for a few minutes."

"Great. We have a plan. Brows first, then *Sunflowers*. All right?"

"Yes. So, you're getting your brows done?" I asked, as she pointed the way to Benefit.

"No. You are."

"Oh." She headed off. I caught up and walked alongside her, then self-consciously touched my eyebrows, wondering what was wrong with them.

"They're not terrible," she said helpfully. "But they could be better."

Well, thank god we were getting them sorted out! How had I survived so long with "not terrible" eyebrows?

*

Less than half an hour later, I admired myself in the mirror. "Your eyes really pop now," said the heavily made up and very pretty woman who'd tamed them. I nodded in agreement. I had to admit, the brow bar people really knew what they were doing. Cat's face appeared next to my reflection.

"You look great. And this is my treat, by the way." She scooted off to pay before I could object, and I met her at the counter where she took her credit card and a small Benefit bag from the cashier. "Here," she said, handing me the bag. I looked inside. It was a peach-coloured blush called "Dandelion".

"That's my fave!"

"Duh!"

I gave her a hug. "Thank you. And not just for the pressie." She looked, as the English say, well chuffed.

Next was a quick trip to the National Gallery. Cat left me alone with my favourite painting—and my thoughts—while she checked out the gift shop.

I sat in front of *Sunflowers* staring at the different hues of yellow. I loved that there was nothing symmetrical in the painting, including the vase. Everything was a little off kilter, but the overall effect was very beautiful.

Everything in my love life was off kilter too, but I was struggling to see the beauty in that.

I hadn't made promises to either man—not really—but I *had* been bitterly disappointed when Josh had referred to me as his "travel buddy" right before we'd said goodbye in Greece. I'd wanted more from him. But that wasn't fair to Josh, especially considering how things had developed between me and James. Josh had even asked me not to see James.

And James had been an absolute gentleman about Josh when we were in Greece, saying he didn't want to get in the way if there was something between us. But he hadn't asked about Josh at all during our week together in London. Was he trusting that I would tell him if there was anything to tell, or did he just assume I'd chosen him over the American boy?

And how could I go to Hawaii with Josh knowing how I felt about James?

And a worse question, how could I not?

I *knew* there was a reason to stay single.

I focused on the painting again. Van Gogh had started to go mad by the time he'd painted it. *Mad*. We'd call it depression now or some other treatable mental illness, the poor man. The struggle, *his* struggle, was right there on the canvas.

Yet, he'd found beauty in the details, even living inside a troubled mind. I was a little in love with Vincent.

I felt someone sit down beside me and knew without looking it was Cat. She moved closer and rested her head on my shoulder. "I love you," she said quietly.

"I love you too."

I was starting to feel the separation already. It sucked.

"We need to start drinking," she said after a moment. I could not have agreed more.

*

We were seated at the bar at Bentley's Oyster Bar (& Grill— don't forget the "& Grill"), a dozen empty oyster shells in front of us and each of us on our third glass of bubbles. It wasn't champagne though, because the prosecco was *way* more affordable.

"I'd like to propose a toast," said my tipsy sister.

"I'll drink to that," I said, also tipsy.

She giggled. Maybe she was more than tipsy. "I haven't proposed it yet."

"Oh. Go ahead, then."

"To Sarah, who is brave and beautiful and is shagging two ridiculously handsome men."

I clinked my flute against hers. "Amen." *Oops.* Maybe *I* was more than tipsy. "We should order a bottle," I suggested, helpfully.

"What about cocktails later? We have to pace ourselves."

"To hell with that. Let's order a bottle."

"Uh, Sez?"

"Mmm." I took a sizeable swig.

"Maybe we need more food."

I sat up as straight as I could and had a little think. Yep, I was very close to the tipping point. I'd soon be drunk. "I totes agree."

She grabbed a menu off the bar and read through it quickly, then signalled to the barman. "Can we get some skinny chips, please?" He seemed to ignore that she'd just ordered the cheapest thing on the menu—*and* a side dish.

"Of course, madam." *Madam*. There was that bloody word again.

He left us alone and Cat raised her eyebrows at me—maybe she didn't like that word either. I noted that her brows were perfectly shaped and guessed she went to the brow bar regularly.

"What on earth is a skinny chip?" I asked, eyeing the menu.

"I doubt the skinny part has anything to do with kilojoules. It's probably just French fries.

"Oh right." I sipped my prosecco, but just a tiny sip. *Not to worry, carbs are on the way!*

We sat in comfortable silence for approximately eight minutes, each of us taking micro sips of our bubbles, until the skinny chips arrived. Cat was right, they were French fries, and they were gone in less time than it took to cook them.

Cat licked salt off her fingers. "So, you've had some time to think about your little love triangle." I cringed at the term. "What are you going to do?"

My mouth formed a perfectly straight line. After a moment of further contemplation, I replied, "I'm just going to see."

"You're just going to see what?"

"What happens."

She shook her head, as though trying to dislodge a bug on her face, or perhaps she was trying to make sense of what I was saying. "So, you're going to continue with both of them and just see what happens?"

"Yep," I said with far more certainty than I felt.

"Huh."

We sat side by side, both of us looking forward.

"That might work," she said eventually.

"I hope so," I replied.

*

We skipped the cocktails at Bar Termini—partly because we'd spent quite a lot of money at the oyster bar, but mostly because we were drunk by the time we left. Skinny chips and oysters do not soak up much prosecco.

We rode the tube, then the train, home. On the train, Cat suggested we open some wine at her place to keep the festivities going. As my bubbles buzz was wearing off, I wholeheartedly agreed.

Jane was home when we arrived, but was heading out for the evening, so it would just be me and Cat. I still hadn't met Alex. I had moved from suspecting he didn't exist to deciding he definitely didn't.

Minutes after we arrived, Cat opened a bottle of red while I rummaged in her cupboards for two matching wine glasses. "Success!" I said, holding up a pair. Cat threw me an odd look. "What? I like them to match." I placed them in front of her and she poured two generous glasses.

"What should we have for dinner, do you think?" she asked. Knowing my sister as I did, I took her question to mean, "what are you cooking for us?"

"Well, we're having a red. Shall I make pasta?" She grinned in response. "You were hoping I'd say that, weren't you?" She grinned even wider, the cheeky thing. I rolled my eyes. "Have you got everything for the sauce?"

"I think so." She went through the cupboards and assembled an assortment of tomato-based goods on the countertop, along with a large green bottle of olive oil.

"Pasta?" An unopened packet of pasta appeared on the counter and she stood up, her cupboard foraging complete.

"What else?" she asked. She couldn't cook, but she was a half-decent kitchen hand.

"Fresh herbs? Veggies—an onion."

She went to the fridge and came out with a zucchini, an onion, and a bunch of slightly wilted basil.

"How about these?" she said, dumping her finds next to the cans.

"Great. Big pot?"

"Cupboard below you." I opened the cupboard and pulled out the biggest pot they had. I knew where they kept the cutting board and the sharp knives, so I got to work while Cat went around the other side of the counter and climbed onto a stool, then watched me in silence while she sipped her wine. It's one of the things I love most about my friendship with Cat—no need to fill every moment with chatter.

Once the onions were cooking, I took my first sip of wine. "Mmm, this is good."

"Argentinian malbec."

"Delish." I took another sip while I stirred the onions.

"I have a couple more bottles. It was on sale at Tesco."

"Let's see how we go with this one first. I don't want to fly with a hangover."

"Noted," said my sister, as she took a generous mouthful of wine, then topped up her glass. I ignored her and got down to chopping and opening cans. In no time at all, the sauce was simmering slowly on the stove and I started cleaning up.

"So, this plan of yours," she said, suddenly very interested in the stem of her glass. "It means you *are* going to Hawaii with Josh in December?"

I drank some more wine and absently stirred the sauce. I wasn't sure I was ready to confront the reality Cat had just raised. When I'd said I was going to see what happens, I'd been half-cut on Italian bubbles.

"Is that what I said?" I asked, not really wanting the answer.

"Well, no, not in so many words, but isn't that what you meant? You're going to 'see what happens'." She put the last part in air quotes. I hate air quotes, especially when they're being used against me. "So, you'll see Josh in Hawaii, and James—well, I guess you'll see him whenever he flies down to Sydney or flies you back here, right?"

I chewed on a thumbnail. *Am I a nail-biter now?* Cat frowned at me and I stopped nibbling.

"Uh, yeah, I guess that means I'm going to Hawaii," I said without any conviction whatsoever.

"You guess?"

"I don't know."

She leant across the counter and poured me more wine. "We're gunna need a bigger bottle."

*

The next morning, we were flying down the M4 in Cat's car, the radio blaring far louder than my poor head would have liked. Why did my sister not get hangovers? She got the good hair. Wasn't that enough? I was hating her a little from the passenger seat.

We'd opened a second bottle of wine—of course we had—which we drank with dinner and finished after dinner accompanied by Galaxy chocolate—not a great pairing, by the way. And we had to open the second bottle, because the first bottle didn't even last until I dished up.

But once I did dish up, I told Cat we had to stop talking about James and Josh. We'd gone around in circles so many times my mind was dizzy and my emotions were in turmoil. Each time I heard either name, a surge of happiness, then confusion, then dread coursed through my veins. I had no frigging idea what I was going to do.

Cat had promised to deposit me in the "kiss and fly" drop-off zone at Heathrow, rather than parking and dragging out our goodbye, and after some pretty colourful swearing at some "stupid bloody idiots"—sometimes she was *all* Aussie—

she squeezed into a kerb-side spot. She put the car in neutral and put the handbrake on, but kept it running, then got out and opened the boot.

My legs felt like lead as I climbed out of the car and found a luggage cart nearby. I rolled it over to the car, its front left wheel wobbling like a crappy shopping trolley. *Wonderful*. I helped Cat drag my giant backpack out of the car and onto the cart—she is just little, after all—and sat my leather handbag on top. We did all of that without speaking and I figured she was feeling as shitty as I was.

It was time.

I leant down and hugged her tightly and she returned the hug with ferocity. "I love you," we both said at the same time. We pulled apart, both laughing through the tears that were streaming down our faces. I wiped mine away, my hangover forgotten for the moment. "Thank you so much. I've had the most amazing time. You're the best sister ever."

"Yes," she said, as she wiped under her eyes with her forefingers. "I'm still waiting for my T-shirt."

I laughed. "Christmas. Keep an eye on your mailbox."

Her face crumpled and she hugged me again. "I'll miss you," she said, her voice ragged.

"Me too." I had to go. The whole thing was excruciating, and I'd promised myself not to drag it out.

"Okay, I'm going to go now."

She nodded. "Travel safe. Text me when you get home."

I nodded back, not trusting my voice. I lifted my hand in a wave, even though she was less than a metre from me, grabbed the handle of my luggage cart, and started to push it away. It took a concerted effort to keep it from veering off to the left, but I pushed it across the crosswalk towards the terminal.

I stopped on the other side and turned around. Cat was still there, smiling through her tears. She blew me a kiss, then I turned and pushed that wretched cart into the terminal.

Goodbyes suck so fucking much.

PART TWO

Chapter 10

"So, what are you gunna do if he doesn't show up?"

I was sitting in the backseat of my best friend, Lindsey's, car on the way to the airport. Her husband, Nick, was in the passenger seat, and it was obvious he was intent on torturing me with ridiculous questions. He's the big brother I always knew I never wanted.

"Ha, ha. You're hilarious," I replied drolly.

Lindsey swatted him as though he was a naughty fly. "Ignore my horrendous husband." Nick turned in his seat and grinned at me. "He'll be there," continued Lins, "*and* you'll have a ball."

I nodded, clinging to her words of encouragement.

But Nick had hit a sore spot. I was only *mildly* terrified he wouldn't show up and I'd be sitting in a hotel room halfway across the world by myself. Self-doubt can be such a buzzkill, especially when you're about to fly somewhere you've never been before, to meet up with someone you haven't seen in months.

Lins snuck her car between two four-wheel-drives and pulled up to the kerb at an odd angle. As always, Sydney airport was brimming with drop-off traffic. "Here okay?" she asked unnecessarily. I was hardly going to say "no" and have her pull back out into traffic to find the elusive "better spot".

She put the car in park and Nick leapt out to retrieve my suitcase from the boot. I grabbed my carry-on from the seat beside me and joined Nick on the footpath.

"Have a great time, Sez," he said, giving me a quick hug that squeezed all the air from my lungs. Nick is a huge guy.

"Love you," Lins called through the car window with a smile. Nick climbed back in the passenger seat and gave me one of his lopsided smiles that said, "yeah, me too."

"Love you back," I said, waving goodbye. "Look after Domino!" I added as an afterthought. My poor cat—he'd become an afterthought. Nick's hand waved out the window as the car pulled away from the kerb and I took a moment to catch my breath.

What if he doesn't show up? Or, what if he does but it isn't the same between us? Oh, my god, what am I doing?

I was having a mini meltdown out the front of Sydney International Airport, that's what I was doing. As I do when faced with situations just like this one, I took a deep breath, adjusted my big-girl knickers, and got the hell on with it. I grabbed the handle of my suitcase, slung my carry-on over my shoulder and, chin lifted, walked into the terminal.

As soon as I was inside, my phone bleeped. I hoped it wasn't Nick laying it on again; I wasn't in the mood for brotherly teasing. I took my phone out of my carry-on.

About to take off. Can't wait to see you!!! Jxxx

So, he really was going to show up. I was both relieved and terrified, which I can assure you, is not a fun mix. I tucked the phone away, deciding to reply after I'd checked in and was through security and immigration. Hopefully, by then, I'd no longer be a giant ball of anxiety.

I looked up at the screen to see where to check in, which turned out to be the counters marked "A". Of course, I was way down the other end near "K". Maybe a brisk walk from one end of the airport to the other was exactly what I needed to shake off my nerves.

What I didn't need, however, was having to navigate through a giant tour group of retirees, all sporting the same red and white polo shirt. They didn't seem to care that I said, "Excuse me!" three hundred times. They were sticking together come what may! I needed Cat. She'd just bully through, elbows out.

I finally made it to the "A" counters, discovering that there was only one person ahead of me in line. My plan to arrive at the airport three-and-a-half hours before my flight—just in case—had paid off! It was only when I took my place behind him, that I saw the sign on the counter saying check-in wouldn't open for an hour-and-a-half.

Hmm.

I'd have to reply to the text. Otherwise, he might take off before I had the chance, and maybe *he'd* spend the whole flight wondering if *I* was going to show up, which would suck. I took my phone out.

Me too! Fly safe. See you there. Sxxx

There. Now I *definitely* couldn't back out. I was going.

I'd take a ten-hour flight, then a taxi from the airport, and I'd meet him at the hotel. Of course, I only realised after our flights were booked that I hadn't timed that very well. He was arriving before me and we'd be reunited before I had a chance to take a shower—after a long-haul flight! What had I been thinking?!

Although I'd paid for my own flight, he had insisted on taking care of the accommodation—apparently, he got good deals through a loyalty program. I told him that was fine *if* we shared the car rental and everything else—going Dutch, holiday style. He only agreed when I told him I wouldn't come otherwise.

My phone bleeped in my hand, pulling me away from my thoughts. It was a smiley face blowing a kiss—no words, just the emoji. Josh was such a Millennial. Yes, I know I'm technically one too, but I'm right on the cusp and most of the time, I feel more like a Gen-Xer.

I smiled down at the little kissy face on my phone. Despite my qualms, I really was looking forward to seeing him. We'd texted, emailed, and FaceTimed a lot in the months leading up to our trip to Maui, but I'd missed *being* with him.

I was also looking forward to the trip because the past few months had been ridiculously busy—in a good way, but I was exhausted and needed a breather. You see, when I arrived home from London, I'd leapt wholeheartedly into that bigger life I'd promised myself.

I had finally said yes to the leadership position my principal had been steering me towards and I was officially in charge of a whole year group. It came with a raise—which I immediately deposited into my travel fund—and a team of six teachers.

The woman I replaced was so relieved to hand over her acting role, I almost took it as a sign to run away. But it turned out I had a knack for handling, and hopefully inspiring, fourteen-year-olds. I loved the role and this coming year— fingers crossed—the kids would be even more manageable because they'd be *fifteen*-year-olds!

For my birthday in October, in the middle of a stunning Sydney spring, I'd organised a huge day out at Centennial Park with all my girlfriends and their families. I'd also invited a few of my younger, single friends from school, telling them each to bring a friend, so they'd be more likely to come.

For food we'd had a massive potluck, and I ordered a side of lamb on a spit. Thank god for Nick who commandeered the carving. "No worries, Sez. Just give me a slab of meat and a huge knife and I'm a happy man," he'd said. Nick's kind of weird, or maybe all men like carving cooked carcases.

Lins helped me organise games for the kids, and we'd all brought our own coolers filled with drinks. And *every single person* I invited came. Even my girlfriend, Jonelle, who had a shift at the hospital later that day, came for lunch before she left for work.

People who rarely saw each other reconnected, and people who didn't know each other, met. It was one of the best days I've ever had in Sydney—and a reboot for all my married-friend friendships. Soon afterwards, the invites started pouring in.

I was invited to weeknight dinners, with kid chaos and bedtime stories and a sneaky glass of wine after the kids had gone to sleep. I was "Aunty Sarah" again, which I'd forgotten how much I loved. My younger friends invited me out to dinners in the city and to pubs on Sunday afternoons, even to clubs from time to time. I didn't always accept, but when I did, I had a blast.

But the most exhilarating thing of all—and the most exhausting—was that I had two boyfriends.

Well, sort of.

Geography being the great leveller between them, I hadn't seen Josh *or* James in person, but I'd carried on with them both. And by "carried on", I mean I was in contact with each of them several times a week.

I also had plans to see them both again. Obviously, I was meeting up with Josh for New Year's in Hawaii, like we'd talked about when we were in Greece. And James had recently called with exciting news. He was coming to Sydney in January for a project with the Museum of Contemporary Art.

I didn't like being duplicitous—actually, that's putting it mildly. I hated that part. But I didn't know what else to do. I'd left London knowing I had feelings for James, and those had intensified over the past few months.

But Josh and I had something special too—even more so after months of lengthy emails and long chats.

Over the past few months, I'd engaged in some intricate emotional gymnastics to give myself as much as possible to each relationship. The situation was emotionally gruelling, but I wasn't prepared to decide between them before I knew who I wanted to be with. The decision loomed ominously, but I *had* to see each of them again before I chose.

And, of course, *way* in the back of my mind was the possibility that I wouldn't end up with either of them. I was a different version of myself now—Sarah 2.0. *I* loved this Sarah, but maybe she wouldn't be a fit for Josh *or* James. And maybe, they wouldn't be a fit for her.

Maybe I'd decide to be on my own.

This was my least favourite outcome, by the way. I'd spent many, *many* hours pondering what my life would be like with a proper partner, someone to love and laugh with, to build a life with. I'd never had that kind of relationship, that kind of life, and I *wanted* it. And, just like in that film, *Sliding Doors*, I'd imagined two version of it.

One in which I went home from work to a stylish flat in the Eastern Suburbs of Sydney—kind of like my current flat, but bigger and nicer—to my tech-geek boyfriend and we drank G&Ts on the balcony and told each other about our days. And the other in which I invited my friends out onto our yacht for a day trip around Sydney Harbour, James at the helm and bottles of bubbles on ice.

And the future I wanted most?

Well, that depended on the day, who I'd spoken to most recently, and what was going on in my life at any given moment. I can't say I liked being capricious any more than I liked being duplicitous. The whole situation, the good, the bad, and the very, very ugly, was like being on *The Bachelorette* and in *The Twilight Zone* at the same time—like I said, exhilarating *and* exhausting.

The other thing wearing me down was that only three people knew about my messy love life—Cat, Lins, and Nick. Until I sorted it all out, I only wanted to discuss it with my closest friends. This meant I was keeping a lot of secrets, which sucked.

Overall, though, life was good. I'd gone from a tiny existence—going to the gym, solo dinners and cask wine, imposing myself on Lins and Nick far too often, and hanging out with Domino—to something much bigger. I loved most of it, but I was shattered, and a trip to Maui over New Year's was exactly how I wanted to recharge. I would make a toast to new beginnings, and somewhere in there, I'd edge closer to one of the biggest decisions of my life.

*

Waiting for check-in to open, I read every post on Facebook and Instagram, every tweet in my feed, refreshing twice, unsubscribed from two newsletters, and started a novel on my Kindle app.

I also had a lengthy texting session with my sister. As (bloody, stupid, frigging) luck would have it, she was actually in Sydney—and she hadn't come alone. Since I'd visited her in London, Cat had gone and got herself all loved up.

Yep! My sister, Cat—sworn to be single 'til the day she died—had a boyfriend.

Actually, I knew Jean-Luc—my whole family did. He'd been an exchange student in Sydney the year he and Cat turned fifteen. They'd been really close back then—best friends—and when he returned to France, they'd written every week for years. It had all gone pear-shaped because her jealous idiot of an ex told her not to write to Jean-Luc anymore—and she'd complied.

Anyway, long story short—too late!—they lost touch over the years and as fate would have it, she literally ran into him when she was in Paris a few months ago. They reconnected and have been going back and forth between Paris and London for the past few months. And now they were in Sydney for the holidays.

When she'd told me they were coming, it was one of the best surprises of my life but, of course, their trip to Australia overlapped with my trip to Hawaii.

I'd agonised over cancelling my trip with Josh—or at least postponing my arrival in Hawaii—but, knowing how much I missed Josh, Cat had insisted I keep my plans. That meant we'd only had a couple of days together—Christmas and Boxing Day— but we'd squeezed the most out of that time, and it was easily the best Christmas I've ever had.

And to see Cat *so* happy with Jean-Luc—okay, this is going to sound ridiculously corny—*that* was the real Christmas present.

They were perfect for each other. He brought out her more vulnerable side, her gentler side, and I loved seeing her be *that* Cat, the one she usually reserved for me. And even though he was now a grown man of thirty-five, Jean-Luc was, at heart, the same person who had fit so easily into our family all those years ago. It was like having a long-lost family member back in the fold. Besides, anyone who could make Cat's face light up with joy just by looking at her, was a keeper.

Waiting in line, I also replied to a passive-aggressive "bon voyage" text from my mother who was miffed that I was missing the traditional family New Year's Day barbecue. I sent her lots of kissy smiley faces and told her to send my love to everyone. Going to Hawaii was *way* more appealing than fielding questions from my relatives about why I was still single at thirty-seven.

If only they knew!

Eventually, airline agents appeared behind the counter and I was called over by a smiling young woman. At the counter I lifted my suitcase onto the scale—a *suitcase*, not a backpack, this time. I was a civilised person going on holiday, rather than a traveller roughing it on a boat. I had no illusions about this trip. It was going to be on the beaten track and replete with poolside cocktails, pricey excursions, and maybe even a spa day. This gal was on HOL-I-DAY!

I handed over my passport. "First time?" asked the smiling woman. I wondered if she could hold onto that smile after checking in hundreds of passengers.

"Uh, to Hawaii, yes, but I've been to the States before."

"Hawaii is just beautiful," she replied. "You'll love it." She was far chattier than any airline agent I'd met before. Maybe she was be a traveller at heart, like me. Her nametag said, "Candyce".

"I'm meeting my lover there," my mouth said without my permission. I don't even like that word and I *never* use it. Yet, there I was telling a perfect stranger that I was heading to Hawaii for a shag.

I wanted to suck the words back into my mouth, but before I could go into damage control, she replied, "Good for you," and added a conspiratorial smile. I beamed. She printed a luggage tag and put it on my suitcase with a practised ease I've never mastered at self-check-in. Then her machine spat out my boarding pass and luggage receipt. She tucked them into my passport and handed them across the counter.

"It's not a full flight, so I've blacked out the seat next to yours. You'll have some extra room to rest up." She smiled again and raised her eyebrows. I beamed even more.

"Thank you!"

"Have a great flight," she called after me.

"I will!" It was possibly the best check-in ever. I gave myself a mental high-five, forgetting instantly that I'd just spilled to a stranger about my sex life.

Once I was through security and immigration, the knot in my stomach started to ease and excitement took its place. I changed some money, so I'd have US cash, then stopped at duty free to pick up a bottle of Bombay Sapphire gin. When Josh and I were in Greece, we'd discovered it was a shared favourite, and I liked the idea of having "our drink" at the ready for sundowners on the balcony.

I filled the rest of the time before my flight the same way I usually do, browsing the latest book releases, stocking up on water, gum, snacks, and trashy magazines for the flight, and settling any lingering nerves by drinking a glass of wine at the bar closest to my gate.

Okay, it was two.

Boarding a long-haul flight just a little tipsy is my preferred way to travel—don't judge me. I know the prevailing wisdom is to avoid alcohol and stay hydrated, but I'd bet a billion dollars that the people who write those travel tips fly business class. *And* that they've never had a peevish seat battle with the person in front who decides to fully recline in the middle of dinner. Those people, the mid-meal recliners, belong in hell with the bad toast-makers.

Luckily, my flight turned out to be quite nice—for a ten-hour flight, that is. No seat war, dinner was served right after we took off, and Candyce blocking out the seat next to me paid off big time! *Both* seats next to me were empty and I got to lie down and sleep, which I did for six hours. Six! That's the economy flier's equivalent of a unicorn sighting.

Immigration in Honolulu was uneventful. We were essentially a planeload of Aussies on holiday, so I can't imagine we posed much of a challenge to the immigration officers. Mine even looked bored as I pressed my fingertips to the little fingerprinting screen and she took my photo. Imagine living in paradise and being stuck inside all day welcoming tourists.

I switched my phone off flight mode as I waited for my suitcase. It bleeped immediately with a text.

Delayed in LA. Sorry! Will be there after you. Room in my name. I called them so you can check in. See you soon. Jx

A Sunset in Sydney

Oh. A wave of disappointment washed over me. I'd landed thinking I would see Josh within the hour, so my anticipation, after months of being apart, was palpable. *It's only a few more hours,* I told myself, and now I'd have time to freshen up before he arrived. Happily landing on the bright side, I thought about what I wanted to be wearing when he arrived.

I decided on nothing.

*

When the taxi pulled up at the hotel, excitement bubbled up inside me. *Hawaii, Hawaii, Hawaii!* I paid the driver in cash and a man in a Hawaiian shirt—do they just call it a "shirt" in Hawaii?—opened my door with, "Aloha," followed closely by, "Welcome to The Waikiki Beach Marriott Resort and Spa." That was quite a mouthful to have to say dozens of times a day.

I climbed out of the taxi and took a deep breath of the warm, fragrant breeze. The man placed a lei around my neck—a real one, made of frangipanis! *How lovely!* I was already blown away, and I hadn't even gone inside yet. I replied with a big smile and said, "Thank you!"

The excellent service continued all the way through check-in—yes, they were expecting me, "Welcome, Miss Parsons"—and being shown to the room. The hotel—the lobby, the room, everything—was over-the-top beautiful. I couldn't remember the last time I'd stayed somewhere as luxurious. *Mental note: fancy hotels are extremely nice.*

Overwhelmed by the view of Waikiki Beach, I only remembered at the last second to tip the bellboy for bringing my suitcase. He smiled politely without looking at the five dollars I'd given him, and I wondered if it was too much, but better too much than too little.

Then it was just me alone in a massive room with one of the most famous views in the world. *Nice digs, Joshua.* Waikiki was only for a night, though, as we were flying to Maui in the morning. From Josh's description, the resort in Maui was even more luxurious. *I could get used to this*, I thought.

As I wasn't sure how long I would have the room to myself, I tore myself away from the view and got busy freshening up. Close to two hours later, after I had scrubbed, lathered, slathered, and prettied myself *and* after I had practised arranging myself on the bed in the most alluring pose possible, still no Josh. I went to the wardrobe, took out a robe, and slipped it on. Being nude for Josh's arrival was one thing, but it felt odd to hang out in a hotel room stark naked.

The wait also gave me time to think, which for me, can be dangerous.

The last time I'd seen Josh, he told me he'd never known anyone like me and that he wanted to know me for the rest of his life. He'd also called me his "travel buddy". I wondered which Josh would show up, especially as over the past few months, we'd become even closer than we were in Greece.

Over email and FaceTime, we'd chatted easily about all sorts of things *and* we'd planned the trip together. Sure, we'd had some discussions—disagreements, really—but we had talked our way through them, listening to each other, respecting the other's opinion.

We were close friends. Close friends who planned on having lots of sex over the coming week. Close friends who may—or may not—end up in a relationship and actually *be* boyfriend and girlfriend.

Or, we'd just stay travel buddies.

Alone in a luxury hotel room, I managed to work myself into quite a tizzy.

Why am I here waiting for a man who isn't sure about his feelings? James sees a future with me. But Josh might too. How can I decide between them if I don't find out?

Around and around I went. I was my own worst enemy. Then my phone bleeped, saving me from myself.

Landed. Should be there within the hour. Can't wait. Jxxx

I replied, relieved to be out of my head.

We're in room 1505. I had reception set aside a key-card for you. See you soon! Sx

I went into the bathroom to check my makeup. Flawless. No matter how much inner turmoil I was in, at least I looked good. Back in the bedroom, I smoothed out the bed covers and fluffed the pillows.

Usually I would unpack and nest a little after arriving somewhere new, but we were only there for one night, so it wouldn't be worth it. I looked around the room trying to find something—*anything*—to keep me occupied until Josh got there.

Next to my suitcase, I spied the duty-free bag that held the bottle of gin. I opened the mini bar—there was tonic. I looked at the clock—nearly noon. "It's five o'clock somewhere," I said to myself. I didn't have a lime, but desperate times and all that. I free-poured a shot of gin into a glass and topped it up with a six-dollar tonic, then took my drink to the balcony to enjoy the view. I sat, then propped my feet up on the railing and took a sip. It was delicious and I sighed a little. *Fantastic. I am officially a day-drinker.*

The view of Waikiki Beach was just like I'd imagined. Palm trees, white sand, clear aquamarine water and surfers riding even rows of waves. From that high up I couldn't hear the hubbub of the tourists, but I could see the hordes milling about. One night was enough, I figured.

The gin started to warm me through and soon my troubled thoughts receded into the background. I knew I'd revisit them another time, but just then, I needed the reprieve. A little while later, after the meditative sound of waves crashing and the gin had lulled me into a peaceful state, my phone bleeped again.

Just arrived! See you soon. Jx

Holy crap! Only a couple of minutes to go!

I ran back into the room, took off my robe and flung it into the closet, then arranged my nude self on the bed and waited.

And waited.

And waited.

More than a few minutes went by, then I finally heard the

key-card in the lock. I sucked in my stomach and pursed my lips.

And then died of utter mortification.

It wasn't Josh. It was the bellboy. The same bellboy. With Josh's luggage. And *then* it was Josh.

They both wore the same shocked expression, while I plummeted into the depths of horror. When I finally came to my senses, I rolled off the other side of the bed onto the floor, grabbing a pillow to cover me as I went.

"Oh, my god," I said to myself over and over.

I heard Josh tell the bellboy, "Thank you. I'll take it from here," which was even *more* mortifying, and then the door closed.

"You can come out now," he said, an annoying lilt of laughter in his voice.

"I'm just going to stay here."

He came around the bed to where I was lying on my back with a pillow covering my torso. "You probably made his day." I squeezed my eyes shut, which was worse, because the whole scene replayed vividly in my mind. I opened my eyes. "Maybe even his whole week." He grinned down at me.

"You were supposed to come *alone*. I thought that was *very obvious*."

"Very obvious? Is that like super-duper obvious." I frowned at him. "I'm really sorry that happened." He didn't seem particularly sorry. "Can I at least help you up?" he said, extending a hand.

"No thank you. I'd prefer to stay down here. It's very comfy." He took a pillow off the bed and put it on the floor next to my head, slipped his shoes off, and lay down next to me.

149

We both looked up at the ceiling. "Hmmm, you're right. This isn't bad."

My giggles started silently and took over my whole body. By the time I was laughing aloud, Josh was too, and we lay there on the floor laughing until tears streamed from my eyes onto the carpet. Eventually, I got a hold of myself and took a few deep breaths.

"Would you like me to go out and come back in again?" That set us both off again and it was another few minutes before I could compose myself enough to get off the floor.

"Close your eyes," I commanded. He didn't even ask why, he just did it. I got up, taking the pillow with me, and climbed onto the bed. I arranged myself as elegantly as possible for a woman who'd just humiliated herself in front of a bellboy and her long-distance boyfriend. I hoped I hadn't scarred him for life—the bellboy, that is.

"Okay, you can open your eyes now."

Josh's head popped up beside the bed and our eyes met. Then his gaze trailed the length of my nakedness and made its way back up to my eyes. "If it's possible, I think you look even better than you did the last time I saw you." That made me smile.

He stood up quickly and walked over to the door. "You don't need to come in again," I said.

"No, but I do need to put out the 'do not disturb' sign," which he did before joining me on the bed. Our reunion—the part *after* the most embarrassing thing that's ever happened to me—was tender and sweet, two close friends who perhaps felt something more, finding each other again.

Chapter 11

"Oh, fuck," said Josh under his breath. We were standing in the security line at Honolulu airport on our way to Maui.

"What?" I asked, turning around.

"I just remembered I put my pocketknife in my backpack last night." He meant the backpack he was using as a carry-on, the one about to go through an airport x-ray machine.

"Why did you do that?"

"Because that's where I normally keep it, just in case, and I stupidly repacked it last night, *completely* forgetting about flying today." It was the sort of dumb thing I'd do, so I empathised, but I was also concerned.

"Shouldn't you tell them? They'll confiscate it, but at least you won't get into trouble."

He scrunched up his face. "The thing is my grandpa gave me that knife. I've had it since I was twelve. I really don't want to lose it." We were getting closer to the front of the line; I was only two people away from the stack of trays. "I think I'll chance it. Maybe they won't find it."

I was doubtful. We were talking about the TSA. In *America*.

You can't take a bottle of hand sanitiser on board if it's over three ounces—you know, in case you're one of those incredibly clever people who knows how to hijack a plane with just your (very clean) bare hands.

We moved up and I took a tray, loading it with my iPad, Kindle, a tube of lip balm, and a small bottle of hand sanitiser—just for hand sanitation, by the way. Josh took a tray and placed his laptop in it, and we remained silent as we moved through the line. I wondered about the worst thing that could happen, which led to a vision of Josh sitting in a windowless room being questioned by TSA agents while our flight left without us.

Our stuff went through the x-ray machine and we walked through the metal detector one at a time.

"Sir, is this your bag?" *Oh, crap*. A TSA agent was looking at Josh and pointing to his backpack. I gathered my stuff and put it back into my carry-on.

"Uh, yes. Is there a problem?"

The woman took Josh's bag to the end of the conveyor belt and sat it on a metal table. "Come with me please, sir." Josh followed and I stood off to the side chewing on my thumbnail.

She rummaged around in Josh's backpack, finally pulling out a giant bottle of sunscreen. "Sir, you can't travel with liquids in containers larger than three ounces."

Josh had seemingly lost the ability to speak, so I did. "I told him not to put that in there," I said. Maybe if I threw him under the bus, she'd be too distracted to search the bag further.

"Well, I'm going to have to confiscate this." She took the offending item and placed it in a bin behind her.

Josh pretended to look contrite and apologised for the oversight while I shook my head at him and tutted, the finishing touches on my obviously credible performance. He took his backpack off the table, slung it over his shoulder and we walked away briskly. When we were out of sight of the security point, we burst out laughing.

"I think playing the nagging wife really sealed the deal." He flung his arm around my shoulder and kissed the top of my head as we walked to our gate.

Wife. Coming from Josh, even in that context, it sounded odd—*extremely* odd.

*

"And here we are, the Honeymoon Suite," said our bellboy as we followed him into the most beautiful room I'd ever seen. The surprise of the room wore off as soon as I realised what he'd said.

"Oh, we're not—" I started to correct him, but Josh cut me off.

"We're not used to such luxury," he said to the bellboy. "This room is amazing." The bellboy looked pleased and lifted our suitcases onto the luggage rack in turn. Josh pulled a five-dollar note from his money clip and handed it to the bellboy.

"Thank you, sir. Anything you or your wife need during your stay, just let us know."

There was that word again, "wife". Josh and I were barely boyfriend and girlfriend, so it didn't sit well with me—*at all*.

The bellboy left, and Josh opened the sliding door and stepped out onto our balcony as though everything was exactly as it should be. "Uh, Josh?" I followed him out onto the balcony, needing to clarify something. "You didn't *book* the Honeymoon Suite, did you?"

He laughed in a way that instantly told me two things. First, he did *not* book the Honeymoon Suite. And second, he thought it was preposterous that I thought he had. The second one annoyed me. Why was it so ridiculous for me to wonder if he'd done it as a romantic gesture? A *misguided* romantic gesture, but even so!

"It's probably just an upgrade," he explained. "It happens sometimes because I have platinum status—I *think* I told you about that." I nodded curtly. "Anyway, I'm guessing he just assumed we were newlyweds. It may mean some perks, though. That's why I didn't correct him."

"Oh," I replied. Was I relieved or disappointed? Perhaps it was a little of both.

Josh, who had either missed my darkening mood, or was deliberately ignoring it, turned me towards the view, then stood behind me and wrapped his arms around me. "Look," he said softly in my ear.

My annoyance dissipated instantly, and I leant into him, drinking in the view. The lush resort grounds lay before us, vast undulating lawns in vivid green punctuated by palm trees and bordered by native shrubs, each with vibrant bursts of flowers. Just beyond, there was a cove with lapping waves and white sand and in the distance, ocean spray rose from the jagged black rocks along the coastline.

Maui was nothing like Waikiki. Both were beautiful, but Maui seemed quieter, more peaceful. I needed some of that peace. I was on edge—a concoction of nerves, excitement and doubt. I took a deep breath of the gentle breeze; it carried briny air tempered with the fragrance of tropical flowers. Divine.

"The pools must be on the other side," said Josh, pulling me from my thoughts. "This is a nicer view than more of the resort, though, don't you think?"

"I do." *I do?* "Uh, yep, yes." Did you know it's possible to roll your eyes at yourself so hard, you see the inside of your own head?

"Want to go explore?"

"Absolutely," I said, with great conviction. Anything to stop *thinking*.

"You know I mean 'go sit by the pool and order cocktails', right?" he added.

"Yep," I replied, winking at him as I slipped past him and went inside.

"Great, and how about I bring my laptop so we can check out some day trips and excursions?"

"Sounds like a plan," I replied. I pulled a tangerine-coloured bikini out of my luggage. "Hey, remember this from our trip?" I asked, holding it up for Josh to see.

"Remember? It's been the sole thing keeping me going through a Chicago winter."

I grinned. "I'll be right back." It wasn't that I was being modest, but it's far sexier to get out of a bikini than into one. Besides, I was hoping to erase the image of me, naked, squealing, and rolling off the bed onto the floor, from Josh's mind. I didn't want to replace it with me wrestling with some scraps of orange lycra.

"Oh, my god!" I stopped short at the door to the bathroom. It was the most luxurious and spacious bathroom I'd ever seen—including the one at James's house. There was a long granite vanity with two sinks and drawers below, a spa bath big enough for two, a rainwater shower—also big enough for two—and a separate room for the toilet. There was even a basket filled with spa products on the vanity. I was in heaven.

"What?" called Josh.

"This bathroom is bigger than the Blue Banana," I called back. I could hear him laugh from the other room.

"Does that make me Richard Gere?" *Richard Gere, a silver fox, like James.* The thought of James in his rainwater shower, water sluicing off his back, popped into my head. I shooed it away and poked my head around the corner, so I could see Josh.

Josh, Josh, Josh.

"Uh, let's go with 'no' on that one. If you're Richard Gere, that would make me Julia Roberts *and* a prostitute. But at least you got the reference."

"*Pretty Woman*? Of course," he laughed. "I wasn't born yesterday."

"But you *were* very young when it came out." I leant against the doorframe.

"What year was that?" he asked.

"1990, I think."

He shrugged. "I was a toddler."

"Right."

"Well, it's not like *you* saw it in the theatre either."

"Yes, I know. I saw it later, when it was age-appropriate," I replied.

"Well, so did I."

This conversation was not going well. I wanted to revel in the glorious bathroom, not discuss the movie about the prostitute with a heart of gold.

And, I still wasn't in my bikini.

"I'm just going to get changed," I said, closing the bathroom door on our tiff.

Surely it was normal for things to be a little awkward at first? And if not, it certainly wasn't helping that thoughts of James kept popping into my head. Why was it so hard to be with Josh and not constantly compare him to James?

I needed to focus on where I was and who I was with.

I wrangled myself into my bikini and opened the bathroom door. Josh was already in his bathing suit and we each took a moment to admire the other. His muscular torso was paler than it had been in Greece, him having spent the past few months in cold weather, but the sight of that waistband slung low on his slim hips made my heart race.

"Just like I remembered," he said, with a smile, indicating my bikini. "Actually, even better."

"What? This old thing?" I did a twirl, basking in false modesty.

"It's not the bikini—it's the woman in it." He crossed the room and pulled me to him, his hands resting on the small of my back, then kissed me. I liked this Josh—he was quite different from the guy I'd met on the dock in Santorini, the one who was shy around women. I wondered if *I'd* had that effect on him. He pulled away, keeping his hands where they were. "Maybe the pool can wait."

"I'm actually looking forward to being in the pool with you."

"Is that so?"

"Uh huh. My legs wrapped around your waist, my arms around your neck, just floating about. Doesn't that sound good?"

His eyes narrowed and a sexy smile rested on his lips. "Okay, pool first, you naked on that bed, later." He nodded towards the massive bed. I'd counted nine pillows earlier. *Nine*.

"Deal." I popped some poolside necessities into my beach bag and slung it over my shoulder.

"Got everything?" He raised his eyebrows at me.

"Yep." I ignored his teasing and offered up an inventory. "Kindle, hat, sunscreen, lip balm, sarong, wallet, phone." I slid on my duty-free Prada sunglasses. "Sunnies," I added.

"You sure you don't want to bring your whole suitcase, just in case?"

"Have *you* got everything?"

He held up the key-card for the room. "Yep." He grinned at me.

"So, no laptop? What about the excursions?"

He made a face. "Oh yeah. Should we just do that later?" I shrugged. I was beginning to think I'd be happy spending the whole holiday sitting by the pool—or in bed.

*

"How about here?" Josh indicated two sun loungers, side by side, with a table in between and an umbrella overhead.

"Perfect." I put my beach bag on one and started unpacking. Josh climbed onto his and watched me. "What?" I said, without looking at him.

"I'm just looking."

"I *know* you are."

"You're very pretty." That stopped me in my tracks.

"Oh. Thank you."

He smiled. "You're welcome."

I went back to getting situated. I squeezed some sunscreen into my hands and slathered it on my neck, my shoulders, and my arms. I sat down and stretched out, covering my legs with the sarong, and then put my hat on.

"You're also pretty funny."

"Funny ha-hah or funny weird?"

"A little of both."

"I like to be sun-smart. I'm Australian. It's drummed into us at birth," I said defensively.

"And you're cute when you're miffed." He stood, then leant down and smacked a kiss onto my lips. I harrumphed in response; I do not like to be patronised. "Now, what would you like to drink?" I do, however, like cocktails. *Good play, Joshua.*

"Well, how about a Mai Tai? That's Hawaiian, isn't it?"

"Sure, I guess so. Two Mai Tais coming up." I watched him walk over to the bar, and I wasn't the only one. Two women, two *young* women, women in their mid-twenties—as in, much closer in age to Josh than I was—also watched him walk to the bar. As he passed them, they made "oh, my god" faces at each other, then giggled.

I frowned at them, but they didn't seem to notice, so I turned on my Kindle, opening it to the home page. I'd downloaded a handful of beach reads, including the latest book from my favourite author about a love triangle. I tapped on the cover. Maybe it would give me some insight into how to choose between two very different men. I was only a few pages into chapter one when a drink appeared in front of me. It looked like a work of art.

"Wow," I said, putting down my Kindle and taking the drink from Josh. "Fancy!" It had two distinct layers, yellow and orange, and it was topped off with a piece of pineapple, a sprig of mint, a slice of lime, *and* a cherry with a stem.

I took a sip just as Josh said, "Cheers." Why couldn't I ever wait for a toast before I started drinking? What was wrong with me?

"Uh, sorry. Cheers," I said, clinking my glass against his. I took another sip. "Yum."

Josh stretched out on his lounger and tasted his drink. "Yeah. Good choice."

I picked up the cherry by the stem and held it out. "Have I ever shown you what I can do with one of these?" I asked, waggling my eyebrows.

"Let's go with no." I knew I had his complete attention, so I put the cherry in my mouth, pulled the stem off and ate the cherry. Then I put the stem in my mouth and used my tongue and my teeth to twist it into a knot. I pulled the knotted stem out of my mouth and held it up for Josh to see.

His expression was one of awe. "How did you ...?" He didn't finish the thought, just shook his head in disbelief, then added, "And, you've *definitely* never shown me that before."

"I can teach you sometime, if you like."

"Yeah maybe." He grinned at me. "You have any more hidden talents?"

"You'll have to wait and see," I said, not really knowing what I meant by that. My flirting techniques were a little rusty. And I didn't usually bust out the cherry trick unless it was at the end of a long, drunken night and I was trying to impress someone. Maybe I was a little hung up on the "younger women ogling Josh" thing.

He flew across an ocean to see you, *Sarah.*

While I wrestled with my insecurities, Josh seemed content to drink his cocktail and take in our surroundings. I took his cue and leant back against my lounger, taking another sip of my Mai Tai. "It really is beautiful here. Thank you again for organising the resort—and the hotel in Waikiki."

"Oh, no problem. It's nice to be able to spoil you." I liked that. "And maybe even impress you a little." He smiled shyly. I liked that too.

"Well, I do feel spoiled and I am impressed, so let's drink to that." I lifted my glass and he touched his against mine.

"What are you reading?" he asked, pointing to my Kindle.

"Oh, uh, just chick lit."

"Chick lit?"

"Yeah, you know, literature for chicks."

"Ahh. Like romcoms, but books?" I nodded. "But why is it 'just' chick lit?"

"I don't know. Some people think it's frivolous."

"Well, you know I'm a fan of romcoms. Maybe I'd like it. What's it about?"

Uh oh. Danger. Danger, Will Robinson.

"Uh, it's about this woman ..." Not surprisingly, I was having a hard time articulating that it was about a woman who thought she was in love with two men. Not wanting to open that can of worms, I lied. "And, she's just moved to this new city and she meets this guy, who's kind of a jerk at first. You know? Typical romcom stuff. I've just started ... so, uh, yeah ..."

"Oh, sure." From the look on his face, he seemed to buy the lie. I sipped my drink and pretended to be very interested in my book, re-reading the same paragraph four times.

"I'm going to take a dip," Josh said a little while later and before I could reply, he did a running dive into the pool.

I caught the young women across the way giggling over him again. Then they looked at me, smiled very unfriendly smiles, put their heads together, and sniggered. It was overtly mean. I know I'm not what anyone would call conventionally beautiful—sure, I'm fit and I'm attractive, but I get that I'm not to everyone's taste. Even so, having two younger women covet my boyfriend *and* laugh at me, was shitty.

I took a big sip of my drink and tried to concentrate on my book, but I couldn't. I looked for Josh in the pool, which had curvy edges, an island in the middle, and a bridge. It was so large, it took me a while to locate him it, but when I did, he was looking my way and waving at me to join him.

I tucked all my things into my beach bag and put it beneath

the lounger. Surely, no one was going to steal my bag at a high-end resort but still, I was a little hesitant to leave my belongings unattended. I took off my hat and my sunglasses and put them with everything else under the lounger.

Then I took another swig of my drink and with my stomach pulled in as tightly as possible, I strutted past those little bitches, did a perfect dive into the pool and swam underwater to Josh. As I emerged, I tipped my head back, so my long hair would cascade down my back, and stuck out my boobs.

"Hi," I said.

"Wow," he said, giving me the kind of kiss you don't normally give someone in public. And just like I'd said when we were in our room, I wrapped my arms around his neck and my legs around his waist. "You're going to give me a hard-on," he groaned into my neck. I grinned. *Suck it, little bitches.*

After bobbing around the pool together—and after Josh swam some brisk laps to cajole his erection away—we made our way back to our spot by the pool. The little bitches had gone. *Good.*

We were just settling in when a waiter appeared with an elaborate cocktail—not a Mai Tai, but something just as impressive. "Here you are, ma'am," he said, placing it on the table next to me.

"Um, I'm sorry, I didn't order this," I said. I looked at Josh quizzically, but he just shook his head. "Ma'am" is just as bad as "madam", by the way, but that was hardly the matter at hand.

"Oh, sorry, ma'am." The waiter looked confused. He checked a small slip of paper on his tray.

Just then we heard, "Yoo-hoo," from a few loungers away. All three of us looked at the yoo-hoo-ing woman. She was tall and curvy and had a shock of super-curly hair like mine, only hers was jet black. "I believe that was mine," she said smiling, her Irish lilt ringing in the air. I really do love an Irish accent.

"Oh, my apologies," said the waiter. He picked up the drink. "Sorry, ma'am." The only thing I wanted him to apologise for was calling me "ma'am"—three times!

"No worries," I said, behaving far more graciously than I felt. Josh leant back and closed his eyes. I pulled out my Kindle and got back to chapter one of my love triangle book.

A few minutes later the same waiter was back, this time with two of the mystery cocktails. I looked at him, baffled. He indicated towards the Irish woman. "From the woman over there," he said, as he placed them on the table.

"Oh, how lovely," I replied. Josh sat up and we both looked over at the woman who'd sent us drinks. She was smiling at us.

"Thank you. That's very generous."

"Just a nice way to say hello," she said. "I'm Siobhan, by the way." For some reason, I warmed to her immediately— perhaps because she was grinning at us in an utterly charming way.

"I'm Sarah and this is Josh," I replied.

Josh waved and said, "Hi."

"Would you like to join us?" I asked Siobhan, suddenly realising I hadn't run it past Josh. I glanced at him and he seemed fine with it. He even added, "Yeah, come and join us."

"Are you sure? I really don't want to interrupt your afternoon. I just wanted to say sorry for the drink mix up."

"Oh, that was no trouble. Please." I indicated the lounger on the other side of mine. Siobhan gathered her things and her drink and made her way over.

"You're too kind," she said.

"So, what have we got here?" asked Josh, holding up his drink.

"Tequila Sunrise," she said. "*Sláinte*," she added, and we all clinked glasses.

I took a sip. *Whoa*. It was strong—like Duncan, our skipper in Greece, had made it and he was known for the kinds of cocktails that could fuel rockets. I liked it, though—a lot. I was starting to think the whole trip was going to be drinking cocktails while I worked on my tan—and sex. How could I forget the "lots and lots of sex" part?

"It's tasty. Thanks again," said Josh. Siobhan waved away his thanks as she took a big sip from her own glass.

"So, Siobhan, can I ask, you're obviously Irish, but what was the toast? *Slancha*?" I asked.

"That's right. It's short for *Sláinte mhaith*, which means 'good health' in Gaelic." She pronounced the whole thing as "slancha vha". I had no idea what it would look like written down. Gaelic was tricky like that, in my experience. Although, I did know how Siobhan's name was spelled despite it being said, "Shevaun".

"*Sláinte mhaith*," I said to myself, so I would remember it.

"So, what brings you to Maui?" asked Josh. At least he had

remembered his manners, making polite conversation rather than grilling the poor woman about Gaelic.

"It's my honeymoon," she replied. I noticed that she lifted her chin a little when she said "honeymoon" and I detected a slight edge in her voice. Josh forged on, not seeming to catch either tell.

"Oh, congratulations. So where is your husband—or wife, sorry, I shouldn't assume, uh, spouse?" I gave him an encouraging smile and he shook his head at me ever-so-slightly, clearly chastising himself.

"Well, I'm on my honeymoon, but I'm here alone, as I didn't actually *get* married, because he didn't show up." She took a long pull on her straw.

I realised my mouth was open and when I looked at Josh, so was his. "Oh, my god, Siobhan, I'm so sorry." And I was. I had only met this woman minutes before, but she seemed warm and lovely, and how awful to be left at the altar!

"That's rough," added Josh.

"Well, yes, but the holiday was already paid for and Maui was my choice, not his, so I thought, 'feck it', and I brought *myself* on my honeymoon." She grinned at us. It was an infectious grin, and we all ended up laughing.

"Good for you!" I said. "That should be our toast—to taking yourself on a glorious holiday." That's what I'd done when I'd taken myself to Greece. It wasn't after being dumped by my groom, but I *had* been in a post-break-up slump, needing something that was just for me.

Taking that trip was one of the best decisions of my life.

Siobhan responded to my toast by holding up her glass

and we clinked ours together. "So, how long are you here for?" Josh asked.

"Eight glorious days. I got here yesterday, so one week more. And do you know how bloody cold it is in Dublin right now?" It was clearly a rhetorical question, so we waited it out. "Bloody freezing, that's how cold. And serves Liam right, the eejit. He's sitting there in his cold little flat all by himself, and I'm in paradise making new friends."

"So, you'll be here for New Year's, then?" I asked.

"Yes, that was the whole reason for taking the trip now, so we could celebrate the start of the new year as husband and wife." Yep, definitely an edge in her voice. It was obviously still a gaping wound, no matter how much good cheer she seemed to have.

It took the rest of that round *and* another round of cocktails to hear Siobhan's story and for us to share an abridged version of ours. It took less time for me to fall hopelessly in love with her. She was effusive and genuine and quick to laugh, especially at herself. I had no doubt Liam *was* an eejit for not marrying her.

They had been together fourteen years—*fourteen years!*—when one night over fish and chips, he'd said, "Do ya tink we should get marrid?" Have you ever heard of a less romantic proposal? Siobhan was still beating herself up for saying yes, but at the time she hadn't realised how much of a rut she was in.

"I have declared war on boredom," she said. "How can we think that life is supposed to be an endless stream of watching rubbish TV, eating fish and chips for tea, and folding someone else's pants? I used to be *sooo* much fun when I was younger."

She took the piece of pineapple from the rim of her drink and chewed on it.

"You know, when Josh and I met, we bonded over something similar. Josh calls it 'having a bigger life'."

He nodded, his brows knitting together. "I haven't been doing such a great job of that, though."

"No?" I asked at the same time Siobhan asked, "Why not?"

He spat out a wry laugh. To me he said, "No, I haven't, not really," and to Siobhan, "That is an excellent question. I've been asking myself the same thing and the truth is, I really don't know. Fear, perhaps."

"Of what?" she asked. She wasn't letting him off the hook and, truth be told, I was with Siobhan. I wanted to know what he was so scared of that he'd let his own life philosophy fall by the wayside.

I was also baffled. In all the times we'd emailed and chatted, he'd never said anything like this. I'd figured that, like me, he was actively making changes in his life. He'd even mentioned some stuff about his job that had sounded really promising.

Josh shrugged and frowned again, but I wasn't going to let it slide entirely. I'd ask him about his not-so-bigger life later.

"Well, at least you have this," she said, indicating me and Josh. "You have each other."

Did we, though? Maybe Josh's great big fear, what was holding him back, was *me*. Yes, he was there on holiday with me, but maybe the thought of something more permanent, more meaningful, was keeping him rooted to the spot.

I didn't dare look at Josh. I just sipped my drink and chewed on my straw. I didn't want to be anyone's great big fear.

Chapter 12

As a surprise, Josh had booked an excursion for the following day—something he'd snuck in while I was getting ready for dinner. We were going snorkelling at Molokini Crater. It was just off the western coast of Maui and was considered some of the best snorkelling in the world. Not only that, the waters between the coast and the atoll were great for spotting dolphins and whales, and on the way back we'd be stopping to look for sea turtles!

He told me at dinner, then added, "I hope you don't mind, but I told Siobhan and she's going to book it too."

"Oh, that's great," I replied, glad we had plans to see her again.

"You sure?"

"Of course! I adore her."

"Oh good—I mean, I do too. She's cool." He took a bite of steak and with his hand over his mouth said, "She asked me about us, you know?"

"What do you mean?"

He swallowed the steak while I waited for him to explain. "Just about how long we've been together."

Be cool, Sarah. "Oh yeah?" I feigned indifference and loaded up a fork with some grilled fish. "What did you tell her?"

"Just that we met travelling a few months ago and that we're good friends. I wanted to clear up the idea that we were a couple."

Oh.

"Oh, cool." I added my very best this-is-not-fake smile.

"That's okay, isn't it?"

"Yeah, of course." *It's. Not. Okay.* I took a bite, even though my stomach had soured with the lie.

"I mean, we can't exactly call it a relationship. More of a *vacationship*." He laughed at his play on words and I nearly choked on my fish. What the hell was he talking about? "I heard that on a podcast. I thought it was a good description of us. Better than 'travel buddies', don't ya think?"

I could only nod in response. He didn't seem to notice that I lost my appetite after that. I sipped my wine, a riesling from Washington. It was over-priced, but tasty. It was also a decent salve for discovering that one of my boyfriends didn't think we were in a relationship at all.

I had a sudden thought. "So, when were you and Siobhan talking about our 'vacationship'?" The word felt awkward on my tongue, and I barely got it out.

"When you went to the bathroom."

"Oh, right." *Mental note: fewer bathroom breaks.*

Dinner conversation turned a little pedestrian after that, and it was my doing.

I just couldn't get past the idea of Josh divesting himself from our budding romance, or at least what I *thought* was a budding romance. I'd been excited about starting the new year with Josh, sharing a new beginning. It was kind of like what Siobhan had said about her plans with Liam.

I had arrived in Hawaii thinking I'd throw myself whole-heartedly into whatever it was between us, but hearing how he'd described it to Siobhan, I realised we had very different ideas about what it was and what it could be. My plans to broach his admission about being stuck in his life were pushed to the far recesses of my mind. It was very clear that I was part of the problem. *I* was Josh's great big fear.

I fretted most of the night, not able to sink into the blissful ignorance of a deep sleep. I woke often and a couple of those times, I watched Josh sleep, wondering what the hell was going on with him. Why had he gone ahead with our trip if all he wanted was to get laid? Couldn't he do that back home? With someone who wasn't falling for him? With someone other than *me*?!

Then I thought about those bitchy young women by the pool and I felt sick. I didn't want Josh to be with someone else—*anyone* else. I wanted him to make *me* laugh, to plan thoughtful excursions for *me*, to make love to *me*. How could he still think of us as just buddies? Even if all the other stuff didn't exist, when we had sex it was more than mere fucking.

At least it was for me.

I finally drifted off to sleep around four in the morning. Josh woke me with tea around seven. "Hey, gorgeous," he said, kissing my cheek until I stirred into consciousness. "I made you some tea, just how you like it."

I rubbed my gritty eyes and pushed myself up to sitting. I

glanced at the clock and calculated that I'd had barely five hours of sleep, most of it broken. *Ugh*. Josh looked annoyingly refreshed. *Double ugh*.

"You've showered." It was the first thing I thought to say. He laughed.

"Yeah, still on Chicago time. I've been awake a couple of hours already."

Of course—jet lag. No wonder I'd had so much trouble sleeping. It also explained why I felt so groggy. I pushed aside all the ugly thoughts from my fitful night, because there was Josh smiling at me and he'd called me "gorgeous" and he'd made me tea. Tea how I liked it, just like a boyfriend would.

I picked up the mug and took a swig. I groaned. "God, I really needed this. Thank you."

"Happy to do it. Take your time getting up. The ride to the boat doesn't come 'til nine. We have time for breakfast, too, when you're ready." I nodded and drank more tea. This was a very different Josh from the day before, the guy who'd called us a "vacationship". I took it as a sign that we had a good day ahead of us.

*

Siobhan and I leant against the railing at the front of the boat and watched a pod of dolphins swimming alongside us, darting in and out of the boat's slipstream. "Oh, my god, look!" she repeated, each time pointing to a different dolphin.

Josh was on the port side of the boat taking photos with

his fancy new phone—it had a better camera than an actual camera, apparently. "Josh," I called, "Mykonos!"

"I know! I was just thinking that." He grinned at me.

On our trip in Greece, we'd sailed into Mykonos accompanied by a pod of dolphins. It was an incredible moment, just like this one. There's something quite magical about dolphins—they seem both cheeky *and* joyful. It is practically impossible not to grin and giggle like a fool when they're so close by.

I caught Josh taking a photo of me with Siobhan and he lifted his eyes to me, then pursed his lips to blow me a kiss. *Vacationship, my ass.*

During my restless night, I'd briefly considered trying to get Siobhan's take on the situation, but it didn't take me long to decide against it. Her marriage had broken up before it had even started. It would have been selfish of me to burden her with my paltry worries. I'd have to work it out on my own.

So, when the dolphins eventually veered off, I couldn't have been more surprised, or more grateful, when she quietly asked me, "So, what is going on with you and Josh?"

I glanced over at Josh and he seemed ensconced in his phone, probably looking at the photos he'd just taken. I didn't think he could hear us from there, but even so, I lowered my voice. "Well, he told me that he told you that we're just friends."

"Yes, which doesn't seem right at *all* considering what I saw of you two in the pool yesterday." I was embarrassed. At the time, I hadn't cared about strangers seeing our slightly-too-lascivious-for-public behaviour, but Siobhan had, and now she was our friend.

"Uh, sorry about that. We were probably a little, um, risqué."

She waved my apology away. "No need. I've got to get my thrills vicariously at this stage. But why is he saying you're just friends, when clearly you're not?"

"I honestly don't know," I replied.

"And I'm not just talking about the physical stuff, but you *seem* like a couple. Even when you told me about how you met on the boat, you shared little looks and jokes and the like. You're just gorgeous together."

"So, it's not just me, then? *You* think that Josh acts like we're a couple."

"Exactly. And then all that shite he was saying about just being friends. If you ask me, he's deluding himself." I was beyond relieved to hear Siobhan's take on the whole thing. Just knowing I had someone to talk to, that there *was* something to talk about, made me feel better.

I looked over at Josh and watched him for a moment, Marie's voice in my head. She'd cornered me on the last night of our sailing trip, asking when I was going to Chicago to see Josh. I'd quipped something about holiday romances and she'd replied—quite pointedly—with, "That boy loves you, Sarah."

I'd played it down at the time, but her words had stuck, running through my head dozens of times since—especially any time I wanted out of my bizarre love triangle.

Yes, living a double love life was my own doing and, for the most part, I loved having Josh and James in my life. But there had been some darker moments in the past few months when it had all got too much, and I'd just wanted to call it quits.

With James, it was imposter syndrome. *What will happen*

when he discovers that I'm nothing like the woman he thinks I am? He's far too worldly and sophisticated for me. Self-doubt really can be insidious.

And with Josh—well, before anything romantic happened between us, he'd been very clear that he didn't want a relationship—*ever*. Like I'd thought at the time, when a man tells you he wants to stay single, it's usually because he wants to stay single. So, why give your heart to someone who doesn't want it?

In those dark moments, I would ask myself why I'd opened my heart in the first place. I had put a moratorium on romantic entanglements and a week into my trip to Greece I'd broken my own rule—*twice*.

But the simple truth was, when you feel something after being numb for so long—something real and vibrant and closer to yourself than you've felt in ages—you can't ignore it. You can't pretend that it was a holiday fling and just something for the memory books.

You have to *see* where it can go, what it can be, if it's as wonderful in reality as it is in your memory. And I *had* felt something—with both of them.

But when I heard the word "vacationship" come out of Josh's mouth, it raised all the doubts I had. What did it even *mean*?

Josh must have sensed me watching him, because he looked up and our eyes met again. He smiled and on reflex I returned it; he had a lovely smile.

He pocketed his phone and headed over, and I reached down and squeezed Siobhan's hand. "Thanks. Let's talk more another time," I said quietly. She squeezed mine in return.

"I got some great shots," said Josh. "I'll share them with you later. I even got some video footage I think you'll love." He threw his arm around my shoulder and kissed the top of my head—*boyfriend* behaviour. Siobhan flashed me a tiny eye roll and I couldn't have agreed more. *This is getting ridiculous.*

Ignoring my astute inner voice, I leant into him, telling myself not to ruin the day. I'd sort everything out some other time. Siobhan seemed to understand without me uttering a word and the three of us stood together in silence, smiling faces tipped to the sun, as we sailed towards Molokini.

When the boat finally approached the atoll, I realised with delight that it was a lush, green crescent. For some reason, I'd been expecting bare volcanic rocks, like we'd seen along the coastline. Offset against the vibrant sky, it was breathtaking. Even the sight of half a dozen other boats anchored in the atoll didn't dampen my excitement.

"This is going to be incredible," I said, almost to myself.

"And look at the water," said Siobhan. "I haven't seen this colour before. It's stunning." She was right. "We should name it," she said.

"What a lovely idea," I said, turning to her.

"Oh, I like to name colours, especially when they're like this, rare, you know?" She stared down into the water. It wasn't just one colour, but a fluid amalgam of many shades of blues.

"Let me know what you come up with," said Josh, taking his phone out of his pocket. "I'm going to get some more shots." He smiled at me before heading towards the bow of the boat.

Siobhan and I were silent while we each searched for the

perfect name for the colour of the water. Just as "fifty shades of great" popped into my mind, Siobhan leant over and in a near-whisper said, "Cobalt from the blue."

I actually gasped. "I love it," I said, and she beamed.

"It's ours." We grinned at each other.

*

It's very difficult to giggle underwater and not fill your snorkel and mask with water. I discovered this while giggling underwater. The fish at Molokini were not just plentiful, they were also very friendly, and when fish are friendly with pretty much *every part of your body*, it tickles, which makes you laugh. I came up to clear my mask for about the sixth time—I'd lost track by that stage.

Josh popped up beside me and we both treaded water, our fins flowing through the water below us.

"You keep laughing," he said, laughing at me.

"I know. They keep tickling me."

"Isn't this incredible?" he asked rhetorically.

I replied anyway. "It's incredible. I had no idea there were places like this. The water is *so* clear." I held my breath and stuck my mask below the surface of the water, so I could see to the sandy bottom below us. The water was around fifteen metres deep where we were, with near-perfect visibility to the ocean floor the whole way down.

I lifted my head from the water just as a woman started screaming, "My ring! I've dropped my ring! Oh, my god, my engagement ring!"

She was one of the honeymooners. There were four honey-mooning couples on board, and I had quickly confirmed to the crew that Josh and I were *not* a fifth one. This woman had obviously ignored the skipper's advice about not wearing jewellery into the water, and I only felt mildly upset for her—the skipper had been quite clear about the risk.

We watched as one of the crew members donned flippers, took off his shirt, and dived into the water. He emerged next to the woman and asked where she thought she'd lost it. She pointed to the area where they'd been snorkelling, which was close to the atoll wall and probably not very deep. Then he took a big breath and went under the water. Josh and I shared a look, then put our masks on so we could watch the rescue mission unfold.

The crew member swam around close to the ocean floor, and it looked like he was being careful not to upset the sand as he searched. He didn't have any breathing gear—he was free-diving—so he had to come up for breath a few times. The woman and her new husband, meanwhile, had re-boarded the boat. She looked like she'd gone into shock, and another crew member wrapped a towel around her as she sat sobbing inconsolably on the deck.

It was all very dramatic, and that's coming from me.

The diver came up for air a fourth time and he must have spotted the ring, because then he swam directly to something, picked it up, then swam to the surface and held up the ring. By this time, most people from the boat were watching—some from the deck and some bobbing in the water like us—and there was a round of cheers and applause.

The bride got to her feet, tears hastily wiped away, and jumped up and down squealing with delight. She grinned at her obviously relieved husband. The crew member climbed on board, slipped off his flippers, and presented her with the ring. She put it on her finger before throwing her arms around his neck and hugging him tightly. "Thank you, thank you, thank you," she said. When she released him, still grinning, he seemed a little embarrassed by all the attention.

That was when the skipper called out over the loudspeaker, "Now the entertainment is over, folks, lunch is served. We have a wonderful buffet for you on the deck. Soft drinks are included, and alcohol is available for purchase at the bar."

"Should we go up?" asked Josh.

"Yep. I'll follow." I swam behind him to the boat where we queued to climb aboard. Crew members were collecting and rinsing our snorkels, masks, and fins, ready for us to use again when we got to the turtle-watching spot later in the day.

We made our way over to where we'd left our stuff and I retrieved our beach towels from my bag. I wanted to dry off and put something on over my bikini, because the sun was high in the sky and I didn't want to get burnt. "Seen Siobhan?" I asked Josh.

He shook his head and ran a towel over his hair. "I saw her in the water earlier, but I didn't see her when the ring was being rescued."

"Fancy wearing an expensive diamond ring into the ocean," I scoffed.

"Fancy *buying* someone an expensive diamond ring," Josh scoffed back. *Wonderful.* So "anti-relationship Josh" was making an appearance. I ignored him and slipped on a T-shirt and a pair of shorts and slid my feet into my flip-flops.

Just then, I heard a huge laugh which I knew belonged to our missing Irishwoman. "Well, we found Siobhan," I said, heading towards the sound of her voice. She was seated at the bar, charming one of the crew members.

"Sarah, Josh, come and meet Paddy," she called out, waving us over.

"Hello Paddy," I said as we got within earshot. Paddy smiled as he cut a lime into slices.

"He's Irish," said Siobhan. I had figured as much with a name like Paddy. She took a sip from a plastic cup and cooed, "Ooooh, this is delicious."

"Would you like one?" Paddy asked me and Josh.

"What are you making?" asked Josh.

"It's a caipirinha," he replied.

"Two," I said, raising my hand. Josh flicked an amused glance at me.

"My treat," added Siobhan.

"No, you got us drinks yesterday," I protested.

She wasn't having it. "Put them on my tab, Paddy." She'd been there long enough to run up a tab?

"Did you like the snorkelling?" Josh asked her.

"I loved it. Beautiful. But I was starting to get pink—I've got my grannie's pale skin, I'm afraid—so I popped back on board. That's when I met Paddy." I was guessing she was on her second drink, or maybe her third.

Paddy shook the cocktail shaker, placed two plastic cups on the bar, filled each with some fresh mint, muddled the leaves, and poured out the cocktails. He added a slice of lime to each and handed them across the bar.

"To my new besties, Josh and Sarah." We three tapped our cups together and Josh and I took a sip.

"Mmm, that is delicious. Thank you."

"A pleasure," Paddy replied with a smile.

A line had formed behind us, so we stepped to the side. "Did you want to come get some lunch?" I asked Siobhan.

"Oh, the buffet! I had completely forgotten. Let's go and see."

"I can take our drinks over to where our stuff is, if you like?" Josh offered. "I'll grab my lunch after you." It was a good plan, as it would be a little tricky to juggle a drink and a plate while trying to load it up. After she paid her tab, I grabbed Siobhan's hand and pulled her towards the line for the buffet.

"So, how are you doing?" I asked. I had been wondering how she felt about being on board with a bunch of honeymooners, considering she was supposed to be one too.

She didn't even pretend that she had no idea what I was talking about. The smile vanished, her shoulders drooped, and she sighed heavily. "Oh Sarah. In truth it's been harder than I thought. I didn't even consider that coming here alone I'd be surrounded by people celebrating their new marriages. What was I thinking?"

I wasn't sure what to say to her, so I just reached over and squeezed her arm. She turned back towards the front of the queue.

My last break-up had been completely different to Siobhan's.

I'd been so furious with my ex that the anger had carried me through the grief. Sure, there were times when I was sad about the break-up, but I didn't really miss *him*. Mostly, because he'd cheated with a friend of mine *and* we'd been together less than a year. Whereas Siobhan and Liam had been together for an aeon. And even if they weren't passionately in love, she clearly still loved him. She must have missed him like crazy.

We eventually made it to the buffet table and let's just say they hadn't scrimped. Even Siobhan perked up a bit when we saw the spread of seafood and salads. I piled as many prawns on my plate as I could, added some salad, and grabbed a knife and fork. If I'd been a more dextrous person, I would have made a plate for Josh, but being a klutz comes with its limits.

We went back to Josh, picking our way carefully around people who were sprawled on the deck of the boat. Not surprisingly, we'd taken so long that his drink was finished and the ice in mine had melted. We sat down as he got up.

"Wow, that looks good," he said.

"There's still lots left and there shouldn't be much of a line now," I replied. When he left, I picked up a prawn and broke its head off. I tossed it into the water and watched as a handful of fish made a beeline for it. I then peeled off the shell and popped the pink and white flesh in my mouth. *Delicious*.

I realised that Siobhan was watching me in horror. "What?" I asked.

"I can't believe you can just rip its head off like that. Don't you get squeamish?"

I laughed. "No, definitely not. I've been eating prawns like this since I was little. Hang on, does that mean you've never had a prawn?"

"Well, no, I have. You know those little tiny ones that come in take-away fried rice?" I knew the ones. I pitied the person whose job it was to take *their* heads and shells off. How fiddly.

"Here." I expertly shucked a prawn and handed it to her. She took it with a slight frown on her face. Then she shrugged and took a big bite. I watched her chew, her expression changing. She swallowed.

"Oh, feckin' 'ell! That's fantastic. That's the best thing I've had in my mouth in ages!" She laughed loudly at her own crudeness, then popped the rest of prawn in her mouth. By the time Josh got back with his plate, we'd eaten all the prawns and Siobhan was a fairly decent prawn shucker. "I'm going back for more," she said, jumping up and taking our plates with her.

"What was that about?" asked Josh.

"Siobhan has discovered the prawn."

"Ahhh, yes, an important milestone in any woman's life." That made me laugh, and he smiled his shy smile—the one where he's trying to be funny, but he's not quite sure if he's pulling it off.

Siobhan came back with two plates piled high with prawns. I should have told her that I'd had my fill, but she was so keen to get her shucking time down, I let her do all the heavy lifting and ate a few more. Josh had some too, but Siobhan ate the bulk of them.

"These are now my absolute favourite thing to eat in the entire world." As someone who's no stranger to hyperbole, I loved her effusiveness. Just then, Paddy arrived holding a tray with three caipirinhas on it. I looked at Siobhan, who looked at me, and then we both looked at Josh.

He just shrugged. "My treat."

"A man after my own heart," said Siobhan taking one of the drinks from the tray. I noticed that she winked at Paddy and he smiled back.

When Paddy left, I turned to Siobhan. "He's cute." I raised my eyebrows at her.

"Paddy? Oh, I suppose if you like tall, handsome men, he's *okay*." I rolled my eyes. "I asked him out, you know."

"You did not!" I laughed when she nodded and sipped her drink. "Good for you, Siobhan!"

Josh joined in, "So, when are you seeing him?"

"Tonight. We're going for burgers and beer."

"Brilliant!" I declared.

She grinned. "And we may get a chance to do some other stuff too," she added, then giggled. Josh and I shared a look. I was very happy that our new friend was getting back on the horse, so to speak.

*

An hour or so later, the boat was anchored just off the coast at the primo spot for seeing sea turtles. We all lined up to collect our snorkelling gear, and I was one of the first people off the boat, eager to see a sea turtle for the first time.

I bobbed in the water waiting for Siobhan and Josh to join me, paddling my flippers slowly to keep me afloat. Just then a head popped up out of the water and an ancient-looking face regarded me. I was so gobsmacked to see a turtle up close, I forgot to call out to my friends. The turtle and I watched each other, and then it disappeared below the surface.

I rushed to get my mask and snorkel on, and when I looked below the surface, there were actually *five* turtles below me! I paddled my flippers gently so I could stay in one place as much as possible while I watched them. They moved so gracefully, their flippers barely moving, almost as if they were swimming in slow motion.

One of the turtles swam too close to another, and the second turtle turned and snapped at the first. It made me laugh, but I stopped as soon as I started. I didn't want to have to surface again to clear my mask. The turtles were moving away from me, so I started kicking my fins to follow. Josh appeared beside me, tapping me on the shoulder. I waved and he waved back. I held up five fingers and pointed at the turtles and he nodded and gave me a thumbs-up.

After what must have been about fifteen minutes, the turtles we'd been following got too far ahead of us. I wanted to turn back, so I stopped swimming, lifted my head out of the water and took off my mask. Josh came up next to me and took his off too.

"Wow!" I said, half-smiling, half-laughing. "That's one of the best things I've ever seen. Thank you again for booking this trip for us."

He swam closer and pulled me to him, our legs entwined underwater. "I'm glad you're enjoying it. It's fun watching you have such a good time." He pulled me closer and kissed me, a kiss that was salty from the seawater and sweet from the cocktails. When he pulled away, he said, "You're beautiful, do you know that?"

I very much doubted I looked beautiful with wet, salted hair plastered to my head, a snorkelling mask resting on my forehead, and no makeup on, but he looked so earnest I just said, "Thank you."

"You *are*. I know you don't think you are, but your joyfulness—how much you love being here—that's what makes you beautiful."

"Oh." It was a lovely thing to say and I rewarded him with another kiss.

The skipper's voice called out over the loudspeaker, "Fifteen more minutes, folks, then back in the boat."

"Let's find Siobhan," I said. I started swimming towards the boat, not bothering with my mask and snorkel. I looked for her amongst the other bums in the air, and saw her red swimsuit and black hair floating close to the boat. "There," I said to Josh and he nodded. We swam over, and I tapped her on the shoulder.

She sputtered a little as she lifted her head out of the water. "Sorry," I said. "I didn't mean to startle you."

She laughed her hearty Siobhan laugh. "Oh, no mind. How brilliant is this, then?" she asked.

"Did you see some turtles?" Josh asked.

"Yes, there's a bunch right below us."

"Oh cool." I pushed my mask down and popped my snorkel in my mouth. Josh and Siobhan did the same and the three of us bobbed next to each other as we watched another pod.

I would find out later from a crew member that it's a "flotilla" of sea turtles. They were my new favourite animal.

We heard the bell ring underwater and lifted our heads. "Time to re-board the boat, folks," said the skipper. There was a collective groan from the group, as though we were school-kids and he'd just shortened recess.

We made our way back onto the boat, surrendering our equipment and gathering our things. The bar on the boat was closed, but we promised to meet for a pre-date drink at the resort before Siobhan went out with Paddy.

The rest of the boat trip and the ride in the van were reasonably quiet. It had been a big day—exciting and fun, but also quite tiring. I was looking forward to a long hot shower before we met Siobhan for a drink.

Chapter 13

So, the hot shower turned into hot sex—one of the benefits of having a shower built for two. We were late to meet Siobhan for the drink, but only by a few minutes. She didn't seem to mind—or perhaps she didn't notice—because when we got to the bar, she was chatting up the bartender.

Just seeing her made me happy. She was one of those people who radiated good humour and joy, and considering what she'd been through, I thought that made her even more lovable. As we approached, she said something to make the bartender laugh and when she saw us, she greeted us with, "Oh, hello you two," and a broad grin.

I gave her a hug as though I'd known her for years, because that's how I felt, and Josh and I sat on the barstools either side of her as she introduced the bartender. "This is Keone," she said, laughter still lingering in her voice. Siobhan was making friends all over Maui.

"Aloha," said Keone. We heard it dozens of times a day, and I didn't think I'd ever get tired of it. Although it's most often used as a greeting and to farewell someone, it actually means "love, peace, and compassion"—isn't that a lovely thing to say to people?

We replied, "Aloha," in unison and Keone asked for our drink orders. I ordered a Bombay Sapphire gin and tonic and Josh added, "Make that two." Sure, we had a bottle in the mini-bar upstairs, but our date with Siobhan took priority over having sundowners on our balcony.

Keone moved down the bar to make our drinks. "So, Keone, huh? You lining up tomorrow night's date?" I asked, pretending to give her a pointed look.

Her response was to laugh. "Maybe. You never know."

"I'm beginning to think you could charm the pants off anyone," I said. Josh chuckled.

"Well, here's hoping," she replied. "I had fourteen years of not getting the pants off Liam as much as I'd have liked, so I've got a lot to make up for." Josh laughed aloud at that. Keone came back with our drinks and Siobhan told him to charge them to her room.

"You've got to stop buying us drinks, Siobhan," said Josh.

"I absolutely do not. Meeting you two has *made* this trip. I'd have been propped up here in this very spot the whole time if I hadn't met you." I was happy to hear that she liked us as much as we liked her. "We should have a name."

"A name?" I asked.

"Yes. You know, like Brangelina, but for the three of us." We were quiet and I trawled my mind for the perfect combination of our three names. After a few moments, Siobhan beat me to it, declaring, "Joshivarah!"

"Oh, my god, that's hilarious," I laughed.

She ignored me, donning a compelling faux serious tone. "We shall from herein be known to all and sundry as

190

'Joshivarah' and no one shall put us asunder." I wondered how long she'd been at the bar, but then I realised this was Siobhan. She was probably more drunk on life than she was on cocktails; I found her verve infectious.

The talk turned to our work lives and we discovered that Siobhan was a teacher like me. Unlike me, however, she worked in a part of Dublin where many of her students were in need of firm guidance to keep them out of trouble. I taught at a Catholic school where the kids had fairly good manners and were only *occasionally* little ratbags. I admired her for undertaking what was clearly challenging work.

When Josh said he was a software developer, her response was hilarious. "Oh great, one of those super-smarty-pants people, and here I am still with a VCR in my front room."

"You do not have a VCR," he said, his eyes narrowing.

"I do! And when you come to Dublin to visit me—and you must—and when you do, you must stay ages and ages—you'll see for yourself!" She punctuated her little speech with raised eyebrows and a sip from her drink. Josh laughed. I could tell he was falling for her as much as I was.

When the time came for Siobhan to meet Paddy, we saw her off with a kiss on the cheek from me and a hug from Josh. "Do everything I wouldn't do," I called out after her, as she strutted across the lobby. Her reply was a hearty laugh and a wave over her head.

"So that leaves us," said Josh, leaning in and nuzzling my neck. It tickled, like the fish earlier in the day, and I shooed him away. He laughed good-naturedly, and I gave him a smile to let him know I was only kidding.

"Actually, it's got to be time for dinner. I'm starving," he said. "I found a sushi restaurant online that's not too far. It's got great reviews."

"I would kill for some sushi."

"Revenge for all those fish nibbling at you?"

"Something like that."

*

When the taxi arrived at the restaurant and it turned out to be Morimoto Maui, I smacked Josh on the arm.

"Ow, what was that for?"

"You didn't tell me we were coming to an Iron Chef's restaurant!"

"Probably because I don't even know what that means." His confusion looked genuine.

"Really?"

"*Yes.*"

"I'll explain later, but we might not get in without a reservation."

"Oh. I just picked the sushi place that got the best reviews."

I couldn't blame Josh. I could, however, be annoyed with myself. How had I missed that we were staying just down the road from a world-renowned sushi restaurant? The taxi driver drove into the parking lot, which was full—not a good sign. I paid him and we got out.

"I just realised it's Friday night too," said Josh. "I'm really sorry about not getting a reservation."

"Don't worry. I should have done my research."

"Well, let's just see if we can get in, okay?" I nodded, even though there was no way we were getting in.

We got in, but only by agreeing to sit at the sushi bar, squished together at the very end next to the door. Quite honestly, I would have agreed to sit in the parking lot if I got some world-famous sushi; I was ravenous. And did I mention *the* Morimoto was the executive chef?

As expected, the restaurant was buzzing, but once we were seated, we were served very quickly. We each ordered an Asahi, then read over the menu. When the waiter brought our beers, Josh asked, "Is there something in particular you'd recommend?" One of the sushi chefs, who was assembling sushi right in front of us, overheard the question.

"The crispy salmon skin roll," he said, continuing the sushi making.

"Oh yeah?" replied Josh. "Good?"

"Like the bacon of the sea," the chef replied. He nodded at us as though he'd shared a trade secret.

We ordered the crispy salmon skin roll and several others, which I couldn't name if I tried, because when I *tasted* the crispy salmon skin roll, I forgot about all other sushi in existence.

"So, you really know who this guy is?" asked Josh as we sipped our Asahis, the second for each of us.

"Who? The chef? Yeah. For sure. Haven't you ever seen *Iron Chef*? The American one, not the Japanese one."

"Mmm, nope, neither." He was quick to add, "but it's your thing, right? You're into cooking shows?"

"Yeah, I guess you could say that. I'm into *food*. I've met a few celebrity chefs. I even collect cookbooks."

"Do you cook a lot?"

"Well, nothing super fancy during the week—that whole 'living by myself' thing—but I like having people over and I'll cook something extravagant then. And you're not really supposed to do this, but I usually try something I've never cooked before."

"What do you mean, 'not supposed to'?"

"You know? It adds to the pressure when you're cooking for other people if you don't know how it's gunna turn out— you're supposed to cook something that's a sure thing."

"So why try something new?"

"I like to live on the edge," I said, laughing at myself. "No, really, it's the best way to expand my repertoire. And most things turn out." He nodded in appreciation.

"It'd be nice to have you cook for me sometime—something other than toast, I mean." He was referring to our time on the boat. Of everyone, I'd spent the most time in the galley, but I was either making a mountain of buttered toast or assembling platters for lunch. I hadn't done any real cooking on that trip.

Remembering that time almost made me miss the thought behind Josh's comment—*almost*. He wanted me to cook for him *sometime*, as in sometime in the future. Huh, so he *did* think about us that way. My mind was a little fuzzy from the gin and the beer, but I was lucid enough to steer us away from his revelation. I'd unpack it later.

"You know, I'll happily sit and read a cookbook," I said, redirecting our conversation.

"You'll *read* a cookbook?"

"Yeah, it's like porn for foodies."

"So, you just read them for the recipes?" he said, teasing me.

"Oh, no, I look at the pictures too."

"Ooh, that's nasty," he said, playing along.

"We need to get the check." I raised my eyebrows at him, eliciting a grin before his hand shot into the air to get the waiter's attention.

I knew we'd have to discuss our future at some point before leaving Hawaii, but not on a date and not after several drinks.

*

Later than night, we were sitting on our balcony in the fluffy white bathrobes we found hanging in the wardrobe, drinking "home-made" gin and tonics. I could just make out the coastline against the inky-blue sky and it wouldn't be long until it was blanketed by blackness. A warm, soft breeze, which smelled of frangipanis, played with the curls around my face. *I could get used to being here.*

"Needs lime," said Josh, regarding his drink.

"It does."

"But it'll do. The view makes up for it," he added.

I kept watching the vanishing light, then looked up at the stars as they started showing themselves. "It is beautiful here."

"I meant you."

I looked over; he was watching me. "Oh, um, thank you."

"Wanna go back inside?"

"Round three?"

"Is that too much?"

I giggled. "Too much? No, we're not having too much sex, Joshua."

"Too little?" I shook my head, the giggle turning into laughter. He smiled, then stood and pulled me up into an embrace, kissing me. "You're so sexy when you laugh," he whispered, his lips brushing mine as he spoke.

I forgot all about my gin and tonic, and the stars, and Hawaii.

He stepped back from me, took my hand, and led me into the bedroom. Standing next to the bed, he enveloped me in his arms, his mouth on mine, the intensity of his kiss building. His hand caressed my hair and he entwined his fingers, pulling me deeper into the kiss. I could feel the strength of his other hand on the small of my back. His mouth left mine only long enough to kiss my neck, trailing down to my collar bones.

He pushed my robe off my shoulders, and it fell to the floor. Then he shrugged out of his own. Our bodies pressed together and I ran my nails lightly along the length of his back. He moaned into my skin, his mouth exploring lower as he took a nipple into his mouth and teased it with his tongue.

I could form no thoughts; I could say nothing. I was completely lost in the sensation of him. And I wanted him inside me. Badly.

"Josh," I whispered, breathless.

He didn't answer. He knelt on the bed as he lowered me onto it, then reached past me to get a condom from the bedside table. He put it on and covered the length of me with his body. For a fleeting moment before he entered me, I wondered who this Josh was and where he'd learnt to do all that.

It was the sexiest sex we'd ever had.

*

"So, your date with Paddy—was it everything you hoped?" I asked Siobhan. She'd joined us for breakfast, ordering tea even before she sat down. She held up one finger. "We're waiting for the tea to arrive, aren't we?" She nodded almost imperceptibly and Josh and I exchanged a look.

The waiter returned soon after with a teapot and poured Siobhan a cup. She stirred in a heaped teaspoon of sugar and seemed to look around for milk. We were in America, where they serve tea with lemon—*yuk*. I looked up at the waiter. "We'll need some milk, too, please."

"Yes, ma'am," he said before disappearing at warp speed. Had I been quick enough to catch him, I would have grabbed his ear and twisted it, telling him never to call me "ma'am" again. He returned moments later with a small jug of milk.

Siobhan, usually so gracious and full of life, didn't even acknowledge the waiter. Instead, she tipped half of the milk into her tea and, not even bothering to stir it, took a giant gulp. She sat back in her chair and, only then, took her sunglasses off.

"Late night?" I teased gently. I was rewarded with a small smile and I was pleased to see that no matter how tired or hungover she was, her good humour was still intact.

"You could say that, yes." She took another gulp of tea. "I'll be right as rain when this kicks in." I'm all about the restorative powers of tea, so I completely understood.

"So, what time did you get in?" asked Josh.

"Five."

"Five this morning?" I asked, incredulous. Siobhan was a few years older than me and people my age did not stay out until five in the morning. And if we did, we didn't roll out of bed until at *least* noon. It was 8:00am.

She nodded again but said nothing. I'd only known her a short time, but she was usually a lot chattier. She must have had a huge night.

"So, lots to drink then?" asked Josh, probing. I threw him another look, this one to silence him.

Siobhan drained her cup and signalled to the ever-present waiter to bring more. He was clearly a smart guy and had already foreseen the need, refilling her cup almost as soon as she lifted her hand to wave him over. She doctored it with milk and sugar and took a sip. By now, I was on the edge of my seat.

"It was a brilliant night," she said, finally and very, *very* quietly. "There was drink, yes, but not as much as you might think. But the best thing was that there was sex, lots of lovely, lovely sex." And then she threw her head back and laughed that infectious Siobhan laugh, the kind that inhabited her whole body. Josh and I couldn't help but join in.

"Ooooph," she added. "I'm not even hungover, just tired. We did drift in and out of sleep through the night—you know, *in between*. I've probably slept about three hours, though, hence the need for gallons of tea." She made a wide-eyed face that made me laugh some more. "I had him drop me off on his way to work."

"He goes to work that early?" asked Josh.

"Some days, yes. Apparently, they do these sunrise sailing trips." Josh scrunched his face up. I was with him. I was a morning person—I was usually at the gym by six—but I wouldn't want to start work that early.

"Oh, and I meant to tell you," she said animatedly. Clearly, the tea was hitting the spot. "There's this massive party on New Year's Eve at a beach house near here. A group of the boys who work on the boats have rented it for the weekend, and we're invited to the party." She grinned and raised her eyebrows a few times.

"Are you sure? We wouldn't want to impose," I replied.

She tutted away my concern. "Don't be silly. We're Joshivarah. You're coming."

Josh caught my eye. "What d'ya think?" I asked him.

"Well, we don't really have definite plans—I thought we'd just have dinner here, maybe go for a walk on the beach, crack open some champagne in our room."

"Sounds very romantic, but you're coming with me. Not quite as romantic, but I promise ye, it'll be mad fun." She smiled wickedly.

We spent the rest of the day alternating between dips in the pool, dips in the ocean, hanging out by the pool, and sipping a handful of cocktails. Don't ask how many cocktails there are in a handful, because I lost track. But for most of the afternoon, I had a nice buzz on.

I also had about fifty photos entitled, "view from a sun

lounger". I posted a few obligatory photos on Facebook, expecting the usual jokingly-jealous-but-not-really-joking comments. My favourite photos were the ones that looked up into the palm trees with the brilliant blue sky as a background. There was something about that sight, combined with the fragrance of tropical flowers, the salty breeze, and the warm sun on my skin that made me unbelievably happy. That and getting to share it all with Josh.

Siobhan joined us post-lunch after a well-deserved nap.

When she arrived, Josh had his laptop out and we were looking into accommodation in Hana on the east coast of Maui. We were driving there the next day, staying overnight, and driving back the following day. It was only about seventy miles between our resort and Hana, but the road was winding and there were lots of places to stop along the way. It could take anywhere from several hours to the whole day.

"So, you won't be staying here tomorrow night, then?" Siobhan asked after we told her our plans.

"No, we won't," I said. I wondered if she was wangling an invitation to join us. As much as I loved her, I was hoping to have some time alone with Josh.

Josh must have been thinking along the same lines. "I hope you won't miss us too much," he said. I thought it was a sensitive way to make it clear we were going on our own, but that we were still, proudly, two-thirds of Joshivarah.

Siobhan replied with a hearty laugh. "I love you two, you know I do, but I have plans with Paddy, so was trying to find a way to break it to you gently."

"Ahhh," Josh and I replied in unison. "Got it," Josh added. "I think we'll be okay, just the two of us."

I was really looking forward to our side trip. I love exploring when I travel and so far, we'd seen a lot of the resort and some of the west coast of Maui, but not much else. And, taking a long drive with Josh was a chance to talk—about life, the universe, and everything, and maybe even about *us*.

*

Later that afternoon, we were standing in the lot of the car rental place, deciding which car to get. We'd left Siobhan to bask in the afternoon sun with the promise that we'd meet up with her for dinner.

"Why not the Mustang? It's a convertible." asked Josh.

I made a face. "*Old* Mustangs are cool. The new ones are ..." I couldn't find words that sounded nicer than "ugly" or "boxy"', so I just made a more extreme face.

Josh rolled his eyes at me. "If you weren't so cute, you'd be annoying," he teased. That was probably true. "They've got an Audi convertible. It doesn't cost much more than the Mustang. How about we just get that?" I jumped up and down and clapped my hands. I'd never driven an Audi.

We finished the paperwork quickly, and Josh drove us back to the resort. At least I thought we were going back to the resort. When we passed it, I gave him a questioning look. "It's a surprise," he said, smiling.

Another surprise. Josh was being very boyfriendly for someone who didn't consider himself to be my boyfriend.

As he drove, I watched the coastline out the passenger window. Maui was so beautiful, especially when everything was bathed in the golden hue of the late-day sun. It was incredible visiting somewhere that was even more impressive than it looked in photos or on film. It was everything I'd hoped and far, far more.

About fifteen minutes' drive beyond the resort and past signs for Big Beach—hardly an innovative name for a beach— we drove into a residential area and parked on the street. I looked at Josh again, but he was giving nothing away. "Come on," he said. He got out of the car and I followed.

He led me down the street along a dark-grey stone wall, then through an opening in the wall and down a set of rustic stairs, where we emerged onto a stunning beach.

It was a small cove with golden-coloured sand and jagged black rocks which trailed into the water. There was an opening in the rock formations, almost a channel, where the water rushed to shore. Cupping the sandy cove was dense greenery, more black rocks, and a random assortment of palm trees.

We weren't the only ones there, though. There was a wedding party having photos taken, but we kept to the right of the beach and found a place to sit where we were out of the way. It was not long until sunset, and the sky was alive with burnt orange, pinks, and the lingering blues of the day.

"Wow," I said as I nestled in next to Josh. He put his arm around me, and I leant into him.

"I thought you'd like this," he said.

"You've been here before?"

"Uh-uh. First time in Hawaii, remember?"

"That's what I thought, but you drove us straight here, *and* you knew where the path was."

"Google. I looked it up before we came."

"Ahhh," I said. "You're full of surprises this trip." I was glad that I'd come around on the whole "I hate surprises" thing, but I didn't dwell on that thought as it was too close to my memories of James.

"Good ones, I hope." There was a hesitancy in Josh's tone that made me lift my head.

"Lovely surprises, very thoughtful ones."

I kissed his mouth with a "smack" and he touched his forehead to mine, closed his eyes, and sighed softly. "Sarah …"

I had no idea if that meant, "Sarah, I'm falling madly in love with you," or, "Sarah, this is the best vacationship ever." I hoped for the former.

The light had shifted quickly, as it seems to at sunset, and I turned to look out over the water. The sun was setting just north of the cove, which faced southwest, but the silhouette of the rocks and palm trees against the darkening sky was breathtaking. We sat silently, soaking it all in. Occasionally, the voice of the photographer permeated the cooling air, but mostly it was quiet.

I rested my head on Josh's shoulder and just breathed.

It was one of the most peaceful moments I'd had in a long time. It wasn't until later that night I realised Josh, always the photographer, hadn't taken any photos of the sunset. He'd just been there with me in that moment.

Chapter 14

I was beyond excited for our side trip to Hana, although packing everything into my carry-on bag for the overnight stay was a little challenging—it's not a big bag. I dressed for a day of driving and adventure, including hiking and swimming.

I wore my bikini, a pair of quick-dry shorts, a tank top, and my runners—I was going for "Lara Croft meets outdoorsy chic". In my bag, I packed a summer dress and a pair of sandals for dinner, a pared-back toiletries and makeup bag, a nightie, clean knickers, and a bra and a top for the next day. Oh, and a little clutch that went with the dress and the sandals.

I put two beach towels from the resort into my beach bag along with two bottles of water, a bag of wasabi peas, a block of dark chocolate, a bag of Craisins, and two muesli bars. Sure, Hana was just on the other side of the island, but you never can be too prepared!

"You two have the absolute loveliest time ever," said Siobhan as we hugged her goodbye after breakfast. Her send-off made me a little sad she wasn't coming with us.

But only a little.

"We will. And you have a lovely time at the spa *and* on your date."

She grinned. "You do know that the spa is just about getting ready for the date, don't you?" she asked.

"Of course!" I replied. "I had my own spa day before this trip. I went in looking like the great hairy unwashed and came out looking as gorgeous as I do now!" I could feel Josh squirming beside me as Siobhan belted out one of her huge laughs.

"Okay, we're going," he said, picking up our bags. He crossed the lobby and headed outside, having called ahead to have the valet bring our car around. I left him to it. He'd probably had enough girl talk for the time being.

I hugged Siobhan again. "We'll be back in plenty of time to share a ride to the party."

"Brilliant." She grinned again. "It's going to be mad fun!" I didn't doubt it.

I went to meet Josh out the front of the resort. "Hey," I said.

"Hey," he said back, leaning down to give me a kiss. "Excited?"

"I am."

"Me too." I earned another kiss, which was interrupted when the valet, a man in his late-forties or early-fifties, pulled up with our car and greeted us with, "Aloha."

We returned the greeting and when we tried to put our bags into the boot, he shooed us away, lifting them both with one hand and making short work of it. I tipped him heavily, then we climbed into the car, and I tucked the bag with the beach towels and snacks behind my seat.

I pulled up the route on my phone while Josh double-checked the seat and mirrors. The route was actually quite simple. We would drive north along the west coast, cut northeast across the top of the island, and then drive southeast along the east coast.

I realised the valet was watching us with what seemed like an amused expression on his face. "So, you're the navigator, huh?" he asked me, indicating my phone. I smiled my reply, even though it was Google doing the navigation. "Navigator through life," he added, nodding his head sagely. It wasn't a question, it was a statement, as though he was offering some gem of wisdom.

Josh and I stopped what we were doing, shared a quick look, then nodded politely at the valet. I didn't think either of us were ready to be someone's "navigator through life". Maybe the valet assumed we were honeymooners. Still, it was a little heavy for first thing in the morning.

"Ready?" asked Josh brightly.

"Ready. Just go out to the highway and turn left." Yes, Google could have told him that, but I liked having a part to play in our adventure.

It was another beautiful day in paradise, and I was glad we'd chosen the convertible. It felt incredible to have the sun on my face and the wind in my hair, no matter how much of a cliché it was. And for the umpteenth time, I mentally pinched myself. Hawaii! I was in Hawaii, and it was stunning.

I was content just watching the scenery go by, but after a few minutes Josh asked, "So, should we listen to some music or a podcast or something?"

"Oh, sure. I've actually been meaning to get into podcasts, but I ... well ... haven't."

"Why not?"

"It's dumb, but I'm a little overwhelmed. There are just so many. And I don't know what app to use." I realised I must have sounded like an old person. *Bugger*. Most of the time I was with Josh, I wasn't aware of our age difference and I didn't want him to be either. "Have you got something we can listen to?" I asked brightly, taking the focus off how ancient I was.

"Yeah, sure. I listen to quite a few. You might like '99% Invisible'. It's about how good design is practically unnoticeable."

"Ooh, that sounds cool."

"Here," Josh handed me his phone and gave me the passcode. "I've connected it to the car's Bluetooth." I gave him a look that said, 'What?' and he added, "So we can listen through the speakers." *Oh, right. I totally knew that.* Okay, that's a lie—I totally didn't.

He then explained how to navigate to the podcasts he'd downloaded. Eventually, I found the "99% Invisible" episodes and scrolled through, feeling far more tech-savvy than I deserved to.

"Ooooh, how about the one on the Sagrada Familia?" I asked. "Barcelonaaaaa," I half-sang Ed Sheeran as I did a little seat dance. "I *love* Barcelona—and the Sagrada Familia. Wowser—one of the most amazing places I've ever been."

"For sure," he said with laughter in his voice. "I listened to that when it came out, but I'm happy to play it again. It's probably a good intro for you."

"It changes all the time, you know, the cathedral."

"Yeah, they talk about that in the podcast." I was amusing him, I could tell.

"You know, I haven't seen it in, like, ten years. It'd be worth going back. Maybe we could go—" I stopped myself too late, the words already out of my mouth. The thing was, we'd never talked about the next trip—or if there would even *be* one. It was like we had an unspoken agreement to see how Hawaii played out first.

Josh laughed uncomfortably. "Yeah, Barcelona's definitely on my list."

Back-pedal or proceed like I'm just a travel buddy? A travel buddy would forge ahead, fearlessly exploring the possibility of travelling to Barcelona together. But I didn't want to be a travel buddy. Too many moments passed, and even if I'd had some clever way to back-pedal, it would have been too late.

Then a worse thought popped into my head.

Oh, my god. Travel buddies plus fuck buddies equals vacation-ship. I was certain I was right. That's how Josh saw us—as a seriously fucked-up equation.

I pressed play on the podcast.

I only half-listened to the first bit, my mind still in over-drive, but after a few minutes it lured me from my sickening thoughts. The episode was so engaging that I ended up enjoying it. When a second episode started up, one about the English road-sign system, I let it play, but at the end of that episode, I stopped the app.

I didn't mind listening to podcasts. It was better than talking myself into an emotional cul-de-sac or being inside my head with those awful thoughts, but I still hadn't asked Josh about the whole "not-so-bigger life" thing. I racked my brain for ways to bring it up casually.

So, Josh, how come you've stalled on the big changes you wanted to make? Why have you abandoned your own life philosophy? I came up with a big fat nothing, so we sat in silence—me agonising over what to say and Josh seeming not to care. I wondered what he was thinking.

My vibrating phone interrupted my thoughts. *Saved by the buzz.*

"Oh, hey! According to Google, this is officially the start of the Hana Highway. Look," I said, pointing ahead of us, "there's mile-marker one!" It was the most excited I'd ever been to see a mile marker, probably because the car was starting to get claustrophobic—my own doing—and we'd get to stop soon.

"Yeah, that's cool," replied Josh.

"Those waterfalls are in about five miles," I said, using miles instead of kilometres for the American. When in Rome and all that.

"Awesome." Josh didn't say anything else and as the road had started to snake, I let him concentrate on driving. Most of the turns were tight and when a car came from the other direction, both cars had to hug the side of the road. There were some worrying places where the side of the road was a wall, or a giant boulder, or a cliff dropping into the raging sea.

Okay, maybe it wasn't *that* dramatic, but it definitely wasn't the best time to start a conversation about important life changes. About fifteen minutes later, we slowly approached the location of the waterfalls. Josh pulled the car off the road as much as possible and on my side, we were so close to a rising rockface, I would have to climb out on his side.

"This is where it's supposed to be," I said, frowning—not a waterfall in sight.

"Let's check it out." Josh looked at me. "You don't trust your directions?"

"*Google's* directions," I corrected.

"Come on, we'll figure it out." I reminded myself that I was an adventurous traveller and to go with it.

Josh took his phone out of the centre console and put it in his front pocket, and I leant over to put mine in my back pocket. We weren't going to lock the car—there was no point with the roof being down—so phones were coming with us. Besides, we'd want to get photos.

I reached around for my beach bag, then climbed out the driver's side of the car. While Josh headed towards the closest bend in the road, which was where the falls were supposed to be, I retrieved the towels from the bag, leaving the snacks behind.

"Sarah! You gotta see this!" Josh was leaning over a railing next to the road and I hurried over. From our vantage point, we could see three distinct waterfalls, side by side, all cascading into a small rockpool. They were officially called "The Upper Waikani Falls" and unofficially, "The Three Bears". I liked the unofficial name, as there was a baby waterfall, a mama waterfall, and a papa waterfall.

I searched for a pathway to the falls—there wasn't one.

There were just a lot of boulders we'd have to climb over to get down to the pool. Josh turned to me with a grin on his face. "This is incredible," and then he was off.

He turned to the left and jogged next to the railing, then skirted around where it ended, and started climbing down a giant boulder. I followed closely but decided to leave our towels at the top of the climb, so I could navigate it more easily.

Josh had the height advantage, being six-one to my five-six, and I realised that for one of the boulders he'd climbed down effortlessly, I was going to have to sit and scooch down on my bum, which I did, my phone in my hand. The manoeuvre left the back of my Lara Croft shorts covered in dirt, which I was going to have to live with for the next two days, as they were the only bottoms I'd brought. *Bugger*.

I met up with Josh at the bottom next to the rockpool. "Let's go in," he said, his eyes alight, and I grinned my agreement. Swimming under a waterfall was absolutely a bucket-list item. He slipped off his shoes and shirt—he was wearing his swimsuit as shorts—and I took off my tank top, shoes and socks, and soiled shorts.

He took the first steps towards the rockpool.

"Josh!" He stopped short and looked at me with a quizzical expression.

"Your phone. It's in your pocket."

"Oh, god, thank you." He took it out and put it in a shoe. "It's water-resistant, but not for full immersion—that would have sucked." I put mine in my shorts pocket. "Oh shit, and this." He held up the fob for the car—now, *that* would have sucked. With the fob and the phone tucked safely away, he took a step into the water.

"God, it's cold." He stood still, not venturing any further. He started laughing, which made me laugh, and I approached the water's edge, thinking it couldn't possibly be that bad. I dipped a toe in.

It *was* that bad. "Oh, my god," I said, jumping back onto dry land. I looked down at Josh's feet. "Are you getting used to it?"

"Nope." He looked towards the waterfalls.

"What do you want to do? Skip it?"

He looked back at me, a funny grimace on his face. "I kinda want to brave it."

I laughed. "Seriously?"

"Yeah. I'm gonna do it." And before I could say anything else, he charged into the rockpool. When he was waist-deep, he lunged forward and swam towards the falls. "Oh, my god," he said, treading water. "Quick! Take a picture!" he called, his teeth starting to chatter. I rushed back to get my phone. "Please hurry!"

"On it!" I retrieved my phone, then took a series of shots in quick succession. "Okay!" I called. Josh wasted no time and swam quickly towards me, style and form abandoned. When he could put his feet down, he climbed out of the rockpool, obviously being careful not to slip.

"I should have brought the towels down. Sorry."

"Don't worry. The air's warm enough. I'll dry off." I went back to my pile of clothes and picked up my tank top to put it back on. "Hey. What're you doing? It's your turn."

"Oh, no," I said, half-laughing. "There's no way. That looked excruciating."

"Yeah, it pretty much was. I don't think we're going to see my balls for a day or two." I laughed. "But you're going in."

He was smiling at me and I was smiling back, but I couldn't tell how serious he was. I shook my head no. He nodded his head yes. I shook my head again.

"Think about it this way. You may never be back here again, and if you don't go in, you will spend your whole life thinking about how you *didn't* swim in that waterfall on Maui and you will regret it forever."

"Wow, that was quite the speech."

"Sarah."

"Josh."

He stood there watching me, his eyebrows raised.

I took a moment to appreciate the sight of his body glistening with water, the not-too-bulky muscles of his arms and taut torso, the benefit of a few days of sunshine evident in his tan, and his wet swimsuit clinging to his thighs. He really was hot. I flicked my phone up and took the photo.

"Hey!" he said in half-assed protest. "Stop stalling. You're not getting out of this."

His posture and his expression hadn't changed, and I actually felt myself give in. "All *right*," I said.

"Really?"

"You're surprised?"

"Yeah."

"After all that 'you'll regret it for the rest of your life' crap? How am I supposed to resist *that*?" He laughed.

Before I could talk myself out of it, I walked past him and handed him my phone. I charged into the water calling out, "Get ready to take a photo, Joshua. This is gunna be fast!" And then I was swimming in the (literally) breathtakingly cold water. He took the shots—me trying to look as natural and as happy as possible—and before I could blink, I was back on land. I think the whole thing took less than a minute.

He wrapped his arms around me as I shivered on the shore. "I'm proud of you," he said. I smiled into his chest.

"I'm proud of both of us," I said, leaning back so I could see his face. He kissed me softly.

"And we never have to do it again," he said.

"I'll drink to that!" We grinned at each other.

"It will be a well-deserved beer when we get to Hana," he quipped.

"Or two."

"Or three."

Thunder cracked over our heads and we both looked skyward. "Where did those clouds come from?" I asked rhetorically.

"Be quick. It feels like it's going to rain." We went back to our piles of clothes and tried to hurry as we pulled them onto our still-wet bodies. When I got to my shoes, they didn't want to cooperate.

"Damn it!" I said, just as I felt the first fat drop of water hit my head. I forced my feet into the shoes without bothering with my socks, which I stuffed into the back pocket of my shorts. More fat drops.

"Oh, bugger it," I said, slinging the tank top around my

neck. I shoved my phone in my front pocket and looked up to see that Josh was way ahead of me, having scaled the first three boulders. He got to the bottom of the biggest one—the one I'd scooched down—and waited for me. I followed as quickly as I could.

"Here, let me give you a boost." He locked his hands together so I could use them as a foothold. I put my right foot into his hands and with his help, pulled myself up onto the boulder. I scraped my knee in the process, but I was up. More and more fat raindrops fell.

Josh followed me and by the time we got to the road, it was pelting down with rain. And we'd left the top down! Josh was first to the car, pulling the fob out of his pocket before he climbed in. He started the car and pressed the mechanism to close the roof. I was left out in the rain, because I was waiting to climb in on that side.

"Oh shit, sorry," he said, realising. He got out of the car, just as the roof was settling into place and I climbed in and slid across to my side, promptly sitting in a pool of rainwater.

Great. Now I look like I shat myself and *pissed myself.*

When Josh got back in the car, I suddenly remembered the beach towels. "Oh crap, crap, crap." I put my hand to my mouth.

He was trying to dry off the steering wheel with his hands. "What?"

"The towels," I said, looking at him with wide eyes and a grimace.

Josh went back for them while I watched the rain cascade down the windscreen. They were sodden, and he put them straight into the boot. When he climbed into the driver's seat and looked at me, he was completely saturated, drops of water falling from his nose and eyelashes.

We burst out laughing.

"It's like that day on Naxos," I said through my laughter, referring to a day out on our sailing trip.

"Oh, my god, yes." We'd been riding scooters up in the hills of Naxos on our way to lunch—me on the back of Josh's scooter—and we got stuck in a massive rainstorm. By the time we arrived at the café, all seven of us were completely wet through. The woman who owned the café, Martika, had given us towels to dry off and clean, dry shirts to put on. It was my favourite day of the trip.

Just then, as suddenly as it had started, the rained stopped. "Shall we chance it?" Josh asked, his finger hovering over the button to put the roof down again.

"Well, if we see any looming black clouds—or feel the first drops—if we're in *any* danger whatsoever of getting rained on again," I said dramatically, "we'll know ahead of time, so I vote for yes."

"And, the air and the sun will help dry us off."

"And there's that."

*

The drive took several more hours, because we'd bookmarked a few more sights along the highway. And each time we stopped we left the roof *up*. Of course, it didn't rain again.

We went to the best banana bread stand on the Hana Highway—according to TripAdvisor, that is—called "Aunty

217

Linda's Banana Bread". I didn't know who Aunty Linda was, but I agreed with the hundreds of other people who'd rated her banana bread as five-out-of-five.

Josh and I ate a slice each, sitting in the car, and then I went back to get two more for the road. It's okay to eat two slices of banana bread for lunch when you've climbed over giant rocks, swum in freezing water, and got caught in a rainstorm—just so you know.

We also stopped at Black Sand Beach. *Seriously, who came up with these names, the Committee of Half-Assing It?* The beach was beautiful, though, and the sand really was black, as were the ubiquitous volcanic rocks. These contrasted against the brilliant blue of the water and the rich green of the foliage that cupped the cove. It was another stunning location on a stunning island.

We parked the car, slipped our shoes off, and locked up, both of us bringing our phones to take photos. Without any discussion, we wandered off in different directions.

I walked the length of shoreline where the waves met the sand, playing a game of tag with the water, and squealing in delight when it nearly caught me. At the far end of the beach, I turned and looked for Josh.

He was further away from the water, his eyes focused on the screen of his phone which he was holding up in front of him. I figured he was taking a photo and it looked like I was going to be in it, so I lifted my hand in a wave. He took the shot, waved back, then jogged over to me. "I'm running out of words to describe Maui," he said, a little out of breath.

"Yeah, I know exactly what you mean."

"I think you're gonna like that shot," he said as we started walking back to the car.

"Oh yeah?"

"Yeah, you look great in it."

"Thanks. And how many have you taken without me knowing?" I teased. He laughed and shook his head.

In Greece, he'd taken some shots of me without my knowledge and when I discovered the photos, I'd thought it was a little stalker-ish. He'd been sheepish at the time—embarrassed that I'd caught him out—but they *were* terrific shots. One of them—me on the boat, my face tipped to the sun—ended up being my favourite photo from the whole trip.

"Only a couple. You look great in those too."

"Uh-huh." He laughed again.

Back at the car, we did our best to brush the black sand from our feet before climbing in, but it was that sticky kind of sand that wants to go home with you. The rental car place was going to love us when we returned the car.

I only realised later, as we drove to our next destination, that there was something quite special about our excursion to the beach. We were there together, but independently, and both seemingly happy with that dynamic—more like a couple than two people in a *vacationship*. God, I hated that stupid word.

Our last stop before we got to our accommodation was actually a little way past Hana. Josh had read about a general store, Hasegawa's, that, *apparently*, we could not miss. It sounded cool, so I was more than happy for the detour, even just to see what they had.

Well, they had everything.

The building itself looked like it would crumble to the ground at any moment. Some of the uprights leant, the tin roof was rusted—just like in that B-52s song from the 90s—and it looked like it would barely withstand the rain we'd encountered earlier. The inside was even more precarious, with shelving units that looked more like the Leaning Tower of Pisa than shop shelves, and goods piled up everywhere.

"Okay," said Josh. "There's a place like this in the small town where my grandpa lives and when we go there, we play this game. Here." He handed me a shopping basket. "You choose the five weirdest things you can find—they should be *really* different from each other—and then we meet back here in five minutes. The one with the best basket wins."

The teacher inside me wanted to know more. *Who gets to decide who wins if we're both competing? Do we have to buy what's in our basket? What if we choose the same thing—is it null and void?* But I had no time to ask these questions, because Josh said, "Starting now," and disappeared down an aisle.

Crap! I told my inner teacher to shut up. I *had* to win this challenge! Josh was practised, but I had beginner's luck and a lifetime of shopping experience on my side. I went the opposite direction to Josh, dozens of weird things catching my eye.

I half-ran from aisle to aisle, only meeting up with Josh twice. Both times I shielded my picks with my arms, and we eyed each other like the adversaries we were. A few times I found something better than an item already in my basket, so I abandoned the lesser one on the nearest shelf.

"Time!" I heard Josh call from the other side of the store.

"Coming!" I called back. Several people turned at the sound of my voice. It was only then that I realised there were other people in the shop. We probably seemed like a pair of oddballs—not that I cared.

We met somewhere close to the middle, both trying to peer into each other's baskets, curiosity trumping fair play. Josh hid his basket behind his back, and I did the same. "Okay, so I'll take you through mine first. Then we'll see what you've got and then we'll decide the winner." Schoolteacher Sarah, the one with all the questions, bit her lip and nodded.

"Here we go." He held up each item as he named it. "Ping pong paddle." I nodded. I had one in my basket too, but I didn't say anything. "Orange food colouring." *Yep, definitely gets a point for that.* "Fishing lure." *And another.* "Cheese in a can." *Geez, America. Good pick, though—another point.*

Then he paused. "And the piece de resistance"—I ignored his mangled French—"and this is totally going to win the game for me—ta da!" He held up a package of floppy discs. Yes, *actual* floppy discs.

"Seriously? How am I supposed to beat that? It's like you caught the Golden Snitch."

"Your turn," he said, grinning at me.

"I'm pretty sure you've already won, but okay." I held up the ping pong paddle first, saying nothing, and the look on his face indicated that we cancelled each other out. Then I held up item two and said, "Box of caps for a cap gun, but I couldn't find a cap gun."

"Nice."

I held up the third item. "Bread in a can."

"What? Is that even a thing?"

"I'm going with, yes, it is. Number four, lime-green nail polish."

"Oh, yeah, that's awful."

"And lastly, this." I held up a magazine in silver wrapping. "Porn."

He threw back his head and laughed. "Oh, my god, that is awesome. You totally win." I was so excited, I actually jumped up and down. "Come here," he said, leaning in for a quick kiss. "You're the best novice I've ever played this game with."

I took a little bow. He looked around. "Now, is there actually anything you want from here?"

"Well, how about we eat in tonight? I know we said we'd go out, but we can get some antipasto stuff and a bottle of wine. What do you think?"

"Yeah, sure, that sounds good." He held up the cheese in a can. "Does this count as antipasto?"

"Uh, no. That's more like antifoodo." He groaned at my play on words. "What? That was funny," I said in my defence.

"It really wasn't."

I poked my tongue out at him. "You get the food. I'll get the wine." I figured I probably had a better idea of what might be a decent bottle, but I didn't say that.

Josh went off to get us our antipasto dinner, and I searched through the small selection of wine. In the end, I chose a rosé by a local winery, Maui Wine. We met up by the checkout, and when it came time to pay and I pulled out my wallet, he waved me away. "Loser buys."

"Did you just make that up?"

"Kinda." I let him pay.

As we drove away from the shop, I leant back in my seat. I had stained my shorts and scraped my knee, my feet were still blackish from the beach, and my hair had dried from the rain into a fluffy mess—but I couldn't have been more content. It had been a brilliant day.

We were back!

Chapter 15

That night, Josh suggested that we get up early the next morning for the sunrise. I thought it was a brilliant idea, especially because the sun wouldn't rise until 7:00am and we could have a bit of a sleep-in. We were staying right on the beach, so we climbed out of bed just before seven. I slipped on my flip-flops, figuring my nightie looked enough like a summer dress to pass any scrutiny. Josh pulled on his shorts and left the room shirtless. I approved.

Forgetting my bed hair and morning breath, I followed him onto the sand. There were a few others on the beach too—another couple, a woman wading in the shallows, and a man with his dog. It wasn't as pretty as other beaches we'd seen, but a sunrise over the ocean is always something special and this was no exception. Josh reached into his pocket for his phone and took a series of shots.

When he showed me later over a mediocre breakfast at a local café, I was blown away.

"You really have an amazing eye, Josh. These are incredible."

"Thanks." I could tell he was a little shy about the compliment. He reached for his phone and I handed it to him. "And, I wanted to show you this."

He scrolled, then handed it back to me. It was the photo he'd taken the day before at Black Sand Beach, the one of me waving. I looked blissful and carefree; it was beautiful.

"I love it." I looked up and we shared a smile.

"It's automatically saved to Google pics—all my photos are—but I'll create a folder I can share with you. Then you can add your photos too, if you like." Wow, we were going to share an online photo folder. I guess you could say that things were getting pretty serious. "Or I could just put them on Facebook and tag you."

Uh oh.

Josh had sent me a friend request on Facebook right after our trip to Greece—actually, even before I'd landed back in London. I'd accepted it, just like I'd accepted requests from Duncan, Marie, and Hannah. At the time, it hadn't occurred to me that it could be a problem, but then I made plans to see James, and I got worried. I didn't want them to cross paths online, especially as I wasn't the only connection between them—there was Duncan too.

But it turned out that James wasn't even on Facebook. So, I didn't have to worry about them seeing each other's interactions with me, or dread that they'd get friend recommendations for each other. Can you even imagine? Cringey.

Still, not even my parents knew about Josh. They thought I was travelling with girlfriends, and most of my friends thought I was travelling alone. All the lies meant that I didn't want any photographic evidence of our trip on social media—

at least, not until I knew what Josh and I were to each other—if we were going to *be* together. And not just in a *vacationship*.

"Uh, the Google folder thing sounds good. I don't really like being tagged in Facebook pics." Well, at least *that* was true.

He didn't seem to catch on that I was actively dodging bullets. "Sure, no problem," he replied.

"So," I said, deftly changing the subject. "The hike today. How long do you think it will take?"

"Looks like a couple of hours."

"Round trip?"

"I think so."

Oh, good," I replied. "That will give us enough time to get back, get clean, and rest up a bit before the party."

"And what time are we expected there?"

"We're leaving the resort at nine."

He nodded. "Did Siobhan tell us what we should bring?"

"She said just a bottle of spirits. They'll have mixers and snacks and stuff."

He made his "that seems cool" face. "We can pick up some vodka or rum or something on the way back."

"Good plan. Okay, let's get the bill, then get hiking!" I was really looking forward to the hike. Waimoku Falls was supposed to be incredible. When the bill arrived, I snatched it up before he could, and he graciously let me pay it—*finally*.

*

So, it turned out that the two-hour-return hike was closer to two hours *one way*.

We left the café and drove straight to Seven Sacred Pools, which was where we would park the car while we hiked. It was also an impressive natural wonder, and I was glad we took the time to see it.

It was a series of volcanic rock pools—seven, if you hadn't guessed—with waterfalls cascading between them, forming a chain all the way to the ocean. But even though it was an incredible place, we only stayed long enough to see it and take some photos. Two busloads of tourists arrived just after us and dodging tour groups is far less fun than hiking.

The hiking trail started across the highway and headed away from the coast. It was around 9:00am when we started and although the morning was reasonably cool, the hike was uphill the whole way. I knew my bum would probably thank me later—great workout, woo hoo—but it was hating me for most of the climb.

After more than an hour of hiking and no waterfall, I dared to say something. "Uh, Josh?"

"Mm-hmm?"

I thought the best tactic was humour, so I went with, "Are we there yet?"

He threw me a look over his shoulder, a half-smile, half-grimace, then stopped walking and pulled out his phone. "I'll check the map." He scrolled and tapped the screen, looking more and more frustrated. "Damn it, no data—and apparently the stupid map didn't cache." He frowned at it, as if willing it to tell him something different.

We're completely lost, I thought. That *may* have been a little dramatic, especially as I knew we were still on the trail, because we'd passed a trail marker only minutes before. I started chewing on my thumbnail, while Josh put his phone away, scowling.

Just then, a young couple appeared from around a bend on the trail ahead of us. "Hiya," I called out. They slowed their pace as they approached. "Just wondering how much further?"

A Californian accent replied, "You're about halfway, but it's totally worth it. Keep going."

"Thanks." I smiled at them as they passed us. I looked at Josh.

He shrugged. "I'm game," he said. "They said it's worth it." He pulled a bottle of water out of his backpack, took a swig, then handed it to me.

I nodded a quick, sharp nod, determined to finish the hike. "Less time to chill out when we get back to the resort, but I vote we keep going. Go on ahead; I'll follow." I took a drink from the bottle and handed it back to him. He put it away, slung the backpack on his back, and headed off. It was starting to warm up.

Not long after, we came upon a bamboo forest. I'd never seen one before and it was *beautiful*. A wooden-slatted pathway cut through the middle, shaded by the bamboo. It was much cooler inside the forest, and even though we were still walking uphill, at least we had relief from the heat.

"First time!" I called ahead to Josh.

"What's that?" he asked over his shoulder.

"Being in a bamboo forest."

"Yeah, me too."

"I kinda love it," I said.

"Yeah, me too. I mean, I wouldn't build a summer home here, or anything, but the bamboo trees really are quite lovely."

I fell about laughing, which made it hard to keep up a decent hiking pace. He hadn't done the English accent, but I loved that he'd quoted *The Princess Bride*. *He's so fun.* I picked up the pace and caught up to him, walking by his side. "Not likely that you'll have to rescue me from an R-O-U-S, here."

"I would, though," he replied solemnly.

"Good to know."

He grinned at me. "I kinda want to run through this. Is that weird?"

No, not weird—awesome. With a quick glance his way, I started running. He was fast on my heels and I squealed in delight. When he caught me around my waist and spun me around, my squeals turned to laughter. He put me down and turned me to him. "You're fun," he said, planting a kiss on my lips.

"I was just thinking the same thing about you."

"We may never get to this waterfall, you know?"

"I kinda don't care right now."

Then he kissed me right there in the bamboo forest. Trust me, it was super romantic.

Eventually, we came to a river. Some might call it a "stream", but we had to cross it, and it was daunting enough for me to think of it as a river, or at least a "river-stream". Josh jumped across three boulders and was on the other side in about four seconds.

I would have followed, but between boulders two and three was a gap I didn't think I could make. For a second, I considered wading across the river, but that would have meant immersing my runners, and they were good runners—I actually *ran* in them. Getting them wet in the rain was one thing, but this was serious adventure stuff.

"You coming?" Josh called from the other side of the river-stream.

"Um, not sure."

He looked at me like I'd grown another limb. "I think we're close, Sarah. Can't you hear the falls?"

I can hear the falls, yes, thank you, Joshua. Grrr.

I looked in the direction of the sound and I could see the top of the falls over the tree line. We *were* close. I looked back at the river-stream. Just as I contemplated ruining my shoes for the sake of the falls, a fellow hiker emerged from the bushes behind Josh. He looked a little older than me—in his forties—and super fit.

"Hi folks," he said. *Mid-westerner*, I thought. "You wanting to cross?" he asked me.

"Uh, yeah, but not totally keen on soaking my shoes."

"No problem. I helped someone across before, and I've got these." He pointed to his shoes which looked like runners, only they were made of neoprene. *Oh, thank god!* He waded into the river-stream and stood between the second and third boulders. "Can you get to here?" he asked, pointing to boulder number two.

Yes, I can do that. I nodded and made the jump from the riverbed to boulder number one. I took a moment to steady myself and then jumped across to boulder number two. My landing was a little wobbly and the man reached out for my hand to steady me.

"Thank you."

"No problem. I'll keep hold of your hand while you jump across to the next rock, okay?" I nodded and bit my lip, unsure. I looked at the distance between the boulders, then envisioned missing boulder number three, slipping awkwardly into the river-stream and knocking my head on a rock. At times, I am quite a talented catastrophiser.

I pushed the ugly thoughts aside, took a deep breath, and leapt to boulder number three, gripping the man's hand. From there it was just a short jump to the other side of the river-stream, where Josh was waiting for me. *I made it! Oh, my god, I totally did it.*

I jumped up and down and grinned madly, then called out an effusive, "Thank you!" to the man in the river-stream.

"Hey, no problem. You folks have a great day. And the waterfall is totally worth it!" He turned and climbed out of the water and went on his way. It didn't even occur to me that I would have to get back across without his help. I was too excited that I'd done it.

Josh beamed at me. "My adventure chick," he said, kissing me hard on the mouth.

I had once been an adventurous chick. I'd travelled incessantly, and I'd hiked, canoed, white-water rafted, abseiled, mountain biked—so many incredible adventures. But all before I immersed myself in a toxic relationship with Neil the cheating bastard and forgot who I was.

A Sunset in Sydney

The woman standing with Josh on the far side of the river-stream, *she* was Adventure Chick (note the capital letters). Adventure Chick was bad-ass. She was brave and intrepid and, most importantly, she was back! I was ecstatic to wear that mantle again.

We headed off down the trail, following the sound of water falling from a great height and a few minutes later, we emerged from the canopy of green into brilliant sunlight. The waterfall loomed above us, a broad crescent of rock and water against the azure sky. The recipient of the water was a very shallow rockpool—in some places only a few inches deep, its bottom covered in pebbles and rocks, some jagged, some smoothed by the water.

I slipped off my runners and socks, leaving them on dry rocks and waded into the rockpool. The water was freshly cool, but not icy like the waterfall from the day before—likely warmed by the sun. I tipped my head to see the top of the waterfall. A dense mist hovered over where the water fell off the cliff, a constant rainbow in the air.

"Oh, my god!" I called to Josh, a lilt of laughter in my voice. I felt the same way I had when we'd swum with the turtles.

Around us, I could hear exclamations from the handful of others who were there, and Josh added his own. "It's incredible!" he replied. We grinned at each other. It was impossible not to be affected by the beauty.

Josh slipped off his shoes and socks, placed his backpack on the rocks, and waded into the water to join me. "Hey, let me get a shot of you looking up at the falls," he said, crouching down.

"How's this?"

"Perfect!" He took a few more shots, with and without me in them. Then I asked if he wanted some of him. "Sure, yeah, that'd be great!" I did my best. I was nowhere near as good a photographer as Josh, so I hoped there was at least one he'd like. Finally, we added a selfie with the top of the falls in the background.

"Is it called a selfie if two people are in it?" I asked.

He threw me a funny look. "Yeah, I think so."

"They should have a different name for it."

"Like what?"

"I have no idea, but selfie doesn't make sense when there's more than one person in it."

"You're weird."

"You have no idea. Try being on the *inside* of this brain." He replied with a chuckle—charity, most likely.

"Is it snack time yet?" I asked. I kept wading in the shallow water, never wanting to leave.

"Sure." He wandered back to the backpack and took out the muesli bars. I dragged myself out of the water found a flat rock to sit on and took in more of the impressive sight while I ate. We'd thought about turning back quite a few times, and I was delighted we hadn't. It was magical there.

I crumpled up my muesli bar wrapper and tucked it into my pocket, then took a swig of water. I didn't want to go. I would happily have spent the whole day there being covered in rainbow-coloured mist, but we had the hike back down the hill, then at least a two-hour drive ahead of us, and it was already close to lunchtime.

"We should go soon," said Josh, standing over me. He reached down a hand and pulled me up.

"Yeah. I don't want to though—not yet."

He took my water bottle from me and tucked it away in his backpack. "Mmm. I know what you mean." We were both quiet for a moment. "So, ready?" I shook my head no. He smiled, leant in for a kiss, then turned and walked towards the trail. I put my shoes on and followed, a little glum. It was hard to leave paradise.

When we got back to the river-stream, I hesitated. There was no kindly hiker wearing waterproof shoes to help me get across. Josh stopped on the bank and I stood beside him. "What do you think?" I asked.

"How about I go first and when I get to the second rock, I reach out for you and catch you when you jump?" I had trouble visualising what he meant, and my concern—okay, it was rampant fear—must have been etched on my face.

"Here, let me show you." He jumped onto the first rock, which was close to the bank, then to the second rock—that was the leap I'd need his help with. "So, you do just what I did, but I'll be right here to help you. Okay?"

Oh, screw it. Come on, Adventure Chick.

I pushed aside my fear, pulled up my big-girl knickers, and leapt to the first rock. *So far, so good.* Then Josh crouched down low and reached out his hand. "All you have to do now is jump to this rock and I'll grab your hand, okay?" Adventure Chick was not having fun. She preferred misty waterfalls to slipping and falling into a raging river-stream.

I took a deep breath and jumped to the next rock, reaching

for Josh's hand as I leapt. He grasped it and pulled me up, just as my back foot slid down the side of the rock. I ended up in an awkward lunge position, but I was safe and without any scrapes or bruises. He helped me stand and we stood face to face grinning at each other like outdoorsy idiots. "Good job," he said. I didn't even find that condescending; I must have been growing as a person.

"You got the last one?" he asked.

"Yep," I said, as I made the jumps to the next rock and then to the far bank, easily. I turned and waited for him, hands on my hips in self-congratulations. He also made the last two jumps easily, joining me on the riverbank.

"We're awesome," he said.

"Agreed."

"Race you," he said, and then he was off along the trail before I could even protest. I followed, watching my step so I didn't turn an ankle on a tree root, and finally caught up to him. He kept up a light jog.

When we came across three sweaty-faced hikers walking uphill towards us, I called, "It's totally worth it," as we passed them.

Josh added, "And you're nearly there!" I heard a half-hearted, "thanks," behind us.

When we came to the bamboo forest and the trail gave way to the wooden-slatted path, Josh picked up the pace. I'd been sorry to leave the waterfall, but running down a shady mountain path was its own kind of fun.

We emerged from the forest into bright sunlight, and Josh slowed back to a jog. I jogged up beside him. "Keep running?"

he asked. We were both fit enough to keep up the pace, but I wasn't sure how wise it was to run in full sun. I figured we still had another couple of miles to go. I dropped back to a fast-paced walk.

"Uh, I need some water." We stopped and he fished out the water bottles—both were more than half empty.

"We should probably walk it," he said after taking a gulp of water. "Obviously it takes longer, but I'm worried about over-heating."

"Yeah, me too." We each drank half of what we had left and continued downhill at a brisk walking pace. When we got back to the car, we were both dripping in sweat, out of water, and grinning.

"That was incredible," he said.

"Agreed. It was brilliant. I need some new words, though. I'm running out of ways to describe things," I replied.

"Yeah." We climbed into the car. "I'll find somewhere to buy water," said Josh, starting the car.

"Also agreed." I leant my head back against the car seat, filthy, exhausted, and gloriously happy. What a wonderful way to see out the year.

*

The drive back to the resort took a lot less time than our drive *to* Hana, because the only stop we made was at Aunty Linda's Banana Bread stand. After our morning of adventure, we had two pieces each. We added some dried pineapple to our order—delicious—and two more bottles of water, having already finished the ones we'd bought near Seven Sacred Pools.

On the road again and contentedly stuffing my face with banana bread, I was in my own little world and wishing I could move to Hawaii. I knew it was a cliché. Surely, everyone who visits Hawaii must think exactly the same thing.

But I also knew, deep down, that the reality was much more like my life in Sydney than the idyllic island life we'd seen as visitors. People had to work and pay rent and shop for groceries and clean their houses and pay their taxes and drive in traffic. They also had to navigate around hordes of tourists whenever they went anywhere. What I was fantasising about, was living a life where I was essentially on holiday— all the time.

"I've had a lot of fun with you," said Josh, intruding on my thoughts.

"Oh, thanks. Yeah, me too." I added a smile and reached over to squeeze his thigh.

"And I don't just mean today. I mean the whole trip so far. Being with you, well, it's ..." He trailed off, then glanced at me and returned his eyes to the road. I knew he had something important to say, so I kept silent, not wanting him to feel pressured to say it.

I was right. After a few moments, he sighed heavily. "Sarah, what I want to say is that I absolutely *love* being with you." My breath hitched on the L-word, but I said nothing. "Thank you again for coming all this way. I can't tell you how much it means to me that you did that."

I squeaked out a feeble reply, on the verge of being overcome with emotion. I understood exactly what Josh was saying.

We'd had a few awkward moments at the beginning, but mostly we were the same "Josh and Sarah" we'd been in Greece. How we were together—that affinity—was what made *me* love being with *him*.

Of course, I'd also come to Hawaii to see if what we had in Greece was real or just a holiday fling—to see if we could be something more. I hoped Josh was there for the same reason. Sitting next to him in the car, having just shared an incredible experience, I wondered if he'd come to some sort of conclusion.

"The other thing is that being with you makes me question what the hell I'm doing with my life." I wasn't sure how to take that. Was that good or bad? Was this conversation going to end up like the time I'd told Neil about getting promoted and he'd accused me of shoving my success in his face? I hoped not.

"You're so *in* your life. You're doing all the things you said you would do when we were in Greece. You're going after your bigger life. And I'm stuck. Other than planning this trip and coming here—and you have to know that this is *huge* for me, and I'm so glad I came—but other than Hawaii, I've been stagnating. Being here with you ..."

I was holding my breath, and even when I realised that, I didn't let it out. Sometimes you really do wait for something with bated breath.

"... It reminds me of what I want. And that *I* need to make it happen. You inspire me, Sarah. You make me want to be better. I'm so glad you're in my life."

So, Josh was not only glad to be there with me, I *wasn't* his big fear. I wasn't what was holding him in place. I let out the breath—probably a little more forcefully than I realised, because Josh shot me a quick look. "You okay?" he asked.

Am I?

A flurry of thoughts and emotions competed for my attention. Tears prickled my eyes, and my nails made tiny crescents in my palm. It wasn't exactly "I love you", but I hadn't expected that from Josh. What he *had* said was that I was important to him, that he was happy being there with me, and he was glad I was in his life. Those were all good things. After a moment, I nodded, then realised he was watching the road and not me. "Yeah, I'm okay," I said.

Or, I will be.

I reached out to put my hand on his thigh, and he caught it with his and squeezed it. He only let go when we approached the next bend in the road because he needed two hands for the sharp turn. I looked out, watching the changeable coastline and then when we turned inland, the sugar plantations.

I was falling hard for the sexy American boy—again.

Chapter 16

We arrived back at the resort around 4:00pm, which gave us just enough time to shower away the grime from our adventures, have a snooze, eat a light dinner—room service that time—then shower again before we got ready to go out. We also managed to fit in our very first quickie, a milestone in any couple's relationship—even though we weren't technically a couple.

We were meeting Siobhan in the lobby at nine so we could ride to the party together, but I had been worried about how we'd get back to the resort after the party. Not being able to find a taxi was always a risk when you went out on New Year's Eve, so I was relieved when the concierge gave us a special number to call—one of the (many) services that came with Josh's Marriott status.

I couldn't help being impressed, and maybe a little envious, that a perk of Josh's job as a travelling software consultant was qualifying for the highest status of an international hotel chain. Whereas, *I* was a schoolteacher. The biggest perk I got was free instant coffee in the staffroom—and it was Nescafé.

I got dressed for the party in the bathroom so I could

surprise Josh with *the* dress, specifically me in the dress. It was perfect for a warm, tropical New Year's Eve, so I hadn't hesitated to pack it. As I stepped into it, it did occur to me that I'd only worn it with James and Josh. It was this odd thread between them, but I tried not to think about that, or James, as I strapped on the sandals I'd bought in London.

Lindsey had lent me one of her clutches in a metallic bronze, and some bangles and earrings in the same colour, to round out the outfit. My hair had miraculously dried into near-perfect curls, so I left it down. A "down-do" was rare for me, and I sprayed so much humidity-resistant hairspray on my curls, I nearly needed a gas mask—but I wasn't taking any chances. I waved a hand in front of my face to clear the air. The price we pay for beauty.

Once I was dressed, I checked my makeup one last time— still perfect. I had gone with a bold fuchsia lip, lashings of mascara, and a dusting of bronzer. Finally, I stood in front of the full-length mirror to see how the whole look came together.

I looked hot, if I did say so myself, and I was ready for the big reveal. If Josh wasn't in love with me yet, he would be when I opened the door. Except that when I opened the bathroom door, he wasn't there. The room was empty.

Where the hell are you, Joshua? Hot Sarah quickly morphed into completely pissed off Sarah. I heard the key-card in the door and went back into the bathroom, closing the door quietly behind me. I really wanted that big entrance.

I could hear Josh moving about in the room and I waited about half-a-minute, so it wouldn't seem like I'd just done the ridiculously vain thing I'd just done. I opened the bathroom door a second time, pretending to fidget with my earring, as though I had only just finished getting ready—so casual—so casually gorgeous—so ...

I stopped in my tracks and stared at the bed. *Oh, my god. What? What?!*

On the bed was a giant, fluffy sea turtle, practically life-sized. It was bright green with beautiful, soulful eyes. My hands went to my mouth. *So that's where he's been.* I dashed across the room, and dropped my clutch onto the bed so I could grab the turtle and hug it.

And, yes, I do realise that most grown women probably wouldn't get that excited about a stuffed animal, but it was so sweet and squishy, and I *loved* sea turtles. Swimming with them had been one of the most peaceful, incredible experiences I'd ever had. It was an extremely thoughtful gift. At least, I thought it was a gift. I suddenly realised that maybe Josh had bought it for himself. He'd seemed pretty keen on sea turtles too.

"Is he for me?" I asked over the turtle's head. In that short amount of time I'd decided that he was a he.

Josh laughed and came over. "Of course! You've stared at it in the gift shop window about a hundred times since we got here." That was true—even before we swam with the turtles, I'd been eyeing him off.

"I love him," I said, hugging the turtle tighter. *I love you for getting him for me.* I didn't say that last part, but it was the most thoughtful and romantic gift I'd ever been given. It was for playful Sarah, fun-loving Sarah, the Sarah who laughed underwater and fell in love with the craggy little faces of sea turtles. It was for *me*.

"I did worry about how you'll get him home. I hope it will be okay. I can help squash him into your suitcase, if you like."

"I'll just take him on the plane with me. He'll be like a pillow." Josh seemed to like that. I tried to ignore the niggling reminder that we only had a couple more days together before the turtle and I would be on a plane to Sydney, while Josh flew off in the other direction. The goodbye loomed ominously; it would be easy to succumb to melancholy if I wasn't careful.

"And what are you going to call him?"

Happy for the distraction, I thought for a moment. "He's called Maui." Josh smiled at me and gave me a gentle peck, leaving my fuchsia lips un-smudged, just like the thoughtful sort-of boyfriend he was.

"I like it, but you may have to leave him here for the night." He was teasing me, but I didn't care. I put Maui carefully on the bed with his head resting on a pillow.

"Bye, Maui," I said quietly. I picked up my clutch and turned towards Josh.

"Ready?" he asked. I nodded. He placed a hand on the small of my back as I walked past. "You look fantastic, by the way."

"I know," I replied playfully.

"And, cool shoes." I nearly stumbled in those cool shoes as I walked out the door, my mind plummeting back to an incredible night in London and the first time I slept with James.

Josh. Josh. Josh. Why was it so hard to just *be* with the man I was with?

I paused to wait for him, taking in how handsome he looked. *It's not always about you, Sarah.* He was wearing a pair of dark-wash jeans, which hugged his thighs just enough to be spectacularly sexy, and a pair of shiny black dress shoes. He wore a crisp white shirt opened to the third button, highlighting the tan he'd got since we'd arrived. He was cleanly shaven, and his hair was still a little damp from his shower, defining some of his curls. And he smelled divine, like sandalwood and sex.

"You look fantastic too," I said with genuine admiration.

He cocked his head to the side. "Thanks!" There was a flash of his brilliant smile and in an instant, all traces of James were erased from my mind. *Josh. Beautiful, funny, adorably sexy Josh.*

*

"And *then*, he took me on a ride along the coast on a motorcycle and we watched the sunset together. It was magic," Siobhan sighed. She'd had a fun couple of days with Paddy and I was happy for her. She was in the front seat of the taxi, and Josh and I were holding hands across the back seat—like a real couple and not just travelling fuck buddies. Yes, I was still a little hung up on that.

"So, Siobhan," said Josh, "do you think you and Paddy will see each other again after this?" I hoped Josh didn't feel me tense up. *Where's he going with this?*

"Oh, like you and Sarah?" I was pretty sure from the tone in Siobhan's voice that she was "Team Sarah". I wondered if Josh noticed, but if he did, he pretended not to. Or, he was back-pedalling like a MoFo.

"Yeah, sure, like us, I guess." *Oh, god, please stop talking. And* please *don't say the V-word.*

Siobhan wasn't having it. "Oh, no, I mean, Paddy and I are just a bit of fun. I mean, I was supposed to be *married* right now. We're a holiday romance—nothing like *you two*."

Bahahahahahahahahaaa. I was laughing on the inside. On the outside, I looked out my window and said nothing. Josh squirmed in his seat a little and I was glad—perhaps a little *too* glad. It was not my finest moment.

"Here we are," said the driver as we pulled up outside a gated home, its gates wide open. When I opened my car door, I could hear music.

Siobhan paid the driver while Josh and I got out of the taxi and waited for her. "Hey," he said, pulling me towards him with one hand. In the other, he was carrying a one-litre bottle of vodka.

I met his gaze. "Hey," I said back.

"You're beautiful, you know?"

I smiled tautly, still stinging a little from how uncomfortable he'd been in the taxi. "Thank you."

"No, I mean that. I'm glad we weren't just a holiday fling." *What?!*

My breath caught in my throat and I stared at him wide-eyed. What he'd said—that meant what I thought it did, right? And had he felt that way since Greece, or was it Siobhan's

246

words that made him realise? Either way, it felt like a pivotal moment for us and tears prickled my eyes. I blinked them away—all that mascara!

"I feel that way too," I replied, my voice thick and raspy.

He kissed me hard—smudging my lipstick, but I didn't care—*just* as Siobhan opened her car door. "All right, you two, the night is young. You've got plenty of time for that," she teased.

Josh and I broke apart, both wearing embarrassed smiles, and his eyes locked onto mine. He seemed about to say something else, but Siobhan broke the spell. "Come on," she said, linking her arm through mine and pulling me away. I linked my other arm with Josh's and the three of us walked up the driveway like we were off to see the wizard or something.

The party was going off, as we like to say in Australia. And the house! It was a gorgeous beach-style mansion decorated in neutral colours, with lots of natural textiles and light-wood furniture. I could have moved in right then had there not been seventy-five people—dancing, drinking and laughing— filling every room.

We were greeted at the door by a stunning Hawaiian woman wearing a bikini top and—I kid you not—a grass skirt. She looked like she'd stepped off a postcard. "Aloha!" she said with a huge smile of perfect white teeth. She placed a lei around each of our necks.

Siobhan leant close to my ear. "Fecking 'ell, how gorgeous is she?"

I turned my head so I could talk into her ear over the music. "I know! Ridiculous."

"Almost as hot as us," she quipped. I barked out a laugh.

"What's that?" asked Josh loudly.

"I said, let's find Paddy," Siobhan practically shouted—the music was *extremely* loud. She grabbed my hand and I grabbed Josh's just as she pulled me through the crowd. We emerged onto a patio that was lit by fairy lights and tiki torches and ran the length of a long narrow pool, girls in teeny bikinis and guys in boardshorts bobbing about in it. It looked inviting, but I was happy to stay dry and looking fabulous.

A bar had been set up next to the pool, and Siobhan squealed—actually squealed—when she saw Paddy shaking a cocktail over his shoulder. She pulled harder on my hand and made a beeline for the bar. "Excuse me," she said, pushing through the small crowd of people lining up for drinks. She reminded me of Cat. Maybe that's why I'd loved her almost instantly.

"Hey!" said Paddy, a grin flashing across his handsome face. Siobhan dropped my hand and grabbed his face with both of hers, giving him a massive smack on his lips. "You look amazing," I heard him say. She grinned, then turned to us.

"You remember my friends, Josh and Sarah?" she asked. I hoped it was a rhetorical question. He must have met fifty new people each day at his job.

"Of course! You're the one who giggles underwater," he said. He did remember us!

"Guilty!" I laughed and raised my hand in a wave. "And thank you for the invite," I added. He shook his head as if to say, "no worries".

Paddy decanted the cocktail he was shaking into a red plastic cup—yes, those cups from American movies are a real thing—and handed it across the bar. I watched the tiny blonde recipient take the drink with a pout, *clearly* disappointed that Paddy only had eyes for Siobhan. Siobhan and Paddy were oblivious.

"Oh hey, we brought this for the bar," said Josh, handing over the vodka.

"Oh, that's grand. Thanks guys."

"So, they've got you working tonight?" asked Josh.

"Oh, we're all chipping in some time behind the bar. There's a few of us here. I'll be wrapping up soon, actually." He turned to Siobhan. "Then I'll be all yours." He leant down and kissed her and she giggled. They were so damned cute together.

"What can I get you?" he asked us.

"Whatever you got going, man," said Josh.

Paddy held up a finger. "Leave it with me." A few minutes later, he handed over three cups. "*Sláinte*," he said, holding up a fourth. We all tapped cups and took sips.

"Paddy," I said, looking up at him in wonder, "it's friggin' delicious." It was also incredibly strong.

"What *is* it?" I asked. He just raised his eyebrows at me and smiled. He wasn't saying. Definitely rum and lots of lime, and a lot of other things I couldn't quite name. I was going to have to pace myself.

I took in more of the party-scape while I sipped my drink. From what I could tell, there was an interesting mix of locals, ex-pats, and visitors amongst the guests. I wondered again what it would be like to live in Hawaii, and I imagined there would be a transitory nature to friendships, and likely relationships, with those three groups constantly in interplay—a bit like Paddy and Siobhan.

Paddy soon handed off his bartending duties, then took Siobhan's hand and pulled her onto a makeshift dance floor. With Siobhan off with Paddy, Josh steered me away from the bar crowd and towards the view. I let him lead me through the partygoers to a low garden wall, where we sat, half-turned towards the ocean. I took another sip of my drink.

"I think Paddy must have gone to the Duncan school of bartending," I said.

Josh took a small sip of his drink. "I hear you. Besides lime, I can't even figure out what's in here."

"Basically, a shit-tonne of booze."

"Well, that, yes. It's good, though. Better than Duncan's." He held his cup aloft, "Sorry, Duncan, wherever you are." I giggled. Even if he was there, I didn't think Duncan would have cared. He probably would have agreed.

I turned to look at the ocean. The sun had set hours before, but there were lights from the houses along the coast reflecting onto the water, and the sky was clear, and the moon was full. How cool to get a full moon on New Year's Eve.

"God that's beautiful!" I said. "Look!"

"I hadn't even realised it was going to be a full moon. Come on." He stood and held out a hand. I tucked my clutch under my arm so I could hold both his hand and my drink, and we found the gate that led out to the beach.

"Hang on," I said, as I stopped to slip off my sandals. I left them next to the gate.

"Oh, yeah. Good thinking." He let go of my hand to take his shoes and socks off, tucking them next to my sandals, then took my hand again, smiling at me. *God, that smile. Utter Swoonsville.*

We walked towards the water and then slowly along the beach, occasionally letting a gently lapping wave catch our feet. The sand was gritty, not the powdery soft sand I'd imagined Hawaii's beaches to be made from, but I didn't mind. It made me aware of every step, a reminder to savour these moments with Josh. We only had two days left together and I felt a sudden twinge of sadness.

It's too soon to have to say goodbye again. We've only just got back in sync.

"So, New Year's resolutions?" Josh asked, a smile in his voice.

"Sorry?" I'd been completely lost in my gloomy thoughts.

"What was it that Duncan would say? 'You off with the fairies?'" I laughed.

"Oh, I miss Duncan," I whined.

"Yeah, he's a good bloke," he said in the worst Aussie accent I'd ever heard.

"Wow, busting out the Aussie-isms. Look at you!"

He pulled me close to him. "No, look at you." Then he kissed me. It was one of those Nicholas Sparks movie kisses, all dreamy and moonlit and scrummy.

"You're a pretty romantic guy, you know," I said, resting my cheek against his chest. He put his arms around me and I sighed. *How lovely to be held like this.*

Especially after I'd spent months going home to my flat alone. Sure, I'd been filling my life with new endeavours and outings, but once I'd realised that I *did* want to be in love, to have a partner and make a life with them, I'd become acutely aware of that empty spot next to me in my bed. No number of cuddles from Domino could make up for what I missed— feeling like I did in that moment with Josh—

"So that's a 'no' for New Year's resolutions, then?"

I broke the hug and started walking again, shaking my head at him. "You dork. We were having a *moment*, don't you know?"

He caught up. "Yeah, but in my defence, this whole romance thing is new to me. Or, at least, I'm a little rusty."

"Dork!" I shook my head at him again and rolled my eyes. I was glad there was a full moon so he could see my face while I made fun of him.

"I wear the mantle proudly."

"You know, I usually *do* make resolutions." I said, getting back to his question. "Actually, scratch that—I don't make them, I *agonise* over them." "But not this year?"

"Well, no. You see, I read this blog post last week about New Year's *absolutions*."

"Absolutions?"

"Yep. That's where you only resolve to *absolve* yourself of something."

"Hah!" he laughed. "Love it."

"Yeah, you like that?" I asked, adding my own laugh. "You're thinking about what to absolve yourself of now, aren't you?"

He nodded, grinning. "Guilty, but I'll wait. Tell me yours."

"Well, the first one is probably obvious. I absolve myself of writing resolutions."

"So, the equivalent of the infinite wishes wish?"

"Exactly! So, with that out of the way, I've been thinking about all the things on my 'should list'."

"Should list?"

"Yeah. You know? I should do this, I should do that," I replied.

"Sounds like you're quite the taskmaster."

"You have no idea. Anyway, the biggies I came up with are"—I held up my thumb—"catching up on *Game of Thrones*—"

He interrupted me. "What's wrong with *Game of Thrones*?"

"Too many characters!" He shook his head at me. "Moving on! Two: drinking kombucha, or coconut water, or apple cider vinegar."

"Well, that's just common sense. Those are all disgusting, especially coconut water."

"Exactly! Not to mention that the so-called 'health benefits' are somewhat dubious." I did the air quotes—don't judge me.

"You're very passionate about this."

"I am." I lifted my chin proudly.

"Anything else?"

"Well, the last one is a little vain and makes me sound like a total chick, so I'm not sure I want to say it."

He laughed. "Sarah, I've seen you without any makeup on many, *many* times." *Okay, Josh, thanks for the reminder—maybe dial it back a bit.* "I think you can tell me your last absolution."

I chewed on my lip, considering it. But what about mystery? Wasn't it the key to keeping the romance alive? I didn't want to become one of those couples who went to the toilet in front of each other— if we actually *were* a couple. I mean, who does that? No, really, *who?*

I digress.

What I didn't want to tell Josh was that I had absolved myself of going grey. I was starting to accumulate quite a few of the little grey buggers, and I'd be damned if I was going to be one of those women who gave in to nature. I wasn't even forty yet *and* one of my boyfriends was a *Millennial*. I was keeping my standing monthly appointment to get my roots done, damn it!

"No, you don't need to know. Consider it secret women's business." I avoided his gaze in case I caved under the scrutiny of those ridiculously gorgeous grey eyes. "So, what about you?"

"I'm letting you off the hook, you know?" I said nothing. "Okay, well, I did think about absolving myself of the whole 'bigger life' thing." I turned my head to him, a frown planted firmly on my face.

He held up his hand as if to stave me off. "Kidding! I'm kidding."

"We're going to have to talk about it at some point, you know." I took the final sip of my drink. Boy, it was potent.

"Yeah, yeah. I know. I'm surprised you haven't asked about it already."

Why haven't I? I tried to kid myself it was because we were having such a great time, and I didn't want to spoil things by bringing it up. But really it was because I was afraid of what he would say—that I might find out we were on completely different trajectories and despite how we felt, we should just go our separate ways.

I was playing emotional ping pong with myself.

"So, yeah, I don't know …" he said, clearly thinking aloud. "I definitely absolve myself of buying those skinny jeans with the low crotch. I know they're kind of the thing right now, but they just look stupid."

I raised the hand that wasn't holding my empty cup. "I couldn't agree more. Anything else?"

"Hmm, I'll have to think about it." That was fair. I'd had plenty of time to think about mine and, besides, none of them were serious. I figured it was time to loop back to what was.

"So, what about the other thing?" I glanced at him and he was rubbing the back of his neck one-handed, his "everything is not okay" gesture.

"Yeah." I waited, giving him time to say what he needed to say. Eventually, he launched into an explanation. "You know, I was so fired up after I got home from Greece. I was going to take charge of my career and do more with my time and start thinking about where to travel to next year—well, now it's almost *this* year."

"And what happened?"

"I don't know. Life, I guess. I know that's a cop-out answer, but routine and work and just *normalcy*. And I didn't have you guys around." I knew he meant the people from the sailing trip, our floating family. And then, "I didn't have *you* around."

Oh, wow. The weight of his words hung between us, a call back to what he'd said when we arrived at the party. Maybe he really *was* thinking about being in a relationship with me.

But I was confused. This wasn't the Josh I'd talked to dozens of times, or the Josh from his emails. How had I not seen what he was going through? "I'm really sorry I didn't realise. It always seemed like you had a lot going on. I've been a crap friend."

"You shouldn't be sorry. *I* should be sorry. I wasn't honest with you. A lot of the time, I was pretending. I mean, I was busy, yes, just busy doing the same old stuff."

I didn't want Josh sinking into a pit of self-flagellation and regret. It was New Year's Eve, a time for beginnings, not getting mired down in what wasn't right with life. "So," I said brightly, and possibly a little too loudly, because his head snapped up at the sound of my voice. I carried on, "What *do* you want to do?"

He laughed and I welcomed the sound. "You mean, what are my New Year's resolutions?"

"Oh, my god, yes! I do. Holy crap. We've come full circle." I let the giggles take hold, and he stopped to face me, smiling.

"I do know I want to do this." He pulled me towards him for another kiss, this one less Nicholas Sparks and more *Fifty Shades of Grey*, if you know what I mean. We both dropped our cups, and I let my clutch fall to the sand, so I could run my hands up his back—he had a lovely back. One of my hands entwined in his hair—he had lovely hair too.

Josh's hands found the slits in my dress and caressed my thighs, his ardour building as he pulled the fabric higher so he could cup my bum with his hands. That was when he discovered I wasn't wearing any knickers.

"You're not wearing any ..." he said breathlessly. I shook my head "no", and he leant in closer to take my mouth with his, his lips and tongue meshed against mine. "I need you," he said, breaking the kiss.

"Here?" He nodded, his eyes alive with wanting. Now, I know this is going to sound super unsexy, but I was not one hundred per cent into the idea of sex on the beach. I mean, there's all that *sand*. Josh was already way ahead of me, though. He slipped his jeans down and, in the fastest recorded time ever, slid on a condom. He lifted me so I could wrap my legs around his waist, then he was inside me. I clung to him, his face pressed against my neck. It was fast and passionate and *so* sexy.

Afterwards, he carefully placed me back on my feet. My legs were a little wobbly and we were both breathing heavily— being joined like that was a bit of a workout. I realised we'd have to deal with the condom and picked up my clutch so I could offer him a tissue.

"Thanks," he mumbled shyly, then sorted himself out. It's odd how you can be so close to someone, so intimate with them, and still be shy about the practicalities of sex.

When he had pulled up and fastened his jeans and after I'd smoothed out my dress, we stood facing each other. He lifted a hand to my face and traced my jawline. I tilted my head and his hand cupped my cheek. Our eyes met and he placed a gentle kiss on my lips, then leant his forehead against mine.

"Sarah ..." he said again, cryptically. I was really going to have to figure out what it meant when he said my name like that—specifically, what it meant for *us*.

Oh, and I should say that I hardly ever do that—go knickerless, I mean—but the dress looked better without them—truly. I hadn't planned on having hot sex on the beach when I got dressed—although, it *was* a lovely outcome.

*

"Ten, nine, eight, seven, six, five, four, three, two, one! Hap-py New Year!" I love the sound of lots of people joyously counting down to the New Year. There's something exhilarating in the collective hope that the year to come will bring all it promises.

And seeing in the year with Josh and our new friend, Siobhan, was more magical than any New Year I'd had in years—particularly as the previous one had been spent with Neil the cheating bastard.

There in Maui, under a full moon and washed in a cooling fragrant breeze, I felt a sense of possibility, perhaps even empowerment. My life had already changed from the stagnant mediocrity it had been the year before—before I'd met Josh and the others on the boat, and before I'd actively started participating in my own life again.

I was happier than I could ever remember being.

After the countdown, Josh and I wished each other "Happy New Year" and kissed—a chaste one compared to the kiss that had led to sex on the beach. Part of me was already excited about sharing that story with Lins and Cat, though I'd skip the details, of course. Contrary to what many people believe, women do not tell each other *everything*. Well, we don't. It's tacky.

Siobhan found us, Paddy following close behind her.

"Happy New Year to my new besties," she said, pulling us in for a group hug. I wondered how many more of Paddy's special cocktails she'd had. We'd stuck to vodka tonics for the rest of the evening and I had a nice buzz going, but I was planning on *not* being hungover the next morning. I wanted to be fresh for my last day in Hawaii.

"Happy New Year to you too!" I said to Siobhan, throwing my arm around her neck. "And you, Paddy." He leant over and gave me a cheek kiss, returning the well wishes, then shook hands with Josh.

"I'm going to stay here with Paddy tonight," shouted Siobhan. The music had started up again and we were being jostled about by revellers who wanted to reclaim our spot as the dance floor. I signalled for us to move away from the thick of the party, not wanting to have a shouting match with Siobhan.

We found a spot away from the noise. The guys followed and were chatting about something—surfing, it sounded like. "So, what time do you fly out tomorrow?" I asked.

"Noon. That's my flight to Honolulu, then I have a couple hours there before the flight to Dublin, via New York."

"Wow, that's quite the milk run."

"Yeah, but it's been brilliant. I'm so glad I came."

"Me too. You know, my sister lives in the UK." *So does James, Sarah.* I pushed the thought aside. I hadn't told Siobhan about James. I'd never had enough time alone with her to go into it—*and* it seemed like a betrayal to talk about him while I was in Hawaii with Josh. Ironic, I know, but it was easier for me to have two boyfriends if I compartmentalised them.

"And I've never been to Ireland," I added. "I should come see you the next time I'm in your part of the world."

"Oh, my god, I'd love it. You absolutely must come—I've told you before and I mean it. You can stay with me. We've— sorry, *I've* ..." I heard her voice catch and I rested my hand on her arm in encouragement. "As I was saying, *I've* got a great little place in the heart of the city, and *I've* even got a spare room. Feels weird sometimes, when I have to say 'I' instead of 'we'."

"It's still very recent—totally understandable. Anyway, we're connected on Facebook and I'll send you my email address too. We can keep in touch for sure."

"Grand." She hugged me. "I'm so glad I found you and Josh." I squeezed her back.

"And Paddy," I added.

We pulled apart. "Oh, yes, and dear Paddy. What a way to get over Liam. My god, that boy has the best abs I've ever felt in my life!" I laughed. "And what about you two?" she asked, leaning in and lowering her voice. I looked over her shoulder at Josh, who was deep in conversation with Paddy.

Looking back at Siobhan, I shrugged, a wry smile on my face. I spoke quietly. "The sex part is good—no, actually, it's *great*—and we're close friends. I love being with him, but I don't know. We still haven't talked about 'us', and if I'm truthful, it doesn't seem like Josh is at the same point in his life as I am. At least, not anymore. And even if he does decide he wants to be with me, he seems stuck, and I'm not sure what that means for us."

It was only as the words tumbled out of my mouth that I

realised what I was saying, and a wave of sadness swept over me.

Siobhan looked rightfully concerned, but I didn't want the conversation to turn even more morose, so I plastered a smile on my face. "But let's not worry about all that—plenty of time to dissect it all when I get home. So, now, you, tomorrow. Can we have breakfast together so we can say goodbye properly?"

"Absolutely—done. I'll meet you downstairs at eight." *Eight? On New Year's Day?? Ugh.* But she was leaving, and I adored her, so I would do it. Josh would too, although he didn't know it yet. "Now, you're not leaving yet, are you?" she asked.

"What? The party?" I looked around. Yes, these people were strangers, but we'd all shared something, a milestone of sorts, and there was a kind of camaraderie in it. *And* someone had started playing dance music from the 90s, which was impossible to resist.

I shook my head. "No way. We haven't danced together yet!" Then I pulled a giggling Siobhan towards the makeshift dance floor, Paddy and Josh following close behind. "Gonna Make You Sweat" by C&C Music Factory started playing, and Siobhan and I squealed, then grabbed hands and jumped up and down in the way grown women do when they're tipsy— okay, *drunk*—and they find out they love dancing to the same song.

The guys joined us—in the dancing, not the squealing and jumping up and down—and Siobhan I shared grins as we danced in the year. I had a feeling it was going to be a great one.

Chapter 17

The alarm bleated like an impaled lamb. I rolled over, threw my arm across my eyes, and groaned.

Well, this is a crappy start to the year.

Why had I promised Siobhan we'd have breakfast together? At eight in the morning on New Year's Day? After we'd stayed at the party 'til two, dancing, and we'd had two more drinks after midnight?

Because I was a moron.

Also, because she was my friend—our friend—and I adored her, and she was flying out in a few hours.

"Are you awake?" I asked Josh, feeling him stir beside me.

"Yeah." He sounded about as enthusiastic as I felt.

"Then can you please turn off that noise?" Sleep-deprived and slightly hungover Sarah is delightful, by the way. Josh turned off the alarm. It was me who'd insisted he set it, so I had no right to be grumpy with him. I mumbled a half-assed, "Sorry."

He rolled onto my side of the bed and played with one of my wayward curls. "No problem. You want the first shower?"

I removed my arm from my face and blinked at him through

the slits of my eyes. "You're a god." He smiled. He looked way better than I felt, and I reminded myself I was quite a bit older than him. *My partying days are OVER! I'm past it!* Sleep-deprived and slightly hungover Sarah is also a drama queen.

I rolled out of bed and dragged myself to the bathroom, then stood under a lukewarm shower until I started to feel some semblance of humanity return.

Why, oh why, do I never learn this lesson? I was fairly certain I'd only had *one* drink too many. I'd been hoping to keep the warm, fuzzy buzz from the evening's cocktails going, but it's always the last drink you should talk yourself out of, isn't it?

"We're meeting Siobhan in twenty minutes," called out my pseudo-boyfriend.

"Okay!" I called back. I turned off the shower and dried off, only then daring to look in the mirror above the sink. To my utter surprise, it wasn't that bad. My hair had behaved itself—for my hair—and was still in its cascading curls. The only tell that I'd spent most of the night out, was some shadowing under my eyes, which I covered with concealer. I rubbed some cream blush into my cheeks, added a few flicks of mascara, tidied my brows with a little brush, and wiped on a slick of lip gloss.

That'll do, Sarah. It's just Siobhan. And Josh, my much younger boyfriend, I reminded myself.

Speak of the devil ...

Josh got into the shower and I watched him as he ran his head under the water, rivulets running down his body and droplets falling from his curls. I could have looked at him naked all day—he was so very, very good-looking.

"I know you're watching me," said the voice from the shower. I'd been sprung!

"Just enjoying the view," I said lightly. I left the bathroom and put on a maxi dress and flip-flops.

At breakfast, Siobhan looked as though she'd had a good night's sleep as well as a good shag, when it was probably just the latter. "Hellooo, lovelies," she cooed at us, waving. We made our way through the tables to where she was already seated. I leant down and gave her a kiss on the cheek.

"Wasn't last night just the most fun thing ever?" Siobhan enthused.

A slew of snapshots from the night before flashed through my mind. "It was the best New Year's I've had in ages," I agreed.

"It was a great party," said Josh. "Sorry we couldn't find you to say goodbye."

"Oh, we were, um, busy," she grinned.

Josh returned the smile. "Yeah, but we didn't get a chance to thank Paddy for the invite. Let him know we had a great time."

"Oh, Paddy and I said our goodbyes this morning."

I was a little surprised at the finality of her tone. "So, you're not going to keep in touch?"

She shook her head. "No, it was just about the sex. We fancied each other. I needed a shag. That's it," she said matter-of-factly. *Oh*.

She picked up her tea and took a sip, reminding me how much I wanted some. I caught a waiter's eye, and when he came over, I asked for tea. "And coffee, please," I added, thinking of Josh.

Tea on its way, I turned my attention back to Siobhan, who looked well pleased with herself. "Well, that's great," I enthused, "good for you." *Do I mean that?* Feeling awash with disappointment, I realised I didn't. I'd been invested in Siobhan finding someone—while she was on her honeymoon—*alone*. It was no fun discovering that I was *that* person, the one who wanted the single woman to find love. At least I'd never said the words out loud!

My tea and Josh's coffee arrived. I added milk to my tea and was stirring it when Siobhan asked, "So, what about you two then?" Josh and I locked eyes and his expression was unreadable. Shock? Fear? Undying love for me?

"Well ..." I said cautiously, breaking eye contact with Josh. Siobhan must have forgotten all about the conversation I'd had with her only hours before. I paused to take a sip of tea while I pondered how to navigate such a loaded question, but Josh jumped in. "We have the rest of today and tonight together, so that's cool." I wasn't sure how "cool" it was that we'd be saying goodbye the next day, especially as we had yet to talk about us. My stomach soured.

"Yes, but what's *next* for you two? Do you have another trip planned?" she probed. Yep, she'd definitely forgotten everything I'd told her at the party.

"Not yet," I said as casually as possible. I caught her eye across the table and she pursed her lips, finally seeming to catch on.

"Well, I meant what I said before. If you're looking for somewhere to go, I'd love to see you in Dublin. And, the spare room has a queen bed," she said, raising her eyebrows at us.

"That could be a lot of fun, Siobhan. Thanks. We'll definitely let you know," I replied, hoping she'd drop the subject.

If I was going back to Siobhan's part of the world, it was unlikely I'd be going with Josh. I'd probably be going to see James—and Cat, of course.

The reality of my tenuous romantic situation was insinuating itself into my holiday *and* into my—dare I say it?—vacationship. Somehow, I got through ordering, eating, and general chit-chat even though I felt like a duplicitous heel. I was actually relieved when Siobhan said she needed to get going and finish packing.

I hugged her tightly. "I've loved spending time with you. You're amazing."

"You too, lovely. An absolute pleasure." She added in a whisper, "I hope it all works out." I knew she meant with Josh.

We pulled back and grasped hands, regarding each other. I really hoped I would see her again; I'd fallen a little in love with her, especially her enthusiasm for life.

She turned to Josh. "Goodbye, you gorgeous, gorgeous man, you," she said, giving him a big hug.

"It was great to meet you," he replied. I could see his smile over Siobhan's shoulder.

We waved her off to her part of the resort and, yes, I got a little teary. Even though I hadn't known her long, she'd become a friend and, besides, goodbyes suck, remember?

"Shall we go see a volcano?" asked Josh. I could tell he was trying to cheer me up, and I decided to let him.

Our plan was to drive up to Haleakala Crater and go hiking—so, not exactly a volcano, but it was supposed to be spectacular up there, and I needed as much spectacular as possible, because the next day was *really* going to suck—another frigging goodbye. *Ugh*.

"Let's go see a volcano," I replied, more cheerfully than I felt.

I needed to change—a maxi dress wasn't a good choice for hiking around a dormant volcano, so we headed back to the room to get ready. I put on some shorts, a tank top, and my runners—basically a replica of my Lara Croft outfit, only not splattered in mud.

We sunscreened up and stocked up on bottled water, then Josh called down to ask the valet to bring our car around. I was glad we'd decided to keep it after Hana. Not only could we get ourselves up to the crater, Josh could drive me to the airport in the morning.

My flight to Honolulu was at 7:00am, with a connection to Sydney at 11:00am. Seven in the morning is a ridiculous time to fly, but I hadn't wanted to stay in Hawaii without Josh, and it had been impossible to coordinate our flights any better than we had.

He was flying out of Maui later in the day, then from Honolulu to Chicago in the evening. His flight was a red-eye, with him landing on the morning of January third, then going straight to work. I felt for him. When I got home, I'd still be on school holidays, meaning I could sleep in until I recovered from my jet lag.

I shoved the thoughts aside. The last thing I wanted to think about was being in Sydney alone—Joshless.

*

The road up to the crater turned into a series of switchbacks—quite different from the Hana Highway, though, because these turns were one-eighties and in many sections, there were no guardrails. We stopped talking so Josh could concentrate. Then it started to get cold—*really* cold. As much as I wanted Josh to focus on his driving, it got to the point where I couldn't stand it any longer.

"Um, Josh? Do you mind if we put the roof up?"

"Yeah, it's getting kind of chilly, isn't it?"

Chilly? Where is this guy from, Antarctica? "Yeah, you could say that."

"It's kinda cool, though, driving with the top down, don't ya think?"

"Yes, 'cool' is the operative word."

"How about I just turn on the heat?" I looked at him as though he'd grown a second head. He didn't seem to notice and cranked up the heater on our feet, and we ended up driving to the top of the crater with toasted toes, but our top halves frozen.

An hour later, we got to the park entrance at the summit, paid for two adult passes, and pulled into the carpark. After parking the car, Josh finally put the roof up. It was far too late for that, as far as I was concerned. I had goose bumps on my goose bumps and my nipples were sore. I knew without looking that they'd turned blue.

When the roof slotted into place, Josh turned off the ignition. "Ready?" he asked with a smile. No! No, I was not ready! I had not dressed for freezing weather. I'd dressed for Maui beach weather. Josh's clothes weren't any more suitable than mine, but he didn't seem to care. *Yep, definitely from Antarctica.*

"Umm ..." I bit my lip.

"What?"

"It's really cold out there."

"It's not that bad."

"It's only fifty!" I said, using Fahrenheit so he would understand. And I knew what fifty meant in Celsius, too. It meant it was frigging cold.

He seemed annoyed with me which, considering the circumstances, I thought was rather unkind. Then he got out of the car and walked off. Well, that was *definitely* unkind. I sat there, pouting, but he didn't come back. I opened the car door and cold air rushed in. Why hadn't we done more research? We were supposed to be hiking the crater for the whole morning. I was going to be lucky to make it out of the carpark.

But still, we'd driven for more than an hour, and even from where I was, I could tell the scenery was worth enduring a little cold for. Unable to lock the car without the fob, I took Josh's backpack off the back seat and got out of the car. No matter how snarky he'd been, I didn't want his backpack to get stolen.

Standing next to the car, I tipped my head to the sun and tried to tell myself that it was warm, balmy—hot even. As convincing as I can be sometimes, I was not having it. Still, I soldiered on. I took my phone out of my pocket and tapped on the camera. Then I set off a brisk pace, determined to get as many photos as possible before other parts of me turned blue along with my nipples. They were hating me, by the way.

Everything I could see in every direction made it look like I'd landed on Mars. Rocks, from small pebbles to enormous boulders, dominated the landscape, covering it in a deep rusty red, and there was absolutely no plant life. Not surprising, I guessed, for a dormant volcano. The observatory rose from the red rock, its foundations in grey-coloured brick and its white domes a stark contrast to the red ground it stood on.

Walking away from the observatory, I stepped off the asphalt onto the rocky rim of the crater and realised we were above the cloud-line. What a unique feeling it was to stand somewhere and look *down* on clouds. I took some photos of the rusty red earth meeting the brilliant sky and snowy clouds—only three colours, but an utterly epic view.

Then I lifted the phone and took a selfie, my smile almost a grimace as my teeth started to chatter. I hadn't seen which way Josh had gone, but I hoped like hell it was to the observation deck, which was enclosed. I walked back towards the observatory and climbed the steps to the observation deck as fast as I could. It was a relief to step inside.

Josh had his back to me and was looking at the view I'd just photographed. A family of four was also there, the boys about four and seven chatting excitedly to their parents, who listened patiently.

I walked up behind Josh. "Hey." He didn't turn around.

"Hey," he said finally.

I stood next to him. "Sorry for being pouty before."

"It's okay," he said, after a moment.

"I was just disappointed. I really wanted to go on this hike,

271

and I'm annoyed I didn't dress more appropriately. Well, that we didn't."

I glanced at him and he nodded, his face set in a frown. "I'm sorry for being pissy."

"It's okay."

He looked at me and saw that I had his backpack. He took it from me. "Hey, thanks for bringing this."

"I didn't want to leave it in the car." Sometimes it's easier to talk about mundane things than about what's really bothering you, like our impending separation.

Josh took a deep breath and sighed, meeting my eyes with a sad smile. "I'm going to miss you, you know." Tears prickled my eyes. *Oh, please don't do that. Please don't say the one thing I don't want to think about.*

He put an arm around my neck and pulled me into a side hug. I wrapped my arms around his waist, and we stood looking at the view for a while. "I took some cool pics," I said eventually, sniffling a little.

"Yeah?" I nodded. "We should get a few more before we leave."

"Okay."

"You ready to go back out there?"

I smiled through my tears and ran a fingertip under each eye. "Bring on the cold!" I said a little too loudly. The family stopped talking and looked over their shoulders at me, which made me giggle. I ran out into the cold with Josh right behind me.

We drove back to the resort with the roof up!

*

Our plans for the day having backfired, we salvaged it by spending the afternoon in a hammock for two.

It was my first time in a hammock—yes, really—and I felt like I could stay there forever with my legs entwined with Josh's, a breeze gently caressing my skin, a good book on my Kindle, and an excellent margarita in my hand. Although, I'll admit that sipping a margarita while in a hammock is a little tricky, and I did spill some of it down my cleavage. Josh very graciously offered to lick it off when we got back to our room, which made me laugh, and that made me spill more of it down the front of me. It was an expensive—and sticky—way to consume a margarita.

As it was our last night together, Josh had booked us a beach-front cabana where we'd have a super-fancy private dinner. *The* dress needed a wash after all the dancing we'd done the night before, but I'd packed another one in a floaty red silk chiffon. It was cinched at the waist, then fell in waves to my knees, and it went perfectly with my strappy suede sandals.

This dress was pretty, rather than sexy, but when I stepped out of the bathroom, Josh whistled and looked at me hungrily. "You look amazing."

"Thank you. You look pretty nice, yourself." He was wearing his jeans with a fitted grey T-shirt under a navy blazer, and the grey shirt made his eyes even more intense than usual. He came over and kissed my neck, and I was glad I'd worn my hair up.

"Thank you," he said, his lips moving to my throat. "You know, we could just stay in and order room service."

"Joshua." The kisses continued. "Josh." I pushed him back

gently and looked him in the eye. "We're going to dinner." A smile curled up the corner of my lip.

His eyes narrowed. "Later, then."

"Oh, absolutely."

Dinner was *incredible*. "Aloha!" called a beautiful Hawaiian woman as we approached. She placed a lei of fresh pink frangipanis around each of our necks, their fragrance heady. Is there a scent that's more evocative of the tropics?

When we were seated, Josh ordered a bottle of bubbles from California. "So we can celebrate the start of the New Year, officially," he said. I thought it was a lovely idea. The waiter brought the bottle, showed Josh, who nodded, then cracked it with a well-practised whisper. He poured into two flutes, allowing the bubbles to settle so he could top them up. Then he disappeared, leaving us alone.

Josh raised his glass. "To the most incredible woman I've ever known." It was a beautiful toast, but heavily loaded with all the things we still hadn't said to each other.

I simply smiled, accepting the compliment, and clinked my flute against his. I took a sip. It was delicious—toasty, dry, and with a hint of honey.

The first course was a tomato stack and I mean, *literally* a stack of tomato slices, one green and others in varying shades of a sunset—yellow, orange, red, deep purple—all drizzled in olive oil and dotted with black pepper. I eyed the stack dubiously.

"What are you thinking over there?" he asked.

"I didn't think Hawaii was known for its tomatoes. Pineapple, yes. Coconut, sure."

He laughed and I was pretty sure it was *at* me. "Well, they're not going to be as good as Greek ones, but how about we just try them."

I picked up my knife and fork and sliced from the top of the stack down, getting several different colours into the one bite. I put it in my mouth, and then a miracle happened. I found out that there were tomatoes in the world as good as Greek ones—maybe even better.

I groaned and met Josh's eyes. He was having the same experience as me, I could tell. We swallowed our respective bites. "Oh, my god," we both said at the same time, and then laughed. We didn't speak as we finished our stacks, each of us savouring every bite.

I sat back, regarding my empty plate. "I can honestly say, if that's all there is for dinner, I'll leave here happy." He smiled, his hand extending across the table to take mine.

The waiter appeared, as if by magic, and cleared the plates, and another waiter came and topped up our bubbles. Josh and I sat in a comfortable silence as we watched the light from the nearly full moon dance on the water and waited for the next course.

It was crab—more specifically, hand-made crab tortellini in a white wine sauce with fresh herbs. The pillows of pasta were brimming with chunks of fresh crab and once again I was in food heaven.

"You keep moaning like that and they're going to think we're having sex in here," said my dinner companion. I smiled, resisting the urge to moan again, as a waiter topped up our drinks. I knew there were two of them, but honestly, I was so focused on the meal, they'd become interchangeable to me.

275

After a respectable pause in the proceedings, dessert arrived—roasted pineapple with coconut ice-cream and toasted coconut flakes. *Are you frigging kidding me?* The meal was battling it out for a place in my top five. Every bite of the dessert was a food orgasm. The only thing that stopped me from asking for another serving was that I was starting to feel full and I was planning on having an actual orgasm— or two—later on. A giant food baby does not make for a sexy time.

"Coffee, ma'am?" asked waiter number one as waiter number two cleared our dessert plates. I didn't even care about the "ma'am". He could have said, "Yo, bitch, want some coffee?" and I would have smiled at him in the same dreamy way that I did.

"No, thank you," I said, completely content and not wanting to taint what had been a perfect meal.

"Sir?"

"No, thank you. You've charged this to the room?" Josh asked.

"Yes, sir. I'll just get the check, so you can sign it."

"Thank you."

We held hands across the table while we waited. "That was incredible," I said. "Thank you so much for organising it."

"It was my pleasure."

"Did you choose the menu?" I hadn't even thought about it until that moment.

"No, it was the chef's choice, but I have to say, it was way better than anything I could have imagined."

"Mmm."

The waiter returned with the check, and Josh added a generous tip and signed it, handing it back with a smile.

"Thank you for looking after us so well," I said, standing up. I felt a little giddy from the bubbles, or maybe from the way Josh had been looking at me all night. He took my hand and we walked slowly back to our room, for the last time.

I had packed that afternoon, laying out my clothes for the plane in the bathroom. My flight was so early I wouldn't even get to eat breakfast until I got to the airport—and probably not until I got to Honolulu.

Whatever Josh and I had to say to each other before parting, we had to say it that night.

Our last time together—at least for the Hawaii trip, I hoped—was sweet and tender and completely different from the night before on the beach. Josh had come to know how to bring my body to the brink and beyond, and afterwards, I collapsed onto him, spent both physically and emotionally. I lay with my head on his chest while he twisted my curls around his fingers.

"I'm going to miss you too," I whispered, finally replying to what he'd said at the crater.

I felt him take in a big breath and I lifted my head. I wanted to see his face. His fingers abandoned my hair and he slipped his hand behind his head and rubbed his neck. I could tell from his expression that he was feeling conflicted; I'd seen that exact face quite a few times over the week.

"What?" I asked, not really wanting to know the answer.

He sighed again and my stomach clenched. Eventually, he spoke. "I know that you want to know what's going to happen next with us. You deserve to know that." I sat abruptly and pulled the sheet up to cover my nakedness, as though it could protect me from his words.

"But?" I asked. *Out with it, Josh.*

"But the truth is, I don't know."

I clenched my teeth as I willed myself not to cry and not to ruin such a beautiful, perfect night. Only it wasn't me who was ruining it. It was Josh. I wanted to tell him to stop talking so I could pretend it was all okay—that it was perfectly normal to want someone who wasn't quite sure if he wanted you back.

But the pragmatist in me knew I had to let him say his piece. I had to know where I stood with him. As much as it would break my heart if he didn't want a real relationship with me, I needed to know before this whole thing dragged on any longer.

His hand reached up to stroke the back of my arm and I tensed.

"Hey," he said. "Come back." He took hold of my arm and tugged gently. I resisted for a moment, then relented, tucking myself back into the nook under his arm, my head on his chest.

"I'm sorry. I know that's not what you want to hear." Still, I said nothing. "Sarah?"

More rejection from the guy who keeps telling me how amazing I am and how much he loves being with me.

"It's okay," I said finally. "I know you're just being honest." I felt an urgent need to distance myself from him, my anger bubbling up and about to overflow. I got out of the bed, making a beeline for the closet where I pulled out one of the white, fluffy robes. It felt good to ensconce myself in it—safe. I sat on the armchair next to the bed and only then did I dare to look at Josh. He was visibly upset, and I felt a twinge of guilt. I'd done that.

"Please come back to bed." I shook my head.

"Look, you're right," I said. "I don't want to hear that you're still unsure about how you feel. I guess I hoped that I would come here, and we would rediscover each other, and you'd finally realise that you want to be with me—for real—and whether you know it or not, Josh, you do. I've felt it." His frown intensified, and I knew I was probably hurting him, but I didn't stop. Instead, I said the one thing that would permanently damage us.

"But you know what? You've actually made it easier for me, because it's been really hard being with two men and now, I don't have to choose."

As the words came out of my mouth—during those very seconds—I knew I'd gone too far. I'd pushed Josh over the edge into full-blown misery. Tears sprang to his eyes and he looked away from me, his face incredulous.

I put my head in my hands, wishing I could take it all back, the tears flowing between my fingers. "I'm so sorry, Josh. I'm *so* sorry." He was crying. I could hear him, but I couldn't bear to look, and I knew I couldn't be the one to comfort him.

Finally, after agonising over what I'd said and the irreparable damage I'd done to him, to us, I heard his voice. "I asked you not to see him." That's all he said.

And it broke me.

All that time since London, through planning our trip to Hawaii, I'd assumed that he *must* have known I'd seen James. And he hadn't.

He climbed out of the bed and went into the bathroom. I heard him blowing his nose and I stood up and got some tissues for my own. I didn't know how to fix it. How could I fix it?

I got into bed and pulled the covers up to my neck, chewing so viciously on my lower lip that I drew blood. I turned off the lamp on my side of the bed and waited.

Eventually, Josh came out of the bathroom and turned off the lamp on his side. He climbed into bed, staying as far away from me as possible, his back to me. I stared at the ceiling, unable to sleep, unable to move, waves of guilt washing over me.

How had I thought I could sustain relationships with two men? What the hell was I doing? How could I hurt him like that? And I knew Josh cared about me—maybe not in the way I'd hoped for, but it wasn't nothing. It still could have worked out between us.

That is, before I'd ruined it.

I felt him shift beside me and a hand reached for mine. I grabbed it tight. "I'm so sorry, Josh," I croaked.

His grip tightened, but he said nothing. Eventually, I fell into a restless sleep, the alarm on my phone screaming at me at 5:00am. *Stupid. Fucking. Thing.*

I leapt up out of bed and turned it off in one motion. Josh didn't seem to stir beside me, but maybe he was just pretending to sleep. I would if I was him. God, I'd been horrible to him the night before.

I got into the shower, a sick feeling in my stomach, but it wouldn't go away no matter how hot I made the water. I showered quickly, got dressed in my travel clothes, and looked at myself in the mirror.

You utter cow, Sarah.

I was furious with myself. I had to at least try to fix things before I left. And I couldn't have Josh drive me to the airport. It was way too much to ask after what I'd said to him.

I didn't bother with makeup, just brushed my teeth and slathered moisturiser on my face. I packed away the rest of my toiletries and taking a deep breath, opened the bathroom door. I had to face him.

Not only was he awake, he was dressed. "I'm so sorry," I blurted, rooted to the spot. His jaw tightened and he nodded a short, sharp nod.

"Me too."

What?

"You don't have anything to be sorry for," I wailed.

"Yes, I do." I shook my head and he put his hand up. "I do, Sarah. I've been thinking about this most of the night, so please let me speak."

"Okay," I said, my voice still croaky. I walked over to the armchair and sat down, pulling my knees up to my chest, building myself a fort against more heartbreak.

"Everything between us has been on my terms, from the moment we met until now. I've been as honest with you—and myself—as I could, but I've always had what *I* wanted." I watched him, his face set in a scowl as he explained his innermost thoughts.

"That you saw James in London, that's on me." I went to speak, to protest, but he dismissed the interruption and kept talking. "That night at dinner on Naxos, when it turned out the two of you had already met"—I could tell that it stung him to think about it—"I didn't want you to go off with him then, but I didn't ask you not to. And I could tell you wanted me to say something. You were almost begging me to. And I didn't. I let you go off with the handsome, rich guy, who made us all laugh, and seemed like a really great guy."

He had worked himself into a lather, and part of me—okay, *most* of me—wanted to go to him and soothe him and tell him it wasn't his fault. But something held me in place.

"And you know, over the past few months, I thought about asking if you saw him in London—and every time I chickened out, because I think I knew. And I can hardly blame you. I mean, if I was you, then I'd be into James too. And it's not like I ever offered you more than this"—he threw his arms out, encompassing the room, the resort, the whole trip—"this *vacationship*." He spat out the word as though it tasted nasty in his mouth.

Then he sat heavily on the edge of the bed, seemingly spent, the tears streaming down his face. It would soon be time to leave for the airport, but that wasn't what I was thinking about. My mind had settled on one nauseating thought.

We're breaking up.

When I spoke, my voice was thick with emotion, barely audible. "So, what do we do now?"

He shook his head, his eyes fixed on his hands which were wringing in his lap. He took a deep breath, then shook them out. "Now I take you to the airport, and we each go home. After that, I don't know." He looked at me then. "Can I come over there?"

I nodded, tears taking hold as I leapt to my feet. He was across the room in a heartbeat and we wrapped our arms around each other, holding on tightly. It was the hug of two people who shared something special, but had no idea what would come of it.

Essentially, we were right back where we were when we'd said goodbye in Greece. Only the feelings were deeper, and the situation was far more precarious.

"I don't want to let you go, but you'll miss your plane," he said after several moments.

"I know. Goodbyes suck and there's so much more to talk about." I pulled away from him, so I could see his face. He looked pale and defeated, his eyes and nose red. It made me feel even worse, but I forced myself to look him in the eye.

"I'm *so* sorry about last night, Josh. I was a complete bitch and I am so ashamed. You didn't deserve that." Fresh tears sprung to his eyes. "I *do* care about you—you're one of the most important people in my life. I hate that we're saying goodbye like this, especially because this week has been brilliant. I have loved being here with you, okay?"

He nodded, much like a sad child would, and sniffled.

"And, I'm going to take a taxi to the airport."

"No, I—"

"Yes, it's just easier that way. I hate long, drawn-out goodbyes."

"Okay," he conceded. "Let me help you bring your bags down, though."

"All right. I just need to splash some water on my face." I let go of him and went back in the bathroom. I washed the tears and snot from my face and patted it dry with the fluffy hand towel. I had no idea what would happen with me and Josh, or if I'd ever see him again. It was a horrifying thought, but it was the truth.

I put on a smile I didn't feel and opened the bathroom door. I was greeted by Maui, flippers out and ready for a hug. I burst out laughing.

Josh's head appeared above Maui's, a shy smile on his lips. "You dork," I teased.

"Maui said it was getting far too heavy in here and he hates it when we fight."

"Oh, yeah? He's very articulate for a turtle."

"Turtles are wise beings."

"Indeed. Come here, Maui," I said, taking him from Josh and hugging him to me. It did feel rather nice.

"Ready?"

"No, but let's go."

We left the room with Josh walking ahead and rolling my suitcase behind him. I carried Maui in one arm with my carry-on bag slung over the other shoulder. My nose was still running from all the crying, and I reached up to wipe it with the back of my hand.

I'm going to miss you so much.

I tried not to think it, but it became a destructive mantra playing over and over in my head. Josh, my bestie, my gorgeous, goofy, funny, sweet Josh.

Once the taxi pulled up and my bags were loaded into the

boot, we sped through the goodbye. Even though there was still so much to say, there was no use making our parting any more excruciating than it already was.

"Thank you again, for everything. I really did have a wonderful time," I said, hugging Maui to me.

"Me too." He pulled me into a final hug, Maui caught between us.

"Love you," I said, just like I would to any of my closest friends.

"Me too," he said. And before it hit me that he'd said he loved me—well, sort of—he bundled me into the taxi, closed the door, and waved me off as the car drove away. Just like he had in Athens. I lifted a hand in a benign final goodbye.

It may have been the saddest, most amicable break-up ever.

And then I realised we hadn't settled the room charges. *Crap*. I pulled my phone out of my pocket and shot him a text.

The room charges! Sorry. Will fix you up when I get home.
S

The reply came a couple of minutes later.

No need. Had always intended to cover that. Love, Josh
x

Love! *Oh, fuck. What have I done?* How had I screwed things up so mammothly? I let loose the biggest boo-hooey cry I'd had in ages—the poor driver. By the time he dropped me off in front of the airport terminal, it had simmered down to a whimpering sniffle. I hoisted my carry-on onto my left shoulder, tucked Maui under my left arm, and grabbed my suitcase handle with my right hand. It was a little awkward, but I only had to make it to check-in.

Once I'd checked my suitcase and was walking to my gate, an older Hawaiian woman stopped me. "You have a honu," she said, a warm smile on her face.

"A what, sorry?" I sniffled, my nose still running.

"A honu." She pointed to Maui.

"Oh, that's what it's called? In Hawaiian?"

She nodded. "They are very special—they are guides, for your life. A honu will show you the way and keep you on your path." I liked the sound of that—I *needed* some of that.

She patted me on the arm and looked into my swollen, red eyes with her deep brown ones. "It will be all right," she said, and I can't explain it, but calm washed over me. I nodded and smiled. She smiled back, then she left me and my honu to get on with the business of finding my path and making it all okay.

I'm not sure how many grown women get on flights with giant stuffed animals, but the flight crews on the island hopper to Honolulu and then on the long-haul flight to Sydney didn't bat an eye. I was glad; Maui was good company and he smelled like Josh.

When the plane touched down on the tarmac at Sydney airport, I reached for my phone and turned it on.

A slew of messages arrived in quick succession.

Lindsey:

Nick is picking you up. Text him when you're through immi-gration. Can't wait to see you and hear all the juicy goss.

I wasn't sure how juicy Lins would find the whole "Josh and I broke up and I'm miserable" thing, but I also couldn't wait to see her—to get a hug and a stiff drink and a heavy dose of Lindsey comfort.

Cat:

So???? How was it? FaceTime me. Soon! I want details.

Maybe I could FaceTime Cat from Lindsey's, so I didn't have to repeat every excruciating detail.

James:

Flights are booked. See you in two weeks, beautiful!

While that message would normally have made me jump up and down with delight, the timing was atrocious. I would have to analyse how I felt about James's upcoming work trip to Sydney later—*much* later.

Then this one:

I miss you already. I'm so sorry about how we left things. I need to go home and think it all through, but don't make any big decisions yet, okay? And let me know that you got home safely. Love, Josh xx

Okay, so maybe we hadn't broken up.

PART THREE

Chapter 18

"So, the old guy is coming in two weeks and you and the young guy are in love?"

Nick, who was in "annoying big brother" mode, was driving me home from the airport. Well, more precisely, he was driving me to his and Lindsey's house, so I could see my cat. I hoped Domino liked Maui as much as I did.

I was also staying the night. Lindsey had insisted after I'd texted her from Sydney airport. Apparently, she didn't want me to be alone after what had happened between me and Josh. To be frank, I didn't want me to be alone either. The plane ride, with only my thoughts and Maui for company, had been hard enough.

Maybe they'd let me move in with them.

"Well, no. Maybe. I don't know, but you're making it sound worse than it is." Who was I trying to kid? It was exactly as bad as he'd said. "And he's *not old*." I heard the annoyance in my voice, I but didn't care. Nick could handle it; he'd been on the receiving end of far worse.

"Isn't he, like, fifty or something?"

Sandy Barker

"He's fifty-two. And he looks really good for his age."

"And how old is the young one?" I sighed an exasperated sigh. Emotional, jet-lagged, sleep-deprived Sarah is an uglier beast than hungover Sarah.

"He's nearly twenty-nine," I said, fudging Josh's age a little. He wasn't even twenty-eight-and-a-half yet. And just so you know, it's possible to grind your teeth when you talk.

"So, the old one could be the young one's dad."

"Oh, my god, Nick. Seriously, please shut the fuck up!"

He chuckled and I rolled my eyes, both of us playing our parts in a routine we'd done a hundred times. Nick knew I really did love him, just like I'd love an *actual* brother who annoyed the hell out of me but would do anything for me— like pick me up from the airport after I'd broken up with my boyfriend in Hawaii.

We were quiet the rest of the way to their house.

Lins came out to meet us after we pulled up in the driveway. "Okay to get the bag, babe?" she asked Nick. It was her not-so-subtle reminder for him to get my suitcase out of the boot, because he was already halfway up the path to the front door when she said it.

He went back for the bag while Lins took my carry-on from me. She eyed Maui curiously.

"He's my turtle," I said, a little defensively.

She shook a flipper. "Nice to meet you, uh ..." She looked at me.

"Maui," I prompted.

"Maui." She smiled. "He's cute. Now come inside before we get eaten alive by mozzies." Nick passed us on the path.

"I'll pop this in your room, Sez."

"Thanks, Nick." They called their guest room "Sarah's room" because I stayed over so much, one of the many benefits of having a cat over a dog. For a single night away, I could leave some food out for Domino, kiss him goodbye and he wouldn't even lift his sleepy little head to say "'hello" when I came home the next day. As long as he got fed, he was cool with my frequent sleepovers.

Inside the entryway, Lins put down my carry-on and I put Maui on top. "Domino!" I called, as though he would come; he's his own cat.

Just then, I heard a high-pitched "meow" and—knock me down with a feather—Domino came running to me from the living room. I scooped him up and hugged him, his purring a much-welcomed welcome home. I nuzzled his fluffy black and white fur, then burst into tears.

"Here," said Lins, taking him from me and putting him down. "Come with me." She took my hand and led me into the living room. "Sit." I sat, immediately grabbing one of their forty-seven throw pillows, pulling it onto my lap, and hugging it. Pillow. Maui. Domino. I just wanted to hug things.

"Tea, gin, wine, or something else?" I looked at my bestie with love and appreciation. When I sniffled, she handed me three tissues. I figured she could sense some serious boo-hooing was impending, and Lins didn't mess about when it came to crying. She was *prepared*.

"Wine. And water. Water first," I hiccupped.

She disappeared into the kitchen, which made up a third of what I called their "great room"—that's the kitchen-dining-living combo for us mere mortals who rent modest little flats. The whole thing was very "Sydney", but the kitchen especially. It was large and impressive and grown-up, with polished concrete countertops, glass splashbacks, and self-closing drawers. It was filled with wonderful kitchen things like an *actual* espresso machine, a hideaway cupboard for the toaster and kettle—yes, really—and a double-door fridge. Maybe that was why I hung out there so much. I had kitchen envy.

I noted that Nick was lying low, leaving Lins and me to talk, and I could hear the sound of the TV coming from the study. See? He's a good guy underneath.

Lins returned from the kitchen with a tray—another super-grown-up thing to have—laden with all the fixings for a good long catch up: two glasses of iced water, two glasses of white wine, and a bowl of Castelvetrano olives. I went for the olives first. Have I mentioned how much I love olives?

"Okay, so how did you leave things?"

It was a seemingly simple question, but the answer churned my insides. How *did* we leave things? Badly. Really, *really* badly. Even though Josh and I had both put on brave faces for our goodbye, I couldn't help feeling that I'd done irreparable damage to us.

Why did I say that thing about being with two men?

Lins was watching me patiently while I ate three olives and spat the pits into my hand. She reached for them and I tipped them into hers. She went back into the kitchen, threw them out, and returned with a tiny ceramic bowl, which she placed next to the bowl of olives. She really was the consummate hostess.

I drank half a glass of water, then took a sip of wine. It was a South Australian riesling—delicious, of course.

Then I wiped my nose and launched into a retelling of the horrible conversation from the night before—at least it felt like the night before, but with the time difference, I wasn't quite sure how long it had been. I finished my tale of woe by showing her Josh's text, the one I'd got when I landed. I took the last swig of my wine as she read it.

She'd been quiet throughout my story—she's an excellent listener—but after I showed her the text, she asked me, "Did you let him know you arrived safely?"

"Oh, no. Crap." I put down my empty glass, then took the phone from her and looked at it, frowning.

"What do I say?"

"Maybe start with, 'I got here safely'."

"And then what?"

"I don't know, sign your name?" She was teasing me a little and I looked up to see her smiling at me.

I nodded and snuffled up some snot. She handed me another three tissues and I blew my nose. Then I wrote a message to Josh. It took me three goes, deleting what I wrote twice, before I came up with this masterpiece:

Hi. I arrived safely. Staying with Lins and Nick tonight. Talk soon. S x

Lins held her hand out so she could see it and I held up my phone. "Good. Right to the point." I tapped "send". "You know, and I don't want to give you false hope, but his text ... it doesn't seem like he's decided it over."

"Really? I mean, that's kind of what I thought too. But then I worried that it was just wishful thinking."

"Well, you probably need to talk to Josh. I mean, I've never met the guy, so I *literally have no idea* what's going through his head, but ..." She shrugged. "Well, you know?" No, I did *not* know. "Now ..." She paused and I could sense what was coming. "What's happening with James?"

"Ugh." I leant back against the couch and put the pillow over my face. "I don't know!" I wailed, my voice muffled.

"Sez." she tugged at the pillow and I put it back in my lap. "You don't have to decide anything tonight, or tomorrow, or even this week, for that matter, okay?" I nodded, suddenly fascinated with the tassels on the pillow. "But you do need to decide if you're going to see James when he comes. And soon." Then she added, "Ish. Soon-*ish*."

I looked at her. "I *have* to see James." I could see she wanted to say something, as a small frown had appeared between her brows. "What?"

She shook her head. "No, it'll muddy the waters."

"Just say it."

"Don't worry about it."

Lindsey was usually free with the truth and *far* more tactful than her husband, but she was hedging, and it made me nervous. "Please just say it."

"Look, I can't imagine what it feels like to be in your

situation. I mean, you obviously have serious feelings for both of them ..."

"But?"

"*But* you got a taste of what it would be like to lose Josh and it *sucked*, right?" I nodded, my own frown deepening. "So, doesn't that tell you something? Doesn't that mean you should let James go?"

Did it? I thought back to how I felt saying goodbye to James in London and tears prickled my eyes. It felt awful, *that's* how it felt. And despite Josh's text, I *didn't* know where things stood with him. Even if I hadn't ruined everything with my horrible outburst, he was still unsure of how he felt about being in a relationship. He'd been very clear about that. What if I let James go and things didn't work out with Josh?

What if I'm left with no one?

It was an utterly selfish and self-pitying thought, and I knew it. So, what I said to my best friend was, "Maybe."

She was kind enough to let me off the hook.

*

The two weeks after I arrived home from Hawaii were an emotional rollercoaster. It's a cliché, I know, but there's no better way to describe the undulations of my love life. I'd talked to Josh a couple of times on FaceTime, but only briefly. Neither of us seemed to want to have the conversation we needed to have, so we just chit-chatted about unimportant things.

He had also sent me a couple of very long emails—one of them obviously written after he'd had a few drinks. The second email, which arrived within two hours of the first and before I read either of them, was to clarify some of what he'd said in the first.

The gist was: he had strong feelings for me (no kidding?); he forgave me for seeing James *and* for telling him about it (but I hadn't forgiven myself); he wanted *my* forgiveness for being so selfish (I'd weighed that up against what I did and Josh came out *way* in front); he asked me if I still had feelings for him (uh, yes!); and then he asked me if I wanted to see him again (definitely, but ...).

My reply was a lot shorter than either of his emails and, of course, I agonised over every word. It took me more than an hour to write this:

Hi,

   You're being gracious saying you forgive me, but I'm grateful—I'll take it. And I hadn't really thought about how we've been together on your terms, but you don't need to apologise for that. I'm a big girl, it takes two to tango, and other applicable clichés. ☺

   I left Hawaii feeling awful, thinking I may have lost you for good, so I'm glad we're okay—or at least, mostly okay. As for seeing you again, I want to. But I think we need to figure out if we're just friends or if we're more than that before we make any plans. Is that okay?

   Sarah x

That last part was the hardest—deciding what we were to each other before making plans to see each other again—and I still hadn't heard back.

The only thing I knew for sure was that I didn't want to lose Josh completely. If it *was* only friendship between us, then I would find a way to be okay with that.

But there was also James to consider. I knew that if he and I worked out—as a couple—then it was highly unlikely Josh would want to remain friends. That thought, when it lifted its ugly, acne-pocked head, made me feel like crap, *and* like a crappy person. I tried to ignore it as much as possible.

And even though Lindsey and Cat were against it—for a fortnight, they'd tempered their comments with concern, but it was clear where they both stood—I knew I needed to see James again. Otherwise, how could I know for sure who I wanted to be with?

My topsy-turvy love life had left me with only one certainty: love triangles suck.

*

I climbed out of an Uber in front of the Ovolo Hotel in Woolloomooloo. James had arrived the night before and had spent most of the day with the people from the Museum of Contemporary Art. We were meeting for dinner, and I was dressed up—*way* up.

I was wearing a floaty lilac dress by Review, which crossed over the bust and was cinched in at the waist, along with my lilac suede high-heeled Mary Janes and a matching clutch.

My hair was pinned up in a French twist, but with my curls being their usual obnoxious selves, I'd made it a loose twist, allowing some of them to frame my face. My makeup was mostly neutral, but I'd gone with lilac-pink lipstick.

I also carried a small overnight bag. James had made it clear he wanted me to spend the night, and I wasn't going to play coy and squeeze a toothbrush and some clean knickers into my clutch, like I'd done in London. There were no pretences this time. I was being a grown-up!

I'd been to the beautician *and* the hairdresser the day before. Wax—check; pedi—check; roots—check. I looked as sophisticated as it was possible for me to look, like maybe you could take me to a polo match or something—actually, not in those shoes. They'd just sink into the grass and get ruined.

Anyway, I looked good, and I was ready to see my fifty-something boyfriend. I really did need to find a better word to describe him. He was definitely *not* a boy.

The hotel was typical of Sydney, chic in its casualness. There was no doorman, so I made my own way inside and took in the funky foyer, which was clearly designed to highlight the features of the heritage building it once was. I approached the reception desk and a woman wearing a crisp white shirt and black trousers greeted me with a polite smile.

"Hi, I'm here to see James Cartwright. Can you please tell me what room he's in?"

Apparently, that's not how things work at high-end hotels, even casually chic ones. "One moment," she said, as she picked up the phone and called James's room. "Hello, Mr Cartwright. I have a Miss ..." She looked at me enquiringly.

A Sunset in Sydney

All the sophistication I'd felt emerging from my Uber dissolved under her overly polite stare. "Parsons," I said, a slight frog in my throat, as though I was unsure of my own name. She repeated my name into the phone, and then said, "Of course." She put down the phone and this time the smile reached her eyes. She gave me his room number and directions.

I had a choice—stairs to the second floor or the elevator. Another time, another occasion, I would have sprinted up the stairs, grateful for the incidental exercise. But I was dressed to woo, and if I was going to spend any time that day panting and glistening with sweat, I didn't want it to be from climbing stairs.

In the short elevator ride, my mouth turned into the Sahara and I felt traitorous dampness under my arms. It had been nearly four months since I'd seen him in person and my stomach added a gymnastics routine to the trifecta of nerves. At James's door, I took a steadying breath, then tentatively knocked.

After a few moments, it opened and there he was. My heart leapt as he enveloped me in his arms. "Hello, beautiful," he said, his lips in my hair.

"Hi," I said, wrapping an arm around his neck. He smelled divine, like he had when I'd met him in Greece and seen him again in London—citrusy and scrummy and undeniably manly.

James broke the hug first and, with his arms still around me, looked down at my face. "I missed you," he whispered, tracing my cheek with his fingertip.

I gulped, his overt masculinity and intense expression working in tandem to awaken my nethers. "I missed you too,"

I croaked. He kissed me then, and I didn't even care that I'd spent ten minutes applying my lipstick. I'd brought it with me. I could reapply.

This man wants you, Sarah. You! Of all people!

My inner voice could be a total cow sometimes. I wished she'd shut the hell up.

The kiss ended and James laughed, and I quickly realised that it was at himself. "I haven't even let you come inside," he said, pulling on my hand. "Or put your bag down. Here, let me." He took it from me. "Terrible manners," he said, shaking his head at himself. "It's this way." *Is he nervous?* I'd seen him like that a few times, and it always seemed incongruous with the confident man I knew, but it was also endearing, and my heart tugged a little.

He led the way from the foyer into the room—a *suite*, actually—and placed my bag at the foot of a staircase. I was too distracted by the grandeur of my surroundings to say anything about his supposed lack of manners.

The suite had a large living room with a fireplace and a bar—an *actual* bar—and the staircase led to a loft bedroom and study, which I could see from my vantage point. The most spectacular feature, however, was the incredible view of downtown Sydney, with the sails of the Opera House peeking out over the treetops of the Botanical Gardens.

The décor was a little more modern than I would have chosen for my own place, but it was stylish and edgy. I eyed the couches suspiciously. They were low, leather, and all right angles. They looked incredibly uncomfortable.

"Can I get you something to drink? Our dinner reservation

isn't until eight." I stopped gawking at the room and turned back to James.

"Um, yes please. What do you have?"

He smiled then and indicated the bar—*Oh right, the bar!* "I think it's safe to say we have many options."

"Well, let's have a look." I walked over and went behind the bar, taking a cursory inventory. It had quite the selection. There were ten bottles of various top-shelf liquors, a fridge full of mixers, and a wine fridge with a dozen bottles of red and white wine and three bottles of bubbles.

"Right, lots to choose from." James sat on one of the stools opposite me, an amused smile on his lips. Perhaps he thought I was cute, playing bartender.

"Lady's choice," he said.

I only knew how to make a couple of cocktails and, of course, I could make a mean gin and tonic, but I'd need limes for that. I looked under the bar. There were limes—a bowl of them, plus a sharp knife and a cutting board. They really did think of everything when you had the penthouse. But it took only a moment to decide that a gin and tonic was a bad idea—too, well, too *Josh*.

"Right," I said. "I'll make a Nineteen Dollars Off."

He laughed. "Is that a cocktail?"

"Yes," I said, a slightly defensive edge in my voice. "Cat and I made it up the last time I was in London. Well, not the *last*, last time, but the time before that. Although in London it's called a 'Nine Pounds Off'."

"Of course it is." He was playing along, even though I was sure he had no idea what I was talking about.

"It got the name, because if you bought it at a bar, it would cost twenty-five dollars or in the UK, around twelve pounds. But if you make it at home, it's a lot cheaper."

"Ahhh," said the wealthy man. I felt a bit daft, realising I should have made up another name for the cocktail, so I moved the proceedings along.

"Anyway, it's got tequila in it. Do you like tequila?"

"Love tequila."

"Good!" I got to work. I sliced up two limes and squeezed them into the cocktail shaker. I added three shots of tequila. It was Jose Cuervo Reserva De La Familia, which was a huge step up from the Cuervo Cat and I had used when we created the cocktail. This one was probably meant for sipping not mixing, but desperate times and all that. Next was a shot of Cointreau. Then I remembered the drink had grapefruit juice in it. *Crap.*

Grapefruit juice is not your usual mixer, but I checked the little fridge just in case. No grapefruit, but they did have unsweetened orange juice—no pulp. It would have to do. I added a generous glug, about six shots worth, then added ice and started shaking. I threw in some flourishes to amuse James, who broke into a wide smile, but I avoided throwing anything into the air. As an amateur, I knew my limitations.

I took two martini glasses down from the shelf behind me and decanted the drinks. Then I popped a can of soda water, topping up each drink with a little fizz. I sliced up a third lime, squeezed in some more juice and added a slice to the rim of each drink. Feel free to write that down, by the way—it's an excellent cocktail.

"Voila!" I pushed one of the glasses over to his side of the bar. "The Nineteen Dollars Off."

He clapped, which could have come off as condescending, but didn't. He seemed genuinely delighted with my little performance. With a smile on my face, I bowed my head to acknowledge my audience. He lifted his glass and I lifted mine.

"To Sarah, who takes my breath away with her beauty and hidden talents." My inner voice didn't make a peep and I accepted the compliment with a clink of glasses and a self-satisfied smile. We each took a sip, James watching me over the rim of his glass.

"That's spectacular," he said, then took another sip.

"Why thank you."

"Definitely worth the whole twelve pounds." I laughed. "Now come around to this side. I don't like you being so far away."

I moved around the other side of the bar and sat on the stool next to James. He sipped his cocktail and looked at me as though he was also drinking me in. His left hand stroked up and down my leg.

"How was your meeting today?" I asked, like a proper girlfriend.

He smiled. "Good, yes. There were several, actually, and the gist is, they want me to curate a collection of contemporary artists, both from Australia and abroad."

"Oh, that's amazing!"

"Which would mean ..." he said, putting his glass down and clasping my legs between his hands. "That I'll be spending quite a lot of time in Sydney over the next few months."

Oh. My. God.

"And," he added tentatively, "I was thinking that while I'm in Sydney, you could come and stay with me here, at the Ovolo." The words hung in the air, his eyes filled with hope and excitement and locked onto mine. I knew I needed to say something, but my mind was brimming with thoughts, each competing for my attention—*We're going to be together, just like he promised. Wait, does the Ovolo allow pets? Why doesn't he just stay at my place? Would he want to stay at my place?* And then this one—*But what about me and Josh?*

I must have looked as dumbfounded as I felt, because he broke into a self-deprecating smile and shook his head a little. "Anyway, nothing has to be decided now ..."

Crap, I'd hesitated too long, and I'd hurt him. "No—sorry, James, I just ..." I leapt off the stool and threw my arms around his neck. "It's wonderful news—really." He hugged me back, his warm throaty laughter echoing throughout the cavernous room. At least one of us believed me.

*

Dinner that night was at Aria. *Aria!* I'd never been, but it was high on my bucket list of Australia's best restaurants. Walking in, I felt like I did the two times I'd been upgraded to business class—trying to look like I belonged while simultaneously gawping at the opulence.

We were seated at a table next to the window, an unobstructed view of Sydney Harbour laid out before us.

There's something you should know if you've never been

to Sydney. There's simply no other cityscape that is quite as spectacular as Circular Quay with its flurry of ferry traffic, the Sydney Opera House, and the Sydney Harbour Bridge together in one vista.

And at sunset, from that vantage point, the sails of the Opera House lit up and the silhouette of the bridge etched against a backdrop of watercolour hues, it was breathtaking.

"This is my favourite view in Sydney," said my date.

It had just become my favourite view too, but I tore my eyes away from the sunset. "So, you've been to Aria before then?"

"I come whenever I'm in Sydney, yes. Matt is an old friend." He meant Matt Moran, the chef and owner, and I geeked out a little. Matt Moran! Maybe I'd get to meet him. Then I remembered our lunch in London at The Summerhouse and Paulie the chef. "James, do you only go to restaurants where you know the chef?" I teased.

"Always," he deadpanned, then smiled. "Actually, I only go to restaurants where the food is exceptional and it feels like home. When you travel as much as I do, feeling like you're at home is important. It can get very lonely." *I know just what you mean.*

He dropped his eyes and I saw the furrow between his brows deepen for a moment. The frown was gone almost as soon as it had arrived, and he pulled his mouth into a faux smile and met my eyes. I laid my hand on his and squeezed it.

The moment evaporated when we were interrupted to hear the specials. Then we looked over our menus and I decided to start with the mud crab, one of the specials, followed by the John Dory for an all-seafood meal. James ordered a bottle of wine without looking at the list and without waiting for the sommelier. The waiter nodded his head subtly and left us to our conversation.

"I completely understand the need to find that sense of home when you're travelling," I said. He tipped his head to the side and encouraged, I continued. "When I ran tours, I would always unpack a few things, even if we were only there for a night—just to create a sense of 'home'.

"The site crew were important, too. They'd welcome us like we were family, even if we were meeting for the first time. Sometimes it was a little forced, the whole 'we're a family' thing, but I did have genuine friends on the circuit. I'd often get a nice surprise when I arrived somewhere and found out who was on site."

He looked baffled. "The company didn't track that kind of information online?"

I laughed. "Uh, no. The company still operated like it did in the 90s. There was no central database or dashboard to log in to, so there was no way of knowing how our tours would criss-cross or parallel with other tours. Archaic, really."

"And you toured for how long? I don't think you've said."

"I just did it for a couple of seasons, although they were quite long—from February to November."

"Why only two?"

"I missed having a real home." He nodded, his lips pulled into a tight, smile—a commiseration from a fellow traveller, I figured. "I loved the actual travel," I added, "but the job was hellishly lonely sometimes, like what you said earlier.

"I mean, my clients were all on holiday and I was working pretty much twenty-four-seven. And I was responsible for *everything*. If it went wrong, I had to fix it. If it went right, it was part of the seamless fabric of the tour. I didn't get credit—not that that's why I did the job—but 'perfect' was the benchmark, you know?"

"I do, yes."

"Is that how you felt about your job in finance."

"To a degree. It was a self-imposed perfection, mostly. Of course, in finance, a mistake can mean millions lost, but I was driven to go above and beyond what was expected—self-imposed and *completely* unsustainable. I was not my best self then."

It surprised me to learn we'd shared similar experiences in such vastly different jobs. Of course, James had had a *career* in finance and being a tour manager was not the kind of job you made a career out of. Well, not for me anyway.

I could have stuck it out a few more years if it hadn't meant selling off a piece of my soul on a regular basis—every time I said goodbye to a dear friend not knowing when I'd see them again, or smiled at a client who was an utter troll, or fended off unwanted advances from certain vendors, or worked twenty-hour days through a head cold or the flu, hiding my misery from my clients with medicine and makeup.

"When I moved home and went back to teaching, it felt right for me."

"From how you talk about it, it seems like teaching is your passion."

"In a way, yes. I enjoy working with the kids, especially

those lightbulb moments when you can *see* that something has clicked for them, or has resonated somehow. They're quite incredible people—the little ratbags," I added affectionately. "They can be exhausting at times, of course—such a diverse group, all with their foibles and insecurities, their dreams—but on the whole, they're the reason I stay with it.

"And, of course, there are parts I endure, like the endless paperwork, but that's the same for every job, right?" Then I realised what I'd said and who I'd said it to. "Except maybe yours."

He smiled a wry smile. "You'd be surprised, I think."

"Oh, really?"

"Two words—customs forms." I made a face and he smiled, his eyes doing that sexy crinkly thing. "Exactly," he added.

I was sure that James had a team of people employed to handle such mundanities as customs forms, but it wouldn't have always been that way. I knew that his success was the result of twenty years' hard work.

Twenty years—geez. Twenty years ago, I was in high school. I was one of those little ratbags who asked a million questions and had ballsy dreams about conquering the world.

James pulled me from my thoughts with another question. "So, with your work, the joy of the lightbulb moment, as you say, it's something you could do from almost anywhere, yes?"

Was he just making conversation, or was he asking because he wanted me to move to London? I'd thought about it, moving back to London—of course I had. If James and I ended up together, one of us would eventually move, right? And yes, he travelled a lot, but we'd still want to share a home base—a *home*—and James certainly had a nice one of those.

"Well, yes, I suppose. I mean, I taught in London, as you know, and I've sometimes wondered about living in a non-English speaking country, maybe teaching English."

"Exactly right. Education will always be a worldwide endeavour, and of course, so much learning takes place online these days. There are those opportunities too." I wasn't sure why, but something about his comment didn't sit well with me. But before I could respond, we were interrupted again by the arrival of the wine and the business of tasting and pouring. James made a generic toast "to Sydney", and after touching the rim of my glass to his, I took a sip. Delicious—but of course it was. It was a Western Australian chardonnay.

"So, Sarah, I was thinking we could head over to New Zealand for the weekend." It was a total non sequitur and I nearly choked on my wine.

Was this what life with James would be like, him whisking me away to some gorgeous destination at a moment's notice? Traveller Sarah was very much on board, so to speak, but practical Sarah—the one who was preparing for the new school year, the one who had brunch plans with her girlfriends that Sunday—wasn't quite so sure. Hiding my raspy coughs behind my hand, I looked up to see those eye crinkles again. "So, what do you think?"

I cleared my throat. "Um, that sounds amazing," I replied, traveller Sarah taking the lead. "I've only been there once, and it was ages ago."

"Where did you go?"

"Christchurch, then up to Marlborough." He nodded. "Have you been to New Zealand?"

"A few times." He didn't elaborate, obviously not the type of person to go on and on about all the amazing places he'd been.

"So where were you thinking we'd go? I asked.

"Well, I'd love to take you to one of the sounds. Milford is probably my favourite."

"Oh, that's supposed to be beautiful."

He grinned and laid out the rest of his plan. "We could fly into Queenstown, stay there, then head down to Milford by car. There are these overnight cruises where you wake up on the sound. It's incredible. Then there's the wine tasting, of course. We'd be right in the heart of the Otago region—great pinots." He raised his eyebrows at me. The trip did sound incredible, but I wondered how we'd fit it all into a weekend. "What's that? You frowned."

"I was just thinking. It's a lot to do in a weekend."

"*Well* ..." He drew it out and smiled to himself. "We could take a little longer. I'll be wrapping up the museum talks in the next couple of days. We could leave Thursday, or perhaps even Wednesday evening, and I'd have you back in Sydney on Monday. We've got time, right? You said you're off work until the end of the month?"

"Well, yes. We don't start the school year until the third of February ..." I was stalling as I thought of all the things I'd have to rearrange and cram into the next few days. Then I realised that when the handsome man, who says he's falling in love with you, wants to take you to *New Zealand* for the weekend, you say "yes".

"Let's do it. Let's go to New Zealand."

"Wonderful," he replied, those eye crinkles intensifying. He raised my hand to his lips and kissed it with a smack, and we shared a smile across the table. I would have to call Lins in the morning to ask her to take Domino again. I hoped he'd forgive me for being such a bad "furrent".

By the time the first course arrived, our conversation had shifted to the sights of Sydney, and I started mentally cataloguing all the places I wanted to take him to. I couldn't believe that someone who'd visited Sydney several times hadn't even been to Taronga Zoo—*or* Bondi.

The mud crab was delicious, by the way, and I thought of Paulie in London praising Sydney's seafood. *With good reason, Paulie*, I thought. Then the moment the plates were cleared away, a tall, elegant woman, who looked about fifty, appeared next to the table.

"Hello James," she said.

Seriously, does he know everyone?

"Antoinette!" He stood and planted a warm, friendly kiss on her cheek. She smiled at him just as warmly.

"Matt's not in tonight, but I called him, and he said to spoil you with dessert later." Then she reached out a hand across the table. "Hello, I'm Antoinette, the *maître d'* and a friend of James's." I appreciated that she didn't load up the word "friend" with adjectives like "old" or "good" or "with benefits". It meant we weren't going to have to play that awful game of "I know him better than you" that some people seem to enjoy.

I smiled up at her and shook her hand as I said, "Hello,"

and James said, "This is Sarah," at the same time. Antoinette was a pro and didn't miss a beat.

"Sarah, it's a pleasure to have you here." Then she turned back to James and included us both when she said, "I hope you enjoy the rest of your meal."

When she left the table, I leant closer to James so I could talk about her discreetly. "Well, she seems lovely."

"She is," he replied, just as quietly. "There have been quite a few nights when Antoinette, Matt, and I have closed the restaurant, sitting right here and solving the problems of the world over a bottle of wine—or two."

The thought made my stomach twinge in a pang of jealousy which surprised me, especially as I hadn't detected any sort of agenda in our brief conversation with Antoinette. It must have registered on my face, because James placed a hand on mine. "We're just friends. Besides, her husband is an ex-rugby player and about twice my size." He winked at me and I laughed.

He's here with you, *Sarah. Please get a grip.*

When the main course arrived, I had to resist the urge to photograph it—the plating was just spectacular—but when you're on a proper date with a grown man at Aria, it's not the time to pad your Instagram feed.

The John Dory tasted even better than it looked and I savoured every bite as we chatted about our respective visits to New Zealand. Although my one trip had been on a budget, I'd been completely taken by the physical beauty of the South Island. It didn't matter that I saw a lot of it from a bus window; I'd fallen in love with New Zealand back then and I couldn't believe I was going again—and in a few days!

The evening seemed to speed by and when I glanced at the view, I was surprised to see that the sun had well and truly set, and the Sydney Harbour Bridge had donned her array of sparkling silvery lights. We'd finished the bottle of wine, and James asked about ordering another. At that rate, I was going to develop a drinking problem. "Uh, maybe just a glass, or something to go with dessert?"

James turned to our waiter, a young guy who throughout the evening had achieved that perfect kind of readiness where he was there when we needed him and discreetly absent when we didn't. *Ahh, Aria.* It had leapt to the top of my list of favourite Australian restaurants. "Would you please check with Antoinette and ask what we're having for dessert, then ask the sommelier to send over liqueur that will pair?"

"Very good, sir." He nodded and left us. "You know, I do eat at normal restaurants too," James said, another non sequitur. I could tell he was teasing himself and played along.

"Oh, yes? You like to slum it once in a while, see how the little people live?"

"I was one of the little people once. I like to remember my roots." We shared a smile. "But really, I hope you know it's not like this is every night. I'm showing off a little because I want to impress you." I was definitely on board with that. "When I'm in London, I will cook for myself, or order in. Janice sometimes cooks, but it's not part of her job. It's only when she gets inspired. Sometimes, I'll come home to a giant pot of something delicious on the stove."

He laughed, "And then, of course, I'm eating lamb stew for three days straight, because it's just me." I had a very clear picture in my head of James sitting at his kitchen counter eating stew and I wanted to be there with him. Maybe I'd make him stew, or cookies, or any of the other things I liked to make.

Our desserts arrived, each a perfect miniature lemon meringue pie. Oh, how I love lemon meringue pie. *LOVE!* The sommelier brought a bottle of Limoncello over, along with two tiny liqueur glasses.

"I think you'll find this is a terrific pairing. I assure you, it won't feel like too much lemon. Instead, they should dance beautifully on the palette together." *What a lovely way to put it.* She poured and I squirmed a little in anticipation.

I took a bite of pie, then followed up with a sip of Limoncello. Oh, my god, the sommelier was right. It was as though one taste continued into the other. It was a stunning pie, by the way, the pastry just perfect—not too doughy—the lemon custard, tart and silky, and the meringue creamy and sweet, the brushstrokes of caramelisation giving it that toasted-marshmallow note. Heavenly.

I cleaned my plate and sat back in my chair, a decent-sized food baby percolating. *Uh oh, I did not think this through.* Lolling about in a food coma until my food baby disappeared was hardly the way to end a romantic evening. And it was probably not what James had in mind when he'd invited me to stay with him in that fancy hotel. *Crap.*

"What's going through your mind? You have an odd expression on your face." I was sure I did, but there was no way in *hell* I was going to tell him what I'd been thinking.

"Just thinking about the last time I had Limoncello." *Liar!*

"It was in the Cinque Terre—Riomaggiore—and I'd just finished hiking the whole thing."

Okay, so that wasn't a lie. I did do that, and I did celebrate with a glass of Limoncello at the end before I got on a train back to Monte Rosso where I was staying. This was years ago, when the track was open the whole way, before the landslides. I was travelling with a not-so-serious boyfriend, who I omitted from the story.

"Really? Now, that's somewhere I would love to go," James said.

"You've never been?"

"Sarah, this may surprise you, but there are many, *many* places in the world I've never been to." Intrepid Sarah perked right up at the thought of travelling somewhere with James and being the experienced traveller, the one showing *him* the way. "Did you do the whole trek in one day?" he added.

"We did!" *Uh oh.* Intrepid Sarah forgot to omit the ex-boyfriend from the story. "I was there with an old boyfriend. Uh, sorry, not that he was *old*, I mean, it was … he was a boyfriend from a long time ago." *Oh crap, does he think that I think he's old?* "Not that I think *you're* …" I trailed off, mortified, and he graciously chuckled, rescuing me from digging myself into a deeper hole.

"I understand. Anyway, so you *did* accomplish the whole trek in a day?"

Relieved, I got back to the story. "Yes! And we did this fun thing where we stopped at each town for a bite to eat or something to drink. First was morning tea, then lunch, then afternoon tea, and at the end, the Limoncello. It's over thirty kilometres and there are a lot of stairs, so it was a massive day, but just phenomenal.

"You'd come around a bend and there would be another town, nestled into the cliffside, these arrays of pastels and primary colours—just gorgeous. And there were so many farms along the way—we'd meet up with people working on their terraced crops. '*Buongiorno*', a little wave, and we'd keep going.

"We also saw quite a few people doing the trek in reverse order—the same thing, '*Buongiorno*' as we passed. It was only when we got to Corniglia, the middle town, that I felt sorry for *anyone* doing the trek north. They'd had to walk up these ridiculous stairs just south of Corniglia—thirty flights, maybe three hundred and fifty stairs in all."

"I didn't realise." A small smiled curled at the corners of his mouth.

"Yes, just brutal, whereas we got to walk *down* them. Actually, I felt even more sorry for the people who arrived on the train to *stay* in Corniglia, especially if they had luggage. Imagine carrying your bags up all those stairs from the train station. It made me glad we'd chosen to stay in Monte Rosso. Also, because it had an actual beach—it's the only town that does." *Am I rambling? For the love of limoncello, stop rambling, Sarah!*

"It sounds like a special place."

"It is."

"I'd love to go there with you."

He'd caught me off guard and I blinked at him like the proverbial stunned mullet. It was one thing for me to go to

A Sunset in Sydney

Hawaii with Josh—we'd made those plans while we were still in Greece *and* before I'd seen James in London. But if James and I were already going to New Zealand together *and* he was talking about Italy, were we going to turn into a vacationship too?

Chapter 19

As I'd anticipated, the next few days passed in a frenzy as I prepared for my trip to New Zealand with James, pinging from one task to the next like a child hopped up on birthday cake.

I called Lins to see if she and Nick would have Domino again and she dryly suggested they just adopt him. *Rude!* And I spent several hours sifting through my wardrobe and trying on outfits to assemble the perfect trousseau for a long weekend in New Zealand with a sophisticated fifty-something. It was more difficult than it may sound.

I moved my brunch date to the following weekend, ran errands and ticked off those heinous online tasks that I usually put off until the last moment, like banking and renewing my car insurance, baked cupcakes for the bake sale Mum and her friends were hosting to raise money for wildlife preservation, and did some planning for the new school year—all things I would have done if I wasn't going to New Zealand, but condensed into three days.

And on the day before I was flying to New Zealand with James, I spoke to Josh.

I know, I know, but there was no way not to. Josh texted to say he had something important to tell me and asked if we could FaceTime. How could I put him off until after New Zealand? "Uh, sorry, Josh, no matter how important your news is, I'm about to chuff off to the ol' NZ for a long weekend away with my other lover. I'll catchya on the flipside!"

My stomach fluttered as soon I heard the ring tone and I took a breath before answering the call.

"Hey!" A massive smile broke across his face warming me instantly. I loved that smile. I missed that smile.

"Hey back! So, what's the big news? I'm guessing it's good since you don't look like you've been wallowing or anything."

"No, no wallowing. I just wanted to let you know that my bigger life reboot has gotten off to a good start."

"Oh, that's fab! Anything in particular?"

"Yeah, actually. And it kind of involves you."

I had no idea if it was good news or bad, but my traitorous stomach defaulted to "bad" and knotted into a tight ball. Damned video conferencing. It took all my acting prowess, which is hardly any at all, to keep a neutral expression and a light tone in my voice. "Oh yeah? How's that?"

"So, you know how I told you that I've been kinda stagnant since Greece?" I nodded in encouragement. "Well, I went to see my career advisor and she told me about this cool new team the company's putting together." The ball started to unknot as I saw his obvious excitement.

"Oh, yeah?"

"Yeah, so it's this innovation team who travels to different geos to work with international colleagues and learn from other organisations, then shares the collective knowledge—kind of like a team of techy diplomats."

"Wow, that sounds incredible."

"Yes! And she convinced me to apply, and I did, *aaand* ... I got accepted!"

"Oh, my god, that's amazing, Josh!" My joy for him bubbled up into a laugh. "Congratulations!" He was grinning so widely that I wanted to zap myself through the screen and be there in person to share his news. "I wish I could give you a big hug. And I hope this doesn't come across as condescending, but I'm really proud of you."

"Thanks!" he replied. "I'm super excited. But, Sarah, that's not all. The team's first trip might be to *Sydney*."

"You're coming to Sydney?!" I started bouncing up and down. And I won't lie, James did not enter my head at all. Josh was coming to Sydney.

"Well, not officially yet and if we do, I'm not sure for how long. It might just be a week, and I'd be working most of the time, but it would be cool to see you."

I stopped bouncing. *Cool to see me?*

Was this more "vacationship" bullshit—just another week of shagging and then he's off? I caught sight of my face in the corner of the screen, and I was frowning. I pasted on a neutral expression and tried to summon some enthusiasm. "So, when will you find out?"

"I should know sometime next week—it's between Sydney and Mumbai. Of course, I'm rooting for Sydney. And if we *are* coming to Australia, it'll likely be in the next month or so."

"Wow, that's soon." And suddenly, James *did* enter my mind. If Josh's company chose Sydney over Mumbai, then he and James would be in Sydney at the same time.

"So, I'll let you know as soon as I do. It would be so awesome, Sarah. You can show me around your hometown. I mean, I'd be working during the day, like I said—and so will you by then—but we can see each other in the evenings. And I think we'd have at least one weekend there. They're even putting us up in an apartment in the city. I'd be sharing, but you could stay over if you wanted."

If I wanted? I wasn't sure what I wanted. And who knew what Josh coming to Sydney would mean for us, how it might affect our friendship, or vacationship, or whatever the hell it was.

As I wrestled with these thoughts, I tried—but failed—to ignore that next to my bed was a suitcase packed to go on a trip with James—who Josh didn't want me to see.

I wasn't sure why I had *ever* thought it was a good idea to have two boyfriends. I sucked at it.

Josh, probably blinded by his excitement, didn't seem to notice how deflated I'd become. Instead, his smile beamed out of the screen at me, making me feel sick. I knew then, right in that moment, I was going to have to make a decision—and soon.

I gave myself an ultimatum: after New Zealand, pick one. *Crap. No, not crap—fuck.*

*

"Hi. It's me."

"Yes, I know. Your name comes up on my phone. It's this amazing technology." Lindsey was in full sarcasm mode. Maybe that's why she's my bestie—she and Cat are practically the same person, right down to the playful sarcasm and knowing whether I need tough love or a soft shoulder to cry on.

"Right. I need to talk to you."

"So, more than what we're doing now?" I could hear her typing, which meant she was only half-listening.

"Yes. Josh called." The typing stopped.

"Oh, yeah?"

"Well, FaceTimed. Whatever. Anyway, he's coming to Australia. For work—maybe—and if it's definitely, then it's happening *soon*."

"Oh, *wow*." I loved her for understanding me when I babbled.

"Yeah. And forget the 'maybe' part, because it's fifty-fifty at the moment, and that's good enough for me to start freaking out."

"Of course you are. They'll both be here at the same time." I loved her even more for following my pseudo-logic and knowing exactly *what* was freaking me out.

We were both silent for a moment—me while I went back over the million and one things I had thought since Josh had called. Lins, I hoped, was quietly formulating the perfect plan to get me out of this ridiculous mess. That I had made. All by my big-girl self.

"You need to come over," she said eventually. "Tonight."

"Yes." I had already decided that. The call was me telling her I was coming.

"It's actually perfect because Nick is going to spin class."

"Spin?"

"Don't ask. Anyway, he goes out for pizza afterwards with a couple of the guys from class."

"Pizza?"

"Again, don't ask. Anyway, come tonight. Seven?"

"Yep."

"Bye." She hung up without waiting for a reply. Best friends can do that without the other one getting pissy. Plus, she ran her own company. She was busy. I'd probably used up a hundred dollars of her time in that five minutes.

I showed up at five to seven with two bottles of wine, an overnight bag, and Domino. I figured that since he was already booked into his home-away-from-home for the duration of my trip, what was one extra night? Besides, I wanted him with me. I'd miss his little face while I was in New Zealand.

Domino always travelled in the car without a cage or anything—he was cool that way—and had spent most of the ride standing on the passenger seat with his paws on the dash watching out the front window. He was squirming in my arms as Lindsey opened the front door, though, so I deposited him on the floor and he ran off down the hallway.

Lindsey took the bag with the wine in it. "Only two bottles?"

"I figured we could dip into yours if we run out."

After stashing my overnight bag in my room, I followed Lindsey into the kitchen. "So, Nick and spin class ..."

She threw me a look. "I know, 'don't ask', but seriously,

spin? When did this start?" You should know that Nick was a surfing rugby player in his younger days. Surfing rugby players were not usually the type of guy you saw in spin class amongst the lycra-clad yummy mummies and the super-fit gay guys. I couldn't have been more surprised if she'd said he was going to barre class.

"One of his friends ... do you know Dean?"

I shook my head "no", then snapped my fingers when I recognised the name. "Yes, divorced guy, speedos, lots of body hair." I described the guy I'd met at their Australia Day barbecue-slash-pool party the year before.

"That's him. So, Dean started going to spin to meet women."

"Ewww."

"Yeah, and he wanted a wing man, so he roped in Nick one week and, *now*, Nick goes to spin."

I made a funny expression, which said "ick" and "weird" and "whatever floats your boat" all at once. It made Lins laugh.

"But the pizza afterwards? What's the point of going to spin if you're just going to stuff your face with fat and dough?"

"I think that's the only reason Nick *does* go. Well, that and he feels sorry for Dean."

"Fair enough." She handed me a generous pour of one of the wines I'd brought. It was a sauvignon blanc from New Zealand. The second bottle was a pinot from California—not quite Chicago, but you see what I did there? New Zealand and the US—I was torturing myself with my wine choices.

Lins put the wine in the door of the fridge, then rummaged around for a bit until she came out with a stack of containers—

olives, sundried tomatoes, marinated artichokes, and tzatziki—with a block of cheddar and a wheel of brie balanced on top.

"Okay with nibbles for dinner? I can't be bothered cooking anything."

"Yeah, totally." Sometimes, Lins is my spirit animal as well as my bestie.

Without being asked, I went to the cupboard and pulled out some toasted almonds, dried apricots, and two types of crackers, and put them on the counter. I grabbed a giant tray from on top of the fridge—I knew their kitchen as well as I knew my own—and Lins and I loaded up the tray.

We settled on either end of the couch with the food between us. Domino was curled up on an armchair opposite us, already asleep. "Okay, spill," prompted Lins.

I told her as many details as I could remember about the conversation with Josh. She nodded and made the appropriate noises as I spoke, letting me know she was taking it all in and musing things over while she piled crackers high with cheese and munched.

"So, when you left Josh in Hawaii, you *really* thought you'd just end up as friends?" she asked, wiping cracker crumbs from the corner of her mouth. The "left Josh in Hawaii" part stung a little, because it made it sound like I'd abandoned him, which I hadn't.

I *had* completely screwed things up by telling him about James, but even though our goodbye was hurried, we'd mostly made things right, and he *had* sent that text asking me not to make any big decisions until he'd thought things through.

So, did I really think we'd broken up for good? Maybe I'd been telling myself we had because it made it easier for me to see James, guilt-free.

I pondered while chewing on a cracker laden with both dip and cheese. Then the truth hit, and I felt ill, that stupid knot making itself at home in my stomach again. "Yes. I did," I said quietly. "I went to Hawaii hoping that Josh had figured things out and wanted to be with me, but ..."

"But he hadn't," she said, finishing my thought.

"Exactly," I said sadly. "And today, at the start of the call, when he was telling me all about this great new job, I was genuinely happy for him—as a *friend*, you know? I was even thinking, 'hey, I can do this. I can be Josh's friend,' but then when he said he was coming to Sydney—"

"Maybe. *Maybe* coming to Sydney."

"*Maybe*, yes, thank you—anyway, when he said he might be coming and that we could see each other and that I could stay over at his place ... well, that was *boyfriend* Josh."

"Or vacationship Josh."

I piled up more cheese and dip onto another cracker and put the whole thing in my mouth. With my mouth full, I said, "Emphatly," which meant, "exactly".

"So, the real question is, are you willing to see how it goes with Josh *if* he comes here and *if* he wants to be more than friends?"

"I think he does."

"Think he does, what?"

"Want to be more than friends. I mean, he specifically mentioned me staying over."

"Maybe he just wants a shag." I threw her a look. She put her hands up—part-surrender, part-apology. "Look, from what you've said, he does seem to have genuine feelings for you—"

"That he can't seem to figure out," I interrupted.

She raised her eyebrows at me. "Is it fair to judge him for that when you're in the same boat?" *Ouch.*

She was right, though. Josh wasn't in the middle of a love triangle, but how could I fault him for being unsure of his feelings when I still hadn't decided which man—if either—to give my heart to? What a selfish cow I was.

Lins got up, leaving me with my thoughts, but taking our empty wine glasses with her. I heard her refilling them, then the sound of the bottle landing in the bottom of the recycling bin. No short pours in her house. She handed me a nearly full glass and I took a sip.

"So, what about James? How is it?"

I looked at her. "What do you mean?"

"Well, I don't want graphic details or anything, but when you're with him, does it feel right?"

She was only asking me the question I'd been asking myself since James had arrived in Sydney, but hearing it out loud made it even more real. And having to articulate a response was an even bigger dose of reality. This wasn't some made-for-Netflix romcom. This was my life. And there were two other lives involved.

I thought back to the night James had taken me to Aria.

After dinner and that mind-blowing dessert, he'd asked me if I wanted to walk back to the hotel or take a taxi. The weather had been mild when we stepped outside—in the low twenties—but I'd just wanted to get to the hotel as soon as possible, so we could go to bed.

That's crass, I know. But it was *James*, and he was ridiculously handsome and sexy, and when he laughed, his eyes crinkled around the corners and he had the most beautiful voice, and I wanted him.

He hailed a taxi and we slid into the back seat, silently sitting side by side and holding hands for the eight-minute ride. I know it was eight minutes because I watched them tick over on the digital clock on the dashboard. James's thumb stroked the back of my hand the whole way and my insides turned to mush.

By the time we reached the room and closed the door behind us, the tension was so high, he pressed me up against the wall, his mouth on mine, and I dropped my clutch without a second thought, throwing my arms around his neck.

He rested a hand on the small of my back, pulling me closer, and his other hand found the top of my zipper. He slid it down my back and, still kissing me, peeled my dress from my shoulders. It slid to the floor and he broke the kiss. Okay, so maybe sometimes my life *is* a made-for-Netflix romcom.

"I want to see you," he said in his honey-gravel voice. He took a half-step back and his eyes ran the length of me, taking in my lacy bra and matching knickers, looking down my legs to my heels. I didn't mind the scrutiny. I'd taken extra care with how I looked and felt every bit as sexy as his smile said I was.

"That's a very sexy look." You see?

"It's just for you." I raised my eyebrows at him, a slight smile on my face. I hadn't been this Sarah for very long—really, I was just trying her on for size—but I relished being her. She was way sexier and far more confident than regular Sarah.

James must have thought so too. He kissed me again, his tongue seeking mine, and his body pressed against me. I could feel how hard he was beneath his trousers. "Bed," I said breathlessly.

James took my hand and led me upstairs. He turned to me and, with an arm around my waist, spun me around and lay me back onto the bed, breaking my fall with his other hand. He held himself just above me and kissed my neck, his lips and his tongue tracking the hollow, then trailing along my collar bone. He pulled aside my bra and took my left nipple into his mouth, making me gasp. His tongue played, teasing me.

I wanted him inside me.

"James," I whispered. "I want you."

He reached underneath me and flicked open the clasp of my bra. He slid it off one shoulder, and I slid it off the other. When it was free of both arms, he took it off me and put it on the bed beside me. His mouth moved to my right breast, as his hand caressed my left. I was in agony for want of him.

His mouth moved lower and his fingers ran gently along the band of my knickers. He slid them off me. "James." I was writhing beneath him and then his mouth was on me, and he took me to the brink, then beyond while I called out his name like they do in the movies.

When I'd climaxed and my senses had returned, I looked down at him as he slowly made his way back up my body, his eyes locked on mine. "James," I said one more time.

"Yes, my darling," he said finally, peppering my face with tiny kisses.

"I want you inside me." This time he didn't hesitate.

"Well, I kind of have my answer there." Lindsey was giving me a scrutinising look.

"What do you mean?"

"I mean, I'm pretty sure that the lost, dreamy look on your face right now is because of James."

I ran my hands over my face and blew out a heavy sigh. "Yeah, but maybe it's just the sex."

She laughed then, a scoffing bark of a laugh, and it pissed me off. "What?"

"C'mon, Sez. This guy flies across the world to see you—"

"He's here for *work*," I insisted. "But, that's not—"

She cut me off. "*And* to see you. *And* he's taking you to New Zealand." I tried to talk again. "*And* he told you he's falling in love with you."

"Are you finished?" She gave me a resigned look. "I know all that, but what if it's just the sex for *me*?" She looked perplexed. I sighed again. "I only say that, because when I'm with him, I kind of feel like an imposter."

"What do you mean?"

"I mean, that *that* Sarah is not me." She shook her head at me. I was obviously not explaining myself very well. I put my wine glass down on the coffee table and sat up straight, gathering my thoughts. "Okay, look. Sometimes when I'm with

James, I feel like a young girl who's pretending to be a grown-up, like I don't belong in that world, *or* with him. Like once he figures out that I'm just me, he's not going to want me anymore."

"Sez?" I detected the hint of pity in her voice, but I didn't mind, because at least it meant she understood—or she was starting to.

"Yes?" I replied.

"Have you talked to him about this?"

"What? No!" I couldn't think of anything more horrifying.

"So, I just want to make sure I've got this straight. James is falling in love with you, but you're not sure it's *you* he loves. Like, *you* you."

"Well, he does say I'm not like the other women he's been with."

"Well, that sounds good. What's bad about that?"

"Nothing. I just—" I let out a heavy sigh. "I'm not completely myself when I'm with him. Not yet, anyway. And what happens if I do show him who I really am, and he doesn't love *that* Sarah?"

"But maybe all these Sarahs are you."

"Maybe." I wasn't convinced.

"Okay, but what about Josh?"

"Huh?" She'd caught me off guard.

"Which Sarah does he know?"

I froze under Lindsey's loving, but potent scrutiny, because what she was asking, was something she already knew—something *I* already knew. *Josh knows you, Sarah.*

"He knows me." It was almost a whisper, but that one

word, "me", was loaded with all that embodied my relationship—my *friendship*—with Josh.

"Well, there you go, then. Maybe *that's* your answer," she said sensibly. Even so, that hard knot in the pit of my stomach was now trying to gnaw its way out.

"Yeah, but *Josh* doesn't know if he loves me. Maybe the *real* Sarah isn't actually lovable." Tears stung my eyes. I brushed them away, annoyed with myself. *Poor me. Two men to choose from and poor, poor me.* I dreaded the dose of tough love I expected to cop from the other end of the couch. Instead, a hand reached out and took mine.

"Oh Sarah," she said, her voice thick with empathy, "That is complete bullshit and you know it." We exchanged a look, then a smile, and then we both laughed long and hard and completely at my expense.

"I'm opening the pinot now. Drink up," she said, as she climbed off the couch. My laughter trailed off and I downed the rest of my wine, not even registering how it tasted. Lins was right to call me out on the self-pity, but I was still stuck in my dilemma.

If I was my true self with Josh, but he wasn't sure how he felt, or if he wanted a relationship with me—and if James was falling in love with me, but there were times with him that I didn't feel like *me*—didn't that mean *something*?

Maybe it meant that I wouldn't end up with either of them.

Was I okay with that?

I probed the thought, and it hurt. I really did want to be in love, in a relationship, but as much as I felt for both men, I couldn't force Josh to love me, and I couldn't pretend that I was my truest self when I was with James—not yet, anyway. Hopefully, I would know more after the trip to New Zealand.

Hopefully.

Chapter 20

"Here you are, sir," said the bellboy as he opened the door to our suite. My eyes flew straight out of the floor-to-ceiling windows to the spectacular view of Lake Wakatipu, which unfurled long and narrow to the south and at a right angle to the west.

The mountains, which in some parts seemed to emerge directly from the shoreline, were reflected in perfect symmetry on the water's surface, and two promontories of low-lying land were covered in dusty dark-green fir trees and chartreuse-coloured grass. Even though it was summer, there was a dusting of white on the highest peaks, and in a feat of magnificence, nature had chosen the same brilliant blue for the sky and the water.

Queenstown was showing off. I hadn't seen this kind of natural beauty since I'd been in Switzerland, and I'm from *Australia*.

The room itself was bigger than my entire apartment in Sydney. Since Christmas, I had been utterly spoiled with lavish accommodations, but realising that made me think of Josh.

James. James. James.

He tipped the bellboy as I admired the view. The trip was his gift to me, I knew that, but I wasn't going to let him pay for everything. I'd be buying us dinner and drinks and whatever else he would let me pay for.

Maybe he'd let me take him to play mini-golf—if we had time and if he didn't think it was a completely idiotic idea. I like mini-golf and Queenstown apparently has an incredible indoor course. But I wasn't sure if James was a mini-golf kind of guy. I'd have to play it by ear, so to speak.

I sensed him behind me, then his arms wrapped around my waist as he nuzzled my neck. "What do you think of the view?" he asked needlessly.

"It's hideous." He chuckled. "No, really. I thought you said it was nice here."

"You are very naughty sometimes, aren't you?"

Why yes, I was, but usually when I was accused of being naughty it didn't turn me on and send shivers down my spine. I bit my bottom lip, not trusting myself to reply. I didn't have a clever retort to hold up my end of the repartee and, besides, it would be bad manners to rip his clothes off less than five minutes after arriving.

"So, do you want to go for a walk and see the town, or would you like to stay in for a bit?" he asked. *Was that a come on?* His hands started to caress me, and the neck nuzzling turned to neck kissing. *Yes, that was a come on.* Maybe it wasn't bad manners to want a shag five minutes after checking in.

*

We did eventually go on a walk to see the town. I'd seen it from the air—incredible, by the way—and some of it on the drive to the hotel, but the walk along the waterfront and through the small, neat streets revealed far more about Queenstown's personality.

It was very pretty for one thing. Low buildings hugged the shoreline, the backdrop of pine-covered mountains dwarfing them. It reminded me a little of alpine towns in Austria or northern Italy, but there was a more relaxed architectural thread in Queenstown, more variety.

I could see the influences of English colonialism in the austere white government buildings, and modernists had stamped their aesthetic onto the skyline with glass and timber meeting at odd angles. Then there were the homages to other styles—a giant hotel that looked like a French *château*, smaller buildings with gabled, shingled roofs, as though they'd been lifted from Cape Cod, and of course, Alpine-cottage-inspired restaurants and shop fronts. There were also some ghastly concrete blocks that had obviously been built in the 70s. And peppered amongst the streets and buildings were trees—conifers, oaks, and willows—and carefully manicured, brilliantly-green lawns.

It all came together in a hodgepodge of styles that somehow worked—Queenstown chic. It was charming.

The cadence of the town, however, was a little odd. The footpaths were busy and there were many times when James and I had to stop holding hands as we walked. It seemed that most people were either gawping or rushing, and it was obvious who was visiting and who lived there. I wondered if the locals wished everyone would bugger off and leave them to their mountainous-lakeside paradise.

James must have been thinking along the same lines. "This is not exactly the relaxing walk I was thinking of," he said, after we dropped hands for the umpteenth time to get around a family of tourists who'd stopped in the middle of the footpath. While we didn't have a destination in mind, just content to see where we ended up, it was becoming clear that we needed a game plan.

"What about over there?" I asked. We were on the waterfront and I could see across a small bay to what looked like a giant park of forested land. "That might have a nicer pace, somewhere for us to soak it all in."

"That's the Queenstown Gardens," he said, adding, "and a brilliant idea." He grabbed my hand again and as we walked briskly around the waterfront, our destination in sight, dodging tourists became a game.

"Seventeen," I said as we entered the gardens.

"What's seventeen?"

"The number of tourist dodges on the way here." I grinned at him and he smiled back, seeming a little less enthused with my game than I was. I suddenly felt foolish.

"There's a track bordering the whole garden," said James, saving me from a bout of self-flagellation. "Let's head this way." We made our way to the track that traced the shoreline of the promontory, and the view back across the water reinforced my impression of the town—it was stunning.

"I never asked you how long it's been since you were here," I said after a few minutes of silence that felt like many more.

"It's been a few years."

"But you've come here a lot?"

"Well, not as much as I would have liked. It's a fair way from London, of course, so I've only really added it as a side jaunt when I've been in Australia, and once when I was in Chile, which I realise isn't *that* close by, but it's in the same hemisphere at least, and I suppose it's all relative."

I wondered if the last bit was about geography, time, or the cost of flying to New Zealand from South America. *It's all relative when you have a bunch of money and get to fly business class.* At least, I was guessing he flew business class. Maybe for long-haul flights he was right in the nose cone.

Even though it had only been a three-hour flight from Sydney, I'd certainly appreciated the wider seats and extra legroom of business class—*and* the endless glasses of bubbles. *If you're with James, you'll always fly like that.* It was a fun thought, but not remotely helpful. I needed to decide how I felt about *James*, not his money.

"You really do travel a lot," I said, purposefully steering clear of my thoughts.

"Yes, but you do too, don't you?" I turned to see a gentle smile.

"I guess. I mean, not as much as you do—and not for work or anything. And, of course, I can only travel in the school holidays, and that's when they hike the prices, so as a teacher I always get stung with the more expensive flights, the pricier accommodation."

I was rambling again, but for some reason I couldn't stop

complaining about the cost of travel—to the wealthy man. *Shut up, Sarah.*

But I didn't shut up.

"And, for most of last year I didn't travel at all—not until the trip to Greece."

"Why's that?"

Without realising, I had painted myself into a Neil-sized corner. *Please, Sarah,* do *shut up.*

"Because of my ex." *Nooo!* He didn't say anything, so I ignored my very loud inner voice and went on to explain how Neil didn't like to travel and how I'd changed who I was to be with him, and how that meant I'd stayed put when all I'd wanted to do was go somewhere. Finally, I wrapped it up with, "So, yeah ..." It was definitely one of my less eloquent moments.

He was quiet for a moment and, predictably, I spent the entire time beating myself up for sounding like I was auditioning for a *Gilmore Girls* reboot.

"Well, I'm certainly glad I had the good fortune of being there when you ventured back out into the world." He lifted the hand he was holding to his lips and kissed it.

So, maybe he didn't think I was a complete idiot with verbal diarrhoea.

*

"So, where are we going for dinner again? I know you told me the name, but is it fancy or caz'?" I was rifling through my luggage and considering what might be appropriate for dining out in a ski town in summertime.

A Sunset in Sydney

I'd packed carefully and had a range of options, but I wanted to be sure we looked like we were going to the same place. It irks me when I see couples out and it seems like one of them thought they were dining at a nice restaurant and the other thought they were volunteering at a community garden.

James looked up from his own suitcase. "I was just going to wear jeans and a dress shirt."

"Okay, cool." *Cool? What am I, twelve?* I took out a pair of skinny jeans, a pair of ballet flats and a flouncy, floral long-sleeved top. Okay, it was a blouse, but I hate that word. It conjures images of pirates or (worse) 80s New Romantic pop groups.

And even though James had seen me naked numerous times, I went into the bathroom to change. Sure, I needed to freshen up, but—truth be told—I was still self-conscious about changing in front of him. It was such a couple-y thing to do and I didn't think we were quite there yet.

I emerged, feeling fresh and pretty, to find him dressed in a dark blue pair of dress jeans and a grey, finely checked button-down shirt, with brown lace-up shoes and a brown belt. He looked ridiculously handsome, but far less caz' than I did. I looked down at my outfit. Flats. I was wearing flats. I needed to change into boots.

I stepped out of my shoes and rummaged in my suitcase for my black boots. James came up behind me and wrapped his arms around my waist. "You look beautiful." I appreciated the compliment, but I was also a *teensy* bit annoyed that he'd interrupted me getting ready. Yes, really—I am particularly skilled at self-sabotage, you know.

He turned me around to face him and out of my shoes, he seemed so much taller than me. I felt my annoyance fall away as he leant down and placed a soft kiss on my lips, seeming to take care not to smudge my lipstick.

I smiled. When a man looks at you the way he was looking at me, you smile, believe me. "Almost ready?" he asked, still holding onto my waist.

"Yes. Just need to put my boots on and grab my hand-bag."

He kept smiling down at me, not letting go. "You're tiny out of your shoes, aren't you?"

"Tiny" was not something anyone had ever called me. I'm five-foot-six. But standing there with James, who was well over six feet tall, and wrapped up in his arms, I did feel tiny. When he popped a kiss on the end of my nose, I also felt cherished. I wanted to forget about dinner and let him cherish me all night long.

He let me go and I felt the sting of disappointment—what a rollercoaster of emotions in just a matter of minutes. I pulled on some socks, then my boots, and checked my handbag for my wallet, tissues, lip balm, phone—the usual. I draped the strap over my shoulder and declared myself, "Ready." James held the door open, his eyes locked to mine and a sexy smile on his lips as I walked past him.

That smile was going to be my undoing, I just knew it.

We were having dinner at Attiqa, which had a rooftop bar and restaurant where we could watch the sunset while we ate. We wouldn't have a direct line of sight to the sun setting, of course—Queenstown is firmly landlocked—but we'd be

344

able to see it disappear behind the mountain range, and I just knew it would be spectacular.

When we arrived, a buzz of energy emanated from the warmly lit restaurant downstairs, with people talking and laughing in groups, and tables filled with platters of tapas. Following the host, we made our way upstairs and stepped out onto the sundeck.

Wow. Just, wow.

With Attiqa positioned at the north-east corner of the water-front, it had a spectacular view of the Queenstown Gardens and of Lake Wakatipu and its surrounding mountains. I paused for a second to take it all in, catching up to James as the host removed a 'reserved' sign from a table in front of a low couch.

"Your waiter will be right with you," she said with a polite smile. I sat down and craned my neck to look around at the other people on the deck. It didn't seem like the kind of place where you could reserve the best seat for sunset viewing, but James had obviously wangled it somehow.

A waiter appeared with menus and he rattled off a list of specials so fast I didn't hear any of them, then disappeared. "I haven't actually been here before, but it was recommended to me," said James. He didn't say who had done the recom-mending. "Apparently, they specialise in cocktails." He flipped through the menu until he found the right page, and I did the same with my own. They had an interesting selection—one was even made with *jam*—but I'm more of a traditionalist when it comes to cocktails.

"Find something you'd like?" James asked, looking up from

his menu. I nodded and as if by magic, our waiter appeared. I ordered the Negroni and James a vodka martini. The waiter disappeared.

"You know, that's cheating," I said.

"What's that?"

"They have this elaborate cocktail menu and you go for something that's not even on it. A *martini*."

He laughed. "Is it too boring for you?"

"No. I mean, I ordered a *Negroni*. I prefer something simple to a drink that arrives with an entourage." He cocked his head at me, his expression telling me to elaborate. "You know, those cocktails that show up and you have to hack your way through an orchard just to get to the drink. They should come with a machete." *Wow, I can be quite hilarious sometimes.* I can also bullshit with the best of them—I had *loved* those cocktails in Hawaii. I wasn't sure why I'd said that other than to be funny. Still, it worked.

"You're quite amusing, you know," he said, chuckling. I decided to go with it.

"I think the word you're looking for is *hil-ar-i-ous*." I said, drawing out each syllable for dramatic effect.

He nodded solemnly, "Right, I stand corrected. You are hil-ar-i-ous." I nestled back against the couch and he put an arm around my shoulders. *Here I am, sitting with my handsome boyfriend in an incredible place, and he thinks I am beautiful and hilarious.* Smugness is not really an attractive trait, but wasn't I entitled to a little?

When our drinks arrived, I realised that we'd sat quietly

for several minutes enjoying the view and I hadn't felt the need to fill the silence with frivolous chitchat—maybe it was more of that "growing as a person" stuff.

"To a beautiful sunset," he said. I clinked my glass against his and took a sip. *Oh, my god, that's strong.* Somehow, I'd forgotten that a Negroni is essentially half a glass of full-strength liquor. I'd have to pace myself.

I took another micro sip and, just as I started to feel the warmth flow through my body, a voice like honey spoke in a way that had my instincts on edge well before my brain caught up. "James?"

My head pivoted so fast I'm surprised I didn't get whiplash. Standing next to our sunset nest was a stunningly beautiful woman with long chestnut hair, large brown eyes, and cheekbones so high, they could have cut diamonds. She could have been cast as Wonder Woman or a Charlie's Angel. I hated her as soon as I saw her. Mostly because I am, at heart, massively insecure.

James, ever cool, ever composed James, coughed on his drink and stood up so quickly, he nearly toppled the table. "Portia." *Portia??? You've got to be kidding me. The goddess's name is frigging Portia?!* "Wow." A laugh I'd never heard from him bubbled out awkwardly. "What a surprise." *I'll say.*

He stepped over my legs—again, he *stepped over* me—and gave the goddess a hug. I hated her even more. And was I supposed to stand or say "hello" or just sit there like a plain little idiot?

The goddess beamed at him, holding his forearms as she

regarded him. "You look well, James," she said in a clipped English accent. *That's something an ex-lover says.* My inner voice could be impressively astute at times.

"You too." James was smiling back at her and the moment seemed to be frozen in time. I still didn't know what to do. Then James seemed to remember himself, "Portia, this is Sarah." He turned around to indicate that *I* was the Sarah in question.

She smiled at me and I couldn't decipher if I saw pity, condescension, or bafflement at what the hell James was doing with me—maybe it was all three. I stood then—literally standing my ground—and when I did, I was glad I'd changed into my boots. I towered over *Portia* by a couple of inches.

I stretched out my hand and positioned a pleasant smile on my face. She had to let go of my boyfriend in order to shake it, so it was a good move on my part. "Hello, nice to meet you," I said in my most grown-up voice.

"And you," she said, her smile blatantly disingenuous. "And this is my husband, Stephen," she said turning towards a pleasant-looking tall man with a mop of curly brown hair. He leant across her to shake James's hand, and I watched James closely. Then Stephen offered to shake mine, which I did as though the whole exchange between the four of us was perfectly normal.

"So, are you on holiday?" asked James, his voice sounding tight.

"Yes, actually. Well, sort of. Stephen had some business in Auckland, and I tagged along. This is our last stop. Isn't it just divine?"

A Sunset in Sydney

I found myself nodding in agreement. Stephen smiled and nodded along with me. Portia seemed to be driving the conversation and I was relieved when she said, "Well, we'll leave you to it. Nice to have seen you, James, and nice to have met you, Sarah."

We said our goodbyes and Stephen threw in, "Enjoy your evening," before they left. The whole thing was ridiculously civilised for what was obviously the reunion of former lovers. Grown-ups do weird things sometimes. James and I sat down and picked up our drinks. He looked out at the sinking sun, a small frown on his face. I wasn't sure what I was supposed to say, so I said nothing.

After a while, he turned to me and met my eyes. "Portia and I used to—" He seemed to get stuck on how to describe what they were to each other and I swallowed a lump in my throat. It was unbelievably awkward, and I wasn't sure how we'd resurrect the evening, let alone the rest of the trip.

"We were involved," he said finally. *Involved*—a word loaded with complication and bad feelings and an unhappy ending. If he'd said "in love" or "in a relationship" that would have been completely different. But he hadn't. He'd said, "involved". It sounded like something out of a night-time soap opera.

We drank our cocktails in silence, and watched the sun descend below the rim of the mountain peaks. With the sun in hiding, the sky looked like someone had torn a jagged piece right off the bottom—a bit like my heart, really. It was beautiful, though—a distraction at least.

"I'm sorry about that," James said, picking up my hand.

I wasn't sure why he was sorry—it's not like he'd planned

349

it. Besides, it had only been mildly excruciating. "You loved her," I said, surprising myself. It was a bold thing to say to your current lover.

"Yes, I did. But quite a while ago. It was just a surprise to see her here, in this context. I wasn't expecting it." And I was *sure* he hadn't expected to meet her husband either.

"It's fine," I said, lying. *It is so not fine.* I told myself to breathe.

"Shall we order something to eat?" he asked.

"Sure." *Yes, let's order food I'll have to choke down.* I hoped I sounded more enthused than I felt.

It was eventually okay between us—*ish*. We ordered food and some wine to go with dinner, then finished our drinks— well, I sipped about half of my Negroni before abandoning it for the wine. We also found something to talk about other than Portia, leaning on the one thing I knew we had in common: travel.

I knew we'd have to talk more about Portia at some point, but I was happy to put it off until I'd had time to sift through my feelings. I'd hated how I'd felt during the whole exchange, and I *certainly* didn't like the look on James's face when he saw the woman he used to love.

I had a lot of sifting to do.

Chapter 21

We didn't have sex that night, which felt strange, but it would have felt stranger to *have* sex.

Our conversation over dinner had an unpleasant subtext of "let's both agree to ignore the giant purple elephant in the room". And that elephant looked like a forty-something super-model.

After we got ready for bed and said our overly polite good-nights, including a kiss I can only describe as "chaste", I lay awake fretting. James, of course, slept.

It will never cease to amaze me how a man can sleep so soundly when everything is utterly crap between you. I'd lost track of the number of times I'd woken from a broken sleep, exhausted and feeling wretched, to have the man next to me say, "I'm sorry about last night," or, "Let me explain ..." or "We should talk about ..." while looking remarkably refreshed. It made me hate him—them—a little. And hate is not a good thing in a relationship, apparently.

Neil had pulled that crap dozens of times. I was practi-cally an insomniac for the better part of a year. After Neil,

I promised myself never again, yet there I was lying on my back staring at the beautifully ornate crown moulding, wanting to poke James in the shoulder and say, "What the hell, James?"

Instead, I ended up replaying the whole evening in my head, over and over. How lovely it was before Portia arrived— would her name ever *not* sound made-up and pretentious? Then "the encounter" as I would think of it forever more. Then the aftermath, which included that worrying goodnight kiss.

James had clearly been blindsided by her appearance, which did sort of make sense. I mean, if I ran into Neil and his wife while I was somewhere across the world, I'd be a little freaked out too. But then again, there was a fragment of me that *wanted* to run into plain, boring, dickhead Neil when I was with James, just so I could see the look on his face when he realised how much of an upgrade I'd made.

By 2:00am, I had turned into a hideous version of myself. I finally fell asleep somewhere around three, as fitful and unfulfilling as it was. James, as I'd predicted, was refreshed, sweet-smelling, and handsome when he kissed my forehead, waking me. My eyelids fluttered open and I frowned. There was no way in hell it could be time to get up. I felt like I had jet lag. Maybe we need a name for that feeling. *Manlag*.

"Good morning, beautiful. I hate to be the bearer of bad news"—*you mean worse than running into the love of your life?*—"but we need to get going soon, if we're going to make the boat." *Oh, that.*

"Yep, I'm up," I said, even though it was plainly obvious I was still prone.

"I'll make you some coffee."

"Uh, tea. Please."

"Oh yes, sorry. Tea."

How could he forget that I drank *tea*? We had enjoyed whole pots of the stuff together! I wondered if *Portia* drank coffee, a snarky thought I held on to all through my shower. When I dried off, I looked in the mirror. It wasn't pretty. Can you have suitcases under your eyes? Steamer trunks? I was certain the word "bags" was inadequate, but then, isn't that what concealer is for? I repaired the damage of a sleepless night, thankful (at least) for my prowess with a makeup brush. Then I dressed in a pair of jeans and a simple top and left the bathroom.

James was zipping up his suitcase. He flashed a smile at me and I returned it with my own facsimile.

"I left your tea on your bedside table."

"Thanks." I walked over and took a sip. Sugar. I didn't take sugar in my tea, but quite frankly, too-sweet tea was the least of our problems. *Is it completely bizarre that we're pretending everything's fine?* Was James also in turmoil and just a phenomenally good actor, or was I cornering the turmoil market with this peculiar mix of panic and fury?

I took another sip of tea—I was going to need as much of it as I could stomach—and then set about the task of packing quickly, which I hate to do. I like ordered, meticulous packing, so I know where everything is on the other end. In a minor miracle, I managed the task in about three minutes.

"Ready?" said the smiling man.

"Sure," said the smiling woman. *Oh boy, it's gunna be a long drive.*

*

That day, we were driving south-west to catch the overnight boat trip on Milford Sound. The route would take us through the town of Te Anau, the last vestige of civilisation on our journey, where we planned to have a quick lunch.

After lunch, we would make the beautiful, but sometimes treacherous, drive to Milford—winding roads, rock falls, sudden changes in temperature. Weren't travel guides supposed to *sell* you on a place, rather than terrify the pants off you? Although, I was sure the risky drive would be worth it. I'd seen those horribly long *Lord of the Rings* movies and the best thing about them was the epic scenery.

Around an hour after we left Queenstown and about halfway to Te Anau, we still hadn't said much. That giant purple elephant was taking up not only the entire backseat, but most of the oxygen in the car. I couldn't stand it any longer.

"James?"

"Mmm?" He kept his eyes on the road.

"Is everything okay between us?" Why mince words, right? I mean, I was in the middle of nowhere, thousands of kilometres from home with a man who may or may not love me. What did I have to lose?

He sighed heavily, and my stomach lurched. "I hope so." *I hope so?* What the hell was that supposed to mean? Had he suddenly turned into an enigmatic teenager? "No, that's not right." He grabbed my hand and pulled it to his lips, kissing it. "We are absolutely okay. That is, if you say we are." *Uh, yeah, that's not gunna fly, mate.*

I channelled every ounce of my teacher patience into what I said next. "I guess what I'm asking is, does running into Portia"—I struggled not to choke on her name—"affect *us* in any way? You seemed a little shaken up by the whole thing. And you've been ... well, you've been kind of strange ever since." I threw a look his way to see his reaction. He had one of those smiles on his face that isn't really a smile, the one where your mouth is stretched back into a straight line and your lips disappear.

"I'm sorry. I really am. I don't want to upset you or concern you. Seeing her didn't change how I feel about you. It just threw me. I mean, I've never run into her in *London*, amongst millions of people, and here we are in probably the furthest place on the planet and it ... it just threw me." *I'll say.*

He squeezed my hand. "I handled it badly, and I've been sitting here wondering how to raise it without making things worse. And, only one of us was the adult, here—you." He glanced at me, clearly not wanting to tear his eyes away from the winding road for too long, and offered me an *actual* smile.

"Forgive me?"

I felt a surge of relief and I imagined the purple elephant popping like a balloon. "Of course," I said. "We're good." I even let myself believe that.

*

355

Nothing could have prepared me for the scenery as we approached Milford Sound, not travel guides or even eleven hours of Peter Jackson's epic tourism commercial.

The road cut through a narrow valley, its floor a carpet of low shrubs, mostly green, but some in a dull yellow. The slopes rose steeply either side of the valley, some tenacious plants clinging to the rockfaces. Mountains in a steely grey climbed into the sky, roughly hewn and inhospitable. I kept my eyes peeled for falling rocks, as if the mountains would spit them at us for trespassing. It was both awe-inspiring and a little terrifying, so I was relieved when we pulled up to where the boat was docked, unscathed.

If I'm honest, it looked like a fishing boat—a super-*fancy* fishing boat, granted, but I wondered if it had been bought from a fishing company and made over. Maybe it would smell like fish. It had two-and-a-half storeys—decks?—and what looked like a third row of smaller portholes close to the waterline, perhaps where the crew slept. Three tall masts promised some actual sailing, which I hoped we'd get to do.

The crew was lovely when they welcomed us aboard, and a steward took our carry-on bags and led the way to our cabin. I only hoped in my hasty packing that I hadn't left anything I needed in my suitcase. If I had, I wouldn't see it until the next day; it was in the boot of the car.

The interior of the boat was far nicer than I'd thought it would be, and it didn't smell like fish—always a good thing when it comes to accommodation. Our cabin was cosy, but we had a queen-sized bed and our own bathroom. The décor was what I would call "Hugh Hefneresque"—lots of heavy fabrics in dark colours. The steward placed our bags on the bed—pretty much the only flat surface available—and welcomed us again. I was prepared with a cash tip and beat James to it. A funny look crossed his face, but he didn't say anything.

Oops—perhaps that was a faux pas.

I still hadn't been able to pay for anything. He'd insisted on picking up the check at dinner the night before, which wasn't overly surprising considering how the evening had played out, *and* he'd paid for lunch in Te Anau when I went to the bathroom, but I wanted to contribute to the trip somehow. Based on his reaction, however, tipping the steward was not the way to do it.

"Shall we go out on deck and watch our departure?" I asked, brightly. His smile returned.

"Absolutely." I turned to leave the cabin, and he caught my arm. "Wait, come here a moment." I looked up at him, his serious eyes sending a jolt of panic through me. *You've changed your mind.* A gentle smile turned his lips up at the corner and reached his eyes. *Or, maybe not.* "I just haven't kissed you today. Not properly, anyway."

"Oh." There was nothing else to say.

He leant down and tenderly pressed his lips to mine. It almost felt like a first kiss, tentative and sweet. As the sweetness gave way to something more intense, rawer, I wrapped my arms tightly around his neck. His hands moved from my arms to my waist, pulling me closer. I could feel him hard against me, wanting me. "We're skipping the launch," he said, his forehead pressed against mine. I nodded, speechless, blinking away the tears in my eyes.

He wants me. He loves me.

Then we made an utter mess of that perfectly made, Hugh Hefner bed.

*

The afternoon was just incredible. Yes, we missed the launch, but the scenery as we sailed the sound—they did put the sails up!—was breathtaking, or rather, breath-*giving*. The air was so fresh, so clean, I could taste it, and I inhaled great gulps of it, clearing my head of all the niggling and nasty thoughts from the night before.

The surface of the water undulated, never breaking, but seeming to move politely aside as the boat made its way into the folds of the sound. The water changed colour seamlessly, nature's depth gauge revealed in the colours of precious stones—sapphire, malachite, and aquamarine. *Siobhan would love this*, I thought.

The mountains rising from the depths of the water were conical and a rich, velvety green, like the kind of mountains small children draw. Where the green gave way to roughly hewn, inky rock, waterfalls fell from great heights, some bridal veils, some brilliant white ponytails, all meeting the water of the sound in halos of mist. There was no need for talking—a shared look said it all—but I did take dozens of photographs.

Dinner was a communal buffet, which was far more fun

than it sounds. We sat opposite each other at a long table, eating roast beef and crispy potatoes, with steamed pudding for dessert. The menu was straight out of my grandmother's playbook circa 1980-something and I loved every bite. We chatted about the day, the incredible things we'd seen, and were engaged in conversation a few times by other couples and a father and son who were travelling together for his seventieth birthday.

One woman referred to James as my husband—isn't it odd when people just assume things like that?—and I glanced at him to see if he'd heard. He didn't seem to have; he was talking to her husband about yachts. I'd almost forgotten that James had owned a yacht. Then that made me think of Duncan, and I indulged in a little nostalgic moment where I missed him and wondered if I'd ever get to see him and Gerry again.

And as James hadn't heard, I didn't correct the woman about being married to him. A sliver of me enjoyed it; it was like trying on a pair of heels that were way higher than I'd normally wear, but made me feel super sexy.

After dinner, the cruise director—that may not have been her actual job title, but in my mind, she was Julie like on *The Love Boat*—announced it was time for games, and she meant *board* games.

"Do you know why they're called board games?" I asked James, a cheeky smile on my face. He shook his head. "Because they're *boring*. Get it? *Bored* games." I waggled my eyebrows and grinned at him, and he smiled one of those half-smiles which isn't really a smile.

Maybe he just was tired—it *had* been a long day—but

whatever the reason for his less-than-enthusiastic response to my pun, my inner voice conjured the most unhelpful thought possible. *Josh would have laughed at that.* I told it to shut up.

As James and I snuck out to avoid the "bored games", I grabbed an opened, but mostly full, bottle of red wine from the bar, adding thievery to my resume. I checked the label as we walked hand in hand to our cabin. It was a pinot noir and I applauded my good luck at snagging my favourite red varietal.

"You are very naughty, you know," James teased, as he opened our cabin door. I slipped into the room past him and plopped down on the bed, grinning. "You know, they would have just given you the bottle if you'd asked. Maybe glasses too."

"But where's the fun in that?" I asked. I may have already been a little tipsy from the wine we'd had at dinner. "There must be glasses in here." I climbed off the bed—ungracefully, I'm sure—and started foraging in our tiny cabin. It only took a few moments to locate the tea and coffee making paraphernalia, and I grabbed the two mugs one-handed, holding them aloft. "See? Perfect."

His response was that enigmatic smile he gave me sometimes, the one that I hoped meant, "you are very sexy and utterly charming". I set about pouring some of my ill-gotten spoils and handed a mug of the pinot to James. He took it carefully and had a sip.

"Probably not the best way to enjoy this, but it isn't bad," he said. When I took a sip, I thought it was delicious. He sat on the rumpled bed and made a nest of pillows for us to lean against. I climbed on and sat beside him and we drank from our mugs of wine in silence.

And as often happens when it's all too quiet and I am wondering what the other person is thinking, I did something stupid. I let myself pore over the previous evening. And *that's* when it hit me. Portia was the woman James had mentioned when we were in Greece.

When I asked him if he had someone in his life—feeling out whether he was actually available—he'd replied that there was someone once, but it hadn't worked out because she didn't want the kind of life he had—it wasn't for her.

It had been obvious from the emotion clouding his eyes that he had loved this "someone" and that she had broken his heart. And in a cabin on a boat on a sound in New Zealand, I realised that Portia was James's "someone".

No wonder he'd been so shaken up.

Without saying anything, I took his hand. He turned his head towards me and I did the same, looking into his eyes. There was love there—and a hint of sadness. He leant over and kissed me gently, a kiss which lasted a long while—not urgent and fraught with need, but tender and loving. We didn't finish the wine, but we did fall asleep wrapped up in each other. The last thing I remembered was James stroking my hair, and me thinking that I didn't want to see sadness in his eyes anymore.

*

I awoke well before sun-up, my head on James's chest and a horrid crick in my neck. That's the part you don't see in the movies. I managed to extricate myself from our tangle of limbs and sheets without waking him. I got out of the bed slowly, hoping not to disturb him, and went into the tiny bathroom. I splashed water on my face and swished some toothpaste to try and shake off the grogginess of poor sleep cut short.

But despite the lack of sleep, when I peered into the mirror above the sink, I didn't look wretched. There was even a hint of colour in my cheeks. I looked like a woman who was falling in love with someone who loved her back. I opened the door of the bathroom and peeked out. James was lying with an arm behind his head, looking directly at me, smiling.

"Hi," I whispered.

"Hi," he whispered back. "Why are we whispering?"

I shrugged and jumped onto the bed, climbing up to re-join him under the covers. I resumed my place, his arm around me, my head on his chest and my leg thrown over his. My neck protested, but I ignored it.

"I wasn't sure if we'd wake up in time," he said, "but now we *are* awake, we should definitely go up on deck to see the sunrise."

"Sounds good." I propped myself up and checked the clock next to his side of the bed. "Still a while, yet, though." I snuggled back under the covers and closed my eyes, basking in the feeling of being wrapped up in him. He smelled so good.

And then, I ruined everything.

"James?"

"Mmm."

"Can I ask you something about Portia?"

I felt him stiffen—and not the good kind. *Uh oh. Abort. Abort. Abort.*

"What's that?"

I couldn't *not* ask the question now, no matter what my inner voice said. I'd already obliterated the mood. "Uh, I just wondered if she was the woman you told me about when we were in Greece."

There was a moment before he replied—only a moment, but it was enough to send a jolt through me and my stomach lit up with nerves.

"Yes, she is."

There was no way not to ask the next question, to just pretend that everything was fine, then get up, get dressed, and go and watch the sound come to life with the sunrise. And even though I dreaded his response, even though some part of me *knew* what was to come, I asked the next question.

"So, it ended because she didn't want a long-distance relationship?"

James travelled all the time. I knew that being with him meant enduring the trials of a long-distance relationship even if we shared a home base. I'd thought about it a lot over the past few months, and I'd decided it would be okay. I could do it. I could do regular bouts of being apart.

That sigh again and my nerves turned to nausea. Then he replied. "No, it ended because *I* didn't want a long-distance relationship. I wanted her with me *all* the time."

All the clichés about the moment you learn something that changes everything—that time almost stands still, that you feel every emotion at once, that you feel sick and exposed and divorced from your body—are true.

And his simple, honest, heart-wrenching reply changed everything.

All I could say was, "Oh," but I'm sure it spoke volumes.

Without discussing it further, we did the things people do on the morning of an overnight boat trip on Milford Sound— as though we hadn't just come to an impasse.

We got dressed and went up on deck in time to see the sunrise—well, the sun lightening the sky. In the sound, there were steep mountains on either side of the water screening the horizon from us mere mortals. But to say that it was "epic" would have been an understatement. I'm sure the word was *created* for moments like that sunrise, but it's been misappropriated so often to describe a red-carpet dress, or an episode of a TV show, or even a burger, that it was not enough.

The light seemed like an entity in itself, as though, if I reached out far enough, I could touch it. The sky above the eastern mountains graduated upward from milky blue to robin's-egg blue and streams of sunlight shot out from behind the mountains as though they were wearing a giant crown of light.

And true to New Zealand's moniker as "the Land of the Long White Cloud", or "*Aotearoa*" in Maori, there were these incredibly low long clouds winding through the sound. They looked like the fake snow people put on their windowsills at Christmas time—dense, fluffy tendrils hovering just above the water.

That I could observe all of this, that I could wonder at the incredible natural beauty surrounding us while my heart was being squeezed in a vice, was a minor miracle. And I held on to that miracle, so I wouldn't have to think about the inevitable conversation that would end us.

When it came, we were back in our cabin, packing in a silence so stifling I couldn't bear it any longer.

"I wish—" I said.

"I'm sorry—" he said at the same time.

We both stopped. I took a trembling breath.

"You go ahead," he said quietly.

I let out my breath as slowly as I could, my insides in turmoil. "I wish I wanted that life. Your life." I glanced up to see him nod, then sit heavily on the end of the bed. There was so much more I wanted to say, but I knew I couldn't say it without looking him in the eye. I went to the door, turned, and leant against it. James looked up at me. There was something in his gaze, in those kind eyes, that emboldened me to speak the truth, *my* truth.

"I had no idea when I went to Greece that I would meet someone like you, or that someone like you even existed. I was not at a good point in my life. I was ..." I paused, trying to find the right word. "... Broken. I wasn't *me*. I'd lost *me*."

Tears prickled my eyes again and I blinked them back, wishing them gone. I needed to get through this. "I was a giant ball of nerves and worry and sadness before I started that trip. But I went anyway. I was brave, and it changed me." I knew if I could just make James understand what I'd gone through, he'd understand *why* I couldn't be with him.

I took a deep breath.

"That whole trip—*everything*—the things we did, what I saw, what I *ate* ..." A smile alighted on my face as I laughed gently at myself. James chuckled, and we smiled at each other through our tears.

"And the *people*—Duncan, my friends from the boat, you, *Josh*—I haven't talked to you about him, because it wasn't right to and maybe now isn't the time, but meeting him was important to me too. And everything that happened, all the laughing and telling each other our stories, the long conversations—some frivolous, some serious—all of that, it *affected* me.

"I remembered who I used to be, that I was adventurous and sexy and *funny*. I mean, I am really fucking hilarious ..." I laughed and James joined in. "I remembered that I had a lot to be grateful for. And I also realised I'd been neglecting my own life."

I was at the hardest part.

"After Greece, after our time together in London, I went home and started participating in my life again—I've told you about that. And, it felt great—*feels* great. I *love* what I'm doing. I love living in Sydney. I love my friends and my job ... my *life*. And I *do* have feelings for you, and I thought I was prepared to drop everything to be with you, if that's how it all turned out, but I'm realising now, almost as I speak, that I can't. I can't pick up and leave the rest of my life to be with you— especially not how you want it to be. I just ... I can't be *that* Sarah again."

I dissolved into sobs. James came to me and held me, and I clung to him. It was the most adult moment of my life, and probably the most heart-breaking.

He held me for some time. I couldn't say how long, as time is hard to discern when your world has been thrust into chaos. He was crying too and when we eventually let go of each other, he rested his forehead on mine.

"Are you sure?" he asked.

It was a fair question. If I'd been in his position, *I* would want to make absolutely sure that the person I loved—who might just love me back—didn't want to spend their life travelling the world with me.

But I couldn't.

I couldn't be someone else's sidekick no matter how appealing James's life sounded. Had he met me right after I'd split with Neil when was wallowing in self-pity and self-doubt, hating my life and wanting to be rescued from it like some modern-day Cinderella, I would have been ecstatic to make a life with a jet-setting, loving, and over-the-top-sexy million-aire.

The thing was, though, I was no longer that woman. I left that woman on a boat in Greece—or maybe I left her on the pier in Santorini. When I met Josh.

Josh.

Oh, my god. Meeting Josh had been the catalyst for living my bigger life, the reason I couldn't be with James.

Now, *that's* ironic, Alanis Morissette.

Chapter 22

Being on a boat in the middle of a remote body of water, several hours' drive from the nearest international airport with a wonderful man you've just broken up with, sucks. I do not recommend it.

As we waited for the boat to get back to shore, we sat up on deck in silence—me (sort of) reading a book on my Kindle and James flicking through a day-old Auckland newspaper. Logistics were the last thing I wanted to talk about, but I had to say something. We were supposed to be in New Zealand for two more days, but I just wanted to go home.

Even so, it shook me when James's voice cut into my thoughts. "I'm guessing you won't want to stay—in New Zealand, I mean—at least with me."

At least with me.

It was one of those definitive moments. I had to be a grown-up, to rip off the Band-Aid. So what if it tore out a large chunk of my heart with it? "I think I should go home," I said simply, stealing a look at him. His jaw tightened and he nodded.

"Of course. We can drive to Queenstown as soon as we get

back to shore. I'll organise your flight when we get to the airport."

"Oh, you don't have to do that—"

He put up a hand and smiled weakly. "Let me." It was my turn to nod.

The time passed as it does. I'm not usually one to wish my life away, but that morning could not have ended sooner. Eventually, we got to the dock and I felt a rush of relief as I stepped onto dry land, one step closer to home.

Back in the car, as we made our way to Queenstown, I sat with my phone clasped between my hands, my knuckles white. As soon as I had service, I wanted to contact Lindsey. Although, what was I going to say?

Hi. James and I broke up so I'm coming home early. He's amazing and good to me, but he wants me to travel around the world with him and give up everything I've only just rediscovered, so I had to end it. Oh, by the way, can you pick me up from the airport?

In the end, what I sent was this:

I'm coming home early—will explain everything then. Will let you know flight stuff as soon as I do. ps it's bad. Sx

I sent it the moment we emerged from the mountain pass, just after we saw one of those big green road signs for Te Anau and my phone started bleeping with all the messages and notifications from the past twenty-four hours.

Then I checked those messages and notifications.
Josh:

I have amazing news! Call me as soon as you get this.

I checked the date and time. He'd sent it at lunchtime the day before, right after I'd entered that very same mountain pass. *Great, he's going to think I'm ignoring him.* I sent off a reply, mindful that James was sitting right beside me.

Hi. Sorry. I'm out of town.

(Not a lie.)

Will call you when I'm back. Excited to hear your news.

There—*almost* honest. I *was* out of town and I *was* excited to hear his news, even though I suspected that when he told me, I'd be playing the role of "awesome long-distance friend".

And then my brain did the thing it does when you're supposed to be in anguish, but it just can't cope, so it takes you somewhere ludicrous. I suddenly remembered the moment in *Clueless* when Cher realises that she loves her stepbrother—her stepbrother called *Josh*.

And just like Cher, I had a flood of memories of *my* Josh—Joshua Walker, the dork who made me laugh so hard I couldn't breathe, who showed me that I, too, wanted a bigger life, the guy who I felt like myself with, and had fun adventures with. And the guy who lived on the other side of the world and was almost a decade younger than me, the one who didn't know how he felt about me.

There I was with the most handsome man I'd ever seen in real life, a man who made enough money for me never to have to worry about it again, a man who gave me mind-blowing orgasms, a man who *loved* me, and what did I realise?

I love Josh.

I said it to myself, over and over—not out loud, of course—but it *was* liberating. I had promised myself I'd decide between my two boyfriends after New Zealand and in a weird way I had.

That said, the one I chose wanted a vacationship, not a real commitment, so what I'd *actually* chosen was to be single.

My phone bleeped twice. They'd both replied.

OMFG!!!!!! Airport—yes, no worries. Love you. FUCK!

That one was from Lindsey.

And this one from Josh:

Sounds great! Can't wait. Jxxx

Three kisses. Three! I figured it must be incredibly big news.

Maybe he's decided he loves me and can't live without me. Sure, Sarah. Get a frigging grip. You haven't even said goodbye to James yet.

I really couldn't wait until I had—said goodbye, that is. I know that sounds awful, but when it's over and you're hurting, you just want it to *be* over.

Again, I strongly recommend *not* breaking up while on holiday—and it was my second time in a matter of weeks. I knew there was a reason I hadn't wanted to meet anyone in Greece.

*

"Do you have everything?" James asked. Everything about his demeanour said "acquaintance" rather than "former contender for the love of my life".

"Yep," I replied, just as benignly. In contrast, an ugly snake of misery was weaving its way through my gut.

We stood next to the security checkpoint, regarding each other awkwardly. I was positive I looked atrocious—like a confused, miserable woman, who'd cried a lot in the last eight hours and needed a giant mug of tea and a lie down.

We started speaking at the same time again.

"Sarah—"

"James—"

We shared a half-hearted laugh. "Please, go ahead." Ever the gentleman, James.

"Okay. I was just going to say that you truly are a wonderful man." His chin dropped to his chest and he sighed. I was screwing it up. *Do not give him the "it's not you, it's me" bullshit, Sarah.* "That came out wrong. Sorry. I mean, you *are*, but ... oh, crap, I'm making a mess of this." That made him lift his head and I was surprised to see a smile—an *actual* smile on his face.

"You are a lovely woman, Sarah Parsons. I am truly, *truly*

sorry that I am not the man who gets to make you happy for the rest of your life, but I *am* glad I've known you." Then he leant down and kissed my cheek.

A gentleman, and possibly the most perfect man in existence.

I dropped my carry-on and handbag and threw my arms around his neck, hugging him tightly. "Bye," I whispered. "And thank you." Then I let go, picked up my bags and turned towards the security line before I could rethink my decision, before I shoved aside everything I truly wanted and stayed with him forever. I didn't turn back as I placed my bags on the conveyor belt and walked slowly alongside them. I went through the scanner and by the time I turned around on the other side, he was gone.

James Cartwright was gone.

Do not cry. Do not cry. Do not cry.

I murmured it as a mantra as I walked away from security and looked for somewhere to buy a drink. I found a bar close to my gate and climbed up onto a stool.

"Hi there," said a cheerful and an impossibly Kiwi-accented guy. I sometimes wonder if the Kiwis are taking the "puss" out of their own accents. "What can I get you?" he said, which sounded like, *Whut cun Oi gat ew?*

"Wine, please. Red. I don't care what kind. And a lot. Of wine."

Maybe it was my tone, or possibly my strange syntax, but his look changed from "cheer" to "concern" in an instant. He reached above his head to take a large wine glass from the rack, then below the counter to retrieve a bottle of red with the cork half sticking out. He pulled the cork and poured me a very generous glass of wine. He pushed it across the bar to me.

"Pinot noir," he said. *Pinot noir*. Of *course* it was. I was in New Zealand and I wanted red wine and they were famous for their frigging pinots and I should have known that's what I would get. But right at that moment, I was supposed to be tasting pinot noir in the Otago region with James and *not* sitting in the airport waiting to fly home early—without him.

Do not cry. Do not cry. Do not cry.

I said thank you to the lovely bartender and took a sip of the wine. It was delicious, which made me feel even more miserable. Maybe I should have ordered a cup of lemon juice as penance for breaking James's heart.

I had gone on a trip to Greece not wanting to meet anyone, and I'd met two men. Two!

What the actual fuck, universe? I've been with the longest list of assholes in the history of the world (that may be a slight exaggeration), *then you send me two awesome men, but they each want different things from me, so I get a taste of what it's like to be with someone amazing, but not actually get to be with someone amazing, and for what? Just to fuck with me? ARGHHH!*

Yep, I was feeling quite sorry for myself.

I fished out my phone and started scrolling through Facebook. It was something normal to do in a moment that was anything but normal. But my mind kept returning to my angry, self-pitying thoughts, the mental version of a mouth sore—the kind you can't help but touch with your tongue, over and over, a kind of masochistic salve, both painful and reassuring at the same time.

Maybe I should just tell Josh that I came to New Zealand with James, so he hates me and leaves me alone.

As I made a serious dent in the wine, my mind flip-flopped.

But I love Josh. And maybe, just maybe, he loves me, and we'll be together—and not just for trips away, but properly.

I finished my wine *way* faster than I should have.

"Would you like another one?" asked my attentive bartender.

The tiny devil and angel on my shoulders went into battle. Red wine makes me loopy lala if I'm already sad. But then again, I would rather feel loopy lala than heartbroken. I was saved from myself by the announcement that my flight was boarding. I picked up my handbag and took out my wallet so I could pay for the wine. It took a few moments for me to catch the bartender's attention, but when I did, he surprised me.

"No charge," he said.

"No, no, it's okay. I'm happy to pay." I waved the card at him. He shook his head and gave me a particularly pitying smile.

"It was the end of a bottle I opened yesterday. It's all good. It's on me." My credit card was still in my hand and he reached across and gently pushed it away. "It's okay."

It's okay. Logically, I knew he meant it was okay to comp me the wine, but my lizard brain, my poor little self who had just broken up with the handsome silver fox, heard, "it's all going to be okay, Sarah—you'll get past this—you did the right thing".

And then I burst into tears.

Somehow, I made it onto the plane. I wasn't even embarrassed by my outburst, which only subsided after I was seated and buckled in; I was too miserable to be embarrassed.

Of course, James had bought me a business-class ticket home. I even had an entire row to myself, which meant that the flight attendants were particularly attentive. Or, that may have been because they took one look at me and decided to rally.

We have a "code blues", people. This is not a drill.

See? Loopy lala.

*

Three hours pass quickly when the flight attendant brings you cups of tea and glasses of bubbles in alternating succession. I thought that if I ever did get married, I should ask her—Dee—to be my maid of honour. Lins and Cat would understand.

When we landed in Sydney, I took my phone out, switching it off flight mode. It started bleeping and lighting up as though I'd been off the grid for weeks instead of hours.

Lindsey:

Text when you've landed and I'll head over. Love you. I'm coming!!!!

Relief flooded through me. In less than an hour, I'd be ensconced at Lins and Nick's and they'd look after me and I could snuggle with Domino. *Domino!* The only man in my life who didn't make me miserable. *I'll be a crazy cat lady for the rest of my life—happily.*

Josh:

Hey. When are you back? Really want to talk to you soon! Jx

Oh, Josh. Joshie. Josharama. I love you. I love your face and your cute smile and your beautiful eyes. But, I'm with Domino now, so we can't be together.

Yep, I was definitely drunk.

My mum:

Hi darling. Dad and I want you to come for lunch next Sunday. We've invited someone we think you'll like.

Good grief. My mum was *still* trying to fix me up. If only she knew! But if she *did* know, I would never hear the end of giving up the millionaire for my cat. NEVER. I decided I could put my mum off for a day or two. She was used to it.

For the first time ever, I was the first person off the plane. I smiled weakly at Dee and thanked her again. The sympathetic look on her face was enough to tell me I was in an utter shambles.

Immigration was quick—those automated thingies—and my bag was the first one down the chute at the baggage carousel—also a first for me. I tried *not* to think about the fact that I could have been flying business class around the world with James for the rest of my life. I wasn't successful, the thought only adding to my misery. By the time I dragged myself through customs, I was pretty sure I looked like Eeyore on a bad day.

Did I have anything to declare? Yes! I declare that my love life sucks and that I am thirty-seven and a hot mess. I didn't say that. Instead, I chose the "nothing to declare" line and went straight through. Lindsey was waiting on the other side of the door and, just like Cat had done a few months before at Heathrow, Lins ignored the signs telling her to stay clear of the area, and came and enveloped me in a huge hug.

I was too tired to cry—and probably too drunk—but I clung to her. She pulled away from me and gave me an appraising look. "Here," she said, reaching for my suitcase and carry-on. "I'll take these. Follow me." I obeyed, following her through the airport like a lost duckling.

Less than thirty minutes later, I was sitting on her couch, a blanket her nana had crocheted on my lap, Domino purring loudly next to me, and a giant mug of tea in one hand. Have I mentioned how much I love my bestie?

Nick had made himself scarce—Nick who usually enjoyed a front-row seat to my love life disasters. *This must be* really *bad.*

"Spill. And don't skip anything. I'll know."

That was "Tough Love" by Lindsey Haskell, everyone. Stick around, because the hits will keep on coming.

She was watching me, her look a combination of "concern" and "don't bullshit me". And even though I *really* didn't want to relive everything from the past few days, I knew I had to.

Lins would listen to me, then help me figure out how to get past this latest love catastrophe. She was good at both those things and when it came to me, she'd had a lot of experience.

I sipped my tea and petted Domino as I walked her through the whole trip, all the conversations and everything I'd felt at the time, only glossing over the sex stuff. I wrapped up by telling her my realisation about Josh.

"So, you love Josh?" I nodded tentatively, no longer confident of my feelings.

"And when you got back from Hawaii, you thought you and Josh had broken up—that you're just going to end up as friends. Right?" I nodded. I was turning into one of those little dogs that sits on the dashboard of your car.

"And then you went to New Zealand with James. Why?" My eyes flew to hers, panicked.

"What do you mean?"

"I mean exactly that. Why did you go to New Zealand with James?"

"Because I wanted to be sure."

"About James or Josh?"

I reminded myself I loved Lindsey *because* she asked the hard questions, because she knew I needed to answer them—for *me*. She wouldn't let me hide from myself. I sat there steeping in the uncomfortable thoughts that tumbled over each other.

Why did I go to New Zealand with James? Josh aside, did I ever really see me and James working out? Have I known all along we wouldn't end up together?

Clarity—even through the fog of fatigue and sadness and

expensive business-class bubbles—smacked me in the head. I looked at Lins who was still watching me.

"Because James makes me—sorry, *made* me feel good about myself. Sort of. I mean, sometimes I felt like an unsophisticated idiot around him, but generally, on the whole, for the most part"—she dropped her head to the side with a look that said, "get on with it"—"he made me feel special and beautiful and desired."

"But?"

"But it wasn't really me. It was exhausting being that person."

She smiled at me, a gentle, loving smile. "You *are* special and beautiful, Sez, but there's something to be said for being yourself when you're with someone—and knowing that they love *you*."

"Yeah. Not that any of it matters now. I mean James and I want very different things and neither of us was going to be happy with a compromise."

"No, probably not. But, from what you've said, Josh knows *you*, Sarah. Doesn't being with *him* feel right?"

"Sort of."

"Why 'sort of'?"

Tears stung my eyes. "Because he doesn't know if he wants me."

"Well, that does seem to be the case—for now, at least. Look, I promise this is the last question, but how long are you going to wait for him to make up his mind?"

I picked up Domino, much to his chagrin, and held him close to me. He wriggled for a few seconds, then succumbed to my suffocating affection. I nuzzled the top of his head with my chin. "Men suck," I said. "Not you, Domino," I added quickly. Lins laughed and I hesitantly joined in with a derisive chuckle. I really did think that men sucked.

"Can we consider the last one hypothetical?"

She got up and patted me on the shoulder as she walked past me to the kitchen. "No. We can't."

I pouted.

"Hey. Can I ask you something?" I asked, twisting around to face her while she put the kettle on. Domino had had enough and jumped down to the floor.

"Yep."

"If Josh does get his shit together and decides he wants to be with me—and *not* as a *vacationship* ..." I heard the bitterness in my voice and checked it.

"Mmm?" she prompted. Her bum was sticking out of the pantry.

"Hey, do you have any Tim Tams?" She stood up and tossed me an unopened packet, which I nearly caught. She rolled her eyes at me; I truly suck at catching things. I picked up the packet from the floor and opened it. "I'll have the broken ones," I called. I hoped they were all broken. I pulled out the first one, which was still intact, and bit off the corner, then spoke with my mouth full. "So, *if* Josh figures out that he wants to be with me ... do I tell him about James?"

I had her full attention then. "You mean about going on a romantic trip with James *after* you went on a romantic trip with Josh, or about James being in Sydney over the next few months, *or* about James wanting to be with you for the rest of your lives?" Wow. That last part really stung. But she was right.

"Yeah, well, when you put it like that ..."

"Sez, you can't tell Josh *any* of it."

"But shouldn't I be honest with him?" I already knew the answer, but I wanted to hear it out loud from Lindsey. Somehow that would justify it, because, despite her bossy ways and her frequent dips into sarcasm, she was the most principled person I knew. Her moral barometer was foolproof.

She came and sat opposite me, leaning forward, her elbows on her knees. "Listen to me. No good can come of telling Josh anything more than what he already knows."

"But—"

"No! There are no 'buts'. It would hurt him. And it would hurt your relationship."

"But what if he asks me a direct question? What then?"

"Lie." *Lindsey* was telling me to outright lie. *How the hell did I get myself into this stupid, crappy, fucked up mess?*

"Are you sure?"

"Yes." She lowered her voice, even though we could hear the TV from the study, and it was highly unlikely Nick was listening to anything we were saying. "There are things I've never told Nick—stuff that would really hurt him if he knew." I frowned. I wondered if *I* knew any of those things. I racked my brain. Did I know anything about Lindsey that would qualify?

"That guy," I whispered, suddenly realising. "The one from Queensland. Before your wedding." Her lips pulled into a taut line and she nodded slightly.

383

"Never told him."

"Oh. Wow."

"Yeah. I knew I fucked up and I knew it would destroy Nick. And I wanted to marry him. So ..."

She let the last thought trail off and took a biscuit out of the packet.

So, Lindsey had never told Nick about her fling with that guy in Queensland the month before their wedding. Right. I was convinced. I would never, ever tell Josh all those things about James, even if we only ended up as friends.

Lins and I finished our Tim Tams in silence. Then my phone bleeped. I dug it out from under Nana's blanket. A text from Josh:

Hey. Just wondering if you're free to FaceTime now?

I must have looked as stricken as I felt, because Lins got up and came to read over my shoulder.

"Apparently, the American boy has something he needs to say."

"But I can't talk to him like this." I indicated my whole self, which was a wretched, *wretched* mess and not fit for other humans to see.

"Text him back. Tell him you'll FaceTime in half an hour. Then get your bum in the shower."

I did *exactly* as I was told.

Chapter 23

Josh had seen me first thing in the morning, no makeup and hair askew. He'd seen me jet-lagged, crying, tired, hungover, hangry, and after a deluge looking like a drowned sewer rat.

But he wasn't seeing me post-break-up until I had showered and put on a *lot* of makeup.

At Lindsey's command, I took myself off to the guest bathroom to shower and tackle the mess that was me. After I dressed, I piled my curls on top of my head in a loose bun—my signature "I don't know what to do with my hair, but hopefully this looks okay" style. I glopped on twice as much moisturiser as usual, hoping it would soak into my skin quickly enough to make me look half-alive.

There probably wasn't enough concealer in the world to handle my tragedy of a face, but I did my best, disguising my red-rimmed eyes and Rudolph nose. I added some mascara—waterproof, just in case—and a swoop of blush. I dotted some translucent powder over the top and appraised my work.

At least it was FaceTime and not face to face. Maybe I could sit next to a window, so he could only see me in silhouette, like they do on *60 Minutes*.

"Lins?" I called out the bathroom door. After a moment, she popped her head around the corner.

"Well?" I asked, holding my arms out wide.

"You look fine," she said.

"Fine? Is that all?" I looked at myself in the mirror. She was right, but sometimes I wished she lie to me. Still, "fine" would have to do as I was running out of time. I sighed. "Okay, let's get this over with."

"That's the spirit," she teased.

I followed her back into the living room, where I rifled through my carry-on bag for my iPad. "You know what I mean. What if his big news is that he's getting married?"

She didn't dignify my idiotic question with a response. I plopped down on the couch and Lindsey sat on the one opposite me. "Are you going to listen in?" I asked.

"I don't have to." She started to get up.

"No, no, stay. Sorry." I stared at the iPad. Then, being the master procrastinator, I called my cat. "Dom-i-noooooo. Here, baby." Nothing. As I said, he's his own cat. I chanced a glance at Lins and she gave me a look that said, "Get on with it, you wuss".

I took a deep breath, turned on the iPad, and tapped the FaceTime icon. I tapped Josh's name, which was at the top of the list, and after two rings, his face appeared on the screen. A wave of happiness flooded over me and without guile or conscious thought, I grinned. It was *Josh*. And I'd missed his face.

"Hi!" he exclaimed. "You look great! How are you?" I laughed; his joy was irresistible.

"Great! Good, yes." It wasn't even a lie. "And thank you," I added.

"So, you're away for the weekend?" I'd already forgotten the lie I'd told to stave him off, but I quickly recovered.

"Yes, sort of, but I'm back in Sydney now." Then I remembered it was only Saturday. "I mean, we just went away for a couple of days." Great, I'd introduced a "we" into the lie. I said I recovered quickly; I did not say I recovered well.

Thankfully, he didn't seem to notice. "Oh, that's right—school holidays. I guess that means every day is like a weekend." He grinned at me from the screen and I felt a pang of guilt for the lie—and any others I'd have to tell to save his feelings.

"So, you said you've got some news?" *Please let it be good.* And by that I meant anything that didn't perpetuate the whole "vacationship" situation.

Because I didn't want that.

I didn't want a part-time vacation lover. If I was going to be with someone, I was going to *be* with them—long-distance, yes, probably at first, but I wanted a proper relationship, a home with someone, a *life* together.

Or, nothing. I was prepared to be on my own if it came to that, but I hoped it wouldn't. I held my breath, steeling myself for the worst.

"Yes!" he replied excitedly. "I wanted to show you something." *Oh-kay.* I let out the breath, intrigue trumping nerves. "Hang on a sec," he said, as he faffed about with his iPad. "Here," he said, finally. "This is what I wanted to show you."

I would never in a million bazillion years have guessed what it was. It was the view of a city skyline and peeking over the top was the Sydney Harbour Bridge.

Josh was in Sydney.

Dozens of emotions flooded through me, each competing for my attention—excitement, relief, bafflement, guilt. In moments, elation barged its way to the forefront. Josh was in my home city.

"Surprise!" he said, turning the camera back around to face him.

I was laughing and heard myself say, "Oh, wow. Oh, my god. You're *here*!" He grinned.

Lindsey's curiosity must have got the better of her, because she was suddenly behind me, leaning over the back of the couch and peering at the iPad.

"Hi," she said to Josh over my shoulder.

"Hi!" said Josh to my best friend. I figured I should introduce them.

"Josh—Lindsey—Lindsey—Josh." They waved at each other. The whole thing was surreal.

Lindsey patted me on the shoulder and left the room. She must have thought I'd be okay on my own and that I wouldn't completely screw everything up.

Then I blurted out my most pressing question. "So, what are you doing here?" *Oops. No, that's not right.* "Sorry, I mean, it's great, but ..."

"But what am I doing here?" He laughed good-naturedly

and I shook my head at my own ineloquence. *It's a miracle that I'm paid to teach English.*

"Well, things have moved incredibly fast with the new team and I'm in Sydney to set it all up. Anyway, there's lots to tell you about, but most importantly, I'm here for another week and I want to see you!"

The details started to sink in. "So, they chose Sydney then?"

"Sorry, what?"

"Sydney over Mumbai."

"Oh, yes. They did. I've been dying to tell you."

Then it hit me with full force. Josh was in *Sydney*. He was just a car ride away and he wanted to see me, and I *so* wanted to see him. I hadn't realised how much I'd missed him, even though it had only been a few weeks since Hawaii.

And yet ...

He was only in Sydney for a week. Then he'd be gone again, and I'd still be waiting for him to figure out what he wanted. I'd still be in a vacationship.

Maybe it was best that I didn't see him. Maybe I really had decided to be on my own. I felt the prickle of tears in my eyes and blinked them back.

Josh must have seen the procession of wretched thoughts register on my face, because he looked crestfallen. "Hey, is everything okay, Sarah?" When had I developed this knack for making the men that I cared about feel like rubbish?

"Yes, yes, it's ... of *course*. It's just so surprising, that's all." I wanted a time out from the conversation so I could catch my breath, but there was no way to do that without making him feel worse.

"But a good surprise, right?" My heart lurched at his earnestness, and I knew then that I needed to give him a chance—to see him, to see about us.

"It's a *wonderful* surprise, Josh."

"That's a relief," he replied with a shy smile. "'Cause, now you're back, I was hoping to take you out for dinner."

"You mean like a date?"

He laughed. "Yes, *exactly* like a date. Tonight, if you're free, but I totally get it if you already have plans." I was guessing he *didn't* mean my plans to curl up on Lindsey's couch and drink myself into oblivion while suffocating my cat with affection.

"Uh, no, no plans. I'm all yours." I mentally slapped myself for the poor choice of words—*all yours?* What if he didn't want me to be all his? Our conversation had more twists and turns than a pretzel.

Josh grinned, seeming to miss my faux pas. "Great. I'm staying at the Star Grand Residences in Darling Harbour. Do you know it?"

"Oh, yeah, I know where that is."

"So, how far away are you?"

"Oh, um, not far. I'm staying at Lindsey's—the one you just met—" *He remembers what happened three minutes ago, Sarah.* "It's near the beach, so about eight kilometres—five miles."

"Well, which would you rather? I can come to you, or you could come to me."

I wasn't ready to introduce Josh to Lindsey in person—or Nick—*especially* not Nick. I mean, who *knew* what he'd say to the "young one"? "I'll come and meet you in the city."

"That sounds great. Um ..." He bit his lower lip. "You could stay here tonight if you wanted." It wasn't an unreasonable thing for him to say since we'd just shared a bed in Hawaii. But before we shared another bed, I knew I had to tell Josh I wanted a proper relationship. If he only wanted to meet up for sleepovers in hotel rooms, I had to end it.

I was staring down my second break-up in as many days— either the unluckiest woman in the world, or a total bad ass for drawing a line in my romantic sandbox.

Still, there was no way I was saying any of that on a call. Despite (some) evidence to the contrary, I was not a total cow and even *I* knew it was bad form to break up over the internet. There was also a sliver of a chance that Josh had changed his mind about relationships. I almost laughed aloud at *that* thought.

But underpinning all this toing and froing, was an intense need just to see him—*badly*. I loved him, remember? I wasn't *not* going to see him when he was just down the road.

We made plans to meet—I stayed noncommittal about the sleepover—and I tapped the big red icon to end the call. Nick chose that moment for a snack run to the kitchen. "Hey," he said, patting my pom-pom of hair on the way past the couch.

"Hi."

"How's it goin'?"

I twisted around to see him elbow deep in the fridge. "Yeah, good, I guess. Um, where's Lins?"

He stopped looking in the fridge and closed it. "She's in our room, but *I'm* right here." He held out his arms like Jesus does in those pictures from Sunday school, but a benevolent being Nick was not, and I wasn't keen on raking through the debris of my love life with him.

"What? I can be a *person*, Sarah."

I sighed audibly, which he took as an invitation. He sat at the end of the couch and looked at me expectantly. I knew Nick's jokey, blokey personality wasn't all there was to him. Deep down—sometimes, *way* deep down—he had a good heart and I knew he thought of me as a sister. I took a deep breath and launched into the digest version of my situation. He listened without interrupting, his brow slightly furrowed, and he nodded in the appropriate places. I wrapped it up with, "So, I'm going to dinner with Josh. Tonight."

"But you don't know if you want to sleep with him, because you're worried he just wants some sort of ongoing holiday romance." It wasn't a question. Nick was just confirming he understood, and hearing it said back to me made me feel better—like my feelings were reasonable and valid.

"Exactly," I said. He nodded solemnly.

"You know, Sarah, we've been friends for a long time." He was right. I'd known him since he and Lindsey started dating more than a decade before. But we'd also forged a friendship separate from mine with Lindsey. Yes, he was a massive pain in the bum sometimes, but I knew that if I needed his help—even in the middle of the night, for whatever reason—he would be there, no questions asked. He really was like a brother to me.

"And I've watched you go out with some of the biggest wankers in Sydney." I laughed at my own expense, and he gave me a warm smile. "No really, I don't know how many times I've asked Lins where the hell you meet these tossers—"

I signalled for him to get on with it; his digression was getting depressing.

"Anyway, you know I love ya"—I started getting teary—"and even if you don't know this, I mean *really* know it, you deserve someone great, someone who loves you, and someone who's going to *be* here. Not some wanker who faffs about and strings you along." It was the most he'd ever said to me about that sort of thing and I blinked back tears.

"So, if this Josh guy doesn't want to get serious, give him the flick. And if he does, I promise to be nice to him." I laughed through my tears.

He scooched down the couch and gave me a Nick-style bear hug. I didn't get them very often, but he seemed to know when I needed them most. The last one had been after my previous cat, Lucy, had died.

Eventually Nick let me go, then stood up, looked over my shoulder and smiled. I turned around and saw Lindsey leaning against the doorway watching us. "She's all yours, love," he said to his wife. He gave her a quick kiss as he passed her in the doorway and followed it up with a smack on her bum. She rolled her eyes, smiling, then came over and plopped down next to me while I blew my nose.

"Two things," she said. "First, no more crying. We're running out of tissues." I nodded and managed a smile. "Second, Josh is *way* hotter than his photos!"

I threw my head back and laughed, and she raised her eyebrows at me. "So, what are you going to wear to dinner?"

*

Five minutes before I was due to meet Josh, I paused in front of the restaurant to steady my breath.

I needed to be a swan—graceful and elegant above the water, when below the water, my stomach was in knots and I was moments away from a full-blown panic attack.

Breathe, Sarah.

I looked at my reflection in the restaurant window. At least I looked good.

I was wearing one of Lindsey's dresses, a 70s-inspired wrap dress by Sass and Bide, which went with the heels and clutch I'd packed for New Zealand. Raiding her wardrobe was far easier than raiding Cat's, because Lins and I wore the same size. It also meant I could put off going home to my empty flat for at least another day.

I pressed my clutch to my chest and took another steadying breath. Before I left Lindsey and Nick's, I'd packed it with a clean pair of knickers and my toothbrush—just in case.

I met my own eyes in the reflection. This was it.

The *maître d'* smiled as I made my way into the restaurant. When I told her I was there to meet Josh Walker, she nodded and led me through the restaurant to a table with a one-eighty panoramic view of Darling Harbour, the top of the Harbour Bridge *just* visible in the distance, and Centre Point Tower standing sentry over the cityscape.

The sun was beginning to set, the sky blanketed in herringbone clouds, and the waning sunlight illuminating them as though they were on fire. The city was painted with countless colours, the hues of orange, pink, indigo, and violet reflecting off the glass towers and dancing on the little glassy water in the harbour.

Sydney truly is a stunning city.

Josh had his back to me, and my breath caught at the sight of his broad shoulders and dark curly hair, still damp from the shower.

He glanced up as the *maître d'* approached and when he turned around, the look on his face as his eyes met mine made me melt. *Oh my, he's handsome.* He stood and enveloped me in a hug, his arms around my waist. I wrapped mine around his neck and held him tightly. *He smells amazing.*

He let go and we stood looking at each other. "God, it's good to see you."

I smiled, and my stomach did cartwheels of joy, the giddiness a welcomed relief from the twisted knots. "Thanks, it's great to see you too." *Understatement of the century.* Part of me wanted to skip dinner and go straight to his room. Instead, I let the *maître d'*, who'd been waiting patiently, seat me and place a napkin in my lap. Josh sat and immediately reached for my hand, squeezing it.

"Nice view, huh?" I said, gazing out the window.

"It's beautiful."

"Sydney does pretty spectacular sunsets," I bragged as my eyes roved the cityscape.

"I was talking about you," he said quietly. When I looked at him, there was a shy smile on his face.

"Oh," I replied, suddenly a little shy myself. "Thank you."

From there, dinner seemed to happen as if it was onstage

and I was an audience member. Josh and I *chatted*, as though we were a normal couple having dinner. We looked at the menu, we ordered food and sake—both came, both were delicious. He asked me about Lindsey and I told him all about her and Nick and how I had my own room at their place.

We talked and laughed and flirted—there was a lot of flirting—and the whole evening felt familiar, like Josh and Sarah from Greece, or from our trip to Hana—like people who met and became friends, then flirted and became lovers, like people who had discovered together that they wanted a bigger life.

But we didn't talk about *us*.

Before I knew it, the bill came, and Josh tucked his credit card into the black wallet, then left it at the side of the table.

"So," he said, turning back to me.

"So," I replied, not wanting the night to end. His fingers found mine and laced ours together.

"There's something I want to ask you," he said, suddenly serious. *Oh, god*. I'd been waiting for him to *tell* me something, to give me some indication about what he wanted, but what could he possibly want to ask me? I dismissed the idea of a proposal. This wasn't a TV movie, and we were nowhere near that kind of commitment.

Maybe he was just going to ask me back to his room. Though, I wasn't sure how I'd respond if he did. My resolve—not to sleep with him again until I knew how he felt about me—had ebbed away over dinner. There's only so much flirting from the man you love that you can ignore.

I nodded, prompting him to ask me his question, while

my tuna carpaccio felt like it had come back to life and was swimming around my stomach.

"It's about James." The tuna flopped about, definitely still alive and fighting for its life. I gulped. I hadn't expected Josh to ask me about James, and I wasn't sure I was prepared to lie like Lindsey had told me to.

"I just wanted to make sure—" He seemed unable to finish the sentence, his expression pained as he concentrated on the candle in the middle of the table. And then I understood.

"It's over," I answered. His eyes met mine.

"Really?"

I knew I needed to reassure him. "Yes. We're not together."

His relief was so obvious that my heart broke a little for him. How had he been so talkative, so charming and attentive over dinner, all the while holding back that incredibly difficult question? I tightened my grip on his hand.

He dropped his eyes, shaking his head as if dislodging something awful. "I was so worried."

"I know you must have been. I'm so sorry."

He looked up and smiled. "It's okay, I mean, you and I, we're not—" He stopped short, and I pulled back my hand as though I'd been burnt. "We're not ..." he'd said. As in, "We're not together, we're not a couple, we're not in a committed relationship ..."

I had the answer to my own question, and I hadn't even asked it.

"No, sorry, that's not what I meant. Wait ..." His face was awash with confusion and frustration. Mine likely looked the same. He took a deep breath. "I don't know how I manage to mess this up every time, but what I meant was, until now I haven't given you any reason to not be with someone else." His syntax was crap, but I was starting to follow his train of thought.

"In Hawaii, I wasn't being honest with myself about what I wanted, which meant I couldn't be honest with you either. I'm just relieved it's not too late—that is, if I don't completely screw this up right now by being an inarticulate dick." That made me laugh, and he joined in.

"You do suck at expressing yourself sometimes, but I do too," I said, letting him off the hook.

He took my hand again and I let him. "What I wanted to tell you, what this whole night was supposed to be about, is that I'm not just here for the week."

"What?" I realised my mouth was hanging open and I closed it.

"Sorry, I mean, I *am*. I am here for this week, and I have to go back to the States for a bit, but then I'm coming back. Sarah, the whole team's moving here in March for a three-month secondment. That's why I'm here this week—I'm making the arrangements."

I was speechless and my mind struggled to process what he'd told me. Josh was coming to Sydney. For a long time. For *months*. It was exactly what I'd hoped for, only …

"But what does that mean for us?" There. I'd asked my question.

He looked confused. "I don't know what you mean."

I couldn't believe I had to spell it out. "I *mean*, if you're going to be here for three months, what do you want to happen between us?" I asked snarkily. I watched his thoughts play across his face. Then a smile, one that lit up his eyes, made me realise I'd been too harsh. I bit my lip, suddenly contrite.

"It means, Sarah Parsons, that I want to be in your life, for real, because you are my favourite person in the world—and I never thought I would say this—to *anyone*—but, I love you."

Well, that shut me up.

He reached for my face, cupping it in his hands, and kissed me while I sobbed into his mouth. I *know*, but I couldn't help it. He didn't seem to mind, though, and I finally pulled myself together enough to kiss him back. When we pulled apart, we were both grinning like idiots.

I love Josh. I love Josh. I love Josh.

And he loves me.

I wiped tears from my face with my napkin. "You know I love you too, right?"

"I had hoped." We shared another smile, and I couldn't *believe* it was possible to feel that happy—or that desperate to get a man naked.

"So, is now a good time to tell you that I packed a toothbrush in there?" I gestured towards my clutch.

"Oh yeah?" he replied, his eyes playful. God, he was sexy.

"Yep, and a clean pair of knickers."

He grinned, then stood and reached for my hand. "Well then, let's get outta here."

Eight months later ...

"Hellooo," I call out.

We're standing on the dock, each of us with our shoes in one hand and a backpack in the other.

A head pops up from below deck and I squeal, dropping everything on the dock. I scamper over the railing and climb onto the boat clumsily, almost slipping over as Siobhan and I throw our arms around each other and bounce up and down.

"Oh, my god! I can't believe we're here!" I exclaim.

She makes a noise that sounds a lot like, "Eeee," but with an Irish accent. We pull apart and grin at each other.

"I know. I've been counting down the days for *so* long now. I actually started at a hundred and fifty. It drove my family mental" I laugh. God, I adore this woman.

"Josh!" she cries.

"Hey!" he calls back.

I realise I've abandoned him with the luggage, and carefully step back to the railing, taking first my backpack from him and then his. He climbs onto the boat, dropping our shoes on the deck.

"Hi Siobhan." He envelops her in a big hug. "Great to see you."

"You too! Joshivarah, back together again!" She lets him go just as Duncan climbs up on deck.

"Hey you two," he says.

"Duncan! Hi!" I am grinning like an idiot.

Duncan and Josh do that man thing where they sort of shake hands and half hug, slapping each other on the back. Then Duncan grabs me in a bear hug and lifts me up, shaking me from side to side.

"Hey! She's taken, you know," jokes Josh.

Duncan puts me down. "Hah! Yeah, mate, so am I!" He holds up his left hand and a gold band glints in the bright sunlight.

"*What?*" I smack him playfully on the arm. "All those frigging emails and you didn't tell us?"

"We wanted it to be a surprise," says a voice I recognise.

"Gerry!" She climbs up onto the deck and we hug tightly. Then she hugs Josh and shows off her own rings, a white gold band and a simple solitaire diamond. Duncan looks more pleased with himself than I've ever seen him.

I'm reeling with excitement. These are some of my favourite people in the world, and we're together for the next ten days to sail the Croatian coast.

"So, we're just waiting on one other couple," says Duncan. I kind of feel sorry for whoever they are, because there's a lot of love amongst the five of us, and I hope they won't be overwhelmed by it.

Just then, I hear another voice.

"Hey, Sez." *What? No!* My mind can't decide if it's a trick or real, but when I turn around, Cat and Jean-Luc are standing on the dock.

I stand stock still, my mouth gaping.

"Surprise," she says, grinning and throwing an arm into the air.

"Ahhh," I yell, jumping up and down so vigorously, the boat starts to rock on its moorings. I pick my way carefully over to the railing and climb over, then ensconce my sister in a massive hug, nearly suffocating her. Her little arms wrap tightly around me and we bounce up and down.

"Did we surprise you?" she asks, her voice muffled by my shoulder.

I finally let her go, a sob escaping my throat.

"Yes, but how?" I seriously can't believe she's here. I last saw her and Jean-Luc at Christmastime in Sydney, but we'd barely got a chance to catch up before I flew off to Hawaii.

"Lots of emails." she wipes a finger under each eye, laughing.

I finally tear my eyes from her and stare up at Jean-Luc. "I—" I'm still speechless and he leans down to kiss me on both cheeks.

"So, Sarah, we have, eh, pulled it off, the surprise, *n'est-ce pas?*"

"Uh, yeah, I'd say that's a big fat yes. Oh, hey—" It suddenly dawns on me that I may be the only one who wasn't expecting them, and I look at the tableau of people standing on the deck of the boat. Siobhan is clapping softly and bouncing on the spot, Gerry's head is tilted as she beams at me, and Duncan and Josh share a look that I can only describe as "well pleased with themselves".

"You all knew!"

"They did," says Cat simply.

"But, how? How did you ...?" I cannot finish a coherent thought.

"It was Josh's idea."

I look from my sister to my love, who shrugs his shoulders as though it's nothing. But it isn't nothing. It's everything.

It's the best surprise I've ever had.

I laugh with glee, touching my fingertips to my mouth, then wrap my arm around my sister's shoulder. "Come on, then. And take your shoes off before you come on board."

The tableau breaks and there's a flurry of activity as Cat and Jean-Luc are welcomed onto the boat and officially meet Duncan, Gerry, and Siobhan.

I sidle up to Josh. "Hey."

"Hey."

"I—thank you. I—"

"You don't have to say anything more. You're welcome."

"I love you."

"I know," he deadpans, Han Solo to my Princess Leia. I roll my eyes and shake my head as his face breaks into a cheeky grin.

"Who's up for cocktails?" calls Duncan, raising a plastic pitcher over his head.

Siobhan calls out, "Me!" and Duncan starts pouring into plastic cups.

"You ready for Duncan's cocktails?" asks Josh in a low voice.

"Oh, god, no. Is anyone ever?"

Gerry hands us cups brimming with greenish-yellow liquid and I sniff mine. *Hmm—like lemonade and paint thinner had a baby.*

"To friends and family," says Duncan, holding his cup aloft.

"To you," says Josh in my ear.

"To *us*," I say, tapping my cup against his. We share a smile, then I take a sip. Yep, exactly like lemonade and paint thinner had a baby.

THE END

A Note from the Author and Acknowledgements

After finishing *One Summer in Santorini*, I knew I wanted Sarah's story to continue and that she'd eventually extricate herself from her love triangle. What I didn't know when I started writing this book was if she would end up with Josh or James—or even on her own, although being a hopeful romantic, that the last option was highly unlikely. And not just for Sarah's sake but for my own.

I wrote most of this book while perched on a sun lounger in Bali—yes, really. It was Spring 2018, and I was on a year-long sabbatical, living in Bali with my partner and love, Ben. For readers who don't know this, Ben and I met on a pier in Santorini just as we were about to embark on a ten-day sailing trip around the Cyclades Islands. If that story sounds familiar, its because our real life "meet cute" was the inspiration for *One Summer in Santorini*, although in reality, there was no silver fox (sorry "Team James").

The sabbatical was Ben's idea. And after some cajoling and reassurance that it would be amazing, I put on my big-girl knickers and we quit our jobs, gave away a lot of our stuff, packed the rest into a storage cage, and bought a one-way ticket to the rest of the world, first stop Bali.

If it wasn't for Ben's bravery, support, and intrepid spirit I would not have gone on sabbatical and I wouldn't have written this book (or *That Night in Paris*). You see, while on sabbatical I gave myself "permission" to be an author, to throw myself into writing, editing, and querying, and to seek out writing as a career.

So, a *huge* thank you to Ben.

You will have seen that this book is dedicated to my bestie, Lindsey, and there is an excellent reason for that. She is one of the most generous, loyal, big-hearted people I know, *and* she has championed my writing since the (very) early days when I was self-published and dreaming of something I never thought would actually happen. She's the person who designed and ordered merchandise for my first book, who had my indie covers printed and framed, and who this past Christmas gifted me a pendant with "One Summer" written in silver. She has believed in me every step of the way, even when I didn't, and she has never, ever given up on my dream.

Thank you, Lindsey. You are an exceptional human being and I am so grateful to have you, Sam, and Evie in my life— our Melbourne family.

As always, thank you to my parents, Lee, Ray, and Gail, my sister, Victoria, and the rest of my wonderful family. I am one of those lucky people who is actually close friends with my family members, and I so appreciate their love, guidance, and support.

Thank you to my dear friends who are scattered across